15 MILES

Rob Scott

The right of Rob Scott to be identified as the author of
this work has been asserted by him in accordance with the
Copyright, Designs and Patents Act 1988.

First published in Great Britain in 2010 by
Gollancz
An imprint of the Orion Publishing Group
Orion House, 5 Upper St Martin's Lane,
London WC2H 9EA
An Hachette UK Company

This edition published in Great Britain in 2011 by
Gollancz

1 3 5 7 9 10 8 6 4 2

A CIP catalogue record for this book
is available from the British Library

ISBN 978 0 575 09387 4

Typeset by Deltatype Ltd, Birkenhead, Merseyside

Printed in Great Britain by Clays Ltd, St Ives plc

The Orion Publishing Group's policy is to use papers
that are natural, renewable and recyclable products and
made from wood grown in sustainable forests. The logging
and manufacturing processes are expected to conform to
the environmental regulations of the country of origin.

www.sailordoyle.com
www.orionbooks.co.uk

and finally, for Mom,
for numbering sands and drinking oceans dry.

From Wibbleton to Wobbleton is fifteen miles,
From Wobbleton to Wibbleton is fifteen miles,
From Wibbleton to Wobbleton,
From Wobbleton to Wibbleton,
From Wibbleton to Wobbleton is fifteen miles.

NURSERY RHYME

INTRODUCTION

December 17th

OxyContin, Scotch, Cigarettes and Sarah

8:53 p.m.

'There he is.'

'Where?'

'There, just coming in with Lieutenant Harper.'

'Who?' Lefkowitz spun in his chair. 'The captain?'

'Fezzamo.' Huck finished his beer and looked for the bartender.

'Old Fezziwig,' I said, trying not to look. The polished bar reflected red and green lights, holiday commercialism awash in conservative mahogany.

'Right.' Huck lit a smoke with a match. He was the only guy left in America who still used matches. 'You know, he even looks like that guy.'

'What guy?' I asked.

'That guy. The guy who played in that movie with the skinny broad who died a while back, the one where they run all over Rome.'

'Jesus, Huck, you're an idiot,' Lefkowitz said. Dr Irving Lefkowitz, a forensic pathologist and deputy to the Chief Medical Examiner of the Commonwealth, was the one Jew in the whole place and the reason the CID Christmas party was now called a *holiday celebration* by the brass. Lefkowitz, a good guy for a doctor, didn't seem to give a shit one way or the other. With a Santa hat, a blinking Rudolph pin on his lapel and a string of sparkling tinsel around his neck, he looked about as ho, ho, ho as any Jew I'd ever seen.

'What do you mean?' Huck said – Sergeant Harold Greeley, my friend and mentor, a forty-eight-year-old Vice/Narcotics cop with a greying ponytail and a backbreaking alimony payment, was called Huck because his retirement dream was to steam up and down the Mississippi River, playing high stakes blackjack and wooing married women on their girls' night out. 'Don't you think he's a dead ringer for

3

the guy from that Fezziwig movie?' He gave me an expectant look, as if I could read his mind.

'Who? The captain?'

Lefkowitz said, 'Huck, you're thinking of Albert Finney, who played with Audrey Hepburn in *Two for the Road*, not *Roman Holiday*. That was Gregory Peck; Atticus Finch, remember? Finney played Ebenezer Scrooge in an abysmal musical version of *A Christmas Carol*. He did not play Mr Fezziwig.'

'That's him!' Huck slapped the table. 'Don't you think he looks like Albert Finney?'

'You need to cut back on the suds, my friend,' I said. 'Captain Fezzamo looks more like Vito Corleone than Albert Finney.'

'Ah, well, at least I had the actress right.' He yelled towards the bar, 'Hey! Who do I have to kill to get a beer in here?'

'There's a waitress somewhere,' I said. 'Kill her.'

The CID Christmas party, an annual barn-burner for anyone with even a remote professional affiliation to the Virginia State Police Criminal Investigation Division, was the one night each year when a Dope cop like me or Huck could rub elbows with the Chief ME, the Richmond lab guys, the ID photographers or even the Homicide Division captain, Arthur P. Fezzamo. Huck, Lefkowitz and I were tucked around a corner table near the bar. There was a starchy buffet and dancing in a banquet room down the hall, but no smoking. Most everyone else was down there, just the smokers in the pub.

In the big room, the DJ cued up a wrinkled Sammy Davis, Jr tune. *Nothing quite says Merry Christmas like a dead Jewish crooner with one good eye.*

'So you gonna go talk to him?' Huck blew a cloud of smoke towards the ceiling fan.

'Nah,' I said, searching my pockets. 'Hey, lemme bum one, will you?'

'Yeah, sure.' He tossed me the pack. 'Why not?'

'Maybe I'll go up to his office next week before everyone clears out for Christ— sorry, Doc, the *holidays*.'

'Whatever.' Lefkowitz waved off the insult. 'Why not tonight?'

'I'm half in the bag already. I'd hate to go over to him and puke, or fart, or start babbling like a common drunk.'

'You are an uncommon drunk, Sailor.' Huck sipped my Scotch and winced. 'And look at him, for Christ's sake. He looks like he's been marinating in Jameson's all day.'

'Sambuca,' Lefkowitz corrected. 'Captain Fezzamo's Italian. Maybe Albert Finney's been in the Jameson's. Do you boys have any idea what those things will do to your lungs?'

'What? These're bad for me?' Huck crushed one and lit another.

'You come by the hospital one of these days when I've got a smoker on the table. You'll quit on the spot.' Doc brushed a dusting of fake snow off a jacket sleeve that alone was worth more than everything I had on.

'No shit?' I said.

'Works every time.'

'Why do you think I've never gone?' Huck covered a belch with the back of his hand. Like any Dope cop who'd been in the game for more than a couple of years he dressed like an ex-hippy with a serious hash problem. His suit was as rumpled as anything you'd find in the back of a garbage truck.

'I tell you what, Doc,' I said, 'you call my cell the next time you're about to do a smoker and I'll come assist.'

'Deal,' Lefkowitz said, 'but as luck would have it, I don't need you to assist.' He stood and waved towards the door. An attractive young woman in an expensive-looking coat smiled and sidled towards us.

I should've worn a tie.

'Holy shit, Doc,' Huck said, 'who's she?'

'My student, at least for next semester.'

'Merciful Bill Clinton's wet dream,' Huck mouthed, and stood as well. 'Please tell me you're riding this pony.'

Lefkowitz frowned and rotated a ruby pinkie ring a half-turn. 'I'm sixty-one years old and forty pounds overweight. That ride would kill me.'

'You've got good hair and a nice suit,' I said, standing too. 'A lot of women go for that distinguished salt-and-pepper look.'

'Let's at least hope my wife still does.'

Lefkowitz outclassed us all by two or three touchdowns.

Huck said, 'You think it's too late for me to go to med school?'

The woman pulled up a chair. 'It's never too late.'

She smelled good – clean – even through the smoke and heady cologne.

Lefkowitz took her coat and said, 'Sarah Danvers, this is Sergeant Harold Greeley.'

'Sergeant.' She extended her hand.

'Huck,' he said, shaking it. 'Would you sleep with me later?'

'Yes, absolutely. I've been standing here for the last eight seconds hoping you'd ask me that very question.'

Huck sat heavily. 'My Christmas wish.'

''Tis the season,' Sarah said. She was maybe twenty-seven, and she wore one of those strappy cocktail dresses that look like someone had ripped it about halfway off without her noticing. She had no visible panty line – I checked while she was watching Huck stare unabashedly at her tits, which were exquisite – and cyclist's legs. Teasing Huck, she flipped her chestnut hair over one shoulder. This was an unexpected and pleasant surprise; I wanted her badly to notice me. I don't know why.

'And this,' Lefkowitz said, 'is Officer Samuel Doyle.'

'Hi Sarah,' I said, thinking, *eyes up, shithead*.

'Samuel, Sammy, or Sam?' She sat down.

'Uh, none of the above, actually. My friends call me Sailor.'

'Huck and Sailor?' She giggled, then tried to hide it. 'Does anyone go by their real name around here?'

'Just the Doc.' Huck grabbed a waitress hustling beers to a bunch of lab guys near the window. 'Let's get you a drink, Sarah.'

'I'll have another Dewar's and soda,' I said.

'VSOP, please.' Lefkowitz handed over his empty snifter. 'Sailor, there are about thirty-nine better Scotches behind that bar. And why the club soda?'

'Just two flavours I like,' I said.

'If you ever get to Scotland, realise that they will beat, cook, and eat you if you order their distillations with club soda, or ice, God forbid. It would be akin to arriving in the US and ordering a Budweiser with a scoop of vanilla ice cream.'

'Now there's two flavours *I* like,' Huck said.

'Beer with ice cream?' The waitress held her pen ready to document the anomaly for alcoholic posterity.

'Just the beer,' Huck said.

Sarah glanced at her cell phone, stashed it in her bag and said, 'A double Bombay gin with a twist, please.'

'Whoa, whoa, sister,' Huck said, 'this is a marathon, not a sprint.'

'What do you mean?'

'CID's picking up the tab. You ought to drink as much as possible. Double gins will have you senseless inside an hour. You don't want to be a cheap date.'

'Thanks for the advice.' She looked to Lefkowitz. 'Is he always this helpful?'

'Narcotics cops are invariably the most amusing entertainment at these functions, yes.'

'Is that what you do?' she asked.

'Yup,' I said. In the banquet room, Jimmy Buffett sang about a beach. *More Christmas music.*

'But not for long,' Huck added, clearly fighting the urge to talk directly to Sarah's dress.

'Really? Where are you off to?'

And she's tan. Who's tan in Richmond in December?

'Sailor's hoping for a transfer to the Homicide Division, and I'm pitching this season for the Baltimore Orioles, middle relief. I'm a bit old for the starting rotation.' Huck was amusing; Doc had that much right.

'Homicide?' Sarah cocked a sexy eyebrow at me. 'Why leave Vice?'

'A lot of reasons,' I said. 'Mostly because we don't really do anything ... wait a minute, that didn't come out right. We do a lot, but we fight a never-ending battle against enemies we can't beat, and to tell you the truth, I don't know if I care to win any more.'

'You sound jaded, Sailor,' Lefkowitz said, our Old Testament sage. 'You're too young to be jaded.'

'Think about it, Doc. First, there's dope. We can't win that. I swear to Christ there's drugs in every car, every house, certainly every medicine cabinet – powerful stuff – and every high school locker in America. And in the end, who really gives a shit? If you're a crackhead or a smack junkie, what do I really care? Take all you want. Smoke, snort, eat, hell, smear the shit on your nuts; I don't care. You're going to end up dead or locked up, anyway. Right? So fuck you; take all you want. It's one less douche bag out there stinking the place up.'

Huck took the drinks from the waitress and passed them around. 'I hate it when he gets like this. He takes it all so personally.'

I ignored him. 'Then there's the sex crimes, and most of that's bullshit, too. Okay, okay, rape is a grotesque thing, but we don't really handle rapes. That's for the city and county guys, and the local detectives. Rarely do we get one that they can't handle, unless it's high-profile: some famous actress gets attacked down at the beach, whatever. For us it's just the lab shit and the DNA tests. So that leaves pornography, and again, who gives a shit? If consenting adults want to oil up and spank each other with flyswatters or sausage links, why should we care if they take pictures and post them on the Internet? Is that a crime? Really? A *felony*? It's more embarrassing than anything, especially given that half these sick bastards should never disrobe with the lights on. But a felony? I don't think so.'

'I'm staggered,' Sarah said. 'What about child pornographers and Internet stalkers luring children into dangerous situations? I see it on the news all the time.'

'Easily solved if the parents would keep the frigging computer in the family room,' Huck interjected.

'True,' I said, 'but she's right, the predators are still out there. As a thirty-one-year-old looking at twenty-four years to retirement, I just don't know that I can chase perverts all day and go home at night without feeling slimy.'

'I would think you'd feel good about yourself, keeping Virginia safe for kids?' Sarah twirled a finger in her gin. Her nail polish matched her dress: Christmas red. And she wasn't wearing a bra. God bless the guy who invented braless dresses – it had to be a guy. Half-drunk and three-quarters fouled on OxyContin, I couldn't help imagining what colour panties she wore. Jenny, my wife, wore the same ones every day: white cotton briefs with wide hips like slats on a farm wagon.

'Sailor?' Sarah said tentatively. 'Any pulse?'

I shook my head. 'Uh, yeah, sorry, distracted. Um, you're right: I might feel good, keeping the place safe,' I admitted. 'But think about it: if you're a guy who wants to whack off to a titty magazine, excuse me, that's fine. Enjoy yourself; it's none of the state's business. However, if you're a guy who preys on small boys, you know, wanting to play with little toy pee-pees, well then, I think you ought to have your head caved in with a brick.'

'That's not motivation enough to stay in Vice?'

Jesus, she's beautiful. Jenny's never looked this good, even the day we got married, she didn't look this good. And she's talking to me.

'In Vice?' I said. 'No.'

'Why not?'

'Because I don't get to cave their heads in with a brick.'

'Oh, right.' She looked down. 'For what it's worth, I think you Vice guys do invaluable work.'

'Yeah, well…' Embarrassed at running my mouth, I swallowed a mouthful of Dewar's. I'd had a couple of pills before coming over from the barracks and shouldn't have. With four or five Scotches in me I was getting slurry and languid. I didn't know where that little diatribe had come from, probably just wanting to impress her. Whatever. Contrary to most junkies, I'm not especially charming on OxyContin.

The rest of them let the silence go on for an unreasonably long period of time, then Huck said, 'So … everyone got their shopping done?'

Again I ignored him. I figured I ought to see if I could rebound. It had been a long time since I had hit on anyone in a bar, especially in front of my friends. 'So, Sarah, how is it that you managed to end up a prisoner in old Dr Mengele's morgue this semester?'

'I'm at VCU, working on my doctorate in biochemistry, one semester to go.'

Shit, she's smart, too.

'Good grief, why?' Huck chugged a few inches.

Lefkowitz fired up one of those cigarillos he pretends he doesn't smoke. They're high-end nails; he gets them from Spain or Turkey, but they smell like burning whale snot.

'I'm interested in forensic chemistry and I want to do research in

9

pathology. I work in serology as well, but my dissertation is on tissues and diagnostic viral stains.'

'So you can work with stiffs for thirty years?'

'For a while. Then maybe I'll teach at a university.' She smiled again.

Nice teeth, too.

'I'll tell you, my dear,' Huck started, 'and no offence to you, Doc, but you can't imagine how shitty your social life's gonna be. I can see it now: "So what do you do?" "I'm a corporate lawyer with a huge yacht and a boner." "Oh, yummy." "How about you?" "Me? I take blood, shit, sperm, tissue, and organ samples from dead people all day and look at them under a microscope." "See ya, sister!" – and that's one who'll smooch you at the dock and sail off to Mardi Gras with that broad from … you know the one … that chesty broad from the movie about the two hillbilly retards in the orange car with the Dixie horn.'

'Jesus, Huck, there's got to be medication for you,' I said. 'Doc, please, prescribe him something.'

Huck feigned a punch at my head and shouted, 'A beer! My kingdom for a beer!'

Sarah didn't know what to make of us. Lefkowitz just grimaced, clearly pleased that the CID holiday party only came around once a year.

'I'll get you one.' I started for the bar.

'Nice to see you respecting your elders.'

'Anything to shut you up. Everyone else okay? Doc? Sarah?'

'I'm good for now, Sailor.' Doc swirled brandy around his snifter.

'I'll have another gin, thanks.'

While Doc sipped his drink and Huck mined for a cigarette, Sarah leaned towards me, loosing her neckline a few inches. 'You need some money?'

Sonofabitch, she's daring you to look. Don't do it, Sailor. She's playing with you. Don't get caught.

'Sailor?'

'Ah … um, no. No, it's … an open bar.'

'Right, thanks.' She sat back again, still eyeing me.

I wanted her right there. Forget Jenny and Ben. Forget everything for ten unholy minutes, and pile-drive Sarah Danvers in her red *holiday* dress, right there on the table.

'I'll be right back,' I said. 'Then I gotta call home.'

For about ten years – *nine years, fifty-one weeks and five days* – I'd been wrestling with what the VSP psychologist called 'self-esteem issues and feelings of self-doubt and loathing'. I didn't mind so much the bouts of feeling low; I mean, every one of us can come up with forty-two reasons why the world should slather us with pity. The problem for me was the surprise attacks. These 'difficult periods', to quote my counsellor, were sneaky bastards, coming out of nowhere to clobber me. Granted, they mostly showed up between two and five a.m., when I was lying there staring at the ceiling, but other times, they'd catch me off-guard, start me sweating, clench up my guts, sometimes even send me running for the can to hurl whatever I'd eaten that month.

The therapist said I had to cut back on the Scotch – like she needed an advanced degree to figure that one out. And although I never came clean to her about the pills, I figure she must have known. A few weeks in Dope and you can see that all junkies do a piss-poor job trying to hide the fact that they're junkies. She probably read the OxyContin all over my face, but I wasn't about to confess. And I was only a pill-popper, an *occasional* popper; I hadn't snorted anything or cruised Shockoe Bottom for real smack.

I suppose I ought to learn my lesson. If drinking and taking pills sends me spiralling, well then, hello shithead, I should cut them out. But it's harder than that, paying up. Sometimes, this feels like exactly what I'm supposed to be doing. How fucked is that?

There was one sure-fire antidote, however. The only true miracle I'd ever known.

I dropped the drinks off at the table, made playful eye-contact with Sarah again – why not? I was already in too deep – and begged a few minutes to call the house, hoping I wasn't too late. I slipped outside, figuring the cold would clear my head.

Jenny picked up on the third ring.

'Hey, hon.'

'Ouch, sweetie, you sound wrecked.'

So much for hiding it. 'Well, yeah, I guess. But, hey, it's a party.'

'Is Captain Fezzamo there?'

'Uh, no, well, I dunno. He might be in the banquet room. I haven't seen him. Huck and I are sitting in the bar with Dr Lefkowitz, the Deputy ME from Richmond.' *Lie number one.*

'How's Huck?'

'The same. He says "hi".' I pulled my jacket closed – it smelled like smoke – and huddled out of the wind. For a place that managed to get so unbearably hot in August, Richmond could be merciless in winter.

'Has he talked with Sandy?'

I chuckled. 'I think he avoids that whenever possible.'

'That's too bad.'

'Yeah, well, what're you gonna do?'

'Everyone having fun?'

'Not really. I'm sorry you couldn't come.' *Lie number two.*

'We need a more reliable babysitter. These high school kids are all over the place, and my mom can't just pack up and run down here on two minutes' notice.'

'I understand,' I said, 'anyway, we don't want her driving down by herself. She's not so great in the snow.'

'You aren't either, Officer Doyle,' Jenny teased. 'If you end up having too many, I want you to crash at Huck's. Tell him I asked while sweetly batting my eyelashes.'

'I'll tell him you flashed your boobs. That'll work.'

'Fine, boobs it is.' She paused a second.

Here it comes.

'And Sailor … please, no pills tonight, okay? I don't want to worry.'

'I promise.' *Lie number three. Jesus, what kind of guy makes his wife beg for something like that?*

'And if you see Captain Fezzamo before you get too shitfaced—'

'I'll ask him, Jenny. I will.' *Lie number four.*

'Good.' She sounded relieved. 'Thanks, baby.' Jenny believed that a transfer to the Homicide Division was going to save my life, our marriage, everything that had got so polluted and tangled since I started in Vice/Narcotics. But that wasn't the reason; we both knew it.

'You want to talk to him?'

'Is he still awake?'

'He was determined to stay up until you got home, but he's fading, so talk fast.'

I heard her moving around. The television was on in the bedroom, some noisy commercial for a fruitcake Chrysler dealer up in Ashland. The jingle was irritating as hell, set to the tune of 'Dixie', some car salesman with a hard-on for the Civil War. Crazy, throw-back sentiment was all over the place down here, as if the South really would rise again. I tried to get the damned song out of my head: two hillbilly retards in an orange car.

Maybe some Jimmy Buffett or Sammy Davis, Jr will help after all.

'Daddy?'

Benjamin Owen Doyle: the one time in my life that I'd been touched by God. For two glorious seconds, everything slipped off me, as if I'd been cast in Teflon. 'Hey, monkey-face!'

'When are you coming home?' Jenny was right: he was barely hanging on.

'You'll be asleep when I get there, buddy.'

'Where are you?'

'In Richmond with Uncle Hucker.'

'That's fifty-eight miles.'

'Exactly!' I beamed to the empty street. 'Are you the planet's most brilliant four-year-old?'

'Daddy …'

'Yes, sir?' I could see him in his Spider-Man pyjamas, buried in a pile of blankets on my side of the bed.

'Mommy made waffles for dinner. I had two with syrup.'

'Mommy needs to eat whatever she wants. Wait a few months and see all the nasty stuff she asks for. When we were waiting for you, she used to eat tuna with cheese and spaghetti *at the same time!*'

'I don't like tuna.'

'Me neither, monkey.' I would have stood there all night, letting the frigid breeze give my soul a much-needed enema, but I heard Jenny pick him up, and whisper, 'Say good night to Daddy.'

'Good night Da— Oh, wait, Daddy?' He was suddenly wide awake, remembering something important.

'What is it, buddy?'

'Daddy, Darth Vader is Luke's *father*!'

My heart broke. 'I know, buddy, but what are you doing watching scary stuff so late?'

'He cut off his *hand*!'

'I know, I know.' I let go with a sound that was trapped between a laugh and a sob. *Go home now, shithead. Get in your car and go.*

'But you would never do that.'

'No, buddy, I would never do that,' I said. 'Good night, monkey-face.'

'Me and you.'

'You and me.'

'Good night, Daddy.'

Jenny took the phone. 'I'll see you later?'

'I'll be there soon.' *Lie number five.* 'How's your belly?'

'Growing and starving and making me pee every eleven minutes.'

'You need anything?'

'I need you to stay at Huck's tonight. You don't sound good, Sailor.'

'I'll be all right. Good night, hon.'

I wandered into the street and opened my jacket. The wind filled it like a cape, clearing some of the smoky stink and freezing me to my bones. A city bus rolled by in the opposite lane, and some kid shouted at me through the back window. He made a face and gave me the finger.

The wind swirled a flurry of snow towards the river. I waited for another gust, then closed my coat and went into the bar.

15

11:56 p.m.

The brass had cleared out, Captain Fezzamo among them. I didn't talk to him, didn't even make it into the banquet room until after most of the officers had left.

I sat with Phil Clarkson, an old ID guy from Roanoke City PD who'd just moved to Richmond to take a job with CID – better retirement benefits, I guess. His wife, a squatty woman in a dress that might have done some moonlighting as curtains in my Aunt Ethel's house, joined us as well. She drank white wine and half-talked, half-mewed through her nose. How anyone drinks white wine for four hours and maintains an active pulse is a mystery to me, but I was too wrecked myself to care much. Bob Lourdes, a muscle-headed road cop from Henrico County and wannabe Dope transfer, had elbowed his way to our table about an hour before. For butting into the conversation, Huck put him in cuffs, said it was a mandatory transfer initiation ritual or some frigging thing. Lourdes sipped at a beer through a curly-Q straw the waitress had found beneath the bar. Even with his hands behind his back, he looked amused at his predicament. I wasn't about to tell him that Huck would probably leave him there all night.

The rest of CID had gone home; only the dregs and the drunks stuck around, waiting for someone to shut down the power, shoot the DJ or kick the keg.

Huck danced with Sarah. I hadn't seen Lefkowitz since about ten. He'd gone off to talk with the Homicide lieutenant – Harper – and disappeared, probably home to Windsor Farms. Sarah, not knowing anyone else, stayed with us. I'd promised Doc we'd get her home all right, but by now I needed a Med-Evac helicopter to get myself to Fredericksburg.

As I watched her and Huck mangle the Fraternity Basement

16

Shuffle I flagged down the waitress, ordered another round and tried hard to Zen out the nasal sound of Curtains Clarkson as she prattled on about her daughter's inept chemistry professor. Sarah's dress was blurry from across the dance floor. It moved in impossible ways, ignoring convention and billowing here and there in some seductive rhythm. I squinted, but that didn't help so I stretched my eyes wide, bugging them out, then blinked fast three or four times, trying to bring the planet into focus. When her dress fell off – it had to; there was so little holding it on – I didn't want to miss a thing. She moved effortlessly, gracefully, as if she was submerged under water while the rest of us were left to stumble around out here under the cruel influence of gravity. Next to her, Huck looked like he had cerebral palsy.

It was easy to covet Sarah Danvers.

With a loving wife, a decent job, a beautiful, healthy son and a supportive group of friends and colleagues, I can't say why I wanted her so badly. But I did. And for all my assurances about my marriage – things I promised myself in quiet moments when I wasn't bullshitting – I would have given almost anything to drop to my knees and savour that woman.

'I gotta get out of here,' I said.

'Where you going, Sailor?' Lourdes asked. 'It isn't midnight yet.'

'I turn into a cantaloupe at midnight.'

'Pumpkin.'

'You eat what you like; I'll eat what I like.'

'Who's eating? I'm starving.' Sarah and Huck staggered to the table. Huck fell into his chair; Sarah, smelling of gin, leaned on me, her chin on top of my head, her hands at my sides.

Don't touch me. Please. I'm going home. Don't touch me.

'Are we done here, my faithful supplicants?' Huck upended his bottle; a dribble of beer skirted over his chin.

'I'm pretty tired,' I murmured. The OxyContin made my arms and legs feel as though they had been filled with sand. 'I promised Ben I'd have breakfast with him tomorrow, so I gotta head north.'

'You're not going anywhere,' Huck said. 'Jenny'd have me in traction if she knew I let you drive to Fredericksburg in your condition.'

17

'I'm a state police officer. No one's going to give me a ticket. If the road guys pull me over, I'll have them run me home.'

'You could kill someone,' Sarah slurred, groping for her gin. 'You could hit some kid.'

'On Interstate 95 at twelve-thirty in the morning in a snowstorm? If I do, I sincerely hope the investigating officer talks with the parents, because someone out there only skimmed *Doctor Spock's Guide to Highway Safety for Toddlers*.'

'Hey,' Huck shouted.

'Too loud, Uncle Hucker,' I groaned.

'Speaking of highways, do you want to drive tomorrow, or should I pick you up?'

'Not now, Huck.' The room tilted, then righted itself.

'Where are you going?' With a twist of her hips, Sarah slid into my lap, ostensibly because there were no other chairs at the table. She draped an arm innocently around my shoulders and I put one around her waist; it seemed an innocuous enough gesture. But I didn't look up at her. Instead, I stared at Huck, all the while feeling her breath on the side of my face. It was about two seconds before I had a blazing hard-on and had to shift awkwardly, shuffling her to one thigh where I could be almost sure she wouldn't notice, or rub up against it by accident. Christ, what a mess. My heart thudded, but my limbs still felt fucked-up, numb, like puppet arms.

'We're making a run to the lab in the morning,' I said feebly.

'Where's that?'

'ATF, up in Maryland.'

'Shit, why?' Lourdes asked. He was a goodlooking kid, too muscular and pretty for Dope, though.

'Gang kid, up in Triangle, shot two MS 13 losers over near Route 1, by the river,' Huck explained.

'So what? Why the ATF?'

'The serial number on the gun was punched out. We figure it might have come from an illegal dealer.'

'How's that?' Sarah said, sliding her leg between my thighs, about two inches from an embarrassing encounter with the old fella. I sat deathly still, holding my breath.

'Most anyone trying to destroy the serial number on a weapon will burn the numbers off with acid. Illegal dealers know that doesn't really work. Our lab guys can get those back. This gang kid in Triangle was too fucking stupid to have punched the numbers out; so that makes it an arms issue, a federal deal. Sailor and I are running the gun up there tomorrow.' For all his posturing as a rank-and-file idiot, Huck Greeley knew felons. I wouldn't have wanted him chasing after me.

I said, 'Bring your truck, and we can drop off that last load of toys in the bin at Potomac Mills. Then my work as CID Santa will be done for another year. God bless us, every one.'

'You're a good man, Charlie Brown,' Huck toasted me.

'Soft spot for needy kids is all.' My ass went numb. I needed to shift in my seat but was afraid to move and risk dumping Sarah into a hot LZ. Pins and needles prickled my backside in a clear warning not to stand up until the coast was clear.

'You're the CID Santa?' Sarah asked, resting her forehead on my shoulder.

'Kringle Kids donations,' I said. 'I missed a meeting about five years ago and got myself elected *in loco* Santa Claus. I've been hosting the CID collection every year since.' I gave a lopsided, lefty shrug. 'I dunno. It's my community service, I guess.'

'Nice,' she whispered, smelling of stale gin and the cosmetics counter at Macy's.

Lourdes sucked beer through his flavour straw. 'Don't let him fool you, Sarah. Sailor sets a donation record every year, keeps a spreadsheet, spends all month on the horn with community organisers. He's like Jerry Lewis — takes it personally if there isn't at least one more toy than last year.' He nodded at Huck. 'Sergeant Greeley's his personal Sherpa.'

'He's the only one with a pickup.' Now I did shrug, maybe waking Sarah. I couldn't tell. 'Anyway, Uncle Hucker, can you bring the truck?'

'Sure.' He dug in his shirt for a smoke. 'But you're buying lunch.'

'I'll take you to that place you like in Fairfax—'

'A peanut butter and jelly stand?' Sarah said.

'Gourmet,' I replied.

19

'Sounds great,' she whispered. Her lips brushed my earlobe; the hair on my forearms stood up.

'Actually, peanut butter and jelly rarely makes much sound at all,' I said, just to be a prick.

'It all depends on what you do with them.' Sarah smirked deviously, then said, 'All right. I'm outta here.' She adjusted her dress, slipped into her coat, and shook hands with everyone, even Lourdes, however awkwardly.

'Pleasure to meet you, Sailor,' she said.

'Likewise,' I murmured, struggling to my feet.

'Huck,' she gave him a polite hug, 'thanks for a great night. I had fun.'

He patted her on the ass. 'My dear, if only you were fifteen years older—'

'I still wouldn't sleep with you.'

Curtains Clarkson howled. 'Oh, shit, oh shit, Huck, she got you there!'

'Good night all. Thanks again.' And Sarah Danvers, stumbling slightly, disappeared into the street, a holiday splash of blinking red and green brightening her way.

The rest of us sat in silence for a minute or two. I sipped at my Scotch; Huck guzzled half a beer. Lourdes used his teeth to move the curly straw to a fresh bottle, closing one eye to target the narrow neck. Curtains Clarkson chuckled absently to herself while Phil looked back and forth between us, wondering what might happen next. Sarah's leaving had punctured a hole in the festivities. The CID Christmas party deflated around us.

Finally, Huck said, 'Should we have one more and then head to church?'

Clearly relieved, Phil said, 'Good idea, Sergeant. Let's go again, a nightcap.'

'Sailor,' Huck said, 'got one more in you?'

I sighed, watching the door and fully expecting Sarah to reappear. She couldn't have left like that, just stood up, said good night and gone home. Wasn't she intrigued by the possibilities? She hadn't mentioned a boyfriend or a roommate. Did she *want* to go home alone?

'What do you say, Sailor? Another Scotch?'

'Uh, yeah, sure.' I used both hands to push myself up, waiting for the room to slant far enough to dump me into the James River. 'But I gotta pee first. I'll be back.'

'Good enough,' Huck said.

I stood at the urinal, dizzy with the aroma of antiseptic pucks, and fished in my pockets for a cigarette. I had a couple left in a pack I had heisted from Huck while he was raiding the buffet table, but no lighter. I checked my jacket for matches – Huck had given me some earlier – and my hand closed around something unfamiliar.

'What d'we got here?' I mumbled into the narrow mirror fixed to the tile wall. Who ever thought that guys taking a piss needed to look themselves directly in the face must have been a pervert, or at least a mirror salesman.

It was a business card. And a key.

Swaying, with the old fella still hanging over the porcelain trough, I read the message scrawled on the back of the card.

I don't normally do this.

A bolt of lightning lanced through me. My stomach rolled over and the old fella gave a half-hearted wave.

On the opposite side, *Sarah K. Danvers* was printed in tiny block letters, just above a Grace Street address.

'Holy shit,' I whispered, barely recognising myself in the mirror. 'Holy frigging shit.'

I never went back to the table.

12:26 a.m.

Driving my car, the state car . . . snow's falling hard; my face is sweaty. I gotta throw up; pull over and puke. Ten and two, ten and two. Don't fuck this up. Don't do anything stupid. Those yellow lights over there: is that Monument? I need Monument, Monument to Grace. Is that Franklin? Ten and two. Where's my gun? Did I bring my gun? Who can take a sunrise, sprinkle it with dew, then do something I don't remember and polish furniture, too? The candy man can. Sing it, Sammy! But can the candy man find Monument? Where's her card? Can't remember the number. Ben and Jenny are sleeping, they're home, safe. Heavenly Father, please take care of Ben and Jenny until I get home. Keep them happy and healthy. The only thing we should be allowed to pray for; the only thing. No praying for the starving, huddled masses, the last second-field goal, the lottery numbers. The only thing we should be allowed to pray for: health and happiness of family. Friends. I don't have too many friends, anyway. There it is: Monument. Arthur Ashe. Did he drunk pray? Monument to Grace. Franklin is too far. God, please take care of Ben and Jenny tonight. Please God, in the name of the Father, the Son, and the Holy Spirit, A-men. My feet are wet. My foot. Just that one, the left one. I stepped in something, snow, maybe. Where's my gun? I'm sick. I can't do this. Go home. Turn around and go home. Jenny and Ben: they're home. They're sleeping. Go home, Sailor.

What? Jesus, what was that? Oh, shit, shit, shit, did I hit that fucking car? Shit, I hit it. Was there anybody in it? I slipped, that's all – it's slippery. I was awake. I was awake. It's slippery. Where the hell does Sarah live?

That's it. This is it. Shake it off, clear your head. Hold the wall just a second. Lean here. Just a second, just lean against the wall. Catch your breath. That's it. Where's the key? Go home, Sailor. Just lean a second . . . sprinkle it with dew. Then go home.

'Sarah?'

She's there. She's awake. Her apartment's dark. What is that? What's she . . . ? Holy shit! Holy shit! Never seen that. That's . . . holy . . . shit . . . what is that?

'Yeah,' I murmur. 'I got your note.'

I'm out of my pants, my jacket. She's on the sofa. Hard-on so hard it hurts. I'm on her from behind, she's working herself from below, on her stomach. I grind as hard as I can, trying to reach around. I get a hand on one tit, almost slip. Her back's sweaty. She's making some kind of primitive sound, like she's got a cold. That's not moaning, that's . . . Ah, shit! she shouts. *We go together. It's maybe thirty seconds, if that. I'm gonna pass out. I gotta puke. She's shouting again. Christ, that's two. I wish I could do that. We go together. Jenny and I've never done that. Not once.*

Then I'm puking. The floor's cool against the side of my face. Just rest here. The tile's white, the fixtures silver. It smells like candles and barf. I think I sleep for a while, maybe just fade out. There's music on. I hear Sarah on the couch again. She shouts for me to join her. I can't do it. She moans this time. That's a moan. I dunno what that other sound was. Christ forgive me. Jenny. Shit, Jenny. I just fucked another woman. I did it. Sarah comes again, a hat trick, then steps over me and sits, naked, on the edge of the tub. She is beautiful; her body's beautiful.

'A few ground rules, Navy boy . . .'

'Right. Whatever.' *All the king's horses couldn't convince me to give a shit about what she has to say.*

Sarah wags a blurry finger. 'I've got one semester left on this motherless dissertation . . .'

'Motherless,' I slur. 'Never had a mother.'

'I'm going to need on-demand chicken wings, on-demand sushi, on-demand Cabernet—'

'Beer.'

'Beer's fine, but don't interrupt,' she giggles. 'On-demand beer, and on-demand sex.'

'My favourite.'

'No one falls in love.' *She leans over, and her tits brush my shoulder, the side of my face.* 'No one falls in love, Navy boy. You hear me?' *Sarah slips off the tub, falls, snorts laughter through her nose.*

'No love. Okay.' *I sleep.*

23

PART I

Friday, July 3rd

The Bruckner Farm

4:18 a.m.

Jenny'd left the closet door open again. I stared into it, a haunted Brooks Brothers cave, rather than watch the unforgiving numbers roll on my bedside clock – the goddamned red eyes of Satan, those frigging numbers. 3:58. 4:07.

Now 4:18.

I'd never been a good sleeper, not since high school. I don't know why: stress, anxiety, feelings of ... what was it ...? *Self-loathing*. Right.

The problem for me wasn't getting to sleep; that I could handle just fine. Most nights, I collapsed into bed with the Angel of Death chasing me in from the bathroom. Falling asleep was *easy*; staying asleep, *that* was the frigging problem. And it was funny. No matter what time I called it a night, whether I went to sleep with Ben at eight-thirty, stayed up watching the idiot box with Jenny, or came home after a bender with Huck, I would wake up between two and five. Most nights it happened more than once.

Tonight was no different. I rolled over the first time at 2:42, then again at 3:28. I turned my back to the clock and snuggled up behind Jenny, my hand draped over her hips. She was still pretty big, especially around the middle. No surprise, I guess. The baby was only six weeks old.

Anna Elizabeth Doyle. The second miracle of my life.

Jenny had been up around two, feeding Anna and checking on Ben. I think that's what did me: when she came back to bed, I woke up. Normally I might have slipped a hand under her nightgown, maybe convinced her to go for an early morning roll, but not tonight. Anna's birth was still too fresh in my mind, hell, in both our minds. My father, that tough-as-nails Teamster in his Dickies and boots, never saw anything like that. He was in a bar across the street when Marie

27

and I were born, probably smoking cigars and drinking bourbon. If he had been in the delivery room with my mother, he would have committed suicide, just opened the hospital window and thrown himself into the River Jordan.

Anyway, Jenny was racking pretty hard. I can't blame her, what with the hours she has to keep with the baby. I figured I'd let her sleep as I slithered up beside her and listened to her snore. Her back resonated with each noisy breath and the air-conditioner kicked on, and the two of them, Jenny snorting through her nose, and the cooling fan droning like a squadron of Luftwaffe, were the final nails in my coffin.

Screw it. What's another sleepless night?

I rolled onto my back, the one place I'm guaranteed not to fall asleep, and let the thoughts come.

And they did, the usual random jumble of fears, to-do items, sex fantasies and bad memories.

Marie — don't think about Marie; anything but Marie. What's it been? Ten years, six months and two weeks. Don't think it, change— Change what? My clothes and my hair. New wool suits. Homicide Division, Lieutenant Harper and Captain Fezzamo. No Huck these days, no Uncle Hucker. No cash, no pills, not in Homicide. It was just easy, too easy: what's he got, Huck? $18,477 in cash, 229 Percocet, 112 Vicodin, 206 Lunesta — that's the pussy drug — 340 Demerol and 841 OxyContin. Oh, for personal use? Sure, they are, dickhead. Bag it for $18,429, beers are on Masterson tonight. Teach him to deal drugs. But that wasn't all. Nope, Uncle Hucker left the room; didn't he, and what'd we do? Bagged him for 733 OxyContin. What's Masterson going to do, tell the Public Defender? Fuck him. Not good, Sailor. Not good. That's 108 OxyContin in your shirt pocket. Fucking stupid — but nobody knew. Nobody but Jenny. Jenny, my own Jenny, over there snoring: Frumpy Alice in that nightgown. RML. No nightgown. Sarah doesn't wear a nightgown. Sarah K. Danvers. Jesus, the body on that woman. What's it been, two weeks? Twelve days — not quite two weeks since Sarah, and not quite two weeks since I've had any pills. Sarah doesn't mind, though. That's fading, fading, fading . . . my fault: too goddamned fat these days. The body on that woman versus the body on Detective Flabzilla — not Hucker yet, but plenty of fat. Fading, fading. RML. What's Sarah want with fat? It's too goddamned hot . . . too hot

28

in Richmond. Fourth of July. I'll need some pills. Goddamned suit. Wool suit today, wool to work – who goes to work on July third? No one. Who wears wool? Homicide detectives. Lieutenant Harper, Captain Fezzamo and the detectives. Detective Me, Samuel Doyle, Detective Flabzilla, Sailor, thirty-one years old, fifteen extra pounds above the belt, screwing a twenty-seven-year-old doctoral student because she has a great body and an awesome sex drive. And a pill problem. Is 108 OxyContin a pill problem? It's been more than 108 pills. Lots more ... lots of wool in a suit. How much wool? How many sheep gave their coats so that I can sweat my nuts off working on July third? Two? Ten? Ten and two. Ten and two. Drive to West Grace Street. Sarah K. Danvers. Christ, I'm getting hard. Jenny? Nah, she's snoring. I can sneak out, call Sarah ... can I get down there this weekend, sneak away? Maybe. No— The kids. I gotta stay with the kids this weekend, promised Ben. We're swimming in the ool. That's right, no P in it. Let's keep it that way, huh, buddy? Okay, Dad. Sarah Danvers. Marie. Anna Elizabeth. RML. What's RML? God Almighty, look out for Anna Elizabeth. Go check on her. That'll clear your head. Check on the baby. What's RML? The sticky note on the fridge; there's one in Jenny's vanity, too. RML. Don't think about it. Get a pill. That'll get you to sleep. That's how we sleep. Get a pill. There's one in those pants, the ones from dinner the other night with Sarah. Sarah. My mistress. Jesus, I have a mistress. Fading, fading mistress. I have a mistress, a pill problem, an alcohol problem, a weight problem, a hot suit problem, a fuckload of problems for a thirty-one-year-old wet-nosed Homicide Division cop at 4:22, no, 4:23 on a sweltering fucking Friday in July. RML.

4:23 a.m.

The phone rang.

I sat up, my mouth tasting like someone had filled it with ashes. I needed a smoke, a Scotch. I hustled downstairs in my boxers, not wanting to wake the kids or Jenny.

'Doyle.' I cleared my throat and scrambled around for a pad.

'Sailor, it's Harper. Sorry, I've got to send you out.'

'No problem, LT – what do we got?' I rubbed my eyes, trying to clear the cobwebs. *Pay attention, dummy. Find a damned pen. Where the hell are all the pens, Jenny?*

'Two bodies, in a bit of a sorry shape. It looks like an old man and his wife, been dead a while. It's a farmhouse, some kind of old orchard, about fifteen miles northwest of Richmond, in St James County, off County Road 183, near the intersection of Goochland Lane and Pitcairn Road. It's the middle of frigging nowhere.'

'Fifteen miles from Richmond? Really?'

'Ever been out there?'

'Nah, not that I remember.'

'Oh, yeah, it's holy banjo-picking Ned Beatty-nowhere, and it's only a stone's throw from the city, on the way to Lake Anna.'

'Hmm.' I switched the coffee-maker on, cracked the kitchen window and searched for a cigarette. 'So shot? Stabbed? Hit by a bus? What's up?'

'We're not sure yet, other than they're in a sorry shape, like I said.'

'Lovely,' I said. 'And in this heat, they'll be ripe as hell.'

'Actually, I don't think so,' Harper said. 'From what Lourdes told me—'

'Bob Lourdes?' *Great, Sailor, interrupt him. Very smooth.*

'Yeah, you know him?'

'Yes, sir.' Failing to find any smokes, I dug in the cabinet for a coffee mug. 'He's around a lot, trolling for a transfer to Dope. He's all right, a tough kid, doesn't take any shit. Huck likes him; he's a bit clean-cut for undercover work, though.'

'Uh huh.' Lieutenant Harper clearly didn't care. 'Listen, I'm going to let you solo on this one.'

'Thank you, sir. I'll make sure I call if—'

'Clarkson, from ID, is going to meet you there. He'll probably be at the farmhouse before you. Follow his lead, Sailor. He's been in ID longer than most of us have been alive. He's worked more murder scenes than all of us put together.'

'Okay.' *Christ, I'm sweating already. I need a frigging drink.* 'So I'll defer to him, then.'

'Nope, no, now don't do that,' he said, trying to clarify his point. '*You're* the detective on the scene; it's *your* scene. He'll do what you tell him, but keep in the back of your mind: Phil's been through this before. That's all.'

'Yes, sir. I appreciate your confidence in me, sir.'

Harper laughed. 'You're going to do fine, Sailor. You've been out on a few, what is it now?'

'Six.'

'Six, in what? Four weeks?'

'About that, yes, sir.' The coffee smelled like a holiday. Upstairs, Ben said something groany in his sleep.

'So you're ready. And, as shit luck would have it, most of the guys are away this weekend, or working that detail down at the Jefferson Hotel tomorrow night. You're the new guy; you get the shit work. We've all been there, Sailor.'

'Sounds great, LT. I'll call you if the Earth crashes into the Sun.'

'I'll be on my boat, but I have my cell. I'll walk you through anything you need.'

'Yes, sir.'

'Doc Lefkowitz is the ME on call this weekend. You know him. He'll take the bodies, but not until you're done. So again, work with him, but don't take any shit; Lefkowitz can be a hardass. And call me with an update before lunch.'

31

'Yes, sir. Thanks, LT.'

'Oh, Christ, I almost forgot,' Harper added, 'apparently, the St James Deputy who arrived first on the scene fired a few shots; wait, let me look here … four shots, I think. Get that gun. Be polite about it, but don't get pushed around by the county lieutenant, the shift sergeant, anybody. Hold their hands; show them the crime scene, but get his fucking gun. Arrest him if you have to, because if we find other shots fired at that location, we'll need ballistics to discern between his and the others. The county lieutenant may want to do that piece of the investigation himself. It'll be a big deal for them; the last shot they fired out there was probably aimed at Ulysses Grant.'

This floored me. *A shooting? By myself?* Granted, it was a holiday weekend and people were gone, but I'd been to shootings before; half the CID always showed up. 'Um, okay; so I should let him take over that piece?'

'Absolutely not, Sailor, and you can tell him I said so. Hell, call me and I'll tell him myself. Get the deputy's gun, get his statement, then send him home.'

'Who'd he shoot?' My bare foot came down in something sticky Ben had spilled, a forgotten popsicle, maybe.

'No one.' Harper laughed again. 'There's some kind of problem with a cat or two, I don't know. Lourdes tried to call Animal Control. They can take care of it.'

Cats? What the hell?

'Very good, sir.' I scribbled a few notes, feeling like I needed to be asking more questions, but nothing came to mind. Then, flipping the page, I saw the letters *RML* scrawled two or three times in the margin. *Jenny?*

'You there, Sailor?'

'Uh, yeah, sorry, sir, just writing this all down. I'll keep you posted when I get there.'

'Let me know if you need anything.'

'Thanks, Lieutenant.' *I'm gonna fuck this up.*

'Call the dispatcher at Division, Julie Largo. She's got the directions. Or hit Clarkson on his cell phone. Apparently this place is buried out in the sticks.'

32

'Will do, sir.' I hung up.

St James County. Doc Lefkowitz and Sarah.

'So wait a minute. *Why* won't they be ripe, Lieutenant?' I asked my empty kitchen.

Upstairs, Jenny was a dishevelled pile of blankets. I shaved, stood under the shower, then in front of the mirror, running through the list of things I hoped I remembered to do when I got to the crime scene. I was getting fat. Four weeks in Homicide and I was putting on weight. Jenny didn't care. She was happy. My hair was short again and I shaved every day: no more going to work looking like I'd slept under the boardwalk. I hadn't realised how much sitting around I'd be doing after the transfer, though, and there was always something to eat. Most days the CID had food out at the barracks: pastries, sugary coffees, cookie or fruit platters, and acres of deli meats and cheese. I hadn't eaten this much since I was in high school. It was no wonder I was hauling around a couple of new lovehandles.

Frowning at my new, definitely not improved pear shape, I snorted disdain at the mirror. I needed some exercise, needed to cut back on the Scotch and the smokes, too. I'd been saying that for years.

Forget it, Sailor. Go to work. I stepped into clean underwear and tiptoed into the bedroom.

'Wear the fawn one,' Jenny mumbled into her pillow. 'It's lighter fabric. I heard it's going to be in the nineties all weekend, hopefully with no rain. I'm still drying out from last week.'

I flipped on the closet light. 'What the hell's fawn?'

'Fawn,' she said. 'Light brown.'

'All right,' I whispered.

She switched on the bedside lamp and sat up. 'Was that Lieutenant Harper?'

'Yeah. Go back to sleep.'

'I'm awake. Where's he sending you?' she asked through a yawn, stretching.

'St James County, northwest of Richmond, some farm. There's two

33

dead; he wasn't sure how, though. Bob Lourdes is there. Remember him?'

'Sure, the goodlooking kid from Henrico. He's nice.' Jenny wrestled with her hair, then left it tangled, her pale Irish face blotchy with sleep. 'Is Harper meeting you?'

'No.' I found my fawn suit in the closet. She was right: it was the lightest of the new ones we'd picked out when my transfer papers came back signed. But I was still headed out into the Virginia summer draped head to toe in wool. 'I'm on my own, so I don't know when I'll be home. Tell Ben I'll try to be at the ool tomorrow, but I'll probably be too late for the whateveritis tonight at Greg and Christine's.'

'It's called a barbecue, Sailor.' She went into the bathroom, left the door open. *Sarah wouldn't do that.* 'Don't worry about us. We're cleaning the house this morning. And I've got to get some things from the supermarket after lunch. Do you want beer for tomorrow? *I* want beer for tomorrow. I miss beer. Does it still taste the same?'

I fumbled a Windsor knot, cursed and tried again. 'No, these days it tastes like breast milk— But Jenny, I don't know about tomorrow either.'

'Really?' She sounded disappointed. 'Ben'll be mad.'

'I'll try to be there, but I'm on my own for the first time on this one. I gotta stick around until it's done right.'

'I know.' The toilet flushed. 'Maybe if we lose this weekend, you can take a day or two when the investigation's over. We'll go to the beach or something.'

'That'll be just grand,' I said, 'the two of us in bathing suits. We look like your parents.'

She giggled, wrapping her arms around me. Her boobs were engorged with milk; I was afraid to squeeze too hard. 'We're turning into my parents.'

'I'm thirty-one,' I said, 'look at me. I'm going to weigh two hundred and fifty pounds working in Homicide, and you—'

'I what?' She shot me a mock scowl.

'You look ... lovely?'

'Nice try, Sailor. I look like a coal barge. Thank Christ there's no Japanese fishing boats on the James River, or someone would have

34

shot a harpoon into my thighs and harvested me for ambergris. Have you seen my thighs?'

'How could I miss them?'

'Smartass.'

I kneeled down and hiked up her Frumpy Alice nightgown. 'I'd love to see them up close, but there are these massive *jambons* in the way. Tell me, did these come with the old lady nightgown, or did you pay extra for them?' I slipped my hands under her panties.

Jenny squealed and dived for the bed. 'Don't! You'll wake up the kids!'

I jumped in next to her and kissed her on the forehead. 'I gotta go.'

She ran a hand between my legs, gave me a quick squeeze and said, 'Go catch bad guys. Call me later.'

'Tell Ben and Anna—'

'I'll tell them you're in a phone booth somewhere slipping into your super suit.'

'Shit-brown wool for the Fourth of July.'

'That's one expensive suit, Sailor – and anyway, most shit is darker than that.'

'Fawn?'

'Fawn.'

'I love you.'

'Well, I don't love you, fatso.'

'Says Mrs Chubby Thighs!'

'Go!'

'There's coffee.'

'I can't have coffee. Your daughter will get one sip and be shrieking two octaves higher than usual. Go on, go to work – keep us safe. Go on, before Ben wakes up. He'll be wandering in here any minute, so you ought to be gone before then or you'll never get away.'

'Bye, hon.' I grabbed my lighter-than-shit-brown jacket and turned to tease her once more before leaving. Then I saw it.

I hadn't noticed it before – I mean *really* noticed it; there were so many things that arrived when Anna was born: new toys, little girl clothes, mountain ranges of infant diapers, all the regular bullshit. I hadn't bought Jenny a present this time around; I don't know why. She still wore the pearls I gave her when Ben was born.

When I saw the anklet, I figured it must have been something someone had given to her. She had probably shown it to me, and I'd nodded, *that's nice, honey*, whatever. But I hadn't really seen it until that moment.

A delicate silver chain held a small circular charm, about the size of a dime. I was glad she'd been wearing it, pleased to see she still felt pretty, despite the lingering baby weight.

But now, in the light from her bedside lamp, I had a closer look.

'What's the matter, Sailor?' she asked.

'Nothing, hon.' I leaned over to kiss her, trying to hide the fact that I was sneaking a look at her ankle. 'I'll call you later.'

'Bye, baby.'

'Bye.' The silver charm was engraved in a fine script: *RML*.

5:17 a.m.

I rolled south down I-95 at ninety-two miles an hour. *God, but I love being a cop.* I figured I'd be in Ashland in half an hour, if that, as I cut across Hanover County to Harper's crime scene – *my* crime scene.

The northbound lanes were already snarled up with DC commuters. Every day it was the same thing, headlights as far as anyone could see, those poor bastards creeping along at one mile every two weeks or so. Commuters get old faster than the rest of us, especially those on I-95 at five-thirty in the morning.

Harper had said there were two dead at the farm, but he didn't say how they'd bought it. An old man and his wife ... I wondered what they were into: old fogies cranking up a meth lab in the barn? It pays a good deal better than shucking corn, even with the federal subsidy. Harper had also said they wouldn't be ripe, but I couldn't imagine why not. Anything dead out here today would surely be ripe as a three-week-old banana.

I was glad Clarkson would be there; he had seemed all right, organised and down to earth. I'd need a leveller in case I got myself too wrapped up with any one detail, too involved chasing my tail around the wrong questions, answers, whatever. Phil would keep *my* eye on the ball. And Doc: I hadn't seen him in a while and I felt better knowing he'd be around, even if it was only on the periphery.

Of course, having Doc involved these days meant Sarah wasn't too far in the shadows. I was half-drunk the last time I saw her. I couldn't remember if she'd said she was going to be away this weekend – I thought she had mentioned something about going home to see her parents, or maybe her brother. I was fairly certain she wasn't going to be in the lab, but I figured I could still sneak back with Doc just to be sure. Tonight would be an easy night to be away late, what with working my first solo murder. Hell, I could probably be gone all week-end without a back-up excuse.

RML. What . . . ?

RML. Robert. Randy. Roger. Red. Roscoe. Shit, not Roscoe; anything but Roscoe.

'Why are you doing this, Sailor?' I asked out loud. 'Why assume it's a man's name?' I fumbled in my jacket for a pack of smokes, but came up empty.

'What are you doing? Let this go, at least for today.'

No one answered me; there was just the inaudible crackle of the radio.

Is someone fucking my wife? Is that why?

'Well, *you're* fucking someone, aren't you, dipshit? Even if it's fad-ing with every pound you pack on, fatty?' I wanted more coffee and I needed cigarettes. Finding coffee would distract me, or keep me sharp, or some damned thing.

'Jenny wouldn't do that. She wouldn't do that to me. She's got to be in love.'

Bullshit.

I wanted a carton of cigarettes right now – I would have eaten them in a bowl with milk if I thought it would get the nicotine into my bloodstream quicker. I promised myself a gallon or two of coffee as soon as I got to Ashland. Whatever – *who*ever – RML was, I couldn't let it screw me up. There were too many things waiting to throw me off my game today, that much I'd already seen in my short time on the job. Buggering up this investigation would not be a wise career choice.

I tried to wrestle myself back to centre, but couldn't quite turn off the faucet yet. Jenny's scribbles came after me again.

RML? Rex. Rodney. Roquefort.

That guy from her office, what's his name? Roger. Roger what? Roger . . . dodger bo-bodger banana something fo-fodger. Rodger. Could it be him? He was . . . well, not young, but still okay-looking.

Two dead people waited for me; ripe or not, they were mine. I had no idea how many cops, St James County deputies, ambulance techs, lawyers, bullpen pitchers or newspaper reporters were already at the scene. Getting focused and staying focused had never been so critical. I had to get my head out of the sand. The radio would help; I'd see if my stiffs had hit the news yet.

Come on down to Ashland Chrysler! General Lee will be here all day Saturday and Sunday! A moon bounce for the kids! Free hot dogs and cheeseburgers from the grill! And, as always, the lowest prices on a new or used Chrysler along the I-95 corridor! That's Ashland Chrysler! Come on down and meet the General! That's General Lee, this Fourth of July!

'Oh shit, and here comes the jingle.'

Come on over to Ashland Chrysler. Prices there have n'er been nicer. Look away! Look away! Look away! To Ashland.

'Jesus, I hate that song … two hillbilly retards in an orange car.'

That's Ashland Chrysler. Just fifteen miles north of Richmond on Route 1 in Ashland.

'Yeah, yeah, we know. You only mentioned it six hundred and—'

The dog lurched across the southbound lanes, appearing out of nowhere at the edge of my vision. He was a big bastard, chocolate-brown, and bounding east in desperate leaps.

'*Fuck!*' I stomped with both feet on the brakes and my cruiser fishtailed dangerously, threatening to roll and end my virgin murder case in a crumple of blue and grey steel. I cranked the wheel left, then right, then left again, over-correcting, and all the while cursing the dog, the breeder, and the first sonofabitch ever to domesticate man's best fucking friend. Waiting for the impact, I had an instant of sick realisation: at this speed the dog's body would act like a ramp and send me sailing nose first into the northbound traffic.

'Shit, oh shit, oh shit!' I yelled, bracing for the worst.

I missed him.

Screeching down below seventy, then fifty, I checked over my shoulder but saw only ribbons of empty macadam, lit smeary-red by ranks of taillights rolling north towards the Beltway. No dog.

'Fuck,' I panted, '*Jesus*, you lucky fucker!'

'Say that again, please.' The air-conditioner roared so loudly I could barely hear the dispatcher over the cell. I finally called in on the phone; the goddamned radio was getting embarrassing. I'd never been so lost, here was me: a state police officer in a fully-loaded cruiser, and I was thinking about getting out and leaving a trail of crumbs.

'It's Pitcairn Road, across the one-lane bridge about a quarter of a mile past the Phillips 66 station. Take that west—'

'Wait, what is west? Left or right? I'm all frigged up out here, and there's no sun, just haze.'

'Right. You're coming south.'

'How is that possible? I just turned north on Goochland Lane.'

'Detective Doyle—'

'Sorry, sorry. I'm just a little ... I'm just ... I should've been there twenty-five minutes ago.' I could see her sitting behind her console at the barracks, fifteen coffee-drinking troopers standing around stifling laughter at the great homicide detective who couldn't find a murder with both hands, a map and a GPS. My lighter-than-shit-brown suit – *fawn*, Christ – had already wrinkled in the heat. I had the AC vents pointed at my face, my pits and my crotch.

'It's fine, sir,' the dispatcher, I think her name was Julie Largo, said, 'you're almost there. It's easy to miss.'

'Sorry,' I mumbled.

'Take a left on Pitcairn, past the Phillips 66 station—'

'You mean that abandoned, burned-out shell that might have been a gas station back when my grandfather was paying eighteen cents a gallon?'

'I can't tell that on the GPS, sir.'

'Right. Fine. Okay, I'm turning left.'

'Now, follow Pitcairn for about a half-mile. There should be an intersection with an unimproved county road; it might be dirt or gravel.'

I drove past the Phillips 66 station, its macadam cracked by an invasion of resilient weeds, into what could only be described as wilderness, not fifteen miles west of Ashland and maybe as far north of Richmond. I was driving through woods and fallow grown-over fields that looked as though they hadn't been tended since the Powhatan Indians moved to Cleveland. The only signs of recent life were two rusty 1950s-era pickups buried to the fenders on either side of a muddy driveway. The drive led to a double-wide trailer with three broken windows and a gaping wound torn through the screen door. It was flanked by a single-room home, built entirely of eight-inch blocks and painted fire-engine red – *Satan-lovin'* red. The roof was tarpaper over plywood, and there were no windows or doors that I could see from the road.

Fifteen miles to Richmond. Jesus, some hardy developer could buy this whole county for the money he makes in an afternoon, build a mansion out here, a golf course, Christ, a theme park.

I drove slowly past the devil worshippers' temple, looking out on both sides of the car for anything that looked like a road. A narrow ribbon of dirt and grass materialised out of the forest. 'Okay, I see the road, goat path, whatever you call it. It's right here, next to my new vacation condo.'

'Good. That's Hadley Road, I think.'

'What's next?'

'The driveway you're looking for is off an unmarked lane about two hundred yards up on the left. Take that about a quarter-mile, past what looks like a pond, then turn right. I don't know if there's a mailbox or not, but you need the first right after the pond.'

'First right after the pond,' I echoed, 'got it. Thanks, Julie.'

'Marie.'

'What's that?'

'I didn't say anything, Detective.'

'What's your name?'

'Julie Largo, sir.'

'I thought so.' I leaned over and let the air-conditioning blow directly onto my damp forehead. *I need a pill, just one, one to blow out the cobwebs.* 'Thanks, Julie. You saved my ass.'

'I'll be here until eight if you need anything, Detective.'

I tossed the cell onto the passenger seat and took a long swallow from the coffee I bought in Ashland. I found a smoke in my briefcase and tried not to think about pills. *I'm hearing things, that's all. She didn't say 'Marie', just 'Julie . . . Julie Largo'.*

The left turn off Pitcairn was barely visible behind a thatch of overgrown raspberry bushes. A two-hundred-year-old stone wall ran between the road and the pond, delineating the edge of a farm probably tilled by Pocahontas. The single lane, rutted and wrinkled from erosion, scraped the undercarriage of my car twice before I reached the driveway, another shrubby path that wound beyond the pond to a patchwork of soybean fields interrupted here and there by clumps of gnarled fruit trees. A tattered calico cat stalked something in the bushes beside the pond. It pounced out of sight behind a stand of bulrushes.

The farm, three hundred acres of untended countryside, sat beyond a mud-and-grass cul-de-sac at the end of the pond road, another half-mile of thick foliage, muggy swampland and bug-infested Virginia summertime. The house slouched atop a short rise, near the edge of a sprawling yard that might have been mowed last when I was in high school. Three rusty bikes and an A-frame swing set peeked above the three-foot-tall sedge and timothy grass like archaeological artefacts. A tyre hung from an ancient oak near the centre of the yard; it swayed listlessly from side to side.

I popped an OxyContin and wiped my forehead on my shirtsleeve before grabbing my briefcase and joining the officers and CID techs already working the crime scene.

Bob Lourdes, looking trim in his uniform, came out to meet me. He wore rubber gloves and a surgical mask.

The humidity hit like an invisible wave. I was sweating inside of five seconds. This was going to be a long day.

Lourdes folded a small spiral notebook closed, stuffed it into his back pocket, and jogged the last few steps to my cruiser. 'Morning, Sailor.'

'Hey,' I said, 'how long you been here?'

'About four hours. What kept you?'

'Couldn't find a phone booth to change clothes.'

'Oh, yeah, I have that problem sometimes too.'

I swallowed hard. 'What in the name of Christ on the cross is that smell?'

Lourdes grinned behind his mask; his voice sounded canned through the cotton shield. 'We have a salad bar of aromas here this morning, Detective. Which particular smell did you mean?'

'Never mind. I'll know soon enough, I'm sure.' I blew smoke out my nose in hopes of sidelining the stench. 'How you been?'

'Not bad,' he said. 'Actually, I've been up your way a lot recently, some training at Quantico, tech and database stuff, mostly.'

'Good. They're a great resource. You ought to grab it when you can.' Jenny was right: he was goodlooking, and he was barely sweating. I'd been outside the car less than a minute and I already wanted to strip naked and jump into a cooler full of beer cans. But I was in charge and I didn't want to be irritated with Lourdes already; I needed to keep things positive. I said, 'Harper told me they weren't ripe! Jesus, I bet you can smell these motherfuckers in Charlottesville.'

'That's not them, Sailor.'

'What do you mean?'

43

'C'mon, I'll show you. Clarkson's already inside. Lefkowitz is on his way.'

'No coroner yet? I figured Doc might try to dodge a bullet on this one, maybe stay home and deal with it on Monday.'

'St James County is screwy, you know that. They sometimes send a coroner, but the guy's a fireman, a paramedic or something – who knows? I guess he's got the weekend off, with the holiday and everything. So Doc Lefkowitz is coming. Clarkson's covering the over-under on Doc's stay.'

'Really?' I pictured Dr Irving Lefkowitz out here in his six-hundred-dollar shoes. 'What's the line?'

'Eighteen minutes from door to door.' Lourdes glanced at his watch.

'I'll bet the over. Jot me down for twenty bucks.'

'The over?'

'Yeah. You don't know Lefkowitz.'

'All right, it's your money, but you might want to hold off until you see what's inside.'

I ushered him towards the wrap-around porch, overdue by a decade for a new coat of paint. 'Let's go.'

'I gotta grab another pen from my car,' he said. 'I'll meet you up there.'

'Hey!' I called after him. 'Who are they?'

'Carl and Claire Bruckner. He's in the sitting room off the back porch. She's upstairs in the hall and the master bedroom, sort of.'

Hall and *master bedroom? Sort of?*

The haze had brightened since I turned west from Ashland, the I-95 corridor and human civilisation, yet the Bruckner farm somehow seemed to shrug off the brightening morning. The house was an antebellum relic that couldn't have been more than ten minutes from termite-ridden collapse. Someone in the St James County Board Office had clearly missed this place on the year's list of demolition projects. The greying, three-level farmhouse would have looked right at home in any Civil War epic – *after* Grant had razed this entire region. The top floor supported three dormers, one of which had broken away from the roof and was listing precariously to one side, the victim of a fallen oak tree which was still lying there. With all the recent thunderstorms, no doubt that end of the house was still dripping wet. The rest of the dilapidated building was rotting way. The wood siding and porch posts were eaten nearly through by legions of hungry bugs. Several shutters hung crookedly; others had fallen into a long-ignored bed of weeds that ringed the house. A shabby, bleached-out American flag, the only patch of colour in the place, dangled limply from a rusting metal rod.

Something bit my neck and I slapped at it. Then I popped the trunk of my cruiser. I would need gloves, hell, a body condom.

Before I ever decided to become a police officer, I understood that death produced its own esoteric odour. I had gutted a few deer as a teenager, had smelled enough summer road-kill while jogging in college, and had even come across a body once beneath a pier on the Jersey coast, near Asbury Park. Some depressed, alcoholic housewife had decided to swim back to the old country; she hadn't made it. When I caught a whiff of her, I doubled over and barfed onto the sand. The smell was astonishing: sweet on the periphery but rancid through its soft centre. She overwhelmed any seaside aromas that morning; even the ozone-heavy breeze couldn't clear her away. I had never encountered anything quite as intolerable: highway wrecks and crimes of passion are generally found quickly, the bodies fresh. Fifteen years later – eight of them as a cop – and that woman's decomposing remains were still the most ghastly thing I'd ever encountered.

Until now.

Slapping invisible insects from my face and neck, I checked the windows. Except for a lightning-bolt fracture across one, they were surprisingly intact, and closed tight, some even painted shut. As foul as the morning smelled here in the driveway, what was trapped inside would be an unchecked nightmare, much worse even than the Jersey floater. This was going to be like walking across a mediaeval battle-field.

All right, let's go. You're in charge.

Lourdes joined me on the porch. I scribbled a couple of observations on a notepad, anything to look like I knew what I was doing.

'Ready?' he asked.

'One second,' I said as I continued writing. A St James County Sheriff's cruiser and a shift sergeant's car were parked on the east side of the house, between the garage and a ramshackle barn. 'Where are they?'

'Out back.' Lourdes inclined his head towards the barn. 'The kid's a rookie. He came out to check on the place when the guy reading the electric meter called in a complaint about the stench. I guess he got here, took a deep breath and knew something wasn't right.'

'Harper mentioned shots fired,' I said. 'Was that this St James officer?'

'Right.'

'Who'd he shoot?'

'No one.' Lourdes started around the porch. About halfway down the west side of the house he sidestepped a broken swing, moved two ceramic planters out of my way with the toe of his boot and pointed into the corner. 'There you go.'

I stopped. 'You gotta be kidding me.'

'Nope,' Lourdes said. 'Those four on the left, they're his. He said they *attacked* him.'

'And the others?'

'I dunno. Clarkson says he thinks they've been dead for a while, the others were eating them. Kill or be killed. You know.'

'Jesus Christ.' I crushed the cigarette on the heel of my shoe and looked around for someplace to get rid of the butt. Not wanting to mess up Clarkson's evidence, I tossed it inside my coffee cup. 'Bring me the St James deputy,' I said, then thought twice. 'No, actually, get his statement—'

'Done.' Lourdes looked like he might injure a shoulder patting himself on the back.

'Good.' I went on anyway, 'Get his statement. Get his gun. Tell his shift sergeant we'll have the mobile lab out here inside of two hours. We'll get the ballistics we need when the trailer gets here, and we'll have the gun back to them in a couple days.'

'He's not going to like—'

'I don't give a shit,' I said, self-conscious sweat running down my face.

46

'He's going to want to talk with—'

'Bob, stop interrupting me.' Lourdes was a damned lapdog, barking for attention.

'Sorry, Detective.' He didn't seem at all abashed. I'd surely beat that out of him before we were done today. I was green, and everyone knew it, and while I might take suggestions, I was not about to get interrupted by a CID wannabe from some pansy-ass gated community in Henrico.

'Get his gun. Tell his staff sergeant to go fuck himself, whatever, I don't care. I know they have their own detectives and their own lab guys, but this is my crime scene, and like it or not, this is a state investigation. His rookie took care of that for us when he started shooting. Be nice about it if you'd rather, but get the gun. What do they give a shit, anyway? He fired four—'

'Um ... six—'

'*Six* rounds ... he'll be riding a desk for at least two weeks. He doesn't need a gun.'

'For this?' Lourdes said.

'Yup.' I opened my pad and scribbled another note. 'Get his name, his statement, his gun, and make sure Clarkson's got photos and notes for each round he fired. Then send him home. We'll be in touch once the lab guys run the ballistics. We might need him out here tomorrow or Sunday for video, but until then, I don't want them hanging around.'

'We need ballistics?'

'Any other shots fired?'

'Not that we know of.'

'Then hell yes. Until we know, we have to be able to discern between his rounds and anyone else's.'

'Got it,' Lourdes said. 'Give me ten minutes. Then, if you don't mind, I'm going to run out for some breakfast, maybe bagels or something.'

'Sounds good. You've been here a long time,' I said. 'Keep the receipt.'

He wandered into the back yard and I crossed the porch and kneeled in the corner. Thirteen dead cats had been lined up in two neat rows.

Four looked freshly killed, nearly torn in two by the St James deputy's .357. The others were in various stages of dismemberment and decomposition, clouds of blowflies and greenheads swarming about them. Some of the cats were bloated to furry balloons, and three or four were already infested with wriggling maggots. I gagged down incipient nausea and waved a greenhead fly away from my face.

Something else stung my neck, and I felt a bite on my wrist.

I lit another cigarette and went inside.

'Phil!' I shouted, then gagged again. The stench of decomposition was only marginally less obnoxious in the Bruckner kitchen, where the heat and humidity trapped the pungent fumes inside. I propped open the porch door, took another look at the cats and called, 'Phil! Where are you?'

'Upstairs,' came the muffled cry. 'Coffee's on in there. Grab some and come up.'

Carl and Claire Bruckners' kitchen was in the same state of neglect and disrepair as the rest of the property. Everything was falling apart, or dusted with a green shadow of mildew. A clock above the chipped Formica table had frozen at 2:27. The refrigerator, an old Frigidaire dotted with condensation, sported a dozen Old Glory magnets, two of which held up a toddler's drawing of a stickman soldier in a cowboy hat with a stickman sabre at his belt. The words *the genrele* were scrawled crookedly across the top.

Tasteful blue-collar curtains hung akimbo from the north window; one was tied neatly, while the other was shredded, most likely by cats, and drooped in ragged tatters almost to the linoleum. The dishwasher and oven both stood open. Dirty pots and pans had been loaded into the washer; those that wouldn't fit were stacked in the sink, some hidden beneath eight inches of grey dishwater. A Pyrex casserole bowl with the remains of someone's last meal sat on a blackened grate protruding from the oven, bloated cockroaches helping themselves to the leftovers. The oven's interior light had burned out. A forgotten potholder and a wooden serving spoon were lying on the stained floor beneath the table. A roiling swarm of fruit flies hovered over three blackened bananas; another cloud filled the air above a plastic trash can. I couldn't see what was inside.

Six cat food dishes, three of which were monogrammed in bright letters – MOOSE, CHICKADEE and POOPSIE – were lined up, empty, beside the refrigerator, and the torn remnants of three fifty-pound bags of dry cat food had been stuffed into the corner near the pantry. There was a massive litter box, filled with so much mummified cat shit that I couldn't imagine a team of engineers could find a place to take a dump, never mind a housecat.

That's the other smell in here, for Christ's sake: cat shit . . . old cat piss. I forced the nausea back down again and continued my inventory.

The wallpaper, a garish floral print from the 1970s, peeled in places, rolling far enough over itself for me to see that something worse, a geometric pattern from the 1960s, had been papered over. More unnerving was an old coffee can of peeled and broken crayons lying on its side, the contents spilled across the table in a swathe of out-of-place colour.

So where's the kid?

I slid an aluminium dining chair against the sink and crossed to the counter. Someone had fired up the Bruckners' coffee-maker.

'Who made coffee?' I shouted upstairs.

'I did,' Phil called back. 'It's okay, but you gotta drink it black; don't even open the fridge. You don't want to smell that.'

'This is a crime scene, Phil – what are you doing using their coffee-maker?' I searched around for a clean mug, regardless. A stack of opened and unopened mail had not yet been dusted for prints. There were a few hunting and boating magazines, two letters from the US Department of Defense, three from the Social Security Administration, and some child's drawings: crayon scribbles of animals, houses, giant flowers, and half a dozen attempts at a white horse, saddled and ready to ride. Across the bottom of several, in different coloured crayon, someone had written *From Wibbleton to Wobbleton is fifteen miles, From Wobbleton to Wibbleton is fifteen miles*.

'Anybody dust in here yet?' I didn't see any residue. The techs were in the living room; one of Phil's team members dusted, labelled, and photographed evidence, anything that might help explain what had occurred.

'Not yet, sir,' a young CID trooper, I think her name was Kay Bryson, paused long enough to answer.

'Then what are we doing leaving prints all over the place just to make coffee?' As much as I wanted to instil confidence in the investigators working the Bruckner house, I didn't want to fuck up evidence by being too lax with them either. Deciding when to encourage and when to shout: *that* was something they didn't teach at the academy.

'The prints are just yours, sir,' Bryson said, albeit politely.

'What?'

'We're in gloves, sir. No prints.' She held up a hand and waggled her fingers at me.

Okay. I forgot to put mine on. So fire me.

'Still,' I said, 'this is a murder scene. Think a little; you get a headache, that's just evidence you're alive, huh?' I found a clean mug in a cabinet and helped myself to the coffee.

'I'm not so sure,' Clarkson called from the upstairs hall.

'What?'

'I'm not sure it's a murder scene, Sailor, at least not what we expected.'

I paused, mid-pour, as Phil clomped down the stairs and into the kitchen. He, like me, was sweating through his suit. He had a digital camera around his neck, two pads in one hand, a pocket full of Ziploc baggies, a surgical mask over his mouth and nose and three pens in his damp shirt pocket: red, black, and blue. He kept a yellow highlighter behind one ear. I hadn't seen Phil in a few weeks, but it was pretty obvious summer wasn't agreeing with him. His skin was pasty, and he'd gained weight. He was in the neighbourhood of fifty-five now, and he owed about a pound for every year since he'd graduated college.

'What do you mean, you're not sure this is a murder scene?' I asked. 'Are they not dead?'

Phil removed his mask. 'Oh, they're dead as hell, but I don't know yet that we can say a murder's been committed.' He pulled out a pen and I winced; he had an irritating way of repeatedly clicking his ballpoint pens. That was Phil Clarkson's background music: nervous clicks.

'Well, who killed them? We've got a St James deputy shooting the

51

place full of holes, two dead people, one of whom apparently is *sort of* occupying two different spaces—'

'She is—'

'And thirteen dead cats lined up on the porch like hunting trophies—'

'Thirty-seven,' he interrupted.

'Thirty-seven what?'

'Thirty-seven dead cats ... so far.'

'*So far?*'

'Right.' Phil refilled his own mug from the pot. 'Thirty-seven dead cats, two dead goats, one dead horse, very grim – and Jesus, that one's hard to look at – at least three dead sheep, a handful of dead chickens, the ones we can find that haven't been eaten – I'm guessing by the cats – and what appears to be the remains of a dead dog, probably a stray, down near the pond.'

'A stray?'

Phil loosened his tie. 'The Bruckners had at least thirty-seven cats, Sailor. They weren't dog people.'

My mind reeled for a moment, taking it all in. 'So what killed them?'

'Beats the shit out of me.' He shrugged. 'Some of them have some kind of snotty, boogery crud coagulating around their nostrils and on their lips, especially the horse, the goats and the dog. The sheep might have been killed by hungry cats.'

'*House* cats? Mother of God! We should have Lourdes call Animal Control.'

'Bryson tried,' Phil said. 'There's no one on until eight o'clock.'

'Okay, but until then, we figure that whatever killed these people also killed the animals, correct?'

'That, or the animals died after these people stopped caring for them. I don't know enough about animals to figure that one out, but they look pretty bad. Apart from the snot, most of them are gaunt as hell, so it could be starvation. And like I said, a few of them have been eaten or chewed up pretty badly.' Phil made a gesture towards the barn. He was right: I didn't want to see a horse that had starved to death while trapped its own stable and then been half-eaten by an army of ravenous cats.

Lourdes said the St James rookie was attacked . . . by house cats. Holy shit.

I scratched another note on my pad. 'So can we determine if these people died of natural causes?'

Phil said, 'Lefkowitz can, and if it *is* natural causes, some kind of sickness, then we've got a righteous mess on our hands, but no felony murder.'

'And if it's not natural?'

Phil lowered his voice. 'Then there is one sick motherfucker out there, my friend.'

'How'd he do it?'

'Could have been airborne, some practise run for a terror attack. Location's perfect for it; you can wipe out a whole area, and no one knows until the meter reader shows up for his monthly tally. Frigging mailman doesn't come within a half-mile of this place, even to drop off the bills.'

'Should we get hazmat suits or something?' I hated sounding like I didn't know what to do.

'Nah,' Phil waved me off dismissively. 'Whatever it was is dissipated by now, all that rain we had last week. These people have been dead for a long time. Well, at least Claire has. Carl's a different story.'

'Show me.'

'All right.' He handed me a surgical mask. 'Put this on.'

I gulped the coffee, poured a refill. 'Lourdes is getting a statement from the St James deputy; I'll go through this mail, whatever's in the box, and any personal effects or paperwork after Lefkowitz leaves. Until then, we're at your disposal. I want to be ready when Doc gets here.'

Phil chuckled and added his coffee mug to the pile sitting in the filthy sink. 'Ready for what, Sailor?'

'How the hell do I know? Look, Phil, I know you've been out on twenty thousand of these things, but this is my cherry, and I don't want to screw it up.'

'So you want me to tell you if you're screwing things up?'

'Exactly, and—'

'And you'll buy the beer later?'

'Done.'

'Well, then, when you arrive at a crime scene as the investigating officer, you really should see the bodies. You know, make it a short-term goal.'

My face flushed. For the first time all morning I was happy for the heat. 'Fine, lead on.'

'Oh, and Sailor, even when we do have terrorists who kill an entire family, including the farm animals, with an airborne biohazard, we rarely – and I do mean *rarely* – lift incriminating prints from the coffee-maker. The toilet, yes, but the coffee-maker, no.'

I slapped him on the shoulder. 'Fine, Obiwan, thanks for the tip.'

I followed Phil along a narrow, cluttered hallway into the living room as all the while he droned on about getting the scene wrapped up soon because his teenage daughter was playing trombone in some patriotic holiday concert down near the James River that night.

More cat bowls littered the floor between the kitchen and the living room: GEORGIE, MARKUS, FLUFFY, one that just said PURINA, and WHISKERS. A charcoal-grey suit, still in dry-cleaning plastic, hung from a nail on the wall. 'That's odd,' I said, checking the receipt.

'What?' Phil asked over his shoulder.

'What's a nice suit doing hanging in a dump like this?'

'Who knows?' Phil shrugged and headed for the stairs.

I pulled the surgical mask over my face and struggled into my examination gloves. Kay Bryson was busying herself snapping pictures, collecting hair samples from seat cushions and rifling through what looked like carbon copies of bills, receipts, or credit card statements. She hummed through her mask as she made notes on a legal pad. She had a laptop, too, plugged into the wall, and she glanced at it periodically. I could see five or six hillocks of cat shit scattered throughout the room, but Bryson didn't appear to care; she was going to make a good detective one day. She was in uniform, so she'd either been working midnights on the road and volunteered to come out and assist Phil – a smart choice for anyone hoping for a transfer – or she'd got the call in the middle of the night and summoned the strength to pull herself into her uniform before driving all the way out here. Either way, I was impressed. I couldn't get a decent look at her; I could only imagine what curves lay hidden beneath that Kevlar vest.

Near the fireplace stood the Bruckners' television, turned on, but with the volume down. A bearded man on a horse, a passable General Lee, rode across a used car lot brandishing a sabre. Graphics flashed on the screen: Meet General Lee! July Fourth weekend at Ashland Chrysler!

I was glad Bryson had muted the sound.

Phil turned up the stairs. Each creaking wooden tread housed another bowl.

'... she was up late last night practising the songs ... getting good ...'

TIGER.

'... thinking about playing in college ... last year of high school ...'

PADDY.

'... our oldest ... more an athlete ... tried guitar for a while ...'

BERT.

'... will have three in college at once ... no idea how to pay for that ...'

MING, and another small mountain of cat shit. The tangy odour intensified as we climbed the steps; heat and grim smells both rise, apparently.

'... wife's back to work ... clerical stuff mostly ... time off when we had kids a hundred years ago ...'

I struggled to breathe through the mask. Sweat soaked my shirt; a trickle ran down the inside of my thigh. I regretted the coffee and badly needed a drink of water, beer, something cold. I was screwing up. I'd been here thirty-five minutes and I'd still not seen the damned Bruckners. Phil was making me crazy, jabbering away about his kids, his wife, whatever her name was – Curtains; that's how I remembered her. We had a farm full of dead animals, two dead people, at least one kid unaccounted for, whoever spilled the crayons – and there was the very real possibility that terrorists had used this place to dry-run a biological weapon. Should I call someone? The FBI? CID headquarters? Captain Fezzamo? I didn't have any of those numbers, did I? Maybe in the car somewhere ... I was over my head.

KARLA.

Karla? Who names a cat Karla?

FERGIE.

That's better.

Phil reached the landing and turned down the upstairs hall. I paused, distracted.

A cluster of framed photos and shadow boxes hung from the faux wood panelling. An overhead bulb cast display-case lighting on the miniature collection. Ignoring Phil, I leaned in to read the citations and certificates. There were a few snapshot photos as well, framed with newspaper articles pasted to coloured construction paper. They were all well cared for, cleaned recently, and the expensive frames in cherry or rosewood were as out of place in this haunted farmhouse as the crayons in the kitchen.

'You see these?' I asked.

'Yeah, um, yes, I did' – Phil started clicking again – 'I noticed them when I arrived. They're Carl's.'

'Captain Carl James Bruckner,' I read, 'decorated Vietnam veteran, US Marines.' I pointed at one of the shadow boxes. 'What is that? A Bronze Star?'

'Yup,' Phil said, 'and with that little V hanging there, that's for valour in combat. The one with the coloured stripes is the Navy and Marine Corps Medal; that's a big deal, and the other, on the left with Washington on it, that's a Purple Heart. He was injured somewhere.'

'Gia Lai Province and Pleiku.' I fumbled the phonics on one of Carl's citations. 'I wonder what happened.'

'Same as every other fucking swampy shithole over there probably,' Phil said. 'We slogged through mud, shot at shadows, sweated until our underwear and socks were soaked through, ate C-rations that looked like baby food and liked them, smoked a shitload of cigarettes – those were hard to quit, lemme tell you – and sometimes we even felt like we were winning. Most of the time, we looked forward to sleep and hot food. Sleep would have made any of us happy, almost as happy as peace.'

'You were there?'

'Just one tour, near the end,' Phil said. 'I was on a zippo down in the Mekong. I think I have clothes that are still wet. It sucked donkey balls.'

'Curious assessment,' I said. 'I wasn't even born yet.'

'Well, be glad you missed it.' He started down the hall. 'C'mon, I'll introduce you to Claire Bruckner.'

'Hey, Bryson!'

'Sir?' She appeared at the foot of the stairs.

'Call Dispatch, back at the barracks, Julie Largo's her name. Let her know you're out here with me.'

Bryson waited, pen poised. 'What do you need, Detective?'

'Have someone dig up Carl James Bruckner's service record, US Marines, Vietnam era. Got it?'

'Yes, sir.'

'Good. Let Lourdes know when you get anything.'

'See?' Phil grinned. 'You're doing fine.'

'What's Wibbleton or Wobbleton? Ever heard of them?'

'You kidding?' Phil replaced his surgical mask. 'Were you raised in a barn?'

I looked puzzled. 'I don't get it.'

'It's a nursery rhyme, you know: From Wibbleton to Wobbleton is fifteen miles. From Wobbleton to Wibbleton is fifteen miles. From Wibbleton to Wobbleton, from Wobbleton to Wibbleton ... on and on like that.'

I'd never heard it before.

Phil's brow furrowed. 'You all right, Sailor? You don't look good; you're too pale for a kid your age.'

Fifty-something-years-old, as ashen-grey as spoiled milk, and Phil Clarkson was suggesting that I looked bad? 'I'm fine,' I said. 'I should've had breakfast.'

'C'mon. She's just down here.'

I took three steps along the hallway and saw Claire Bruckner.

7:10 a.m.

Claire Bruckner looked like a figure stolen from a wax tableau outside one of those cheap seashore funhouses. Her face, tanned to football leather, was frozen in a silent wail. Her eyes – the eyeballs themselves dried to tiny marbles – were empty sockets, cast into shadow by the summer haze through the window. She looked as though she had been dead for the better part of the last millennium. I understood now what Harper had meant when he said the bodies weren't ripe. She didn't smell at all.

Claire's upper body was sprawled across the hall, as if she had been trying to drag herself to freedom while slowly succumbing to mummification. Her brittle hair was wrapped in a tight bun. She was wearing a blue dress, which had been pulled down to her waist, exposing the white bra now about eleven sizes too big, a gaudy crucifix hanging on a gold chain around her emaciated neck, and her naked torso ... and the marks where someone had tried to saw her in half with a carpenter's handsaw. Her legs, still clad in pale stockings and covered demurely by the blue dress, jutted awkwardly into the master bedroom. The saw remained lodged in her lumbar vertebrae, looking like one of Houdini's illusions gone horribly wrong.

A grass frond, like those Christians collect at Palm Sunday services, was pulled into a complicated-looking knot and tacked to the bedroom door. The door itself had been duct-taped shut, then forced open with a hammer or a crowbar, neither of which were lying around. On the door someone had scrawled:

> Rest in Peace
> Claire Ellen Bruckner
> Beloved Mother and Wife

in indelible ink beneath the frond.

Phil stepped wordlessly over the body. I followed him into the master bedroom, equally silent. The carpet was dotted with cat shit; I stepped around and over it. There were piss stains as well, though they were, for the most part, confined to one corner of the room. An end-table held an open Bible, a family photo and a vase with a bouquet of dead wildflowers. Small clouds of blowflies swarmed around the cat shit, but there were no insects, flies or maggots on Claire Bruckner at all. The wall behind the master bed was littered with mismatched framed photographs of the Bruckner family, most looking like vacation snapshots. There were the obligatory pictures of sunny beaches, snowy mountainsides, red clay deserts – even an eight-by-ten of a midtown Manhattan restaurant with the Empire State Building in the background.

The queen-sized bed, still draped with a frilly quilt and accented with four neatly arranged pillows, had been covered with hundreds of pounds of cat litter. In the centre of the grim mound, a Claire-Bruckner-sized indentation showed where she had been laid to rest, perhaps years earlier.

'Not sure if a felony has been committed?' I pulled the surgical mask beneath my chin. 'I've lost count of the felonies I've witnessed in the last eleven seconds, Phil. Have you lost your mind?'

'I never said felony.' Phil held up one hand in a peace offering. 'I said *murder*. Think about it, Sailor. You're a homicide detective. Do you see a murder here?'

'She's got a handsaw stuck in her bones! You call that "natural causes"?'

'No, but I certainly don't call it murder. Someone tried to cut her in half, but it was long, long after she was already dead – look at the sawdust on the floor; that's her! Even the goddamned bugs aren't interested.'

My head throbbed. I needed another OxyContin. The first one wasn't working for shit. My stomach roiled over and back; I should have eaten breakfast. 'So she's dead, entombed in here for God only knows how long, while her family makes waffles and plays card games and watches Oprah Winfrey on TV downstairs. They eventually decide that she's got to go. We're not sure why, but it may be because someone has got wind of the fact that she's been missing her dentist appointments. They come in, try to heave her out the door, but she's stiff as a railroad tie; so the only option is to saw her into more manageable pieces. How'm I doing so far, Phil? Sound about right?'

'Or they're screwballs, Egyptian mummy freaks, whack jobs determined to find an afterlife with Ra the Sun God or that crazy actress who keeps getting reincarnated.' Phil moved to the window where he watched a brown spider working on a web that already covered most of the space between the curtains.

'Nah, she's wearing a crucifix and there's a Bible on the nightstand.'

'That's *her*,' Phil said, 'not necessarily the ones who killed her, mummified her, entombed her in kitty litter, and then tried to saw her into kindling.'

I sighed. 'Then we need the damn shootin' match: the whole place dusted, footprints, anything we can lift from the floors or outside that doesn't match shoes in the closets or the mud room downstairs, tyre marks, hair and fibre samples from this entire room. If there's any blood, anywhere, we need to find it. Anything that might have been used as a weapon or to bash open this door, especially after Doc gives us an idea about what might have killed her, let's look for it, inside, outside, in the barn, anything with a hair sticking to it, with a bit of dried blood on it, I don't care if it's dental floss, we need to bag it.'

'Way ahead of you, Sailor.'

Another bug bit my neck. 'Yeah, well, I got lost on the way here.'

'Really? I'm surprised. It's such an easy place to find.'

'How'd she die? Can you tell?' I slapped at whatever it was before it could sting me again. 'Fucker, that one hurt.'

Phil pulled a handkerchief from his jacket pocket and mopped his face. 'No, I can't tell. She doesn't appear to have any knife or gunshot wounds, no obvious blunt trauma, but she's a wreck; her skull could be fractured in nine places for all I can tell. If you look at her back, you can see where the skin is darker, there around her shoulder blades. That's the lividity, but even that's been dry for a while. You've seen bodies. Lividity is purple at its darkest; that blood is fixed and dried in there like paint.'

'Okay, so we wait for Lefkowitz,' I said. 'You done in here?' I wanted out. My head hurt and my stomach hadn't settled. I wiped my eyes; the sweat stung.

'I've got a bit more to do.' Phil clicked his pen in anticipation.

'Is the mobile lab coming?'

'Nah. They can't get that thing in here, Sailor. We'd have to set them up out on Pitcairn or maybe at that abandoned gas station a couple of miles back. We'd have to shuttle the samples out in one of the cruisers.' He paused a moment then said, 'You really want to call those guys? Or should we wait for Lefkowitz to give his opinion?'

'Get them here.' I reminded myself that it didn't do any good for me to get angry, but downplaying this investigation, assuming the Bruckners died of natural causes and had been entombed by a nutty relative short on cash for funeral expenses was a sure-fire guarantee that we'd fuck this up. 'I'll call CID myself,' I added. 'He's a retired Marine officer; she's obviously a Christian, a Catholic ... nah, this whole thing stinks. Something's not right.' I needed an excuse to get out to my car. *One more pill, just one, then I'll eat something. That'll do me all right.*

Phil severed the web with his pen, then stepped on the spider before it could scurry under the bed. 'Now that you mention it, I really should introduce you to Carl.'

7:17 a.m.

I staggered a little as I stepped over Claire into the hallway and used the wall to keep on my feet, but I had to clench my teeth against my roiling stomach and tunnelling vision.

'You all right, Sailor?' Phil's voice came from behind me, somewhere down the hall, across the yard, out near the pond.

I tried to answer. 'Okay ... should've eaten ... where's the can?' My voice was a five-Scotch garble, on just one OxyContin and a barnyard full of rotting meat.

'Second door on the left. You can flush with your pen tip, but don't use any hand towels and don't run the water – not until we get in there and dust the fixtures.' I felt him go past me. 'I'll wait downstairs. I've got a couple of chocolate bars in my briefcase.'

'Got it.'

In the bathroom, I ignored Phil's orders and splashed water on my face, as cold as I could get it, until I felt better. When my thoughts cleared, I noticed the hand towel: Minnie Mouse hugging Mickey's dog: Plano, Pluggo, whatever. The toothbrush was a ballerina, her pointed toes for ever moulded to the base of a discoloured splay of bristles. A colourful sticker took up the lower right-hand corner of the mirror. A cartoon rabbit, shouldering a yellow toothbrush like a rifle, wagged a finger imperiously and in red bubble letters reminded me to *floss after every meal!* A bathmat with a group shot of the seven dwarfs, each of them playing a musical instrument and dancing, had been spread outside the tub, and a huge towel with a unicorn leaping over a cartoon rainbow hung from a silver hook beside the toilet.

I borrowed a plastic cup embossed with another image of Minnie Mouse and chugged some metallic water.

'That's better,' I said to the mirror. 'Now, where's the kid?'

Behind the unicorn towel, a back door off the bathroom led into a bedroom.

'In here, Sammy,' someone whispered.

It didn't sound like Phil or Bryson, neither of whom called me Sammy. Hell, my own wife didn't call me Sammy. This was a raspy voice, a two-pack-a-day scratch that reminded me suddenly and unnervingly of my father after a long night playing cards at the Freehold Teamsters' Hall back home in Jersey.

'Who's that?' I called as I opened the door— and froze. The springs and cogs keeping me upright all failed at once and I fell against the door jamb, gasping for air.

Emerging from the shadows was an elderly woman – or what remained of a woman after time and something unspeakable – leprosy, scabies; I don't know – had their way with her. A pallid, skeletal face was framed by a wild shriek of white hair. The woman's mouth hung open; her eyes were flickering pinpricks of frozen ice-blue; her nose was rotted off. In a watchman's black topcoat she flew at me, her arms wide, screeching a mind-blistering cry that crescendoed between my ears, nearly knocking me senseless.

It was a second, maybe two, before I managed to slap on the light switch; it saved me. If I'd listened to that sound, her monstrous, hopeless wail, for even ten seconds more, I'd have been dead.

The light, a Disney princess lamp – Belle, I think – banished the horror, and the woman was gone.

Instead, a black raincoat, a full-length woman's coat, slipped off the peg beside the door and fell in a heap at my feet. I hugged the door jamb until my heart had slowed down, then shouted towards the hallway.

'Phil!'

'Yeah? You all right?' he called up the stairs.

'Where's the kid?' It was hard not to sound out of breath.

'What kid?'

I took quick stock of the room. 'The ... daughter ... from the look of things in here.'

Phil hurried back up the stairs, while I checked out the bedroom. There were six stuffed dogs, as many stuffed horses, cats and rabbits, a plastic horse – white and saddled for a miniature rider – two Disney posters, a Minnie Mouse bedspread, a princess pillowcase, and two dozen colouring books and drawing pads stacked on a kid's writing desk beside a shoebox filled with coloured pencils, markers and crayons. Three Barbies slept on the bed, each in various stages of undress. One had lost an arm in some gruesome accident, and another had a haircut that couldn't have cost more than a couple of dollars from a street-corner barber. A plastic mirrored vanity with a toy Biedermeyer chair housed a collection of colourful hair brushes, barrettes, fancy perfume and nail polish bottles, and a girl's ransom in plastic and costume jewellery. Any of this stuff might have come from a Kringle Kids donation, the sort of thing Huck and I harassed out of the troopers for the holidays.

A yellowing diploma from a Richmond junior high school hung from the vanity mirror.

The floor was strewn with paper: dozens of sketches, drawings, coloured pictures and toddler paintings of a white horse, rigged with a leather saddle and awaiting a rider. I rifled through them while waiting for Phil; most carried the same nearly illegible footer, scrawled in crayon or marker: *From Wibbleton to Wobbleton is fifteen miles. From*

Wobbleton to Wibbleton is fifteen miles. A few read: *The genrele is coming!*

Phil appeared in the doorway and read my mind. 'Shit.'

'You're thinking my thoughts, cousin.' I passed him a stack of horse drawings.

'We've got a missing kid.'

'We're going to need every-goddamned-body out here,' I said. 'Get on the horn. Have Julie call—'

Something moved in the closet.

Phil, at fifty-five-plus and carrying forty extra pounds above his belt, was past me in a flash, his gun drawn.

I crouched and drew my Glock 21. Sliding along the edge of the bed, I made eye-contact with Phil, glanced at the doorknob and nodded.

Something thumped again. There was a rustling sound, a thud, and then silence.

Phil held his pistol in one hand and reached tentatively for the doorknob with the other. 'This is Sergeant Phillip Clarkson of the Virginia State Police, Criminal Investigation Division. Come out of the closet slowly and lie face down on the floor with your hands extended,' he called.

Nothing.

Phil raised his voice. 'This is the Virginia State Police. Come out of the closet and lie face down on the floor!'

A faint rustle; then nothing.

Phil looked back at me and when I nodded he yanked the door open, shielding himself behind it.

'Christ, look out!' Phil screamed.

I fired twice, wildly, in self-defence before falling as three battered-looking house cats leapt howling from the closet shelf. One clawed at my face, another my sleeve, and the third clung to my shoulder, scrabbling for my exposed skin with a naked talon. The cats were all over me, scratching, biting, and clawing their way into the flesh on my face, the soft skin beneath my eyes and the fattest parts of my cheeks and neck. One sank its teeth deep into my lower lip. I

66

screamed, ripping it off and tossing it towards the closet. This was no hallucination.

Phil's gun roared twice and I heard him kicking and stomping at something before he half-dived, half-fell on me, his hands slapping and tugging near my face.

A cat that had been clawing at my neck was suddenly gone; there was another explosion as Phil fired again, leaving just one ghastly smelling creature gnawing at my cheek, its claws embedded deep in my neck and forehead as it fought to hold on. I rolled over hard onto a Bugs Bunny rug and managed to break its grip. Drops of blood stained Bugs' chest, making it look like Elmer Fudd had finally connected with one of those shotgun blasts.

Raising myself on one elbow, I managed to bring my gun around and found the cat scrambling to its feet, ready to attack again. This time I fired deliberately, sending it somersaulting backwards into the hallway. A splash of blood stained the wall as the cat was turned nearly inside out; it twitched unnervingly, then went still.

Bryson burst in with her semi-automatic drawn, looking around, searching the room for anyone that needed killing. 'What the fuck's going on?' she cried. 'Where'd he go?'

Still figuring we'd been shooting at someone, Bryson vanished into the hall; I heard her bounding towards Claire Bruckner's tomb, shouting all the way, 'Virginia State Police!' She crashed into each of the upstairs bedrooms in turn.

'It's okay,' Phil said, panting, 'we're okay. Bryson! We're fine! But get a first-aid kit, Bryson, hurry up!'

I touched my face. My hand came away bloody. 'Shit!' I rolled onto my back. 'Jenny's gonna kill me if I get blood on this suit.' I lifted my head to check the closet. Six pairs of different-coloured Converse All Stars were lined up in a neat row. The yellow ones sported fresh stains: cat blood. There was a floral print pair; I'd never seen that style before.

Phil sucked in a couple of laboured breaths. 'Stay there. I'll get you a towel.'

'They dead?' I asked, my .45 still clasped tightly in my hand but feeling awkward, *as out of place as Carl's citations or those crayons down-stairs.*

'Jesus, I hope so.' He grunted, found his feet and staggered into the bathroom.

7:24 a.m.

I lay on my back, still sprawled across the Bugs Bunny rug, with a wet towel on my face. The cool dampness felt good on my skin, despite the stinging pain of multiple puncture wounds and slashes, some of which were still bleeding. I closed my eyes and tried not to picture the cats, blinded by hunger and rage, leaping out at me, but that memory was one that would stay with me for a while; I'd be ninety-eight years old and still stepping to one side before opening closet doors. Thankfully, Jenny was always leaving ours open, my haunted Brooks Brothers cave.

My lower lip was slow to clot. I sucked on it, tasting blood. Bryson sat beside me. Through all the death, the stale piss, the decomposition and the putrefying farm animals, she smelled good: some musky perfume I doubted I'd find on the racks at Walgreen's. I inhaled as deeply as I could without getting caught. She was literally a real breath of fresh air.

'Was it just those three?' she asked.

Phil moved furniture, checked beneath the bed, and dug around behind the plastic vanity. 'Yeah,' he said, 'and a good thing, too. Between Sailor and me, we only had twenty-eight shots. We'd've been goners if there'd been many more in there.'

'It looks like there were.' Bryson moved away, her scent replaced by cat urine and mouldy carpet. Her voice came from inside the closet. 'But these two ... sorry, *three* ... are already dead.'

'Six cats in a closet,' I murmured into the towel. 'Three kill the others, probably for food, then strike a temporary truce. It won't be long until another of them is on the menu, but before they have to fight it out—'

'We come along,' Phil finished my thought, 'bursting with real meat flavour!'

'Lovely.'

'Damn, but these things are in sorry shape,' Bryson said from the hallway, retrieving the cat I'd shot.

'They were killed at close range with a .45,' Phil said. 'Did you expect them primped for a cat food commercial?'

'*Before* you shot them,' Bryson said, 'they were still alive, which means they hadn't been neglected for too long, but they were beat to shit, which means they've probably been fending for themselves for a while.'

I sat up and removed the towel. 'How long do you figure they've been in that closet?'

'Why does that matter?' Phil asked.

'Because that'll give us some idea about when the daughter went missing.'

'You think she locked them in there?'

'Look at her room,' I said. 'There's no cat shit in here. This is probably where she was hiding.'

'Hiding?'

'Sure,' I said, 'a little kid trapped in this nightmare, both parents dead, and eight hundred cats hunting for food. It looks like these six might have got in recently … maybe they forced her to take off.'

'Where?'

'That's the next item up for bids on *The Price is Right*, my friends,' I said.

'At least that explains the strips,' Bryson said.

'Strips?' I asked.

'Downstairs,' Phil said, clicking his pen. 'Someone was feeding the cats, probably to keep them at bay, even for a little while.'

'It makes sense,' Bryson added, now cradling a furry carcase in one gloved hand. 'The animals in that closet haven't been dead long. Whoever locked them in there can't be far away – especially if it's a little kid.'

'Put that thing back,' Phil said. 'We need photos before we move them.'

'Right, sorry.' Bryson returned the cat to the hallway floor, trying to get it exactly where it had been.

I ignored both of them. 'Strips? Strips of what?'

'Of Carl,' Phil said. 'You haven't been down there yet.'

'All right, give me a second. I need to patch myself up a bit. Bryson, Phil's right: photograph the shell casings, document each of the shots in here, and get photos of the cats before you move them. When you get that done, bag them and take them down to the porch. We'll have Animal Control get rid of the others, but the ones that were shot are getting bagged and iced until further notice.' I dabbed at my lip with the towel; it was swollen and still oozing blood.

'We're keeping frozen cats?' Phil cocked an eyebrow at me.

'The ones we've shot, yes.'

'Phil, get Julie Largo on the phone. Tell her that we've got a girl ... wait ... what do we know about her?' I remembered the photos in Claire Bruckner's homemade sepulchre. 'Hold on a minute.' I kept the towel against my lip and hustled down the hall, hurdling Claire a third time, and took up the framed photograph of the Bruckner family from the bedside table.

'Oh shit,' I whispered, then ran back to the child's room and tore the faded diploma from the vanity mirror. The paper was brittle, the writing faded and difficult to make out.

'What's the matter?' Bryson looked over my shoulder.

'Phil, how old were these people?'

He checked his notes. 'Um, Claire Bruckner, born in November, 1935. That makes her ... what?'

'Mid-seventies,' I said. 'And Carl?'

'June, 1936.'

'Shit, and he was a US Marine captain in Vietnam, right? No high school kid, nineteen and drafted before he lost his virginity, no. Carl was a career man, thirty-something before he went over there. Bronze Star. Purple Heart, the works with olives and pepperoni.'

'So what?' Bryson asked. 'They're still dead. What difference does it make how old they are?'

'Their daughter,' I said, gesturing to the room, the Minnie Mouse toys, the stuffed animals, and plastic jewellery. 'Molly Bruckner finished eighth grade at Jefferson Junior High in June, 1973. So she's ... what ... ? Forty-nine years old, maybe fifty—'

Phil brushed past me, taking the diploma. 'That can't be right, Sailor. I mean, look at all these toys. This kid is six or seven, tops.'

'A granddaughter?' Bryson craned her neck to get a better look at the picture.

'No,' I said. 'It's her.'

The photograph was an 8 x 10 from a formal family shot, one of those $12.99 deals at Wal-Mart with the muted blue background, like twilight in Antarctica. Carl sat square-jawed and tough-looking, wearing a tight-lipped smile. He was probably sixty-five in the photo, his grey hair cut high and tight, probably five years down the road from his retirement party. He wore a navy suit, off the rack, that hugged him across the shoulders, and a red tie. In lieu of a wedding band, his Naval Academy ring shone prominently on his left hand. Claire was rail-thin and blotchy, in a floral print dress, displaying a modest crucifix, nothing like the post-and-beam model she wore now. With horn-rimmed glasses and her greying hair in a bun, everything about Claire Bruckner screamed Ladies' Auxiliary. I was surprised that she wasn't clutching a Bible, or perhaps a pitchfork. Yet my eyes weren't drawn to Carl or Claire, in their salt-of-the-earth Sunday best. Rather, I studied the heavyset woman seated between them.

Molly Bruckner. She might have been forty years old when the photo was taken, and would have been within spitting distance of fifty when her parents died. She wore a hundred extra pounds like a parka, a meaty woman through the shoulders, torso and hips. Her face, while pudgy and round, remained childlike, and she stared in mute fascination, her attention for ever focused on something behind and above the camera, despite what must have been the photographer's best efforts to have Molly 'watch the birdie'. Her mouth was caught somewhere between a smile and a dull gape; someone had said something funny. And her front teeth, yellow and askew, peeked from beneath her upper lip. She wore a linen dress and a green cardigan that so clearly clashed with every other article of clothing in sight, it must have been her favourite. I imagined Claire trying to convince her to take it off, *just for the picture, honey*, and Carl finally giving in, frustrated and angry, *Oh, for Christ's sake, Claire, just let her wear the damned thing!*

Phil wasn't convinced. 'C'mon, Sailor, look at her. She's got to be forty-five or even fifty by now. This isn't her room.' He gestured to the cartoon knickknacks and toys as if I hadn't been in there, shooting cats, for the past fifteen minutes. 'Maybe it's her daughter's room ... you know, their granddaughter.'

'Nope.' I felt my suspicion lock into place. I was right. 'It's her. There's something wrong with her. What do they call it these days? Down Syndrome?'

'Nah,' Bryson said, 'that's those rolly kids with the fatty eyelids and the goofy I-love-everybody grin. She's got something else.'

Phil's brow furrowed. 'You mean, like a retard or something?'

'Exactly,' I said. 'But I don't know the word for it. I'm pretty sure "retard" doesn't capture it.'

'Instead of the granddaughter idea?' Phil looked to Bryson for support. 'What do you think? Take a look at her.'

'Well, I've never really—'

'Here,' I interrupted, pulling out one of the dresser drawers and tossing a pair of woman's panties to Phil. He caught them, uncertain at first what they were, then held them up for the rest of us. They were a triple-XL, with slat sides, *like Jenny's pregnancy panties. Sarah could use those as a tent.*

'Holy shit,' he said.

I tried another drawer. 'Here's a sweater. It's a 26-W, just a smidge too big for a six-year-old granddaughter. This woman, Molly Bruckner, lived in this room, with her kids' toys, her princess pillow case and her fifty-nine drawings of Wibbleton and Wobbleton horses, whatever the hell that means. She appears to be in her late forties, and she is missing. I'm afraid—'

Phil finished my thought, 'That we have to presume she's dead.'

I looked back at the picture, into Molly's dull gaze, and said, 'We're gonna need some help. Bryson, call Julie at CID Dispatch; get some road guys out here, whomever they can spare. Those cats had been in the closet long enough to kill three of their own, but the dead ones are fresh.'

'You think she's alive?' Phil asked.

'If she is, she's scared, probably hurt or all scratched up, maybe bitten badly. You saw what they did to me in eight seconds. Who knows what she saw here in the past few weeks. She might have been locked in this room for days, a retarded woman with no food and two mutilated parents hanging around like the Ghosts of Christmas in Hell.'

'I'm on it.' Bryson started down the stairs.

'No,' I called after her, 'actually, let's have Lourdes do it. He should be back in a couple of minutes. I need you to come with me and Phil. I want to see Carl before Lefkowitz gets here.'

On my way downstairs, I forgot about the dollop of cat shit sharing the tread with MING's food bowl. I stepped in it and nearly went ass-over-handlebars into the living room.

'Careful, Detective.' Bryson grabbed my elbow from behind.

'Sailor, please.'

'Fine,' she said, 'Sailor it is.'

'Can I ask you something?' I paused to clean my shoe and hunted around for a bit of tissue.

'Sure,' she said, 'what do you need?'

'Just take it off, Sailor,' Phil interrupted. 'I can't have you tracking cat shit all over the house.'

I sighed. 'Okay, Mom, I know.' I kicked the shoe off and nudged it behind the bottom step. 'Not that supply lines for cat excrement are thin around here.'

'You know better,' Phil chided me. 'You'll be leaving shitprints all over the place.'

'Yeah, yeah. You had me at hello.' I was secretly relieved that my sock didn't have any holes in it.

'You do look good, though,' Phil said, 'with all those Band-Aids on your face.'

'It's an improvement; I know.' I hiked my sock up a bit and thought about kicking off the other shoe.

Bryson led us through the living room. 'This area is about done, Sergeant.'

'Good, thanks,' Phil said.

'I'm afraid most of the fibre samples we've collected are going to come back as animal hair, however.'

'That's for the lab to determine,' he said. 'We don't tell them how to do their jobs, and they don't tell Sailor where and when to shoot a cat.'

'Right,' Bryson smiled. She was about my age, and looked stocky in her vest – the uniform didn't do much for female troopers, which was probably a good thing. She was sweating and obviously uncomfortable, although not as crippled by the heat as Phil or me. She looked at me expectantly, perhaps thinking I might share some wisdom regarding homicide investigation, little realising I had about as much insight into this crime scene as Claire Bruckner. I hated to let her down, though; enthusiasm is important in troopers who've been on the road long enough to want a transfer for the right reasons. CID wasn't a bad place to end up. I caught myself unconsciously standing a bit straighter, trying to suck in my gut.

Bryson let Phil slip by. 'You had a question?'

'What? Oh, yeah, sorry,' I said. 'Do you have any idea what the initials RML might mean?'

'Like, what?'

'Nothing. Just RML. Ring a bell for you?'

'RML? Out-of-the-blue RML, not linked to anything, just RML, take-a-wild-shot RML?'

'Exactly!' It was the first genuinely amusing thing I'd heard since I'd arrived.

'Not a clue.' She pulled a spiral pad from her breast pocket and scribbled *RML?* officiously on a blank page. 'But if I think of anything or come across anything, I'll let you know.'

'Fair enough,' I said.

'You want to come into the sun room?' She started after Phil.

'Just a second.' In the untidy living room a threadbare, tartan sofa sat at right angles to a rickety wooden rocker and a once-green love-seat with duct-taped patches on both armrests. An oval rug covered the worn plank floor. The furniture had been arranged to give an unimpeded view of the small television standing on a low bookcase in the corner. A brick fireplace that might have been cosy if only the temperature would drop sixty degrees flanked the furniture on one wall. A framed print, farmers toiling behind a horse-drawn plough, hung crookedly on the other. Mismatched lamps on twin end-tables had been lit earlier but now the morning sun through the window illuminated the room in tapered rectangles. Dust had accumulated on everything; the only clean places were where Lourdes and Bryson had begun collecting evidence. Scores of scrawled-upon bits of evidence tape were stuck to the walls, floors and furniture. There were photographs here too, on the walls, the mantelpiece and on the book shelf: Carl and Claire outside a whitewashed church, Molly cuddling a pair of cats, and Carl and Molly paddling a canoe. Two deer heads were mounted, one on either side of the fireplace. They looked to have been there for decades: both had cobwebs growing between their ears, and one, a big buck, judging from the thickness in his neck, had a few bits of sparkling tinsel dangling from one antler point.

I called after Bryson, 'We find anything in this room?'

She opened the pad again. 'Not much. Someone, I'm guessing Carl, was an avid reader of hunting and fishing magazines. There's a stack of them, some quite old, in the rack beneath the TV. They kept newspapers beside the fireplace, the *Times-Dispatch* and the *Herald-Progress*, probably to get the fire going. There were docs in the bottom drawer of that end-table ... receipts, deposit slips, credit card statements, utility bills, the normal stuff.'

'Any weapons? Guns?'

'Upstairs. Two shotguns, a 12-gauge and an old .410, a Ka-Bar knife, military issue, a .30-calibre Winchester rifle, and a .45 semi-automatic pistol. It's a 1911, an old one, but polished up, recently oiled, and loaded.'

'Anything else? Anything out of the ordinary?'

'Nah.' She frowned. Her brow furrowed, highlighting a tiny indentation between her eyes. Somewhere there was a boyfriend who had it on a tally of his favourite things. If he didn't, he was an idiot.

Bryson said, 'It looks like both Carl and Claire were on the company dime. He had a military retirement, plus social security, not much, and Claire was drawing social security. There's a small office beyond the sitting room at the other end of the house. I'm afraid much of what's in there is wet, though, with all the rain we had last week. There's a hole in the roof, a broken dormer, and a goddamned river managed to run through there.'

'You been in there yet?'

'Just to peek in. I figured with the water damage I ought to focus elsewhere.'

'Box it up, anyway,' I said. 'Anything that ought to have a second look.'

'Okay,' she said, then added, 'actually, Detective—'

'Sailor—'

'Sailor . . . there were a couple of brochures, magazines. I don't know what you'd call them, advertisements, maybe.'

'For what?'

'For wheelchairs, specialised furniture, ramps and prosthetics.'

'What do you mean, someone's physically screwy, too?' I said. 'It wouldn't surprise me; they were older. Did you find a wheelchair?'

'No, but the toilets and shower stalls all have "oh-shit" bars, you know, those grab bars in case you're about to fall. They're drilled right into the tile, and there are a couple of canes in the mud room and that one there, leaning against the fireplace.'

'So someone struggled to get around,' I said. 'Which one? Do we know yet? It could be Molly. I'm going to call that school, see if anyone there still remembers her. If you find anything in the office from the family doctor, we can check with them, too, although probably not until Monday.'

'Will do,' Bryson kept scribbling to-do items in her pad.

I said, 'I don't know that it matters now, but make sure you get started in the office. Grab one of the sealable plastic containers from my cruiser. Put anything of interest in there, even if it's wet. We'll deal with it at CID or hand it over to the mobile crew when they arrive.'

'Got it.'

'What do we have on Carl's military record?'

She shrugged. 'Sorry, Det— Sailor, no idea yet. Julie Largo's working on it. I'm not sure we'll hear back today.'

'Let me know if we don't. I'm not sure why, but there's something odd about those frames, those citations, everything hanging up there,

all polished and shiny, in the middle of this junkyard of battered shit.'
I tried to get a deep breath in, then coughed. 'We need some damned
air in here. This is like being in a frigging catacomb under a cathedral
somewhere.'

'With cat poop.'

'Lovely.'

The Bruckners' sitting room was an unconventional little space off the dining area, created by adding a covered sun-porch to the back of the house. It faced a crowded orchard grove and a large soybean field, now grown over with meadow grasses, timothy and sedge. The room widened out near the sun-porch, as if the Bruckners had used a faulty level; they must have failed geometry miserably in high school not to have noticed the discrepancy. It was too small for even an intimate cocktail party; the room must have been used as a quiet place to read or play a game of cards.

Floor-to-ceiling book shelves lined three walls, and an antique china cabinet full of holiday plates and cups and saucers stood against the fourth, further narrowing the space. Two wooden chairs stood beside a round café-style table, and a massive hope chest had been pushed against the base of the far book shelf, nearest the sun-porch. White evidence tape striped the floor in a widening pattern of long strands that looked like a child's drawing of the sun, *the sun over a white horse, saddled and ready to ride from Wibbleton to Wobbleton. It's only fifteen miles.*

Carl Bruckner, his arms spread wide, lay half-in and half-out of the chest. His hands, which had matching Ziploc plastic bags over them, secured at the wrists with rubber bands, were curled like prehistoric claws. His head, also bagged, in a larger Ziploc, hung suspended about four inches off the floor, making Carl look like a bloated half-naked jack-in-the-box.

Like Claire's dress, Carl's blue flannel shirt had been pulled down to his waist, exposing the former Marine's lean back and shoulders. His stomach, creased neatly by the front lip of the hope chest, was roundly distended where bacteria were breaking down his innards. From across

the room I could see that long strips of flesh had been sliced from between Carl's shoulder blades. There was no sign of the strips themselves.
The dry grey stripes of subcutaneous fat and occasional bits of naked
bone marked a permanent bar code pattern across Carl's upper back.

A stillness lay over the room; for a moment nothing moved but a
legion of ravening blowflies. Lieutenant Harper had this one all wrong:
the stench here was excruciating. I shifted uncomfortably.

Phil Clarkson kneeled in front of the hope chest. He was searching for something, but he looked so much like a supplicant at some
macabre altar that I instinctively took a step backwards, not wanting
to interrupt.

'Mother of God,' I whispered.

'Yes, this one's ugly,' Bryson said, almost too loudly, as if breaking
the silence on purpose.

'The tape on the floor? You vacuumed?'

'The bags are numbered one to four with five the area immediately
around the chest.'

'Nice job.'

'The room is so small, and the killer would have had to do so much
to get him in here, get him propped up like that, and then to cut away
those parts of his back, it seemed sensible to vacuum our way in, out,
and then back and forth to the chest from each corner. I switched
bags after each strip and labelled them. They're in the sun-porch, over
there.' She pointed towards the bright space beyond Carl's body. 'If
there were fibres, tissue samples, anything, we have them.'

'You photograph everything first?' I stood on my toes to get a look
atop the china cabinet.

'And video,' Bryson said.

Like Lourdes, she wanted my approval, my gratitude for doing a
thorough job. It hadn't crossed my mind that there would be troopers who looked up to me, not yet, anyway. It was a lot less irritating
coming from her than when Lourdes did it. But I was convinced I was
fucking up my first murder scene, and desperately needing another
OxyContin, at least a handful of ibuprofen for my face and anything
with alcohol to settle my stomach, and right now I honestly didn't
give a shit.

I stayed positive, though. 'Nice job, Bryson. You stick with Phil and you're going to learn everything you need to be a top-flight homicide cop.'

'Thanks, Sailor.'

'Who bagged him?'

'The sergeant did,' she said. 'He was going—'

Phil interrupted, pushing himself up with creaking knees, 'I was going to take his trace scrapings here, but this place is such a frigging mess, and he's got so much shit beneath his nails, I figured we'd do it at the morgue. With his head hanging over like that, he's got froth built up in his nose and throat, probably filling his sinuses. The blowflies have been laying eggs on him for a couple of days, but there aren't any maggots or beetles, so he hasn't been in here too long. Doc can scrape him for larvae when he arrives.'

'Fine.' I kneeled down myself now. The chest was partially closed over Carl's waist, and it was dark inside. 'Gimme a flashlight, will you?'

Bryson pulled one from her belt.

I shone it inside the hope chest. 'Well, whaddya know?' I reached for the lid. 'This been dusted?'

'Yeah,' Phil said, 'we lifted about thirty prints off it. Everyone in the Commonwealth seems to have come in here and left a handprint on the damned thing.'

'At least three of them, anyway,' I said, and pushed the varnished cedar lid up against the bookshelf.

The hope chest had been filled with cat litter and from the waist down, Carl Bruckner was metamorphosing into a mummy to match his wife. I dug in a few inches, far enough to determine that the body had been arranged in what we used to call sitting Indian-style. (Jenny told me that wasn't PC any more; I had to call it criss-cross-applesauce before Ben went to kindergarten or we'd all get hauled into the principal's office on racism charges.) Carl was wearing light cotton pants and a brown leather belt. His shirt had bunched up in places around his waist and he wore a Saint George medal on a cheap chain around his neck. It dangled below his chin inside Phil's Ziploc baggie.

'I want to get a look at the top of his head,' I said as I carefully slipped the bag free from the rubber band Bryson had used to hold it in place. 'If he died in here, the skin on his head will be darker … although I can't begin to imagine a former Marine captain and decorated veteran would climb into a cedar chest, fill it with cat litter and lean over like this while waiting to die.'

'That's a tough one to swallow.' Bryson looked down at me and smiled. *Number two on the Boyfriend's Tally: that grin.*

I moved the bag out of the way and slowly lifted Carl's chin, just far enough to shine my flashlight on his bald spot. I didn't want to cause any froth to drain from his mouth or nose. Stiff with rigor, his shoulders and arms rose slightly like a mannequin's. The smooth skin of Carl's head shone deep purple with lividity – *you called it, Phil* – but it was not as dark as the skin between Claire's shoulder blades.

'Look at that,' I said. 'If he didn't die in here, he wasn't dead long before he ended up in this very spot.'

Phil pressed on the purple skin. The colour didn't change. 'Livor mortis like that, in this godforsaken swamp … the killer had maybe two or three hours to get him in here for that much blood to drain into his head. With it dangling above the floor, he's a textbook example.'

'And his hands are the same way.' Bryson borrowed the light and shone the beam onto Carl's left hand. The Naval Academy ring was missing, but I could see the knuckles and flesh that hadn't rested on the floor were also purple with blood that had seeped into Carl's tissues. His nails had been gnawed down: the farmer's manicure.

'Nice job,' I said, and rebagged the head.

'We aim to please,' Phil chuckled and swatted at a blowfly that had landed on his legal pad.

'So where'd he die?'

'Don't know yet,' Bryson said.

'We were hoping you'd help us figure that one out. You are the homicide detective, after all.' Phil trailed a gloved finger through the cat litter.

'Any sign of the knife used to cut these strips out of him?' I pushed the edge of one wound open, hoping to see evidence of serrations. There were none, but I was a rookie and I would need Lefkowitz to confirm my suspicions. 'From the look of these slashes, it was a smooth blade, and thin, about half an inch across, and as sharp as Jack the Ripper's shaving razor.

'And we have a winner!' Phil said. 'Come here.' He offered me a hand up and I was glad for it. Kneeling like that always made me a bit dizzy, and it was worse now that I'd gained some weight. I saw flashes of yellow burst like fireworks in front of my face and wiped my forehead dry on my sleeve again. I'd need a dry-cleaner with an Olympic gold medal in Fawn Wool to get my suit back to normal. A bug bit my leg, just above my sock line; I tried to crush it with the toe of my remaining shoe.

Bryson, seemingly out of sympathy, slapped at something on her own neck.

'Welcome to homicide,' I said. 'The glamour, the romance, the blood, gore and shit.'

'I don't mind the blood and gore,' Phil said. 'I could do without the frigging bugs, though. Twenty-nine years later, and I still can't abide the frigging bugs.'

'Where's the knife?'

'Over here.' Phil stepped into the sun-porch, past a stack of books and papers on the floor. A puddle of morning sunlight coloured the splotches in Phil's cheeks.

'What're these?' I asked.

'Probably what had been in that hope chest,' Bryson said. 'I'll go through them this afternoon or tomorrow, whenever I get done with the office.'

Phil said, 'Here it is,' and crouched beside another café-style table, this one with three chairs around it, on the porch. Resting crookedly against one of the table's wrought-iron legs was a fisherman's fillet knife, thin and razor-sharp, as advertised.

'We aren't sure how it got here,' Bryson said, leaning against one of the porch windows.

'Probably thrown from over there.' I crawled under the table and checked the line of sight into the sitting room. A lefty with a good aim could have made the toss easily. 'Why's it not bagged?'

'We took photos and videoed the room,' Phil said, 'but I wanted you to see it before we dusted it.'

'Thanks,' I said. 'Lourdes can do it when he comes back in. Unless our boy was wearing gloves, I'm betting that these prints will bring us our winner. Let's lift what we can and run them today. If we get the mobile lab out here, we can hit the database from their wireless. We'll have a name before dinner, if we're lucky, and dredge up someone with priors.'

'Why'd he throw the knife?' Bryson asked after a moment, not sure if the question would make her look ignorant.

'Why do these people do anything?' Phil shrugged. 'Who knows? Maybe he went wild, got scared, angry, sick of himself … it could have been anything.'

'I don't think so,' I said. 'You saw those slices in Carl's back. This motherfucker was meticulous. He was shaving even portions out of what must have been a ripe and rotting corpse and either eating them himself or feeding them to a legion of ravenous felines. Either way, there's no trace of Carl's missing bits.'

'Could he have kept them, like a trophy?' Bryson asked.

'Bullshit,' I said. 'You're watching too much TV. This guy left a saw stuck halfway through Claire's mummified spine. He wasn't after trophies. He was doing something, building something, arranging these two just right.'

'Why?'

'Again, why do these people do anything?' I said, echoing Phil. 'But I'm guessing he got done slicing in here and tossed that knife, probably left-handed, from the angle between Carl and the table.'

'Unless it bounced.'

'True.'

'But you said he was meticulous,' Bryson pressed. 'Do meticulous killers throw their knives away like that?'

'No,' Phil said, 'but it's probably Carl's knife. You said he was an avid hunter and fisherman. He read all the magazines. He's an ex-Marine, retired – I'm sure he got his share of fishing in, which is why Sailor thinks we'll find prints on it. Am I right?'

'Bingo,' I said. 'If the killer brought the knife with him, he might have planned to wear gloves. Picking up Carl's knife isn't anything this guy expected to do. I'd wager the prints on the knife will match the ones we lift from that saw upstairs, too. But, what the hell, any fourth-grader could have figured that.'

Phil crossed back into the sitting room and stood looking down at Carl like a visitor at a modern art museum. He propped his chin on one fist and said, 'Unless he was attacked.'

'What do you mean?' I asked. 'Attacked by whom?'

'We said upstairs that the strips might have been used to feed the cats, to keep them at bay for a while.'

'Disgusting, but it makes some sense.' Bryson and I joined him over the corpse.

Phil went on, 'And there's no cat shit in this room.'

'Hell no,' I said, 'are you kidding? If this room had been open, those scavenging mothers would have eaten him down to the bone, like frigging piranhas. The fact that he's only been strip-mined, not completely consumed, leads me to believe that someone was living in this room, eating Carl here, and sneaking out when the cats were occupied elsewhere.'

'But if they got in somehow,' Bryson said, 'if a few of them made it in here and attacked whoever was slicing Carl up, either to feed them, to feed himself, or just to make ornaments for the Christmas tree ... if cats got in here and attacked—'

Phil turned towards the sun-porch. 'Our boy might have got scared, overwhelmed, and thrown the knife, or dropped it while making his escape.'

'Escape where?' Bryson said.

'Upstairs,' I said, 'into Molly's room.'

'Molly did this?' Phil's already pale skin lost more of its colour. 'The retard daughter?'

'Not necessarily,' I said. 'If Molly's dead somewhere, maybe she wasn't the one who trapped the last six cats in the closet. Maybe it was someone else ... our killer, body arranger, Egyptian mummy freak, whoever this is.'

'But wait,' Bryson interrupted, 'if cats got in here, wouldn't they have eaten Carl? Why chase a living person upstairs if they have two hundred pounds of fresh meat dangling right here?'

'Because, my dear, cats are by nature hunters, and pushed to rely on their most primitive instincts, as these felines almost assuredly were, they would trust their ancestral directives to provide them with food. They might have scratched and nibbled a bit on this unfortunate fellow, as a closer inspection of his body will probably reveal, but warm meat on the bone, fleeing, would have been too difficult to resist.' Doctor Irving Lefkowitz, accompanied by Bob Lourdes, joined us in the sitting room.

'Doc!' I said. 'Lemme tell you how glad we are to see you.'

'Detective Doyle.' He shook my hand, latex on latex. 'What have you done to your face? One last hurrah with our friend Huck before the transfer? I see you finally convinced Captain Fezzamo to sign your papers.'

'About a month ago.' I made introductions. Doc greeted everyone in turn, commending Phil and Bryson on the condition of the evidence thus far. It was good to see him, and all at once I felt better, downright glad that the St James County Coroner was out on his boat or barbecuing with his neighbours. While we all watched, Lefkowitz lifted Carl's head and shoulders, cut a small incision with a scalpel and stabbed a core temperature thermometer into the dead man's liver as easily as if checking a Thanksgiving turkey. 'There we go,' he said, letting the body hang once again.

I said, 'Let's start upstairs, Doc. There are a few things you should—'

'Hold on a moment, Detective Doyle,' he cut me off, taking me by the elbow.

'Sailor, please, Doc.'

'I'll call you whatever you like after hours, Detective, but out here you are Detective Doyle,' he whispered. 'Authority's hard to come by; don't give it up on purpose. You need to remember that, my boy.'

'I will, Doc, thanks.'

'Now, outside, to my car.'

'Why?'

'*Outside*, please, Detective.'

I turned to the others. 'We'll be right back. Bryson, Phil, grab a bagel. Lourdes, dust and lift whatever latents you can from that fillet knife. I want them ready when the mobile techs arrive.'

'Got it.'

'What's the word on help finding Molly?'

'CID is sending a couple of road units, but Sergeant Dallek said we had to bring in the St James sheriff if we want to report Molly as missing.'

'Sonofabitch,' I said. 'Um … all right, give me a minute to think on that. But get those prints.'

To Phil, Lefkowitz said, 'Take another look at his arms, maybe hidden by hair, or the backs of his hands. Look for scratches or small bite marks, but they won't be red or discoloured at all, because—'

Phil suddenly understood, 'Because he was already dead when the cats started nibbling on him.'

'Top marks, Sergeant Clarkson. It's hard to catch in this lighting; I'll show you later at the hospital.' Lefkowitz wrapped an arm around my shoulders and ushered me outside.

'What're we doing out here, Doc?' As much as I welcomed the chance to take a full breath without the risk of ingesting a blowfly, I was nervous leaving the house.

'I need two minutes alone with you.' Lefkowitz opened the back of his BMW and dug around for something. He shifted a few cardboard boxes, moved a briefcase and what looked like a small cosmetics case and finally said, 'Ah, here it is.'

'What's that?' I scrubbed the sole of my shoe on the grass and tugged it back on my foot.

He rooted in his shirt for one of his imported rancid-smelling cigarillos. 'This, my boy, is for live people. I get to use it so rarely that it's usually buried beneath all the accoutrements of my dead trade, so to speak. Got a light?'

I lit the nail for him, and asked, 'What live people?'

'You, my friend.' He blew a cloud of smoke towards Richmond. 'You look like shit, Detective; you're on the verge of passing out. I could see it five seconds after I entered that room. Now, take off your jacket and roll up your sleeve.'

I checked the farmhouse to be certain no one was watching, then complied. 'Look, Doc, I know I'm a bit off my game this morning, but I think most of it's just stress. I'm worried as hell about this whole investigation. Harper sent me out here as a virgin, and this thing is a mess. Phil is shrugging it all off 'cause his daughter's playing trombone tonight down on the river, Lourdes is auditioning for cop of the year and Bryson doesn't know murder from a road-kill possum. I don't want to call in the St James County sheriff because I just sent two of them home, including a shift sergeant, minus one gun. They'll be cursing me all the way to Goochland and then laughing at me all the way back.'

'You're too self-conscious.' He wrapped a blood pressure cuff around my upper arm and pulled on a stethoscope. 'Or too self-confident, or maybe—' He stopped to listen, then continued, '—too self-absorbed, I don't know which. 160 over 100. That's near death for a thirty-one-year-old.'

'It's a stressful job, Doc.'

'What happened to your face?'

'Cats. Angry, starving cats who smelled like the ass-end of North Philly.'

He looked mildly amused, then asked, 'What are you taking?'

'What do you mean?' I felt like a high-schooler caught with his hand up a blouse.

'Don't bullshit me, Sailor. What pills?'

I felt my face redden. It was already damp. 'I took an OxyContin this morning.'

'What the hell for?'

'I hurt my back in a 5k a couple of weeks ago. It bothered me a bit when I got the lieutenant's call, and I didn't want to be distracted by it today.'

You're lying to a doctor who likes you, shithead.

'You eat anything?' He felt the glands in my neck and looked hard at my pupils.

'Not yet.'

'Coffee?' His hair was thinning, but perfectly combed off his forehead. Like Lourdes, Doc barely sweated.

'Two or three cups, one big one from the 7-11 in Ashland.'

'Cigarettes?' Doc asked, his own chocolate-coloured nail dangling from the corner of his mouth.

'Sure.'

'How many already today?'

'Christ, I dunno. How many are in a pack? I smoke them until they're gone and then I buy more.' I wanted to get him to laugh with me; it didn't work.

'I need you to listen to me, Sailor, not because I'm a doctor, but because I am an old man, an old *Jewish* man—'

'Does that make a difference?'

'Hell yes! Old Jewish men are the smartest men on the earth; everyone knows that.'

'Because you know that old Jewish women are always right?' I tried for another joke.

This time he cracked a brief grin. 'That's part of it, yes, but in this case immaterial. I was thirty years old half a millennium ago, Sailor. You are heading down a dangerous path.'

'What do you mean, booze, pills, smokes? All of it together? It's going to kill me? Shit, I've known that for a long time.'

For ten years, six months and two weeks now.

'That's not the half of it, my friend. You will not be a successful homicide investigator until you learn to share some of the accountability, some of the work and some of the stress.'

'Hey, I've been doing okay this morning. Phil's a great ID man. He has his shit togeth—'

'Not out there, Sailor.' He took me by both shoulders, like my father – my two-packs-a-day-Dickies-wearing father – might have, once or twice a hundred years ago. Tapping a finger on my sweaty forehead, Lefkowitz said, 'In here. This is what's going to get you. I've been there myself.'

'Ah, c'mon, Doc. This is my first—'

'You throw up this morning?'

'No.' *So there, Dr Holier-than-Thou.*

'Want to? Feel like it?'

'Yeah, okay, a bit, but Doc, trust me, it smells like a rotting-meat-cat-shit-dead-Marine stew in there. Anybody would—'

'Your arms or legs feel funny? Like they're someone else's, or that maybe it takes a second or two for directions to get there from your brain?'

I held my breath. *That's enough, old man.* My mind was racing around, a Tasmanian devil whirlwind searching through old bits of witty, distracting things I might have heard, or read, or said myself in awkward situations before now, hunting for a tip-of-my-tongue word in a dictionary, something robust. *Nothing. I have no response to that question.*

'Your silence is telling.' Doc smirked, and I felt myself relax, however slightly, like a kid hearing thunder moving away a few miles. It was still there, but bearable. Doc packed up his medical utility belt. 'Get off the pills and then start working on the cigarettes. You're swimming in shark-infested waters, okay? Right, sermon's over. Let's go bag some bodies. Later, if you're in town, I'll let you buy me a brandy and I'll give you my initial opinion on what sent these nice – however aromatic – folks into the promised land.'

'Deal.' It was all I could say. He had my number, and as pissed as I wanted to be at him, I found I appreciated knowing he could see inside my head. I felt a little better about wandering near the edge of the cliff knowing someone was around to warn me when my toes were hanging over the side.

Doc grabbed a leather case with one hand and a large cardboard box with the other. 'Do me a favour,' he said, 'grab that rolling suitcase there, and another of these boxes. I'll meet you back inside.'

'Hold on,' I said, 'I'll come with you.'

'Call your wife first.' He started up the drive. 'I'm sure she's waiting to hear how it's going.'

'Old sonofabitch,' I said to the back of his head.

'That's old, *still-married*, sonofabitch to you, Detective Doyle.' He blew another lungful of that wretched-smelling smoke into the morning and said, 'Then come in and tell me about Huck. I haven't heard from him in a while.'

'Doc,' I called after him, 'I need— I need this— I have to be able to ...'

He turned back to me. Laden with boxes and bags and smoking the snub of a cigar, he looked fallible, human, even in his three-thousand-dollar suit. 'You're smart and arrogant, Sailor, and God bless you for it. All thirty-year-olds should be smart and arrogant; I swear it. But at some point you'll realise that the *smart* you need to keep but the *arrogant* will ruin you.'

I called Jenny. Doc was right: she was happy to hear from me, her good mood from earlier hanging in there. We talked for a minute or two; then she begged off to load Anna and Ben into the car. The grocery store was waiting.

It would take a few drinks to get me to Sarah's tonight.

But I'd order them. As much as I wanted to believe otherwise, just like Doc, I had my own number.

By ten-thirty Doc Lefkowitz had left, easily clearing the eighteen-minute over/under. I collected my twenty bucks from Phil and Lourdes, but had to promise that I'd buy the first round – which in copspeak means the first *few* rounds – when we finally wrapped up. Two morgue techs from the Medical College of Virginia arrived in a State Medical Examiner's Office van and loaded the Bruckners, now in plastic body bags, into the back. While no one mentioned it, Lourdes, Bryson and I all found it disconcerting how easily the two staffers were able to carry Claire Bruckner's shrivelled body. They were sharing the load out of respect or decorum, but either of them could have hefted the mummified remains under one arm like a stack of firewood. Phil was a jaded veteran of too many crime scenes; he didn't seem to notice or to care.

We did have one surprise when we helped Lefkowitz prepare the bodies: Carl Bruckner had lost a foot. Doc removed the prosthetic and examined the stump; proclaiming it to be from a prior trauma. Indicating large whorls of scar tissue with his pen, Doc said, 'It's easy to determine, even given the mummifying condition of the lower extremities. See how the skin here is still white, while the moist flesh on his back is putrefying and turning green and his veins are marbled? It'll all be black in another few days. I'd say this injury is much older – years, perhaps decades. You dig around enough in his past and you'll find it. People don't lose limbs without documentation, disability applications, the lot; you'll get it all readily enough. It's funny: we're forbidden to tell anyone if you come in with flu symptoms, something contagious and genuinely dangerous, but get an arm or a leg ripped off, and all the applications, all the soft money, all the documentation is a matter of public record. God bless America.'

'Little pink houses, for you and me,' I said.

'That explains the canes, the "oh-shit" bars and the brochures,' Bryson said.

'It might explain the Bronze Star and Purple Heart at the top of the stairs, too,' Phil added.

'Waiting on his military records,' Lourdes said quickly, reminding us that he had done his job.

'Whatever.' I shrugged it off. 'Foot or no foot, it doesn't help us find Molly's body or bring us any closer to answering why someone would want to create two mummies and then move them around the house.'

Before Doc left he took me aside again, this time to tell me that he would need to complete an autopsy to work out exactly when Claire Bruckner died. 'Immersed in cat litter like that, she might have died a few months ago, or it could have been years. That stuff is an outstanding dehydrator; someone knew what they were doing – made it impossible for me to use the usual run-of-the-mill crime scene indicators. No bugs, flies, or maggots – even her bacteria have moved on to greener pastures.'

'You think it was the family?' I asked. 'With the epitaph on the door and the duct tape? Did they inter the body upstairs and then someone else desecrate it like that?'

'That's for you to determine, Detective Doyle.' He hit me for another light, another imported smoke. 'After all, you're the homicide investigator. I'll tell you how and when they died. You go catch the bad guys.'

'How about Carl?'

'His death was more recent, a couple of days, tops. With all that cat litter drawing moisture from his extremities, he hasn't rotted as quickly as normal in this humidity, but with that said, it hasn't been long since Carl signed his bill.'

'The moisture from his upper body is getting sucked into the cat litter?'

'Didn't you go to high school?' Doc looked askance at the cigar, frowned, and crushed the butt on the heel of his loafer. 'That moisture was drawn downward, for the most part, as his legs and lower back were sucked dry. The kitty litter acted as a big organic sponge.'

'From a high concentration to a low concentration,' I said.

'Sort of,' he said. 'It wasn't perfect, but it would have taken longer for Carl to rot away than a handful of raw hamburger you'd leave out on the kitchen counter, simply because so much of the moisture in his body was draining into the hope chest.'

'Then why wasn't Carl like Claire? You know, like a shoe left out in the rain or dipped in the ocean and hung up to dry?'

Doc raised a finger, as if lecturing. 'Time mostly. He's still fresh. Look at the bugs he's attracted; blowflies and houseflies are always first in line. But also because so much of him was hanging over the lip of the chest. That litter is an effective dehydrant, but gravity is a merciless bedfellow.'

'So half-mummy and half—'

'Tapioca,' Doc said. 'Be glad you arrived when you did. Things would have been much worse in another three days.'

Phil, Lourdes and I helped Doc get Carl's body – sculpted by gravity, rigor mortis and cat litter into criss-cross-applesauce – zipped into a Virginia CID body bag. Doc supervised as we tugged and pushed to get the knees extended straight enough to fit properly. I had the misfortune to get the footless leg, but I marvelled at the resilience of his corpse, and the sheer muscle and will it took to convince Carl Bruckner to get inside that bag. When my hand passed over the knuckles of oddly shaped scar tissue I felt sorry for Carl, a mistake on any homicide detective's part. With one foot ripped off, most likely forty years earlier in the murky, haunted swamps of Gia Lai Province, Carl came home to eventually die in his own swamp, his body interred in an organic dehydrator, to be slashed into strips and either eaten or fed to a battalion of maddened cats. I pressed down on his knee, then pulled with both hands until his leg finally succumbed. I made myself look him in the face, all bloated, and discoloured with what might as well have been grape juice or cheap merlot. His mouth hung open like the banshee woman I'd imagined in Molly's room. I sighed and took a half-hearted swipe at a buzzing fly as Doc finally zipped the bag closed.

In the driveway, Doc said, 'Call when you're done for the night. Get cleaned up and meet me in the city. VSOPs are on you.'

'Harper never told me how many drinks I'd have to buy in this job.' The morning sun had burned off the haze and was now bringing a full-court press with temperatures already in the high eighties.

'Occupational hazard,' he said.

'Your wife going to let you out?'

'I'm a bachelor this weekend,' he said. 'Esther's in New York, visiting her sister. I managed a get-out-of-jail-free card until Monday night. I'll be in the hospital all day. I want to get a head start on our new friends.'

'Working on this today? You're shitting me – why?'

'Your first investigation, Sailor. It's the least I can do. I'll bring anything I get done with me later.'

That was outstanding news, but nonsense, nevertheless. I pushed him a bit. 'C'mon, Doc. A free weekend, and you're going to the morgue to work? I know July fourth is a busy time for you, but these two aren't going anywhere, and you know I'll be out here at least until Monday sifting through all the trash and papers and dead animals.'

His faced changed; just for a moment I thought maybe Lefkowitz looked frightened. Then it was gone. He threw his hands up. 'You caught me. I'm a little worried. Call it a professional concern.'

I tensed up. This wasn't what I needed to hear. Doc Lefkowitz was supposed to be my leveller, this investigation's bastion of calm and organisation. 'What do you mean?'

'Those animals ... sheep don't just drop dead in the field like that. Horses don't starve to death in two days ... two weeks, maybe ... Something's wrong.'

'Shit, Doc. You think it's terrorists? Some kind of field test for a pathogen?' Phil guessing wildly was one thing, but Lefkowitz's *professional concerns* made it real.

He gave me a disconcerting look. 'It might be. I took blood samples from the big animals and two of those cats you shot. I'll call a couple of friends and see what I can eliminate.'

'Eliminate?'

'I start with my worst fears and work backwards.'

'Thanks Doc, truly. And yes, I'll buy the VSOPs, whatever the hell those are.'

He climbed gracefully behind the wheel of his BMW, looking more like a corporate CEO than a medical examiner. 'Goyim. Raised in a barn.'

'See you later.'

'Find that girl, whatshername, the daughter.'

'Molly.'

'Find her, Sailor,' he called through the window. 'If she's not off with relatives somewhere, she's probably here. If you find her body, call my cell. I'll come back out.'

'Thanks, Doc.' I watched him go, his German luxury liner scraping over rocks and ruts as he drove.

With the bodies gone, I felt a weight lift from my chest. In my shirt-sleeves, I was still sweating, still uncomfortable, but feeling less like I was destined to botch this investigation beyond recognition. Having Carl and Claire lying dead in front of us brought a deeper sense of urgency to our work; with them gone, things changed. Now we were cops working a crime scene together, but the spill had been cleaned up. We could ratchet the tension back, however slightly, while we read, labelled, photographed, bagged and reviewed evidence. Doc Lefkowitz would take care of the Bruckners and share his initial thoughts in an air-conditioned Richmond bar-room later that night.

Phil and Lourdes made phone calls. They tried Animal Control about seventeen times between eight and nine-thirty, leaving messages, some patient, some less so, and then gave up to work on coordinating with the CID mobile lab. Phil had ample evidence – blood, hair and tissue samples, dozens of fingerprints, including the victims' – and he needed the lab close to the Bruckner farm to make analysis and data-base searches feasible. At one point, frustrated and cursing under his breath, Phil took off in his car, hauling one of the living room lamps along with him to determine if there was electricity available at the abandoned gas station out on Goochland Lane. If so, he'd have the lab set up there. While labs had generators, he explained, electricity could keep them running on site for days.

Lourdes coordinated the search for Molly. I gave it to him because I didn't want to deal with the shift sergeant who'd been out here earlier, or any I-told-you-so lieutenant from St James County. I had kicked them out, and I stood by my decision. Bringing them back to search for a missing person, while important, wasn't part of the immediate homicide investigation. If they found Molly alive, terrific, I'd call the news crews and even shine their buckles and badges for them. If they found her dead two hundred feet out in some soybean field, fuck it, they could be heroes. Either way, I had a team of locals to wander around the property sniffing for a dead fifty-year-old retarded woman. Even better, they knew the local game warden, a kid with a listless hundred-and-thirty-pound bloodhound who could try like hell to differentiate between the aroma of dead woman and dead every-goddamned-thing-else. It was the perfect assignment for Bob Lourdes. He was young, attractive, pretty enough for television, actually, and he desperately wanted a transfer to CID. Well, this was his chance: follow the evidence to Molly Bruckner and provide leadership to a team of St James County deputies while you're at it. Lieutenant Harper would be thrilled if Lourdes pulled it off.

While everyone moved around me, I took a few minutes alone on the porch to review the morning so far. Flying solo on this investigation, I found myself face to face with every misconception I'd ever had about homicide detectives. Hollywood couldn't have it more wrong. All the courtroom dramas with the neat, linear, perfect-puzzle-piece presentations of evidence, all my classes at the Academy with the step-one, step-two, step-three PowerPoint presentations on how to approach a crime scene and meticulously collect and eliminate evidence. What a crock.

So far this morning I had got lost and shown up late, after the CID techs had already wandered all over the scene. I had taken a powerful narcotic and drunk coffee from the victims' kitchen in the victims' mug. I had been second-guessed by and deferred to Phil Clarkson on multiple occasions, clearly because he needed to be out of here by three-thirty this afternoon to get to his daughter's music recital.

I had considered that terrorists might have used the Bruckner farm to test an airborne biohazard, but I hadn't called anyone – not the Centers for Disease Control, the World Health Organisation, the Federal Emergency Management Agency, not even the Girl Scouts of America – because I was too proud, and too frightened that any of those organisations would laugh and hang up. Fear is a powerful motivator, after all. I had stepped in cat shit and wandered around the first floor with one shoe off. I had been attacked by cats and fired my gun three times. I'd alienated the St James County Sheriff's Office and had ordered people to do things that I wasn't certain they knew how to do – or that were even part of their professional experience. I was relying on a dispatcher I barely knew to gather critical background evidence on one victim. And as I reflected on my morning, I realised that of all the people working this crime scene, I was about the furthest from a neat-and-tidy presentation of evidence about anything at all, never mind whether or not a murder had been committed.

I remembered being at the Academy and taking notes as fast as I could scribble when one of the old homicide guys – the real detectives, guest speakers, not the regular Academy teachers – would talk about crime scene investigations and the medical-legal investigation of murder. I could still picture my notebooks, everything outlined: A, 1, 2, 3, B, 1, 2, 3 for pages and pages. It was a fundamentally quantitative, structuralist process, investigating a homicide. In the past four weeks, I'd been to six murder scenes with other detectives from CID. Each of those cases had worked out neatly: husband gets drunk, shoots wife … gun's on the floor; bullet's in her chest … collect evidence, talk to witnesses, get a warrant, zip, bang, boom, thanks for coming; try the veal. No one shot anyone's pets; no one hallucinated decomposing banshees, and no one showed up for work half-stoned on illegal prescription meds. Everything was as neat as a Hallmark commercial, all tied up in a bloodstained ribbon.

But this was different.

Here, *I* was the narrow portion of the hourglass. There were eight thousand grains of sand above me, bits of information that had to move through me, the CID filter for all of them, before they could be passed along. Some of them were hard and fast facts: blowflies on

Carl's body, but no maggots, a fillet knife under the porch table, a saw stuck in Claire's backbone – solid pieces of evidence that would undoubtedly play a role in the neat and tidy presentation I hoped to make before a grand jury one day soon. Other grains of sand were more qualitative: a retarded, fifty-year-old daughter, now missing, a shrine to a Vietnamese skirmish, a farm full of dead animals, some apparently killed for food, others dying of starvation or disease.

And who was coming to help me sort through it all? None of my Academy instructors would be stopping by any time soon. Huck was working some detail in Richmond – no matter, this whole place would have him signing on to Dope for the rest of his career. Lieutenant Harper was fishing on the Chesapeake.

So I had Phil, Bryson and Lourdes. Later, I would have Doc, the planet's most reliable sounding board.

And even later, Sarah. She might help, too.

But that was it. News, innuendo, evidence, questions, theories, guesses and speculations were coming at me from all sides, and I had to find a way to throw a net around them all; fit the puzzle together without forcing in pieces, and without overlooking anything important.

I didn't know how to do that. Nothing had prepared me for this. I silently promised to smash my television with a hammer the next time a crime scene cop show came on. *Just the facts, ma'am.* I supposed that was as good a place to start as any, but there were no flashing lights, no bright yellow stickers affixed to the facts. I had to find them, and out here, most of them were either putrefying in the sun or covered in cat shit.

I flipped back through my notebook as Phil pulled up the dirt drive. He climbed out of his car, clumsily balancing two cardboard drinks holders, each with four styrofoam cups. He had a small paper bag in his mouth. He closed the door with his hip.

'Come on up,' I called. 'If that's coffee, I'm sending your name forward for a commendation.'

He grunted something and thumped up the porch steps. His jacket sported matching sweat stains beneath the armpits and between the shoulder blades.

'Lemme help you.' I took the bag from his mouth and relieved him of one of the cup holders. 'You read my mind on the coffee.'

'I got water, too,' he said. 'It's in the back seat. We can throw it in their fridge.'

'After we shoot whatever's evolving in there, right?'

'I'll do it. I'm a better shot.'

'Not fair.' I dumped a few sugars from the bag into his hand, then mine. 'I had a cat on my face the last time I had to shoot anything. That's a ... what would Jenny call it? A mitigating factor.'

'Any progress on Molly?' he asked.

'Lourdes has St James working the fields with one of the game wardens. He's inside digging through the office with Bryson, looking for relatives.' I stirred the coffee. 'I'm hoping she's with an aunt or a cousin somewhere, maybe even at a home, some kind of facility, maybe in the city.'

'That would make things easier,' Phil said. 'What do you figure, they have about three hours left before it rains?'

'Maybe a bit longer.' I lit a smoke. 'It's gonna piss down, though. They won't be able to search for anything out there if it hits like last week. That was a frigging monsoon. This place'll be a mud hole; not even that dog'll be able to smell his way back to the pickup.'

'Given this heat I almost don't mind,' Phil said.

'Me neither, but I worry about anything outside, anything we might be missing.'

He looked across the uncut yard towards the orchard. 'If it was out here last week, it's already flooded out, anyway.'

'Good point.'

Phil rooted in his back pocket. With one hand, he flipped open a spiral notebook. 'I stopped by the closest neighbours, about a half-mile out on Hadley Lane, Hadley Road, whatever it is.'

'The red block place that looks like Satan's vacation home?'

'I tried there, nobody home.'

'That's probably for the best.'

'There's a fruit farm: peaches, pears, apples, on Pitcairn the other way, north. Michael Caldwell and Henry Felten. Two ex-hippies from the looks of them, dope smokers, probably dope farmers posing as apple-pickers trying to get away from it all out here. They had the hair, the tie-dye, the broken-down guitars on the porch, the organic tomatoes growing in the yard, the whole nine yards.'

'Gay?'

'I didn't ask, but it seems likely, you know: floral print on the porch chairs.'

'What'd they know of the Bruckners?'

'Not much,' Phil said. 'They had some kind of run-in with Carl a few years back, something about a field he was working. They seemed to think it was theirs, a regular old-time border dispute. Words were exchanged, insults, threats, whatever, no axe handles or shotguns as far as I can tell.'

'Carl didn't like gay men? Hippies?' I put two and two together.

'Again, I didn't ask, but that might have been at the root of it. Anyway, they haven't spoken with any of the Bruckners for a few years, and claim they haven't even seen anyone over here for the past year. Granted, they're almost a mile away, as the crow flies, further in a car.'

'Any word on Molly?' I finished the coffee and lit another cigarette, trying not to think about Doc's little lecture.

'Nothing. Henry Felten claims he would see her out and about from time to time, but that he didn't know what was wrong with her, you know, what kind of disease she had. I don't know what to call it.'

'Disorder, disease, whatever. I'm not from the Community Services Board.' I twirled two fingers in a get-on-with-it gesture.

'I guess Henry used to talk with her, help her pick apples and take care of her cats. He's one of them, you know, hippy-Jesus-freak types, liberal, open-minded. He wouldn't judge her, might even have enjoyed passing the time with her, felt like he was serving the community, you know.'

I laughed through my nose. 'Phil, I love it when you try to act politically correct. It's a language you just don't speak.'

He frowned. 'Oh, and you're fluent?'

'Shit no,' I said. 'I hate everyone equally.'

'Anyway,' Phil got us back on track. 'Henry didn't give me much useful information on Molly or where she might be today. He talked about her as "special" and "disabled". He even said it that way: a "woman with a disability". It seems like a lot to say. I think the word "retard" has never crossed his lips.'

'And no idea where she might be?'

'Nope.'

'No word of relatives or visitors, doctors, teachers, therapists, anybody who might have taken Molly out of here when Claire died?'

'Nothing.'

'Shit.'

'Hopefully someone from that school will have more information,' he suggested. 'You tried calling yet?'

'Yeah, I got a secretary a half-hour ago. She's going to have someone call me back,' I said. 'I'll throw it to the St James sergeant, whatever his name is. He can chase it down.'

'Good enough.'

Bob Lourdes emerged through the kitchen door. 'Sailor, your phone's been vibrating for five minutes.'

I had left it in the kitchen, not wanting to be interrupted while I thought back over the morning's débâcles. Lourdes tossed it to me, then asked, 'This coffee up for grabs?' He took two, dumped sugar into them and headed back inside.

I flipped the phone open and checked the messages, two calls from Jefferson Middle School in Richmond. To Phil, I said, 'Give me a second to call them back.'

'There's still electricity running through that Phillips 66 station so the mobile lab will have someplace to hook up. I spoke with them on the way back from the diner; we can expect them in the next hour.'

'Right on time,' I said.

'Hey, it's a holiday weekend,' he said defensively. 'They'll call when they get here. Bryson and I can start ferrying boxes back and forth. Until then, I'll keep trying Animal Control.'

'Good enough. Thanks.' I dialled the number on the screen and waited.

'Good morning, Jefferson Middle,' said the same person I'd spoken to earlier.

'Dr Grace Wentworth, please. This is Detective Samuel Doyle of the Virginia State Police calling again.'

'Oh, thank you, Detective Doyle. Dr Wentworth is waiting for your call. I'll put you right through.'

The line clicked, hummed a few bars of muzak – Me and Bobby McGee – then clicked again.

'Hello, Detective. This is Grace Wentworth. How can I help you?'

11:37 a.m.

'Hello, Dr Wentworth.' My jacket was draped over the porch rail. I dug in the pocket for a pen. 'My name is Sam Doyle and I'm a homicide detective with the Virginia State Police. Do you have a couple of minutes, ma'am?'

'I do, Detective,' she said, 'but please don't worry about calling me ma'am. I've been down here most of my life but I'm originally from up north. If they knew someone was calling me ma'am, they'd alert the editors, teamsters and congressmen.'

'Sorry, ma—'

'Hard habit to break, huh?'

'It is,' I said, 'and sadly, I'm from New Jersey. We never had many ma'ams up there either.'

She tittered and sounded like an old lady. I guessed she might be in her sixties. 'Either way, Detective, I'm sure you didn't call me to discuss differences in regional pleasantries.'

'No, ma'am,' I said before I realised I'd slipped back into localspeak. 'Actually, I'm calling to ask if you can shed some light on a murder – well, *potential* murder – I'm working here in St James County.'

'Potential murder? I'm not sure I understand what you mean, Detective Doyle. Has someone been killed? Someone I know?'

'Um, yeah – well maybe yes, and perhaps not.' I sighed. 'Sorry. I'm not making any sense.'

Goddamned idiot. Can't even conduct a frigging phone interview.

'I have a few minutes before my next appointment.' I imagined her leaning back in her chair, trying not to get distracted by the paperwork on her desk. 'Why don't you start again?'

'All right,' I said. 'Carl and Claire Bruckner, of St James County, were found dead this morning in their farmhouse. I'm still determining whether they were murdered, and I was wondering if you might recall their daughter ... at least, I think she's their daughter—'

'Molly.' Her voice was all at once grey and toneless.

'Yes, Molly.'

'Has she been killed?'

'Not that I know of, no.'

'I see.' She hesitated, then said, 'So she's still alive then.'

'As far as I know, yes,' I said, and tried to explain. 'Claire Bruckner appears to have been dead for some time, perhaps even months, while Carl might have been killed in the past two or three days. I have enough evidence to believe that someone was in the house recently, and I wondered if you might remember anything about Molly or be able to wager a guess if Molly still lived here.'

Grace Wentworth made a sound that I had heard many times as a road cop: the noise people made when they knew a victim, but didn't know them well, or maybe hadn't seen them in years, a sound that meant 'Christ, what a tragedy' or 'I hope the family is okay', but without all the awful emotions layered on to intensify things.

She said, 'Carl and Claire Bruckner were both quite active here while Molly was a student. I think it must have been ...'

'Early 1970s?'

'Merciful heavens, am I that old?'

'Sorry, ma—'

'Not your fault, Detective. Time gets us all in the end, damnit. Excuse me.'

'So you remember Molly?'

'I taught Molly,' she said, sounding a little proud. 'She was one of my students for four, maybe five years, a couple of centuries ago.'

'Five years in middle school?'

'We weren't a middle school back then, Detective. We were a junior high, and students like Molly stayed on with us until they were either ready to go to high school – which Molly did not – or they entered the vo-tech programme for job training.'

'Great. This is great.' I caught myself, coughed and said, 'Sorry. I just ... well, I'm glad to find someone who knew the family.'

'I knew them as well as any teacher knows her students, her special students,' she said, 'but I wasn't close to the family. Carl Bruckner spent some time volunteering in my classroom. He had just retired from the military, after his return from Vietnam. He wasn't working at the time, and he came around quite often to assist. Odd for a father to do that, back in those days. As I recall, Claire Bruckner was often busy with the local churches. She was invariably organising a fund-raiser, roast beef suppers, benefit concerts, mission trips and whatnot. Carl mostly took care of the farm and tried to do what he could to look after Molly.'

I wrote as fast as I could, not wanting to miss anything that might emerge as important later on. I said, 'Can you tell me a little bit about what Molly had, what disease, or why she might still be living at home in her late forties? I don't know what to call it, but was she some kind of ... well, a retard or something?'

'Oh, Detective, *ouch.*'

'Sorry, I know that's not the right word for it, but among the crew up here this morning, we don't have a thimbleful of experience with retarded people.'

'People with cognitive disabilities,' she corrected me.

'Got it.' I wrote it down.

'Molly Bruckner had a childhood seizure disorder, a rare form of epilepsy. I suppose these days we'd call it Lennox-Gastaut Syndrome—'

'Can you spell that for me?'

Jesus, Sailor, you're a dipshit. Google it later.

She did, then continued, 'Back that long ago, we didn't know what to make of Molly's condition. We could tell that she was having multiple seizures every day, little ones, seizures we used to call petit mal but now refer to as myoclonic or absence seizures.'

'When you say "multiple seizures"—'

'No one knows, Detective. It might have been ten or fifty or three hundred.'

I wasn't sure what to ask next. 'So ... would she fall on the ground and shake like they do in the movies?'

'Not too often, actually,' Dr Wentworth said. 'Those are grand mal, what we now call tonic-clonic seizures. Molly had those too, an alarming number for you and me even to consider, but it was the small ones that got to her in the end. Each day was like starting over. I'd teach her something; we'd review and review and review it again and again, and she'd go home for the night, have a few dozen seizures, some too small to notice without an EEG, and come back to school the next day with her internal blackboard erased.'

'Erased?'

'She'd forget everything. Only the blurry edges of what we'd covered would stick. So I'd break out the toys and games and blocks and markers and we'd start all over again. And the good news for me was that I knew her as a junior high student. It would have been worse for her in grade school.'

'Holy shit,' I whispered, then said, 'Sorry. Excuse me.'

'Oh no, Detective. That about hits it on the head.'

'How long did this go on?'

'For as long as I knew Molly, and if you say it was the early 1970s, then I suppose I kept in touch until maybe '75 or '76. After that, I'm not sure what happened to her. They tried all sorts of job placement schemes, internships, training and work coaches, but back then those programmes were in their fledgling stages. No one wanted to acknowledge that our friends and neighbours had cognitive disabilities, never mind give someone like that a job bagging groceries or playing cart jockey in the store parking lot. It embarrasses me to say that back then young people like Molly either went to special schools or they stayed at home. The Bruckner farm was the perfect place for Molly with its predictable daily routines, repetitive tasks, simple jobs that need doing every day. With her parents there all the time she probably had a decent life.'

'You're talking about her in the past tense,' I said. 'She might still be around someplace.'

'That's true, Detective.'

'Any idea where?'

'Me? Oh, goodness no.' She took a moment to think, then said, 'I don't recall other relatives, certainly not any brothers or sisters. Claire might have had a sister from out near Danville or maybe Roanoke, but that's me guessing based on a shadowy recollection seen through thirty-five years of pretty thick fog.'

I smiled. 'That's fine, Dr Wentworth, thanks.'

'I have to admit that I'm a little surprised Molly is still with us. Not many Lennox-Gastaut victims make it to their fiftieth birthday. That blackboard can't take too many erasures. After a while, the seizures start winning, and victims experience a regression, often an insurmountable regression. It's a sad and tragic thing to watch, Detective.'

My stomach fell. 'So what you're saying is that if Molly is still alive, chances are that she's regressed to ... what? Teenage behaviours? Younger?'

Not with a princess pillowcase and a Minnie Mouse drinking cup. She's younger than that. From Wibbleton to Wobbleton is fifteen miles, after all.

Dr Wentworth confirmed my suspicions. 'Molly never reached teenage behaviours, Detective Doyle. If she's regressed over the decades, you can expect that she'll be exhibiting behaviours you might find in a three-year-old, maybe a five-year-old.'

'But you said the blurry edges of things would stick over time,' I tried to quote her and gain myself an ounce of credibility. 'Does that mean that she might have learned some things just through repetition that she can still do?'

'Oh sure.' Dr Wentworth sounded relieved to take the conversation in a positive direction. 'My students learned to shop on their own, to count money, to make simple recipes, to match directions and steps with physical behaviours, all manner of productive skills ... as long as they were repetitive and predictable. Lots of skills managed to stick over time.'

'Can Molly care for herself?'

'I haven't seen her in over thirty years, but I'd have to say no. She needed someone with her long-term. I'm sure she can set the table, make toast, use an ATM and maybe sign a cheque or a credit card slip, but she won't be able to do much more than that, I'm afraid.'

Countless questions lined up in my mind; foremost among them was how to find Molly out here in a hundred square miles of nothing. 'Dr Wentworth, can I come see you? I have a number of things I'd like to discuss, and I don't really want to do this over the phone. I can't get a decent cell signal out here and I could use a few minutes to get my thoughts together. This isn't exactly what I expected to hear when I drove to work this morning.'

'Certainly,' she said. 'I'm at your disposal. It's Friday and this place is a ghost town already. What can I do for you?'

'Are you free for lunch? I'll buy.'

'I never turn down a lunch offer from a younger man; it's on my list of Old Lady Directives! Can I come to you?'

I caught a whiff of something rotting in the sun and said, 'The last thing you want to do is come out here.'

'I might surprise you, Detective. I've worked with teenagers for the past thirty-eight years. Stephen King couldn't kill me.'

'Halfway. How about the State Police barracks on Route 1 near the I-295 interchange? Can I meet you there at twelve-forty-five?'

'I'll be there.'

'Thank you, sincerely. You're helping me more than you can imagine.'

'And getting a lunch out of it! This is my lucky day.'

'See you in an hour.' I hung up and shouted for Phil.

'What?' He came running from the opposite side of the house. 'What is it?'

'Get on the horn to ... shit, I don't even know ... maybe someone in Lefkowitz's office. We need anything they can dig up on a child-hood seizure disorder called Lennox-Gastaut Syndrome.'

'What the hell?'

'Molly.' I started towards the driveway. 'I'm going to meet the old teacher. She's the principal now at Jefferson Middle School. I'll be back by three-thirty. I've got my cell if the Earth crashes into the Sun.'

'Okay,' he said, 'we'll be here.'

'And see if you can find any medicines stashed in the kitchen, maybe the upstairs bathroom, probably not in Molly's bathroom if Wentworth's description holds any water. I want to know what she was taking.'

In the car. AC on full. I thought I'd never feel a cool breeze again, even one sponsored by the Ford Motor Company. I had to get to a mall or a men's store, somewhere I could find a new shirt. I'd sweated through this one three times already. A dress shirt and new deodorant.

Then to the barracks. If I got there early enough, I could lean on whoever Lourdes had looking for Carl's service record. Wentworth mentioned Vietnam. I wished I'd asked her if she knew about Carl's foot.

Okay. Line it up: St James is working on the missing persons, but I'll get this piece. I don't know why, but there's more to this Wentworth woman than meets the eye. Call it a hunch, a feeling in my balls, whatever. I need to talk with her.

Lourdes and Bryson are bagging and tagging.

Phil can hold down the fort and get shit rolling back and forth between the farmhouse and the mobile lab. We need latents off that fillet knife. That's number one.

Phil's also on the Animal Control fuckers. Where the hell are they today? Probably some dumb-ass on duty answering phones figuring some suburban-ite pussy's poodle, Cocoa or Fifi, got away to dry-hump the neighbour's guinea pig. If I think of it I'll get the afternoon Dispatch to call them every five goddamned minutes until they call back on the cell. Better yet, I can send one of those St James roadies over there. That'll stir 'em up.

My car bottomed out on a pothole. I could have sworn the god-damned things were moving around to break my back. I already had to piss, making every rut a bladder control commercial. 'Fucking Oregon Trail out here! And these goddamned bushes – is this really what the eco-green assholes want? Do they truly want a planet overgrown with underbrush? Because on my scorecard, there are about nine giant redwoods here on the Blue Planet and nine trillion prickly, pointless, thorn-covered shrubs. This is what we'd have if we got rid of all the lawnmowers and parking lots, my friends: impenetrable jungle brush less than fifteen miles outside Richmond, not Petropolis, Brazil, no, no, no ... Richmond motherfucking Virginia.'

Anyway, Doc's got the bodies. I need to learn how to move through a crime scene like he did. He was a damned virtuoso. It was like watching one of those cooking shows where the shit always comes out of the oven looking better than you could do with six months of trying. He's smooth as silk, all the silk in one of those suits he wears. He's not out here in wool, sweating like Phil and me, shit no. Silky-smooth Doc, with his great hair and his Italian shoes. Nice. Of course, he did yank that saw out of Claire's backbone – did it without blinking, too. I felt my damned bowels contract just watching him. I'd have soiled the old pyjamas if I'd done it.

Maybe Doc's seen his share of horror. Yeah, I bet he has.

Anyway, another pill. Fuck it. Two. That'll do me through lunch.

I need a shirt, some deodorant.

Then food. I'll shit liquid Drano for three days if I don't eat some solid food.

Lennox-Gastaut. What the hell is that? Some retard syndrome. Got to call it cognitive disability, whatever that is, out wandering around the farm ... ought to be in a facility. Make a note to ask that: could Molly be in a facility somewhere? Maybe, maybe she's fine in Richmond or somewhere, some home for Lennox and Gastaut and myoclonic-tonic seizures. Tonic. Gin and tonic is about the only tonic I know.

Where's Sarah? Need a shirt and a deodorant. Two pills. Hit the barracks bathroom. Liquid Drano shit, new shirt and lunch.

Lennox-Gastaut Syndrome. LGS. RML. What's RML?

I took two OxyContin with a swallow of coffee and drifted back in time.

July 28, 1998
Asbury Park, New Jersey

Two runners materialised out of the morning fog. Their feet hidden in low-scudding billows, they appeared to glide, phantom-like, over the perfect sand. Behind them, Asbury Park's boardwalk rose, colourless, above the dunes. The hollow shell of the old casino looked as much like a ruin from a war epic as a Roaring Twenties hotspot left to rot in the humidity.

Frothy grey tide clawed its way up the beach; there would be little time left this morning to run on the hard-packed mud down near the breakers. In another hour, the runners would be forced inland. Just a few paces, and they'd be ankle-deep in unforgiving sand, and dodging the first of the day's sun worshippers, weaving between them like a slalom course. Near the jetty, an elderly man scraped the hull of a dory with grainy sandpaper, each stroke sounding like a sneeze.

Sailor Doyle wouldn't make it another hour, there wasn't a chance. The mere fact that he had dragged himself – relatively sober – out of bed at five a.m. to run ... to *jog* ... that was accomplishment enough for a summer morning. He felt shockingly good after four or five miles, and had no plans to press his luck by extending himself for too long.

Beside him, Marie ran on the balls of her feet, barely touching the ground, a physical anomaly.

Sailor sucked in a deep breath through his nose, and blew hard out of his mouth. Asbury Park smelled of bacon and sewage. 'How far you going?'

Marie looked up at him. 'Why? You feeling good? Wanna come with me?'

He snorted. 'I want to collapse here until Sue and Kara wake up, drive to Dan's and bring me back a half gallon of coffee and a half-dozen doughnuts, *that* is feeling good.'

'I've got a couple bucks; I'll take you to Dan's.' Marie spoke easily, breathing with little effort. 'You've earned it this morning.'

'Bullshit.' Sailor crossed behind her, determined to find the hardest sand on the beach. 'I've done nothing but slow you down.'

'That's not true,' Marie tried, 'I mean ... well, look, I'm breathing pretty hard.'

'How fast are we going?'

She peeked at her watch. 'Nine-minute miles. That's not bad.'

'Yawn. How fast do you run on your own?'

Marie tugged at the zipper on her windbreaker. 'Oh, I don't know.'

'C'mon.'

'Six-forties, or thereabouts, depends on the day, the workout.'

'Jesus! Why? You got a hot date or something?' Sailor tried running on the balls of his feet, and failed. 'How far are you going?' he asked again.

'I'm going to run down to Spring Lake. I'll turn around at that big hotel, the one with the cupola on the roof. If I meet you back at the car, that'll be about fifteen miles.'

'Fifteen miles,' Sailor echoed. 'You're out of your mind.'

'It's really not that far.'

'Sure, if you weigh a hundred pounds and run eighty miles a week.' He dragged a sleeve across his forehead. 'You've got to remember, I'm carrying a fourth grader on me, compared to you.'

'And you smoke,' she said, 'that's why you can't breathe, shithead. Lots of big guys run just fine, but they don't smoke.'

'Ah, well, I've got to die of something,' he said. They crossed from Ocean Grove to Bradley Beach. 'All right,' Sailor went on, 'how far will I have gone if I wait for you on the Belmar boardwalk, like, by Seibert's seafood place?'

'Six ... six and a half, maybe.'

'Really? Holy shit.' Sailor roused himself for the challenge. 'That'd be an all-time personal best – that's a frigging beachfront marathon for me.' Without realising, he picked up the pace.

Marie easily stayed abreast of him. 'I'm nervous about next week.'

'C'mon,' Sailor chided, 'you're running eighty miles a week—'

'Sixty.' She gnawed on her bottom lip.

113

'Sixty. Same difference.' He watched a teenage girl jogging north along Ocean Avenue for a moment. 'You're three-times regional champ, and state champ, and you've wiped the floor with any number of sinewy-looking creatures at any number of big invitationals in the past two years. And I should know, because I was there at all of them, checking out all those freakish, Holocaust babes. Yikes! The things I do for you – not a curve among 'em.'

'If you haven't noticed, I'm not particularly curvy myself.' The sun sneaked above the horizon, bluing sea and browning sand, and promptly disappeared behind an uncooperative wisp of fog.

'I hadn't noticed,' Sailor said. 'Don't be gross.' He cast around for something to say to cheer her up. 'You look good – at least you're tanned after a summer on the boardwalk.'

'I'm going to get my ass kicked,' Marie said.

'How many races have you or your team lost all year? Three? Five? *All year?*' Sailor tugged at the neckline of his T-shirt, anything to breathe easier.

'Yeah, but—'

'Yeah, but nothing.' Bradley Beach gave way to Avon, then Belmar. A young couple made out beneath a blanket, while a vagrant drunk slept off a bender, his dreadlocks and beard dusted with sand. 'Your coach. Your teammates. Everyone is going to love you. You're fast, the greatest runner I've ever seen.'

'You don't know anything about running, Sailor.' Marie's shoulder-length ponytail jounced in time with her stride, the waves, the salty breeze, the cawing gulls. She was a work of art. Once, maybe twice in his life had Sailor been as perfectly in sync with the world around him.

'I beg to differ,' he retorted. 'I know a great deal about running. Those of us who suffer with every flatfooted step, *we* are the experts. You and all your slide-along-on-your-tippee-toe friends, you're the ones who don't know squat about running. Until you've dragged your ass a few miles in my shoes, all panting and blurry, you'll never understand running.'

'Always the philosopher, aren't you?'

'It's my Ninja skill,' Sailor smiled. 'Now go: run your fifteen miles.

You won't be hailed as the Freshman Phenom this semester if you can't manage a measly fifteen miles. I'm going to crawl up the beach and beg a cigarette from a homeless person. I think there's one around here who went to Rutgers. We'll wait for you and, I don't know, maybe parse some sentences together.'

'All right, if you're sure.' Marie pressed a lap timer on her watch and pulled away as easily as if she had just switched up another gear.

Her brother slogged to a stop and bent over, his hands on his knees, listening to his arrhythmic wheezing over the rolling breakers. Once he'd cleared his sinuses, he walked slowly up the beach, watching Marie until she disappeared into the fog hovering over Shark River. She'd be gone in another week, off to East Stroudsburg for the August workouts with the cross-country team.

Silently, he promised he'd get out of bed again tomorrow, and the day after, and log as many miles with Marie as he could before she left.

At Division Headquarters I hurried to the locker room, stripped off my shirt, rinsed it in the sink and then wrung out as much water as I could. I hoped I wasn't leaving indelible wrinkles. I shook the shirt out, nodded to a couple of road guys who looked at me as if I was performing ritual sacrifice of a squirrel, and then dunked the shirt again, this time with soap from the dispenser.

It was a pain in the ass to get all the suds out of it, and I left quite a puddle on the locker room floor. But when I was done, I hung the shirt up in the back to dry. If I didn't make it home that night – *you mean hopefully, shithead* – I figured I could bum an iron off Sarah and have a halfway decent shirt to wear back to the Bruckner place on Saturday.

I cleaned up in the sink, dried with a handful of paper towels and slathered a ton of deodorant under my arms. I'd been so immersed in foul aromas all morning that I had no sense of whether my suit smelled like a rotting corpse or if it was me. The more Old Spice I could get to stick the better my chances were of not curdling milk at the restaurant.

I took a moment to splash water on my face. The damp, blotchy, overheated red colour I'd sported all morning faded, and my normal colour, Irish Summer Burn, returned.

The water felt good. I cupped another handful and drank. I stuck three Band-Aids over the slashes and the deep bite marks. It was like pasting them on a storefront mannequin.

Dressed again and feeling better, I ran my fingers through my hair, wrestled a few curls into submission and then drew my fingertips down from my forehead to my chin. I was feeling someone else's face. That's the OxyContin, a sainted wonder drug, the best pharmacological advancement since the antihistamine. My favourite thing about

OxyContin was that gloriously distant feeling it provided, not to rookies or first-timers, but to veteran users – like me, sadly. When I first started on the pills, it was like getting hit in the head with a brick. I'd take one when I needed to separate myself from work and Jenny and our routines around the house. I'd take another when I couldn't sleep; they were particularly suited for those occasions. OxyContin, in the beginning, is a bit like getting punched in the head by Evander Holyfield. If Evander isn't around to kick the snot out of you, that little green pill will do the trick.

But after a while, one or two wouldn't beat me into the ground. Instead, they'd sneak up on me. It was a fun game, because I knew they were coming; hell, I'd invited them. They'd come up from behind, low and quiet like a bank of warm fog over a beach – Asbury Park – and in twenty minutes all the dials would be turned down, just a few notches, but enough to smooth the frayed edges of my life.

I captured that feeling in the car on the way back to the barracks. It had taken three pills before noon to get there, I'm not sure why, probably because I hadn't eaten and was running in the red on coffee and stress. Real anxiety. The nasty shit that follows you home and sneaks into your nightmares is OxyContin's one mortal enemy, and I'd had a king's ransom in stress so far that morning.

But what the hell, two pills or three, who cares? On my first solo investigation, I wasn't about to split that hair.

When I pulled into the men's store on Route 1, I knew I'd hit one out of the ballpark. The seat of my cruiser, normally about as comfortable as a wooden bench in a boarding school cafeteria, had moulded to my ass and thighs, wrapping around them like a comforter. And the clerk in the store, a teenage kid hawking men's socks for the summer, had smiled at me. Not two feet away, she looked and sounded as though she was on the other side of Alice's looking glass. I didn't feel fucked-up, not any more. I'd done enough pills by now to keep Evander Holyfield against the ropes. Instead, I was dully sharp, sharply dull, with it enough to calculate the quadratic equation, but detached enough not to give a shit what a quadratic equation was.

With a couple of cold beers, I could sleep all night in what Jenny called a death nap: no dreams, no rolling around, no staring into the closet, and no glowing red numbers ticking off the minutes of my life.

But Doc knew, the old bastard. I don't know how. I guess it was just too many years of medicine, too many dead bodies on that slanted table of his. Doc had a sixth, seventh, eighth sense, some damned thing.

What are you taking?

What do you mean?

Don't bullshit me, Sailor. What pills?

I took an OxyContin this morning . . .

I'd have to be careful around him in the future, keep both hands on the wheel.

In the lounge, the TV was on. A couple of the three-to-eleven guys dressed in workout clothes sat around a table eating burgers and fries from styrofoam take-out boxes. They looked pumped-up in their T-shirts, barbell babies ready to kick the shit out of someone. I thought about grabbing another coffee from the pot on the counter, but passed it by. That damned commercial was on again. I hated that fucking song.

Come on over to Ashland Chrysler. Prices there have n'er been nicer. Look away! Look away! Look away! To Ashland.

I asked the two troopers, 'Anyone seen Huck Greeley this morning?'

Dave Stephens, a young bruiser in his second year, said, 'Yeah, he stopped in early, on his way down to the Jefferson Hotel. He's working that dinner tomorrow night, the Bob Lake thing. The Secret Service is paying a bunch of the guys from Dope to be outside in plain clothes, work the streets and alleys, watching for terrorists, snipers, angry VCU kids, whatever.'

'The lone gunman,' I said. 'Did he mention coming back out this way?'

Stephens said, 'Nah. Hit him on the radio. He's probably got one with him.'

'I'll do that, thanks.'

Tony Cotillo, a wiry road sergeant, originally from Boston's North End, asked, 'What the hell happened to your face, Sailor? You dive into the shallow end of the pool?'

'Occupational hazard,' I said. 'How's it going, Tony?'

'Can't complain,' he said. 'In exchange for my wise mentoring, young Stephens here is teaching me how to lift weights as a forty-two-year-old. It's an entirely different game twenty years down the road.'

'So I hear.'

'What're you workin', Sailor? That thing out in St James? We heard something about cats, some deputy shooting cats?'

I went over to the table but didn't sit down. 'Yeah. Lourdes is out there with me, and Clarkson from CID. It's a frigging nightmare: thirty-seven dead cats – actually, forty-three after the ones Phil and I shot and the three they had been snacking on in the closet.'

'Holy Jesus,' Stephens said, 'sounds like a cat ranch.'

'Something like that.' I stole a French fry from him. 'Hey, on that note, do you happen to know who was chasing down that military record for Lourdes? I think he called it in when Julie Largo was on the board.'

'Uh, yeah, Shantal is out there now. Ask her.' Cotillo poured Diet Coke into a styrofoam cup. He wore a Celtics T-shirt with a bright green shamrock on the chest.

'Will do, thanks. And if you see Huck, tell him I'm looking for him.'

'Good luck out there.' Stephens smeared ketchup on his burger. 'It's a hot and shitty day for it, huh?'

'No kidding. You guys working that Senator Lake thing, too?'

Cotillo crumpled a napkin and shot it towards a corner trash can. 'Nah, just a few plain clothes guys from Narcotics. Huck said the Secret Service had a pre-game crew at the Jefferson today, sweeping the place, shutting down the adjacent buildings, moving the trash cans and running routes to the local hospitals. MCV Medical is right there, three minutes tops.'

'Nobody inside?' I asked.

'Nope,' Cotillo said, 'just Secret Service in the hotel. Our guys can't get near it, Richmond PD, neither. I heard they were going to shut down Franklin, West Main, Jefferson, and that one by the old library …'

'Foushee,' Stephens supplied.

'Right, Foushee,' Cotillo went on. 'It's going to severely fuck up Saturday night traffic down there.'

'The Jefferson.' Stephens furrowed his brow. 'Isn't that the one from *Gone with the Wind*, the big dance scene in the beginning?'

Tony shook his head. 'A popular legend around these parts, my young friend, but inaccurate. I think the good folks at the Jefferson would like people to think so, however.'

'Keep the tourists coming in for photos,' I said.

'And convince them to stick around for brunch.' Tony winked at me conspiratorially.

'Hey, where else can you eat pheasant and quail's eggs? Certainly not in the residence halls at VCU,' I laughed.

Stephens said, 'Good thing there's only a handful of kids on campus this weekend, or they'd have a mess on Monument and West Main, given how most college kids feel about Bob Lake.'

'Is that how they're coming in from the airport?' I asked.

Cotillo shrugged. 'Damned if I know. The Secret Service doesn't tell us much. I bet anything the colonel or the governor will get their marching orders some time tomorrow morning, like when Clinton came down for that dinner in Windsor Farms, you know: roads to close, escort stuff.'

'Shouldn't Richmond City handle that?' Stephens asked.

'Depends on which way they come,' Cotillo said. 'I-64 and 95 are ours.'

'But Monument, Grace and West Main—' I started, not really caring any more.

'Right. That's Richmond's nightmare.' Stephens punctuated his thoughts with a French fry pointer. 'That makes sense, then: why they don't want any uniform guys down there.'

'State troopers.' Cotillo nodded. 'It makes Lake look scared, militaristic, paranoid, too reliant on uniformed muscle. With Richmond PD on the street, it could be anything. Hell, even the city basketball championships have uniforms and cruisers at every corner, blue lights and all.'

'That's smart,' I said. 'So even if the college kids burn sofas in the street, it doesn't look like Lake's brought in any hired guns. Just our Dope guys working the crowd from the inside. I like it.'

Cotillo laughed and drained his Diet Coke. 'I'll alert Bob Lake's campaign manager: Sailor Doyle, homicide detective and cat killer—'

'Alleged cat killer,' I cut him off.

'Fine, *alleged* cat killer approves of his political posturing.'

Stephens leaned back, folding his fingers behind his head. He had big arms, enviable biceps.

I don't look like that. I've never looked like that.

He said, 'I've got to admit; I'm voting for him.'

'Me too,' Cotillo said without hesitation. 'You heard him on crime? He doesn't dick around, and you look at what he did in the Senate, his voting record, he's good for cops: cop pay, cop pensions, cop benefits, he's all about cops, and he goddamned hates criminals and terrorists: no negotiations, no aid to their countries, nothing like President Baird.'

'Well, criminals and terrorists are easy to hate,' I joked. 'But that surprises me about you, Tony. Aren't you from Boston? I thought most everyone up there was a democrat.'

'A common myth, but admittedly part of the reason I live down here,' Cotillo said. 'And Bob Lake's got a plan to get rid of the fuckers—'

'The democrats?' Stephens elbowed him in the ribs.

'The criminals.' Cotillo threw a backhand at Stephens' head. 'I'm not even that worried about the terrorists. Not down here, anyway. When I was stationed up in Fairfax and we worked Arlington, Alexandria – just the highways – that was a frigging frightfest every night. I still hate driving in Crystal City; you're constantly waiting for the sky to light up, the big boom, you know? But down here, it's more the thug assholes and gang bangers. And while the city guys take care of most of the neighbourhood shit, I worry when we pull them over on the highways.'

'Huck used to say the same thing when I first went over to Dope,' I added. 'A car full of street thugs on the highway are going somewhere. That's never good news.'

'What do you mean?' Stephens asked.

'Criminal thugs fight for a neighbourhood, a school yard, a stretch of road to sell drugs and enjoy worry-free partying. When they get out on the highway, they're doing business somewhere,' Cotillo explained.

'That means stolen cars, drugs, guns, money and bad attitudes,' I said.

'Oh, right.' Stephens burped into the back of his hand. 'They're probably never on their way to Epcot.'

'Not often, no.'

Cotillo stood. I didn't know if he was that passionate about Bob Lake or if he was just throwing away his lunch trash. He gathered up the remnants of his burger and said, 'After four years of liberal bullshit, *reforming* criminals and *treating* drug addicts on the taxpayers' kindness, I think America is ready to start hauling some of these losers back to prison.'

'Thus the animosity from the college crowd,' Stephens concluded.

'Exactly, but that's all for nothing. November will be a walk for Lake. He's already got it wrapped up. I don't even know why they're paying all that money to have a convention next month. They ought to funnel it into his campaign.' Cotillo did finally crumple his trash and stuff it in the bin. I hadn't noticed his shamrock tattoo; this was one serious basketball fan. He went on, 'Yet with that said, I'm staying home to barbecue tomorrow night with my wife. Let the Narcotics guys infiltrate the angry mob, however small. I'll watch it on TV.'

'Me too,' Stephens said.

'You both got the night off?' I asked.

'Yeah, but back on Sunday, three-to-eleven.' Cotillo tugged a Red Sox cap over his thinning curls and shouldered a gym bag.

'I'll be elbow-deep in cat shit and dead people.' I waved and started towards the door. 'Who'd you say is on the board?'

'Marie.' Dave Stephens faded from view, suddenly shrinking to a point. He was small, like a doll, and hard to hear. The lights dimmed and I staggered a step, gripping the back of the chair to hide it. An echo of the decomposing woman's shriek thudded around inside my head and my mouth tasted funny, like warm river water.

I swallowed and felt sweat break out on my forehead again. 'What did you—? What was that?'

'Shantal. She came on at eight.' Stephens, back to normal now, tossed me a mock salute. 'Stay clear of those cats, Detective.'

'Um ... heh, yeah ... um, okay, I'll see you guys.' I rubbed my eyes and pinched the bridge of my nose hard enough to hurt. 'I'll go find Shantal then, thanks.' Needing something to do with my hands, I cinched up my tie, then headed out front.

Shantal Whatshername, the afternoon dispatcher, sat behind a U-shaped computer terminal with GPS screen, tape and digital recorders, and a phone, satellite and radio communications console. It looked like the nose cone of the space shuttle, and I swore I would never go in there. If I were in charge, troopers across the state would find themselves at risk, waiting for back-up, holding for tag or registration information, or dialling 1-800-FELON-NEWS to learn if a suspect had priors. The buttons, dials, lights, screens and various sundry coloured labels all required some organisational gene that was absent the day they compiled my personal double helix. At the centre of it all, looking old-fashioned beside all this state-of-the-art technology, was a plastic hand-held microphone, like something John Cameron Swayze might have used back in the 1950s. Shantal wore a headset with a mouthpiece strapped in place, though she didn't seem to need it.

She was short, broad across her ass and shoulders, with stumpy legs that barely reached the plastic mat beneath the chair castors. She looked like she had shown up for work in her younger sister's uniform, and every time she looked at me, I could see glimpses of her bra trying to burst free from the VA State Police blouse holding it hostage. Yet she was definitely on her toes; she spun and whirled, all the while keeping one hand on the TALK button of Swayze's microphone. She punched in tag numbers, checked GPS information, scribbled notes to herself, and never needed more than a few seconds to respond to a road trooper's radio call.

It was a job I could clearly never pull off, and for the first time all day, I didn't envy someone the work they did compared to mine.

No thanks, ma'am. I'll take the mummies and the rotting farm animals.

Shantal waved me over. Punching numbers into a laptop, she said, 'Detective Doyle?'

'Yes?'

'There's someone here to see you, sir, Dr Wentworth, from—'

'Yes, thanks,' I interrupted, genuinely not wanting to distract her. 'She and I have a meeting.'

She spun back to the microphone, pressed down with an ornately polished fingernail, and said, '275, I show no outstanding summonses on that vehicle. 12:44.' She checked the computer screen, whirled to her GPS and punched a button that marked the position of a cruiser somewhere on the Interstates around Richmond.

'Um, Ms ... Shantal?' I was embarrassed that I didn't know her last name.

'Yes, sweetie, what do you need?' She spun to face me, letting go of the microphone for a moment. 'Great Jesus of mercy, Detective, what happened to your face?'

'I get that a lot,' I said. 'Just another day in homicide.'

'You need anything, sweetie? An ibuprofen or some peroxide?'

'No, but thanks, anyway. Hey, did Bob Lourdes call in about military records for—?'

The speaker behind her cut me off. 'VA674 on a stop.'

Shantal held up a finger, spun to her console, pressed the GPS again and struck the ENTER key on her laptop. 'Go ahead 674. 12:45.'

The voice warbled. It would be difficult for someone off the street to understand what the trooper was saying; deciphering the radio was every rookie's closet fear, but after a few weeks in a state police cruiser, we all managed to figure it out. This was a highway stop, probably a speeder or a beach traffic fender bender on I-64.

'On a stop. I have a green Dodge Ram, New Jersey tag number Four, Two, Nine, Charlie, Charlie, Zebra ...' The trooper, a woman, noted her location and waited for Shantal to respond.

She typed in the tag number, hit ENTER, spun back to me, and said, 'Yes, the fax came in about forty-five minutes ago. It should be in a manila file on the shelf above the Xerox machine across the hall.' She glanced at the laptop, then said, 'That all you need, sweetie?'

I tried not to look at the prisoner bra, tugging her blouse buttons apart. 'Yes, thanks. I'll just—'

'Okay, then, have a good day. Take care of that face, sweetie.' She whirled back, using her toes for leverage. '674, I show a registration to a Roger Beechwood of 6112 Parker Road, Hackettstown with no outstanding summonses. 12:46.'

I backed across the hall and collected my fax. It was definitely time for lunch.

Dr Wentworth waited for me in the lobby. She was in her late sixties, verging on emaciated, with short but gravity-defying hair that looked so stoically held together there might have been an aerosol hole in the ozone layer with her name on it. She wore glasses low on her nose, with a second pair dangling from a beaded chain around her neck. Her necklace, earrings and bracelet all matched: some sort of turquoise Southwest Indian motif with little stickmen dancing around ancient firepits. None of these wore cowboy hats or carried stick sabres, I noted. Her dress was a noisy floral explosion, and she had a Richmond City Schools ID tag with a faded mug shot of herself affixed to a spongy keyring around her wrist. She was talking on a BlackBerry when I came out.

'... just have to retake it in summer school ... well, I don't care if he's decided to do the work now ... it's July, that's too damned late, isn't it?'

I liked her already.

'... have to go now ... back when I can ... not sure how late ... okay, bye-bye.'

What sixty-plus-year-old principal says 'bye-bye'?

She slipped the BlackBerry into an expensive-looking case, grinned, and said, 'Detective Doyle?'

I took her hand; it was tiny in mine. But she had a strong grip, and shook with enthusiasm. She didn't mention my face.

'Yes, ma'am,' I said, then caught myself. 'Sorry.'

'Are you hungry? Because I am hungry. And I never get up here, but there is a restaurant down on Route 1, just a few miles from here, that is to die for. It's a bit of a greasy spoon – hell, greasy floors, walls, and I don't even want to think about the rest rooms – but they do have

126

glorious food, if you don't mind anteing up for coronary bypass surgery later this afternoon.'

Yup. I liked her. She couldn't have weighed ninety pounds in a wet wool sweater, and she had immediately taken over the conversation, the lobby, the afternoon. I was at her disposal. I managed to get my hand free and said, 'I'll buy the food, but the vascular surgeon is on you.'

'Deal,' she said. 'Shall we go?'

'Please.' I ushered her towards the double doors.

She moved past me, talking all the while, 'You know, I've driven by this place dozens of times in my life, but I never realised how large it all is. This is quite a barracks, isn't it?'

'That's my fault.' I pushed open one of the doors, but Dr Wentworth shouldered her way through the other. 'I should have been more specific in my directions. This is Division Headquarters, home of all the brass offices and the state crime labs, not to mention the road barracks serving the north side Interstates, and I-95. It's a big complex.'

'No matter.' She shrugged it off. 'I managed. Now, who's driving? I'm over here if you want me to drive, but I don't suppose State Police officers are much for being driven around.'

She led me towards a two-door Mercedes convertible, something from the early 1960s that was probably worth more than Jenny and I made together in a year. As a cop, I couldn't help but check out the vanity tag: *PRVB 226*. I said, 'You're right, Dr Wentworth. I'll drive; my car helps clear some of the noontime traffic out of the way.'

'Yes, I suppose it does, doesn't it.' She dug in her purse, withdrew a leather glasses case and traded the specs on her nose for a pair of trendy sunglasses.

'That's three pair of glasses already,' I teased. 'You have another in there somewhere for emergencies?'

'You're observant.'

'I'm a detective.'

'Touché.' She snapped the case shut and dumped it into the purse. 'Don't get old, Detective Doyle. Honestly, it is such a bore getting old.'

Flashing back to my days in junior high school, I was secretly glad

127

Dr Grace Wentworth hadn't been my principal. Somehow, I'm certain she and my mother would have been on regular speaking terms.

'Come on.' I opened the door for her; she nodded politely. 'I'll let you play with the siren.'

'Will it make me feel younger?'

'Works for me.'

'Then you're on.'

As tired and numbly stoned as I was at that moment, I enjoyed myself. We rolled onto Route 1 towards Richmond and I regretted not letting her drive. The ragtop Mercedes would have masked any lingering aroma of Claire and Carl Bruckner trapped in my suit and it would certainly have been more enjoyable, zipping along like whatshisname from that movie with Audrey Hepburn, the guy who played Ebenezer Scrooge in the musical version of *A Christmas Carol*.

Dr Wentworth had been right: the Northside Café was more the
grease-pit diner she described than the themed throwback grease-pit
diner its owner envisioned. Bored-looking waitresses in poodle skirts
scratched burger and milkshake orders with bowling pencils. Tiresome
1950s music rang from overhead speakers, and a few flat-panel TVs
showed an old creature feature with a rubbery fish-faced monster chasing a busty blonde through a swamp. I ordered a burger with extra
onion rings and iced tea. Dr Wentworth, without even glancing at
the menu, queued up meatloaf with gravy, mashed potatoes, carrots,
cornbread and coffee. Where she planned to put it all inside that
diminutive frame remained one of the afternoon's mysteries.

She stirred sugar into her cup and said, 'I take it you haven't found
Molly?'

'I was hoping you could help me with that,' I said. 'I don't know
enough about her, or about Lennox-Gastaut Syndrome, to begin to
guess where she might be. Is there a chance she's in a facility someplace?'

Dr Wentworth wrinkled her nose. 'I doubt it. You didn't know Carl
Bruckner. He'd have gone to his grave before sending Molly to a treatment centre. I can't imagine she's anywhere but that farm. And like I
said before, I don't recall any relatives, certainly none nearby.'

I mopped my brow with a napkin. The café was air-conditioned,
almost cold inside, and the sweat on my neck and chest chilled to
cool droplets. Dr Wentworth began fading from my field of view,
falling towards the false horizon between the back of our booth and
the bottom edge of an old movie poster of Gary Cooper. It was like
Dave Stephens after telling me that Marie was working the board at
Division Headquarters – *he didn't really say that, Sailor.* I fought off

129

the hallucination and pressed my wrists against the Formica table. The mild shock of cool against my veins felt good. Through a speaker behind me, Bobby Darin crooned a line about dancing with a homecoming queen named Marie.

I blinked twice and said, 'You mentioned before that you didn't know of Lennox-Gastaut victims who lived to see their fiftieth birthday. I've got to admit I haven't had two minutes to Google it, so I don't know much more than the nothing I knew when I called you this morning. But can you tell me why that is? What is it that kills them? Is there a chance that it caught up with her parents, too? Maybe some kind of recessive gene that finally jumped out from behind the couch?'

She looked at me like any number of teachers had looked at me back in high school. College professors didn't perfect that look, largely because most of them never gave a shit if we learned the material or not. But public school teachers were downright gifted at it. It was a look that said, 'You're a dumb-ass, but I'm going to give this one more try, and maybe, just maybe you'll catch up with the rest of the class.'

Dr Wentworth said, 'No. Lennox-Gastaut Syndrome is a childhood disorder. How long it lingers varies from victim to victim. Most begin experiencing seizures around three or four years old; it's rare to start later than six or seven. What kills them in the end is their mind's inability to learn, to adapt and – eventually – to maintain their body's homeostasis: chemical, emotional, hormonal. I remember back in the 1960s when troubled psych patients would undergo electro-shock treatments. It gave them what they believed was a psychological purge, a clean slate, fresh start, whatever you want to call it. It didn't work. Oh, sure, some zealots still hold fast to the notion, but they're not terribly credible. Modern medicine understands that the human brain can't take that kind of neurological upheaval and continue ticking like a Swiss watch. What Molly Bruckner experienced as a child and through her teenage years, as I understand it, was significantly more disruptive than electro-shock treatments.'

'Damn,' I whispered. 'Why is that?'

'Because Molly's seizures were uncontrollable, too frequent to tally, given the old means of observation – especially in a victim's home in the 1970s. Her brain experienced horrendous trauma, week after week, until it faltered and finally settled in a niche where only her basic needs and wants were addressed.'

'Like breathing and eating? Walking around?'

Dr Wentworth skewered a piece of meatloaf, chewed, then held up a manicured hand, begging a moment. After swallowing, she dabbed at the corners of her mouth with a napkin and said, 'Molly might have maintained other skills. She probably can't read more than a few sight words, or write much more than her name and the alphabet. But I bet she can identify coins and bills, maybe match kitchen tools with key words in a recipe, wash dishes, rake leaves, other tasks around the farm. Her parents – her *father* – worked with her tirelessly thirty-five years ago. I have no reason to believe he ever gave up on her.'

I tried to picture Molly as a little girl, playing with crayons, drawing horses and writing capital letters while Carl looked on, encouraging her from across the kitchen table. It was hard to imagine. I kept seeing Carl as a Marine captain, a hardass with a nasty injury to his leg, the toll exacted by a Vietnamese landmine or a grenade. He was a redneck, a farmer who didn't let something as insignificant as a missing foot keep him from tilling the fields, harvesting the orchard or milking his cows. He didn't strike me as a PTA dad, someone who volunteered in his daughter's retard school – *cognitive disabilities*, whatever. It didn't add up.

I asked Dr Wentworth about him. She confessed to only knowing Carl for a few years, but she was certain that he doted on Molly ...

Why? How could anyone do that, be around a retarded kid like that every day?

... and would for the rest of his life. She hadn't known him before his tour in Southeast Asia, but she told me that he had come to the school most afternoons. Claire dropped Molly off in the mornings while Carl was working in the fields. By early afternoon, Carl's leg was ready for a break. He'd come into the classroom where he could loosen the straps on his false foot, sit with the students, read stories, or help Molly and her friends with crafts or cooking projects. He was a mainstay in Dr Wentworth's former classroom and she ranked him as one of the most helpful and compassionate parents she'd ever known in her thirty-eight years at Jefferson.

I asked, 'Did he ever seem angry about his injury, resentful that the war had cost him a limb?'

Dr Wentworth stopped chewing and looked at me over her glasses. 'You know many Marines, Detective Doyle?'

'A few, sure,' I said. 'Enlisted guys mostly. A lot of troopers are ex-military.'

'Any Marine officers, Annapolis grads?'

'Nah.'

'Carl Bruckner was a Marine through and through. I never heard him gripe about that foot, never saw him take assistance from anyone, never noticed him struggling with his prosthetic. He wouldn't even carry a cane, never mind use it for balance.'

'Proud, tough—'

'A fire-eating jarhead to the very end; don't doubt it,' she said.

I grinned. 'You know many Marines, Dr Wentworth?'

She waggled her ring finger at me. 'I married one forty-two years ago.'

'I thought you said you'd been at Jefferson for thirty-eight years. Don't Marines have to move around a lot?'

'Not the ones who die in Laos, Detective. Not those.'

'Sorry,' I said.

'Oh, don't think twice about it. I remarried in 1980 ... never able to take this old ring off, though. Thank God my Ken's an understanding guy, huh?'

I wanted to change the subject but I felt an irritating knot of ambiguity tightening in my guts. Something about Carl Bruckner was out of focus.

Dr Wentworth interrupted, derailing my thoughts, 'You don't know what killed them?'

'Carl and Claire? No,' I admitted. 'They're in bad shape. Claire's been mummified in cat litter. She probably died months ago. Carl's been dead for a couple of days, three tops, given the insects in the room—'

She looked horrified at that.

'Sorry.'

Dr Wentworth swallowed uncomfortably. 'Was there ... I don't know what you call it ... foul play involved?'

I nodded and ate an onion ring. 'Almost certainly. Carl's half-buried in a hope chest full of cat litter, and he has ...' I decided not to mention the strips cut from his back. While I couldn't imagine Grace Wentworth telling anyone what we'd discussed, I needed to withhold a few details, something only my perp would know. The strips from Carl's back and the fillet knife would do nicely.

'He has what?' she asked.

'Never mind.' I brushed her off. She obviously didn't appreciate it. I don't believe many people were able to ignore Dr Wentworth when she wanted something. I backtracked a bit. 'It isn't good lunch conversation,' I lied; most days this was exactly what I discussed over lunch. 'Certainly not lunch conversation for anyone who knew him personally.'

'Fair enough,' she said, giving in. Upside down, one of the Southwest Indian stickmen on her bracelet appeared to be humping a stick caribou.

'And we have an excellent medical examiner handling the case,' I said. 'I'll join him tomorrow for the autopsies. That should uncover a lot, hopefully all we need to know.'

'You mean sometimes an autopsy fails to deliver the goods?'

I finished my burger and chuckled. 'That's funny. I've never heard it described like that. Uh, yes, sometimes we have autopsies that are no help, and we have to sit around for weeks waiting for lab results, chemical tests, fibre analyses—'

'Like the TV shows?'

'No,' I said, 'rarely like the TV shows. Most of our suspects are identified within twenty minutes of our arrival at the scene.'

'But not today,' she pressed.

'No, not today.'

We chatted for another half-hour. Dr Wentworth did her best to answer my questions and I enjoyed a crash course in cognitive-developmental disabilities over five iced-tea refills. I managed to keep her, the dining room, and my food in focus throughout the meal. I tried to ignore the music, though I couldn't help but keep an ear cocked for phantom lyrics taunting me from a bygone era of sideburns and Lucky Strike cigarettes.

To her credit, Dr Wentworth made an effort to answer all my questions, but in the end, she had little more to offer. Her insights into Lennox-Gastaut Syndrome were interesting, but what captured my attention was her recollection of Carl Bruckner. There was more to him than a ramshackle farmhouse and a few dozen dead cats.

I thanked Dr Wentworth, promised to keep her apprised of our efforts to locate Molly Bruckner, and drove her to her fancy Mercedes in the Division Headquarters lot.

The day had grown heavy with imminent rain, but the heat persisted. Even blowing full on, my cruiser's air-conditioning did little to slice through the grey pall hanging over Richmond. I gave up trying to keep clean and sweated openly through my new shirt.

Dr Wentworth leaned in before closing the car door. 'Thank you for including me in your investigation, Detective Doyle.'

'Thank you,' I said. 'You've shared critical information that will help us track down Molly Bruckner, I'm sure of it.'

'I hope so.'

'Dr Wentworth, can you tell me what your vanity plate means?' I asked. 'What's *PRVB 226*?'

'Oh, that's from the Bible,' she explained, 'something I came across about a hundred years ago. It's from Proverbs, chapter 22, verse 6. *Train up a child in the way he should go: and when he is old, he will not depart from it.*'

'Words to live by for a teacher, I guess.'

She handed me a business card with a cell number scrawled on the back. 'You'll call me when you know where Molly is.' It wasn't a request.

'Absolutely,' I said. 'Thank you again, Dr Wentworth.'

'Keep well, Detective. Marie forgives you. It's important you understand that.' She closed the door and waved before turning away.

I gripped the steering wheel with both hands. A raindrop splattered against the windshield, followed by another on the hood, then a quick drum roll on the roof, harbingers of the approaching torrent. 'She didn't really say that, Sailor. You know better. It's just the ... what is it? The pills? It's gotta be the pills today. That's all. Pills and stress and the stink of that fucking farm stuck in my suit. That's all. She said, "Keep well, Detective." Nothing else.'

I watched Dr Wentworth pull out of the lot and turn south towards the city. I didn't move, still reeling from what I thought I'd heard. With my foot on the brake, my cruiser in drive, I double-parked and listened to the rain roll over Interstate 295. The wind picked up and the skies dimmed to Confederate grey. I listened to myself breathe and tried to get a rope around my thoughts.

Back when I was a road cop, one of the guys – it might even have been Tony Cotillo, who knows a little about a lot of different things – told me that Virginia was geologically unique. The eastern part of the state has a clear delineation between the piedmont region and the coastal plain, right down to certain plants and trees that grow on one side of a road or a field but don't show up on the other. All right, that might have been an exaggeration, but I got the basic gist of what he meant, even though I was only half-listening at the time because I never cared about geography past what was required to graduate from high school. So I wasn't about to start once I'd navigated my way, without a compass, into adulthood. But one of the points Tony made was that a rainstorm in eastern Virginia can be as vicious as anywhere on earth, Brazil, Bolivia, wherever, because of our peculiar geography.

This storm was all at once a noisy brute, with dangerous lightning and cracking, resonant thunder. Staring at a massive VA-DOT snowplough parked behind the barracks for the summer, I barely heard the rain as it roared east, soaking the metro area, washing away evidence out at the Bruckner farm and casting me back three years to a similar day when Huck Greeley, in a show of confidence, left me, a twenty-eight-year-old CID narc, alone in a drug dealer's walk-in closet.

It was July then, too. Huck and I were working an investigation in Northern Virginia, a little town in Fairfax County. A group of recreational drug users – lawyers, sales managers, professors, mostly rich assholes from one of those gated golf communities surrounding DC – would party together on weekends. They had started years earlier, smoking a few bowls of imported weed when their wives weren't looking, nothing serious. After a while, one of the golf pros from the local club, a loser named Roger Masterson, suggested they branch out a bit, expand their party circle and maybe pick up a few dollars for beer and blow jobs. Masterson had connections in Prince George's County, people he'd met when he toured as a wanna-be pro until he blew out his knee sneaking down the back steps of some sponsor's wife's bungalow. He hooked the suburbanite crew up with minor scores, coke and pills, and the raves continued, cycling from one tastefully finished basement to the next.

The guest lists grew until most of the neighbourhood was invited – Friday night at Mark and Billie's; Saturday at Ken and Kellie's; Sunday afternoon at Terry and Rob's – and it was all in good fun. Masterson, in covert, always polite exchanges, passed drugs for cash. No one got hurt. The get-togethers were the talk of the town, and all the forty-somethings felt a bit younger, a bit thinner, and a bit more attractive for a few hours each week. No one cared that it was illegal. They had all come from similar working-class roots, had scratched and clawed their way to the upper rungs of the middle-class ladder, and they reckoned they'd earned the right to ignore a few laws, providing they kept it under control.

And then God invented Methadone, Vicodin, Demerol, and our heroes: the OxyCodone family of Percocet, Percodan and OxyContin. I don't know what it is about rich white people that makes them lean towards prescription drugs. Huck claims it's their educational level:

they're smart enough to know that science can provide a high that Mother Earth can't touch, even with her finest poppy, hemp and coca fields. Poor blacks and white trash rarely stray from the old standards: coke, smack, dust and booze. But we uptight whities can't get enough of experimental, prescription bullshit: ketamine – Special K – what shithead ever decided that if it's strong enough for a thoroughbred racehorse, it's strong enough for his ninety-eight-pound girlfriend? I don't know.

Anyway, Masterson soon realised that while his buddies were happy to drop twenty bucks here and there for a bowl of decent weed, their wives and girlfriends were willing to sell the family SUV, refinance their mortgage or whore themselves out for a steady supply of pills. Lunesta and white wine became the Tuesday afternoon cocktail. Hubby in a traffic jam? Travelling for business? Stuck in the city? Fuck it: Oprah's on; have a Vicodin and a Pinot Grigio. Text your friends and have a satellite party, just a couple of glasses of wine (and maybe a pill or two) until the kids get off the bus. Then it's back to wifing and mothering, no bullshit.

Everything was going well for Masterson. Granted, a few parties stretched through the wee hours; some even wrapped up after dawn. A punch was thrown now and then, and plenty of vomit was mopped up before bedtime, but no one, certainly not the Virginia Criminal Investigation Division or the FBI, would have known or cared less about Roger Masterson if Mark and Billie Hoover hadn't moved to Montgomery County, Maryland.

I never met Billie Hoover, not even at the trial eight months later, though I wished I had. Huck and I tag-teamed our part of the testimony on that one, so Billie's and my paths never crossed. Clearly delineating who does what at a crime scene makes it tougher for a defence attorney to beat you up at trial. Too often during cross-examination you can shrug and say, 'I don't know. That wasn't my responsibility.' It throws off their timing. Huck taught me that.

Anyway, to hear Huck describe her, Billie was a forty-five-year-old housewife and mother of three who was determined to hold tight to the twenty-seven-year-old single life until gravity and nature ripped it away by force. She'd had her nose, her lips and her tits done, and from the stories, she must have lived on chicken and egg whites after humping her way up the Sisyphean stair machine for several hours a day at the country club. When she felt herself losing a step or two, or felt her ass stretching out her old college jeans, or maybe caught Mark peeking at the younger wives around the neighbourhood, Billie, a downright sexy middle-aged mom, had a quiet breakdown.

Roger Masterson, enjoying the ample spoils of his newfound career, was quick to respond. At first it was just cash for pills, with Tuesday and Friday drop-offs outside the club locker room. When Billie's discretionary funds ran dry and Mark got suspicious, Masterson started delivering pills right to the house, 10:15 a.m., between workouts and lunch, in exchange for a hand job, a peek at Billie's sculpted tits, and after a while, a blow job or a quickie lay for each baggie.

Billie had started as a Demerol junkie. She moved on to Vicodin and finally OxyContin, because it didn't fog her instrument panel quite so badly. Demerol is a great high if all you have planned for the afternoon is sleeping or watching old reruns of *WKRP in Cincinnati*. OxyContin was easy to get, and Masterson, figuring he'd push the pills on other wives and mothers feeling old or ignored, was happy to keep supply lines greased.

Of course, Mark Hoover caught them mid-blow job. *Christ, how do you ever get past that in a marriage?* He left for work one morning, hung around the local Starbucks for three hours, probably dropping twenty-two bucks on non-fat decaf mochachinos, and sneaked in the patio doors to find Billie going down on her drug dealer – the same guy who had taught Mark how to hit a flat sand wedge. In typical suburbanite fashion, there was plenty of yelling, maybe a shove or two, but no shotguns, no butcher knives. None of those pussies really have it in them when the smoke all clears. Mark put the house up for sale. Billie spent twenty-eight miserable days puking in rehab, and the kids' grades dropped from As to Cs that semester.

So far just another family chasing the American dream, still nothing for Huck and me.

In Maryland, Billie Hoover held it together for about five months – I'm sure she knows the exact number of weeks, days and hours she was sober – but then something happened, I don't know what. If I'd met her, I would have asked. It's always the damndest things that push addicts off the wagon; Huck collects those kinds of stories and threatens to document them for posterity: *Sergeant Greeley's Top 100 Excuses to Get Shitty*. He's an amusing guy. It'd probably be a bestseller.

Billie's first call to Roger Masterson was in May, about two months before we busted him in a torrential rainstorm.

Roger was thrilled to hear from her, even more enthused at the prospect of visiting the fellatio fairy twice weekly. He had a closet full of cash, pills, Gs of weed and baggies of coke and a neighbourhood jammed with discreet customers rolling in legitimate money. He didn't need Billie's business, and although he never admitted it during questioning, we could tell that old Roger knew the risk he was taking every time he transported drugs into Maryland. He did it anyway. Billie must have given astonishing head.

It was Kyle Brenner, an FBI agent out of the Fairfax field office, who called us in. Roger had graduated from golf-community shithead to Interstate felon, so Huck and I went in with the feds when they kicked the door in. Brenner, a hotshot agent with a boner for narcotics, was busy with about fifty-six other investigations and didn't want to be bothered with the mop-up interviews, all those chicken-shit suburbanites and their lawyers. So we agreed he'd bust Masterson, the big fish, on Interstate trafficking; we'd participate, take care of any ancillary pinches that needed to be made, and help track the drugs back to Prince George's County. The FBI and the VA State Police looked good together and shared some decent press – newspapers are downright bloodthirsty when we focus our microscopes on the upper crust. Thanks to Roger Masterson's fixation with Billie Hoover's fake boobs, it all worked out swimmingly that July afternoon.

Until Huck left me alone.

Brenner, in a nice suit with his FBI shield in the breast pocket, kneeled on Masterson's back in the living room, cuffing him and reading his Miranda rights. I ran upstairs, gun drawn and my heart thudding as I followed Huck from room to room. We cleared the master bedroom together, and I discovered Masterson's stash in the walk-in closet. He had about twelve pairs of mismatched golf shoes tossed haphazardly on the floor, and seven shoe boxes stacked neatly against the back wall behind a suitcase: some hiding place. I don't know if Masterson planned for it to grow into such a monstrous business, but those shoe boxes contained $18,477 in small bills, a half-key of weed, a few dozen eight-balls already measured and bagged, and 841 hits of OxyContin, 340 Demerol, 229 Percocet, 112 Vicodin and a handful of Xanax, just in case anyone got jumpy reading the stock reports in the Sunday paper.

Huck hooted, a funny sound, a shrieky vowel that in narcotics cop language means, 'We're burying your ass now, motherfucker!' I felt the weight lift from my chest, and kneeling on the carpeted floor of Masterson's walk-in closet I planned what I'd say to Jenny when I called, shitfaced, from the Innsbruck Tavern later that night. There was no way I was going home sober; this celebration would be historic.

And then Huck said the words they'll inscribe on my tombstone some day: 'Bag it up, Sailor. I'm going down to taunt Masterson a little.' He tossed me a roll of Ziploc baggies, a pair of rubber gloves and a permanent marker. 'What's there in cash?'

'Lemme see . . . $18,477.'

'Perfect. That's a fucked-up number,' Huck said. 'Bag it for $18,429. Beers are on Masterson tonight. Pocket $48. That'll get us started.'

And I was alone. The rain soaking Fairfax, Virginia, that day was a frigging deluge. Through a Scotch-and-soda fog eight hours later, I heard the local news guy say that five inches had fallen in two hours: goddamn rain forest numbers. It hammered Masterson's house, washing away everything, flooding all my illusions of what it meant to be a state trooper, gathering them up and dumping them in the overflowing Potomac River.

I could no more stop myself then stop that rain. I flipped open the shoe box full of pills, bagged about a hundred OxyContin – one hundred and eight, to be a stickler about it – and stuffed them inside my shirt. What was I going to do with them? I honest-to-Christ didn't know. I certainly wasn't planning to develop my own addiction. Ben was a baby; maybe I thought I'd sell them, grab a bit of cash from a dealer somewhere and put it away for a new minivan or a college fund. Maybe make a dent in a vacation or a timeshare down in Florida. Maybe grab a few stocks or part of a mutual fund.

But not really.

I took those pills that day because I wanted them. I wanted something more, some edge only I knew about. I was a kid left alone in a candy store; I saw the opportunity, felt the urge, and folded like a five-year-old.

Six months later, I took my first pill – six months with a hundred and eight OxyContin zipped in the pocket of my old letterman jacket hanging in the darkest corner of my own walk-in closet. In that time I had probably fifty opportunities to sell them, to trade them for information, to grease an informant or bribe a corner dealer. But I never did. Instead, I just left them there, like hidden cash or found money that no one knew about. They were mine, a measly two grand in prescription pills, but they had my attention. I couldn't throw them away; that'd be a waste. I didn't want to take them, not at first, and I never managed to sell them. Why? Because I always knew I'd end up hitting them to take the edge off my life when I felt like running away. Too many dirty diapers, too many anger lines in Jenny's face, too many weekends with Huck in Shockoe Bottom, too many glimpses of myself in the mirror: fifteen pounds overweight, blotchy, sweaty, tired all the time, working all the time and still goddamned broke.

It was raining again today. I'd had three pills already and was paying for it. Phantom shadows, misplaced song lyrics, hallucinations and imagined comments from friends and colleagues. I mistrusted my wife and her RML anklet. I had low expectations of my co-workers and a medical examiner who visited a crime scene with two mutilated bodies and decided, before doing anything else, to take my blood pressure.

And now I was trapped in my cruiser, listening to the wind and rain batter an abandoned VA-DOT snowplough that looked like a hibernating monster crouched behind the barracks garage.

My cell phone buzzed, snapping me back to Richmond, to CID and to the dead Bruckners. Another cruiser pulled up behind me and stopped, unable to get to the state gas pump with my car in the way. I pulled into a free space, shook my head hard and flipped open the phone. 'Detective Doyle.'

'Sailor?' Lieutenant Harper shouted into his cell phone, somewhere on the Chesapeake.

'Yes, sir,' I said, trying to sound clear-headed. 'How's the fishing?'

'Oh, it's miserable, and now it looks like we've got weather blowing in.'

'Yes, sir. It's coming down in buckets now, Lieutenant. You should expect it out your way in the next hour or so.' I turned the car off. The rain intensified. Lightning crashed nearby; it was hard to hear.

'That's just great news, Sailor. Thanks.'

'Sorry, sir.'

'How are things going out there? You have a suspect? The whole thing wrapped up nice and neat for me?' He laughed a little too hard, but I appreciated him trying to put me at ease. If he felt guilty for being on his boat while I slogged through blood and dead cats on a holiday weekend, I didn't care. He'd done his time.

I briefed him on our progress so far. He seemed pleased with Phil and Doc Lefkowitz, but cursed when I told him about Molly.

'You think she's dead?' he asked.

'Not much survived out there, sir,' I replied. 'Whatever killed those people probably killed a farmyard full of animals as well. I don't see how a retarded woman with the issues Dr Wentworth described could have made it out.'

'But no body?'

'Not yet, sir,' I said. 'St James County is helping with the search, and Phil may have additional game wardens out there by now as well.'

'I'm sure the rain isn't making things any easier,' he said.

'No, sir,' I said, 'but Phil believes that if it was an airborne agent, the rain last week would have cleared any vestiges of it. So we're waiting on Doctor Lefkowitz to complete the autopsies. Should I call someone about this, sir? The CDC or the NIH?'

'Not yet,' Harper said. 'Lefkowitz will alert them if he thinks it was a terrorist on a trial run. I thought Lourdes said the animals had starved to death or killed each other?'

'Perhaps some of them, and certainly a number of cats died hungry, but there were other animals as well: sheep, goats, and a horse.'

'Holy Jesus,' he said, 'they died of *starvation*? On a farm?'

'I dunno, sir,' I said. 'We've had some trouble contacting Animal Control. I think they're on site now, and we ought to have a mobile

142

lab hooked up soon. I'll check with them and get back to you.'

'Do that, Sailor, all right? But let's not get things stirred up if we don't have to. I'd hate to call in the feds and have it be a case of animal cruelty or neglect. These hillbillies might have starved the damned animals to death three months ago for all we know this early.'

'That's true, sir,' I said.

'So let's not jump to the assumption that we have terrorists at work in rural Virginia. Jesus, John, Paul, and Ringo, that'd be a media orgy.' He laughed, this time genuinely. 'Things'll be bad enough tomorrow night with that Senator Lake nonsense down at the Jefferson. If we cry terror attack the day before his speech in Richmond and then come to find out it was animal cruelty or neglect or the frigging chicken pox we'll have a shitstorm from Lake's handlers and campaign people. They'll be on the six o'clock news claiming we're all zealot democrats who dreamed this up to divert attention away from his ten thousand dollars-a-plate dinner. You ever eat anything worth ten thousand dollars?'

'Not me, sir,' I said. 'Most of the food Jenny makes has been in flames for twenty minutes. I don't think I'd get more than a few dollars for it.'

'Ten thousand dollars a head. What can they possibly be serving?'

'A bright new future for America, to hear Lake describe it.'

'Bullshit,' Harper grunted. 'It's probably mac and cheese.'

'Well then, my son would love it,' I said. 'Anything else, sir?'

'Nope. Stay on it, Sailor. Find that girl … whatshername … Molly. It sounds like you're doing a good job. Keep working with Phil, and you two will have this wrapped and stamped by breakfast. Call me later with an update.'

'Will do, sir.' I hung up, dug around under the seat for my umbrella, and ran for the barracks through the torrent.

By two-forty-five on Friday, July 3, most of Division Headquarters was quiet, but I wanted to check on the progress of our mobile lab unit, if anyone was still around the CID offices upstairs. If they weren't on site yet, Phil would be nervous and cranky. Since I was already late getting back to the farm, I assigned myself pushy-pain-in-the-ass duty.

Shantal worked her magic behind the communications console. I waved to her and took the stairs to the third floor. Pushing through the steel fire door, I realised that the rain had loosened the Band-Aids on my face. The one on my forehead flopped up and down with every step. *Need to get a couple more before I go home,* I thought and snuck towards the far end of the third floor hall and Captain Fezzamo's offices. While the newest wings at Division Headquarters were comfortable, with carpeted lounges and posh locker rooms adjacent to the gym, the brass offices remained a 1970s-era tile-and-sheetrock cave. My wingtips clicked on the scuffed chequerboard pattern.

To get to CID, I had to pass the Internal Affairs and Intelligence Offices, the very worst place to be as a trooper, bleeding from the face, high on illegal pharmaceuticals and wearing a soaked and rumpled suit that smelled like decomposing farm animals. The last thing I wanted to do was come face to face with their major, whatever his name was, working late on some internal investigation when he should have been home barbecuing steaks with his kids. My shoes were clickety-clacking so I rolled up on my toes – not quite tiptoeing, but I was glad none of my friends were around to see me creeping along like Scooby or Shaggy through a creepy haunted mansion.

Down in CID, Fezzamo's secretary, an elderly, reed-thin woman with pockmarks across her forehead, stammered something about the captain signing out for the weekend. I wasn't surprised. I told her I knew that Lieutenant Harper was already gone and needed someone to lean on a mobile crew to get out to the Phillips 66 station near the Bruckner farm. Still struggling to find the right words, she shuffled a stack of papers noisily, closed a *Movie Review* magazine and quickly hid an open jar of nail polish behind a rainbow print can full of sharpened pencils. Clearly, she wasn't expecting company this afternoon.

'Sorry,' she said, embarrassed she'd let her usual level of decorum slip a notch or two. Her face flushed and she looked away from me.

'Hell, don't worry about it … sorry, I forgot your name—'

'Cheryl,' she said. 'Cheryl Baskin.'

I snapped my fingers. 'Right, right – sorry, Ms Baskin, that's embarrassing.'

'Oh, don't worry about it. Working with Huck Greeley all that time, you hardly get down this way, certainly not into the offices.'

I took a seat across from her and tried to press a few wrinkles out of my suit lapels. 'I won't forget again, Ms Baskin.'

She finally looked directly at me, and noticed my face. 'Good grief, Detective, are you okay?'

'Fine, really,' I said. 'You should see the other guy.'

'Let me get you some fresh Band-Aids.' She fished around in her desk and produced a tube of antibiotic ointment and a box of bandages. I fussed with them while she recovered her composure and went about locating my mobile lab in the CID computer network.

'Any luck?' I said after taping myself up again.

'Yes.' She clicked on various links in her system, something grunts like me couldn't access. 'It looks like you have a mobile unit, V-ML 4, en route to St James County right now. They left about one. Oh my, they should be there, I would think. Have you called?'

'Not since before lunch,' I admitted. 'Do you have my techs, too?'

'Yes. You have two: Gretchen Kim … oh, she's good. I hear great things all the time about her. And Steve Cornwell, another real talent, to hear Lieutenant Harper go on about him.'

CID was one of the only offices at Division Headquarters to have a bunch of officers housed in the same building: Homicide, Vice/Narcotics, Arson and the Bomb Squad, the Fugitive Unit, Missing Persons, and Cargo Theft and Robbery dominated most of the third floor, sharing a suite of offices and a clerical staff adjacent to Captain Fezzamo's corner digs. Yet apart from a few secretaries and assistants who hadn't sneaked away early for the long weekend, the CID suite was quiet.

With my mobile lab all but on site, I didn't need to play pushy-pain-in-the-ass, and I couldn't think of much more to say to Cheryl Baskin. I thanked her for the help and wished her a good holiday. 'What are you doing here so late anyway? Is your family waiting for you someplace? Got a party to get to tonight?'

She blushed again.

Shit, Sailor, what the hell did you do now?

Cheryl said, 'My kids are grown, Detective—'

'Sailor, please.'

She smiled, deepening her wrinkles. 'Sailor. And my husband left me years ago.'

'Oh.' Now *I* was stammering. 'Um ... sorry.'

'Do you have children, Detec— Sailor?'

'Two. Ben's about to turn five and Anna was born about six minutes ago.'

'Do you love them?' she asked without warning, then backtracked in a noisy flurry of paper and coffee mugs and spilled pencils. 'I'm sorry, Detective, I'm sorry.' She stared at an ink stain on her desk blotter. Her hands were shaking and she laced her fingers together tightly. 'I'm sorry,' she whispered.

I didn't know what to do. In shock and mild surprise I watched myself reach over and put my hand on the back of hers. 'Yes, I do, Ms Baskin. I love them more than anything I've known in my lifetime. I think of them as the only time I've been slapped squarely in the head by God. They're His most effective wake-up call. Is that nuts?'

She had tears on her face, and I felt about as awkward as a boner at a funeral. Finally, she said, 'No, that's not nuts, Sailor.'

'Are you—? Do you need—? I mean, I can—' I wanted to be helpful, but I sure wasn't going to win any awards. 'Can I get you some tea or something?'

She waved me off. 'No, this is silly. I'm sorry.' She wiped her face, blew her nose – more demurely than I've ever managed – and finally looked up. 'Your mobile unit should be on scene, Detective.'

Fine. Let's work.

'Thank you, Ms Baskin,' I said. 'I'll be back soon to see you again.'

'That'd be nice.'

I stole a glance at the photos on her desk. A thirty-something man with her eyes had his arm wrapped around a pretty woman in a San Diego Padres T-shirt. They stood together outside Petco Park, both wearing ball caps and carrying bottles of beer. It looked like a fun afternoon, but Cheryl obviously hadn't been invited. Next to it was a picture of a youngish version of Cheryl on skis standing beside a neo-Tudor lodge in a pine grove. From the sign above the bar in the background, I guessed it was Aspen, or maybe Vail or Breckenridge, another enjoyable day when one of the Baskin kids forgot to invite Mom. A mouthful of tangy Northside Café onion rings bubbled up on me; I swallowed with a grimace.

Are my kids going to forget me some day? Am I going to be sitting here at CID while they traipse around the world, forgetting to call, not bothering to invite me to come along? Shit. Probably.

I started towards the door.

'Detective?' Cheryl said.

'Yeah?'

'That's good that you love them so much,' she said. It was different now: Cheryl had regained herself, and she spoke to me officiously, as if she was sending me down the hall to pull an old file. 'It's the most important thing you can do for your wife. Did you know that? I don't think many men do.'

'Thanks, Ms Baskin. Have a good weekend.' She was pale in the fluorescent light, and too thin. With her hair wrestled into a severe bun, Cheryl looked like Claire Bruckner might have looked before someone interred her remains in three hundred pounds of cat litter. A blast of air-conditioning wafted in from the hall, chilling my skin beneath my damp suit.

Did Claire love Molly? Carl seems to have been the caregiver. What was Claire's story? What kind of mother was she? Did she have photos of Molly on her desk at work? Or did she silently pray that Molly would fall victim to the big one . . . what's it called? Tonic-clonic? That blackboard can only be erased so many times. Was Claire keeping track? Did she have a scorecard in her desk? She might have. I would have.

'And Detective,' Cheryl Baskin called into the empty third-floor hallway, 'Marie forgives you. She does.'

I nodded to a bulletin board littered with anti-drug pamphlets and missing persons flyers. 'I'm sure she does.' There was no need to tiptoe past Internal Affairs or the Intelligence Office on my way out. No one was coming.

3:16 p.m.

The rain had stopped by the time I crossed the Division Headquarters parking lot. The VA-DOT snowplough was still there, dripping from its rusty snout and looking upset enough to lumber over and crush me to jelly. I felt it in my bones, a fat, broken-down workhorse, watching ... appraising ... me. Spinning on my heel, I had what my sister used to call a hissy fit. 'What? Do you know Marie as well? Is she here? Is she? Is she out at the farm? With Molly Bruckner? What is it?'

I yanked off my suit jacket and threw it into the back seat. It lay in a wrinkled pile, looking a mess, looking like ... a failed career, a drug problem, a mistress and a fucked-up marriage.

Then I saw it, forgotten beneath one crumpled sleeve: Carl Bruckner's military record.

I inhaled as deeply as I could, and wanted a cigarette. The city smelled clean, but the bright sunlight, in the wake of the torrent, caused the heat to blossom into something truly oppressive.

Back to work, Sailor.

I saddled up and drove for St James County. I had two dead bodies, a missing retarded woman, a farmyard full of dead animals, no suspects, no motives, no cause of death, no murder weapon, and no one coming to help me.

On my way out Goochland Lane, I tried not to think about the hallucinations. I silently promised to lay off the pills for the rest of the weekend. It had been a while since I'd had any – *12 days, and you know it* – not since I'd last seen Sarah, and I thought that perhaps the combination of heat, humidity, stress, caffeine, nicotine, lack of sleep and OxyContin might be the salad bar of culprits leading to my hearing and seeing things that reminded me of Marie.

I lit a cigarette. With the air-conditioner blowing, the smoke roiled around the inside of my cruiser like fog in a horror movie where some fish-faced monster chases a busty blonde through a swamp – although the reels of my own movie didn't project a chesty blonde running through bushes until her top ripped halfway off; in *my* film the busty blonde wasn't blonde and she wasn't especially busty. She was nineteen, with shoulder-length brown hair that she was always brushing away from her face. She was a distance runner who loved espresso, seventy-five-cent vocabulary words and licorice ropes, and hated cigarettes. In my horror movie, the not-so-busty brunette studied Sociology and thought she might be falling in love with a guy named Mitch from Pennsylvania. And Mitch had no skeletons in his closet, either. He'd never journeyed to Egypt and got himself saddled with an ancient mummy's curse. Mitch had never been bitten by a werewolf, hadn't fought zombies, hadn't been attacked by vampires while rescuing his high school sweetheart on Lovers' Lane. Nope. Mitch had been headed for law school and was now an attorney with two kids, a minivan and a mortgage, somewhere outside Philadelphia. At least he had been the last time I'd bothered to ask.

My horror movie didn't end with a stake through the heart or a silver bullet, in fact, it didn't end, not until Evander Holyfield came by to punch my lights out. But even then, my film didn't end so much as go into an extended intermission – *Grab extra hot dogs and popcorn, kids: this one's a triple feature!* – only to start up again, generally between two and five a.m., when the red eyes of Satan spied on me from the bedside table and demons shuffled around inside my closet, trying on all my new suits.

I crushed the cigarette, cracked the window and flipped the butt onto Goochland, lit another and called Jenny. I needed a distraction.

She picked up on the second ring. 'Hey.' I heard all the frustration in that one syllable. We'd been married long enough for that one syllable to tell me how her morning had fallen apart. It wasn't an 'I'm pissed right now' sound but the road-weary 'hey' that whispered: 'I don't know how I'm going to make it through the day.'

'Hi,' I said, 'what's wrong?'

She sighed: a good sign. She was taking a few seconds to regroup. 'Nothing, I guess. The grocery store was a nightmare. Your daughter wouldn't stop screaming and your son kept asking for things and then wandering off. I had to stop three times to point out strangers to him, just to get it through his head that even the grocery store can be dangerous, but he doesn't listen. Actually, that's not true. He listens like you do: he grins and nods and says "Okay, Mommy" and then he goes right back to what he was doing. Then we had to go into that foul bathroom to change Anna's diaper, and Ben was touching everything. So when his fingers rot off in the next two weeks, we'll know why.'

'Wow, sounds rough. However, you're not being fair,' I said. 'I never call you Mommy.'

'Go to hell.'

'Already been there this morning. And guess what; it doesn't look anything like an eighteenth-century oil painting. It looks a lot like an old farmhouse.'

'Really? What happened?'

'Not much more than I told you earlier: two dead people, one missing daughter, about nine hundred dead cats, a few of which I shot with my own gun—'

'You shot cats?' She sounded incredulous.

'Not the fluffy kind eating Friskie's Buffet on TV. These were more the leap-out-and-eat-your-face kind from Jason Voorhees' basement.'

'At least we know your gun works!' she joked, but we both knew she was relieved that no one was firing back.

'Yeah, who'd have guessed,' I said. 'Doc Lefkowitz was there for a while, and Phil Clarkson and Bob Lourdes have been there all day. Lourdes was the first officer on the scene after the St James deputy called it in. So he's wanting to hang around.'

'He's nice, though,' Jenny said. 'Or is he being a pest?'

'A pest? No, I guess not,' I said. 'It's just not like I imagined it would be, you know, sitting in the front seat on this one.'

'Well, Sailor, nothing ever is— Hang on a second.'

She dropped the phone. In the background, I heard her talking to Ben.

No, I don't know where Captain Blake is.

He was waiting on the couch when we were at the store.

Did you bring him in the car?

He wanted to watch TV.

I'll help you look when I hang up with Daddy.

Is that Daddy? Can I talk to him?

In a minute, monkey. Just wait here.

I couldn't hear Anna, which meant that she'd either been abducted by aliens or she was sleeping in the playpen.

Jenny picked up. 'Sorry, but he was getting ready to melt down over that damned stuffed dog. I swear he loses that thing eighty-six times a day.'

'Staple it to him.' I coughed on a prickly puff of cigarette smoke.

'I'll try that after— Wait, do you have a suspect? Did you catch anyone?'

I shook my head at the dashboard. 'Nothing. Not a whiff. It might be a number of things, maybe easy or maybe a nickel-plated shitstorm.'

'So we won't see you.' Like Dr Grace Wentworth, Jenny Doyle had her own way of asking a question that wasn't really a question.

'I don't think so,' I confessed. 'Because I'm ...'

Because I'm using this investigation as a great excuse to go see my girl-friend who isn't carrying around fifteen pounds of leftover baby fat. Christ, just run my car into a goddamned ditch and kill me, right now.

'... um, because I'm going into the city to meet with Doc later and then we'll probably head back to the mobile lab after dinner. Those techs'll keep working until they have everything done or prepped for the lab at Division. After that, if we don't have a suspect, I'll crash at Huck's for a few hours.'

'Ooh, Sailor, that sounds tough, baby.' She was concerned for me. I was planning a tryst, I was lying to my wife, and she was worried about me. 'Try to get some rest, and eat something decent, will you? Even if Lieutenant Harper won't cover it. Just put it on the bank card, not VISA, not this month.'

'I will.'

'And call me later.'

'I will.'

'You want to talk to him?'

'Sure, but quickly. I'm almost back to the farm now. I've got to review this dead guy's military service record and see if anything in his personal effects and papers might give us a suspect. We have a knife but no prints yet, at least not that I've heard.'

'Aren't you in charge?' she asked.

'Well, yeah.'

'Then how can you not know?'

'I had to go to lunch with a middle-school principal from Richmond. She knew the family about thirty years ago. The daughter, the missing one, is pretty screwy, some kind of seizure thing she had as a kid that turned her into a whack job, like a pure-bred retard, but old now, almost fifty.'

'And she's missing?'

'Probably dead on the farm somewhere. The house wasn't a very hospitable place to spend any length of time.'

'Um, okay ... well, good luck. We'll be here.'

'Thanks, baby ...'

Who's RML? It's a guy, isn't it? RML. They're initials, and they're all over the house. Tell me.

'... can you put Ben on?'

'Yeah. Here he is—'

'Hey, wait, Jenny—'

'What is it?' I heard her shush Ben. *Just one more second, buddy. Daddy's right here.*

I took about two seconds to wonder if I might regret asking my question, but I jumped in anyway. 'Can you think of anything we might have seen or done recently that would get me thinking about Marie, more than *thinking*, to be honest, more like *perseverating* on Marie?'

Jenny took a deep breath and tried to hide it. I heard her blow out slowly through her nose. *Nice try, sweetheart, but I know you.*

'Jesus, Sailor. I don't know what gets you going on that. It could be anything. Hell, I've seen you struggle after spicy Chinese food. But now that we're talking about it, you haven't been sleeping ... at all.'

'You noticed?'

'I'm the one next to you in bed.'

'Sorry.'

'And I know it's bothering you, because when you're up at night, you never ... you know ...'

Don't say it, Jenny. Just leave it out there, between us, like a coffee table that's too big for the room. We've got to keep dancing, just keep dancing around it.

'Sorry,' I said. 'I never know when you're awake. I don't want to wake you just for that. You're always up with Anna, and—'

'And I'm fat. I am, Sailor, but it's coming off. If I keep breast-feeding, you'll see the pounds just fall off me. It won't take long.'

'That's not it, Jenny.' I pulled over to the side of Pitcairn. A patch of raspberry bushes scraped the passenger side of my car. I cracked the window and lit another cigarette – I was chain-smoking now; Doc would be thrilled. But if I have any rules that govern my life, one of them is always chain-smoke immediately upon making your wife feel bad about her baby weight. That's a lot to say in one breath, but it's an important one. I stuffed the pack back in my shirt pocket and said, 'It's not you, hon. It's just that I've been so stuck on Marie, and I don't know why. It's been such a long time.'

'You need to get off the booze and the pills, Sailor.'

A warning light flashed in my head. 'I know, Jenny, and I don't want to fight with you today. I just wanted to know if you'd noticed anything recently. We don't need to make a big deal out of it. And as for the pills, I can't even remember the last time I had any pills.'

Twelve days. Not to mention the three you've had today, shithead. Or was it four?

She backed off a bit. 'What's this about, Sailor? You been distracted today? On your first solo investigation? That's shitty timing, love of my life.'

'Yeah, and maybe more so than normal,' I said, and suddenly wanted to be done with this conversation. It wasn't heading anywhere productive. 'Look, don't worry about it. I'll check in with you later. I'm back at the farm now and have to go.'

'Okay, but—'

'Sorry. I gotta go. Here comes Phil.'

I flipped the phone shut without talking to Ben.

3:48 p.m.

The rain hadn't been kind to the dirt driveway stretching past the small pond into the Bruckners' front yard. I drove slowly, keeping my wheels turning to avoid the deeper patches of soft mud. The big Ford was heavy enough, but if I sank, rear-wheel drive would ensure I was stuck in this St James jungle for the rest of the afternoon.

I slowed down as I saw a shadow flit between tree trunks and move off towards the edge of the water. I squinted through the rays of sunlight piercing the foliage to brighten the muddy ground in flickering patches.

The shadow moved again, further off to the left, near a stand of bulrushes.

'What is that?' I found a section of high ground, parked the cruiser and got out.

The air beneath the tangled brush was equatorial, almost too thick to breathe. I broke out in sweat again, this time smelling distinctly of onion rings. A trickle ran down the small of my back. 'Fucking summer,' I swore as I pushed my way through the bushes. 'I swear to Christ if I ever get this murder solved we're moving to the Arctic. I'll raise reindeer in Lapland.'

The shadow blurred and slid behind the rushes. I heard a rustle and listened for footsteps, but a legion of grumpy locusts and a swarm of hungry mosquitoes covered most of the ambient sound. I slapped at something on the side of my face and came away with a gory palm.

'Shit.' I wiped it on my pants. 'Who's over there? Molly? Is that you? Molly Bruckner?' Ducking and weaving beneath the scrubby brush, I made my clumsy way to the pond.

'Molly?' I tried again. 'My name is Detective Doyle, Molly. I'm a trooper with the Virginia State Police, and I'm here to help you.' Standing still, I listened for anything behind the locusts. 'Molly?'

The smell of organic decay – nothing quite so egregious as the Bruckner farmhouse – wafted about the pond like the grim wake behind a sanitation truck. I crossed to where I had seen one of the cats pounce into the sedge that morning and remembered Phil's briefing:

. . . and what appears to be the remains of a dead dog, probably a stray, down near the pond.

A stray?

The Bruckners had at least thirty-seven cats. They weren't dog people.

On cue, a throaty growl, clearly a warning, rumbled from the bulrushes.

'Molly?' I took a wary step back, nearly falling over a bulging root. 'Are you in there? Is that your dog?' I drew my Glock and chambered a round, wishing I had brought a handheld radio.

'Molly, I'm coming in. Okay? Don't be nervous. Everything's fine.'

A bat-length branch jutted from a rotting hickory stump. I snapped it off and with my left hand used it to poke and prod inside the thick stand of rushes. I thought I heard another growl, but the locusts fired up again, drowning out anything else. I aimed my gun into the shadows with no idea what I might be hunting.

Something rustled on my left, near the edge of the pond. 'Fuck it!' I shouted as I pushed the rushes aside with the hickory stick and half-jumped, half-stepped behind them, my gun still drawn.

My left foot slid along the bent rushes, tipping me to one side; my right landed ankle-deep in viscous black mud, stirring up a swarm of no-see-ums and spooking a bullfrog as big as a third-grader.

No one was there.

'Sonofabitch!' I shouted at the glassy flat water. 'Ruined my goddamned shoe! Sonofabitch! Out here traipsing around in the mother—'

Another growl cut me off.

I whirled, levelled my gun and searched the bushes.

A once-brown dog, a chocolate lab, incurably mutilated, crouched in the shadows. *Just like that motherfucker on the highway this morning.* It watched me through one bloodshot eye – its other had been ripped out, along with most of one ear and ragged sections of its coat. One foreleg looked like it had been broken in multiple places, and its nose

157

was striped with deep gashes, claw marks. It bared its teeth, rising as if to attack, and growled menacingly again.

I aimed at its broad chest, praying that a shot to the lungs or the heart would kill it for good. My foot sank further into the mud. Warm water filled my shoe, soaking my sock and pants leg; I wouldn't get it out without tugging. As much as I wanted to slip away quietly, right now I was going nowhere.

The dog wheezed, a sickening sound, still warning me off.

'Easy, easy,' I said. 'Take it easy, boy. Okay? I don't want to shoot you. So what do you say we—?'

The cat attacked from above. It had been hiding on one of the few remaining branches attached to the dead hickory stump. It landed on the dog's muzzle with a grisly, unnerving shriek and the two animals, battling noisily, rolled into a patch of fern and poison oak. I yanked frantically at my ankle until I felt my foot come free with a sucking sound that sounded impossibly like the cry of the crazed banshee woman in Molly's room. Stumbling through raspberry thorns and pernicious Russian olives, I made my way back to my car, collapsed into the driver's seat and slammed the door.

My face dripped and I panted hard, trying to catch my breath. I dropped my .45 on the floor and pressed as hard as I could on my chest with one hand until I began to feel better. The air-conditioning was blowing so hard I couldn't hear myself breathe. It made me nervous, but I didn't dare turn it down for fear of a heat-induced heart attack.

When my heart finally slowed and I could think straight again I reached back for my suit jacket and mopped my face with one sleeve. My latest Band-Aids wiped off; I tossed them on the floor.

It was another ten minutes before I felt calm enough to put the car in gear and drive to the farmhouse. Insects gnawed at my bare ankle until I found Carl Bruckner's garden hose and washed away the mud.

Lourdes' cruiser was gone, but three St James County police cars and an Animal Control van had taken its place.

4:11 p.m.

Phil found me while I was wringing excess water from my sock.

'Welcome back, Sailor,' he said. 'I've got a sitrep for you whenever you're ready. What the hell happened to your foot?'

'Didn't you say something this morning about a dead stray down by the pond?'

'Sure. He was torn to shreds, probably by cats scavenging for food. Why?' He had his ubiquitous pen in one hand and was clicking away nervously.

'You certain it was dead?' I asked, hoping my hands stayed steady. An attack of the shakes would give me away.

'Yeah. Jesus, Sailor, the thing was a maggoty shell. It had one eye ripped out, a bunch of fur torn away, a busted leg, and all these—'

'Gashes across its snout.' I finished for him.

'That's him.' Phil clicked again. 'Why? You see him down there? Are there other cats snacking on him? If so, we can get these Animal Control guys to scrape him up.'

I sidestepped the question. 'Nah, never mind. I got out of the car, just to look around, slipped in the mud and messed up my shoes.'

'You see the dog? He's lying down there beside a big patch of bulrushes. Bryson spotted him on our way in this morning. She's got younger eyes than me.'

I nodded and forced a nonchalant laugh. 'Yeah. No worries. I saw what I thought was a dog down there, in the brush, but maybe I made a mistake. You said the dead stray was a collie, right? Light brown and white? A little guy?'

Phil frowned. 'Nah, a big mother, brownish-black, like a chocolate lab.'

Icy talons gripped my heart. My skin felt cold and my nipples hardened beneath my shirt. I was losing it, having a full-on psychotic episode. I stammered, 'Oh ... okay, then ... there must be another dog running around down there. That's all.' I sat heavily in the grass, ostensibly to pull my sock back on. I wrestled with it for a few seconds to let the dizziness clear, then changed the subject. 'So what's the update?'

If Phil was suspicious of my dog story, he hid it well. 'Lourdes has gone back to the barracks to sign out and leave his car. He said he'll find you later, after he gets a shower and changes into his civvies.'

'He doesn't need to,' I started.

'He wants to, Sailor. You know.' Phil politely reminded me that we were all road guys fishing for transfers once. 'He was the first trooper on the scene. He wants to see the whole shooting match. What the hell.'

'Okay, fine.' I was hearing things, and seeing vicious phantom dogs; I didn't have the strength to argue. 'What else?'

'Bryson's inside documenting some of the Bruckners' personal papers. We'll need to make some calls, credit cards, banks, utilities, family doctors, and so on, but with the holiday weekend, some of that shit'll have to wait until Monday. There's still nothing on any next of kin.'

'How about meds?' I asked. 'Anything out of the ordinary?'

'Molly was using a frigging salad bar of prescription dope: Klonopin, Depakote, Topamax, Phenytoin, you name it. But they're all epilepsy drugs. We called one of the docs over at the county free clinic in Ashland. He said it's quite a laundry list but nothing alarming, unless she misses too many doses; then she's screwed. Carl had wicked hypertension, he was on ACE inhibitors and beta blockers, but nothing recently. It's been a while since he had his prescriptions filled.'

'No medical insurance?'

'He's a retired officer.' Phil shrugged. 'He's gotta be covered, right?'

Carl was dead, and Doc had the body. He'd tell us what we needed to know. I changed the subject. 'Any latents on the fillet knife?' The one piece of evidence we had that could provide a shortcut to a suspect. I held my breath as I tried to read Phil's face.

'Yeah, two or three decent prints,' he said. 'Lourdes dropped a couple of boxes at the lab on his way out. I'll stop there on my way to Richmond, just to answer any questions the techs have. We got Gretchen and Steve. You know them?'

'Not really,' I admitted. 'I just got to homicide a month ago.'

'We got lucky – they're good, both of them. This is a shit weekend for drunks, car wrecks, family fights, stabbings, muggings, drugs, maybe even some other murders as a side dish, so we're real fortunate to have these two working our little corner of the world. Lourdes was going to have them run the prints right away. Did you know that with a satellite link in that mobile lab they can run those latents against all known prints? It bounces off a satellite dish somewhere and hits a database on a hard drive at Quantico. Takes seconds.'

'The miracles of modern technology,' I said. 'Next thing you know they'll make a toasted oat cereal that doesn't go all soggy in the milk. What else?'

'What else is there?' Phil cocked his head towards the farmhouse as if a suspect might step out the front door. 'That knife is the whole enchilada if we're looking for a killer. We've got hair, fibres, prints, photos, personal effects, blood and Carl's insect larvae all collected and ready for Gretchen and Steve. There were essentially no bugs on Claire; larvae are no help anyway, having been dead for the better part of the last millennium. But if there's a print match or an oddball blood type, those two will find it this weekend. You've got a wrap-up with Doc tonight – unexpected, but nice of him – and autopsies are on deck for tomorrow, thanks to Doc's wife's propensity to stay close to New York City for the holidays.'

Phil was proud of himself. He and Bryson had done a good job in miserable conditions all day. He knew I was nervous flying solo and wanted to be close to done in time to get to his daughter's concert. I decided not to make him ask for it again.

I said, 'Excellent, Phil, truly. Now, don't you have to get out of here for Dad duty?'

'I do,' he said to his shoes. 'If it's all right. I need to get to this show. My wife'll have my ass in traction if I miss another game, concert, teacher conference, you name it.'

I hit him in the shoulder. 'Go. Hurry up. You smell like a corpse, though. It'll take three hours to scrub that smell off. You need all the time you can get.'

He looked visibly relieved. It was an easy thing to do: give him a break. I could stay on all weekend if necessary, and now I'd get the reputation for being a good guy, an okay detective to work for in the field. I'd known about troopers no one wanted on their detail. Letting Phil sneak out to hear his daughter play the bugle, or whatever it was, scored me some points. He wouldn't forget it.

'Thanks, Sailor,' he said, shaking my hand. He was still wearing rubber gloves.

'Shit, Phil, don't thank me. You've saved my ass thirty-six times today. I'd've been crying for my momma if you hadn't been here this morning.'

'You'd have been fine.' It was his turn to be gracious.

'Whatever.' I waved him off. 'What's on my list before dinner? I've got to hit the lab, see if they have a match on the knife, check over Carl's military records for anything helpful or suspicious, get Bryson back to the city, meet Doc and Lourdes ... I'll keep Bryson if she doesn't have any plans—'

'She doesn't,' he said. 'She's expecting to be here until you call it a night.'

'Good,' I said. 'And she's got bills, credit card statements, all the recent mail, files, photos, the works, right?'

'She's in there cataloguing right now.' Phil had taken his jacket off and rolled up his shirtsleeves early that morning. He rolled them down again now, buttoned the cuffs and pulled his jacket on as if he were heading to the White House for tea.

I asked, 'What are you doing? You got a hot date in that suit? I hope she's lost her sense of smell.'

'Force of habit,' he said. 'Married too long, I guess. Kathy's rules, even all the way out here. Funny.'

Not Curtains – Kathy! *Kathy Clarkson!*

'Go,' I said, trying to imagine Jenny ever dictating my wardrobe like that. 'I'll have Bryson bring me up to speed.'

'Okay,' he agreed as he started towards his car. 'What'd you get on Molly?'

'Nothing that'll help us find her, unless she's in a facility, some nut house somewhere,' I said.

I'll be with her soon enough, arguing over who gets the last pudding, if I keep pulling my gun on ghost dogs and imagining Bobby Darin lyrics.

'You want me to—'

'No,' I interrupted, 'you go do Dad duty. I'll give the information to the St James guys and let them chase her down. I've got to admit, I'm only really interested in Molly if she's out here dead somewhere.'

'What?' Phil's face wrinkled into a disappointed expression that I hadn't seen on anyone since my father died.

'Shit!' I backtracked. 'Sorry, that didn't come out right, but c'mon, you know what I mean.'

'Yeah.' He raised his eyebrows and sort of grinned, pretending he could separate Dad duty and Dead duty in his mind.

I hadn't wondered why Phil stayed with ID bureaus for so many years – avoiding Homicide – until just that moment. It was all dead bodies in the end. What difference did it make if you were on point or in a supporting role? I didn't know, but I'd clearly touched a nerve, and I felt shitty about it. I half-raised my hands as if to say, *Sorry. I know I'm an asshole.*

Phil clicked his pen twice and gave me a way out. 'Whatever, Sailor. Just hit me on the cell if you need anything. I'll be back here first thing tomorrow morning.'

'Thanks, Phil. Thank you,' I said, and watched him drive off, my embarrassment still stark, another unembellished screw-up to add to my list.

Halfway up the porch steps, I remembered my fax from St Louis. I jogged back to the car, my damp shoe squishing with every step, and grabbed the folder off the back seat. My gaze fell on the rutted lane leading through the knotted brush beside the haunted pond. I listened for a second, half-expecting to hear Phil firing at rabid canine shadows. Instead, I heard the steady braying of a search-and-rescue bloodhound coming from the soybean fields behind the farmhouse. I hadn't noticed it before. The St James lieutenant had called in a dog of his own. 'Good,' I said to no one. 'One less thing on the list. Let them find Molly.'

'Sammy?' The voice came from behind me. It was different from the wild-eyed apparition that morning, not distinctly male or female. But it certainly wasn't the wind, it wasn't the bloodhound, and it wasn't Bobby Darin.

Moving slowly, I placed the manila folder on the roof of my car and pressed my hands flat on the warm metal above the door. I closed my eyes and waited.

Don't look, Sailor. There's no one there. No one calls you Sammy, not since—

'Sammy.' It wafted over the farmhouse yard, brushing the overgrown timothy stalks like a gust of humid breeze.

'I'm not turning around,' I whispered. 'I'm not.'

I waited again. It might have been two minutes or ten; I'd lost count of breaths, heartbeats. The wind lifted a corner of the manila folder containing a few sheets of fax paper from the barracks clerical office. It fell back, then rose again with the next breeze. I reached out with two fingers, opened the file and lifted the top page, just far enough to read without craning my neck.

Rage hit me like a fist. 'Fuckers!' I shouted. Ignoring my poltergeist, I grabbed the file and took the Bruckners' porch steps three at a time.

'Bryson!' I yelled.

'In here,' she called. 'In the office, past the sitting room.'

I snaked through the house, managing to avoid the cat shit this time. Carl's hope chest was where we'd left it, but now it'd been dusted for fingerprints, bits of white evidence tape and rectangular patches of sticky residue showing where someone had attempted to lift latents. In the office, Bryson had set up two fans at opposite windows to create a cross-breeze. She had moved her laptop from the living room and was typing notes to herself as she reviewed the Bruckners' mail and bills. She sat on a threadbare orange couch, something dating from the 1970s, from the look of the yellow sunbursts and connect-the-dots stains. An antique wooden desk littered with paper took up most of the room, while a circular rug with three dry cat turds covered the wooden floor. What appeared to be another cat corpse lay with its hind paws and snub tail poking out from beneath the couch like a forgotten woollen sock. A ragged, discoloured hole perforated the ceiling; milky rainwater dripped onto a garbage bag tarp Bryson had draped over one corner of the desk.

'How'd you make out?' she asked without getting up.

'Fine, fine,' I said, irritated. 'Never mind that, but fine. Here, take a look at this.' I handed her the fax from the National Personnel Records Center in St Louis. 'Does this say I'm going to have to wait six frigging weeks to get these records?'

She flipped through the pages. 'It's an application, an official request form. Holy crap, it's long. Look at this; it goes on and on!' She wrinkled her nose. 'Our tax dollars at work, huh? I bet most people are so discouraged by the forms they don't bother following through on the request. Look at this: you've even got to have someone co-sign it, like you're a kid applying for a car loan.'

'Do they not know someone's been killed, one of their veterans? Did we not tell them that?'

There was no sarcasm in her voice. 'Actually, that's probably the only reason these forms showed up today. If you were a potential employer or a law office you'd probably be on hold for hours just to get this far. I bet the vets themselves have to order a couple of months early.'

'Shit.' I sat in a worn but comfortable rocker with a knitted blanket folded over the backrest. 'Maybe Fezzamo or Harper could lean on them.'

'On Interstate 70 at four-thirty on Friday July third? I don't think so.' Like most female cops Bryson had short hair, but as she hunched over the fax she had to push both sides behind her ears. It was a slight gesture, but endearing. She said, 'The person who faxed these pages is probably a clerical worker in some pencil pusher's office and long gone for the weekend by now. You'd be starting at square one again – *if* you even got anyone to answer the phones over there.'

'It's the army. They're open twenty-four hours,' I said.

'Sure, if the embassy in Uzbekistan is attacked. This crew' – she waved my pages over her laptop screen – 'checked out about half an hour ago. They are now sitting in shitty traffic beneath the Gateway Arch, considering a transfer to a base in the Solomon Islands.'

'Serves them right, the bastards.' I rocked back in the chair and yawned. 'How are you doing? I like the fan thing.'

She handed the folder back to me. 'Cools it off a bit, but it still smells like an afternoon in Hell. Remember I mentioned the roof leaking? Well, that's where it's coming down from, the attic.' She nodded at the ceiling; many of the documents piled underneath the hole were obviously damp; some were already sprouting mould.

Bryson had organised two piles of papers – notebooks, legal pads, envelopes full of receipts, bank statements and old letters – on the sofa. I watched her read through a VISA bill, type a few words into her computer and then replace the bill, face down, on the second, smaller, pile. It looked like tedious work, but I was glad she'd taken

166

it on, even though the repetitive process might have done me some good. I asked, 'You finding anything interesting?'

Typing again, she answered without looking up, 'I think so. Look at these.' She handed over a stack of bank deposit slips and paycheque receipts.

I paged through them, looking for anything at all that might link them to our mummy-maker. 'I don't get it,' I said. 'What am I missing?'

'Look at the two most recent receipts.' She pointed at the pages in my left hand with her pen. 'Check out the dates and the accounts.'

I found them. 'Okay, they're both government cheques deposited into the same savings account at Virginia Federal. One is from the Veterans' Administration, presumably for Carl, and one is from the US Social Security Administration. I figure that one is Claire's. Both were deposited ... wait a minute—'

'Uh-huh.' Bryson hadn't struck me as someone who acted smug, ever. But the sly grin she shot me over her laptop made me want to toss her neat piles to the floor and ride her right there on that old Partridge Family sofa.

'This isn't right,' I said.

'No, it isn't,' she said. 'That's why I'm going through the rest of this stuff page by page.'

I continued reading. 'It looks like Carl deposited a Veterans' Affairs cheque two weeks ago. Then, three days later, Claire sent her Social Security cheque to the same account.'

Bryson's matter-of-fact demeanour returned. I missed the sexy smugness almost immediately and tallied it as Boyfriend's Favourite Trait Number Three. She said, 'You can call me crazy, Sailor, but I don't believe Claire Bruckner was in any shape to be signing deposit slips a week and a half ago.'

'Yeah, and her parallel parking had gone to shit as well.' I flipped back through six months of similar deposits into the Virginia Federal Credit Union. They all had the same signature: a loopy C-L followed by a scribble and then a large B heading a flat line, sometimes interrupted by the stalk of a K and other times not. 'These were all signed by the same person,' I said.

'That's right,' Bryson said, 'but it wasn't Claire Bruckner. Look.' She handed over a number of cancelled cheques, some dating from the 1980s. Why people hang on to shit like this escapes me, but the old cheques were clear evidence that Claire hadn't signed a deposit slip for her own Social Security in at least six months.

'Nice job, Kay.'

'Thanks, Sailor.' She beamed like a high-schooler who'd aced a maths test. 'I'll go through the rest of this. I'm documenting the whole works, so you need to give that pile back to me in chronological order. I'm already done with those.'

'Sorry,' I said, rearranging the slips and receipts. 'So … fraud, then.'

'Felony fraud.'

'They needed the cash, couldn't live without it,' I said. 'Hell, they barely lived *with* it in this shithole. We need to check county records. I bet you dinner no one knows she's dead.'

'I'm not taking that bet,' Bryson said. 'I'm sure that's the case. Carl's been signing those for months.'

I checked my watch. 'It's four-thirty now. See if you can get anyone in the St James Board of County Supervisors' Offices. I don't know who the rep is for … wherever the hell we are … but ask them. Beat it out of them if you need to. I don't care. I want to know when and *if* St James County ever became aware that Claire Bruckner had fallen off the radar.'

'For dinner?' she said.

'No.' I got up to leave. 'You've already earned dinner, on Lieutenant Harper. Your choice.'

'Where are you going?'

'Upstairs,' I said. 'I want to get whatever information I can from those shadow boxes and citations on the wall – Carl's military stuff. It's like a damned shrine in the middle of a pigpen. I want to know why. What's a decorated military veteran doing – with his medals and citations all polished up and displayed on the wall – defrauding the government out of a measly eight hundred dollars a month?'

Bryson went back to her paperwork. 'Who knows? Buying beer? Paying for groceries? Cat litter? He certainly didn't invest in furniture.'

'Wait!' I stopped. 'Say that again.'

'Furniture.' She thumped the couch with her palm. A miniature cloud of dust rose up and blew away on the fan breeze. 'Look at this couch, will you? Charlie's Angels might have got laid on this thing.'

'Not that,' I said.

'What?' She paused to watch me.

'Groceries,' I said, and started towards the front of the house. 'Can you get the Internet in here?' I shouted over my shoulder.

'No,' she called back. 'But Gretchen or Steve can get you online from the mobile lab.'

'Good,' I said, climbing upstairs. 'Call St James County, and stay on that paperwork. I want the whole thing when you get it done.'

'All right,' she shouted. 'And dinner's on you! My choice.'

'Your choice.'

On the upstairs landing I stepped aside for two Animal Control officers removing dead cats from Molly's bedroom. They had them wrapped in what looked like plastic and then taped into brown paper, looking horribly like macabre sausages. The paper was labelled with letters and numbers, some code system I didn't understand. The guys were muscular, mid-twenties, in bullshit rent-a-cop uniforms. Neither looked thrilled to be on clean-up duty. 'You guys been to the barn yet?' I asked.

'Nah, still finishing up in here, Detective,' one of them said. His name tag read WILKES. 'You know, we normally handle live animals, rabid dogs, poisonous snakes in the family garage, that sort of thing. You need a garbage truck out here for this mess.'

'Yeah,' the other, MARTIN, added. 'Any live animals left, or did you shoot 'em all?'

'Hey, I need grief from you guys like I need a damn abscess in my rectum. So pay attention. I want to know what killed the horse. Ideally, you'll give me some idea about the sheep and the goats and whatever the fuck else is lying dead out there. I watch your show on TV. I know you guys are on duty all the time dealing with malnourished pets and whatever. So I want your professional opinion as to whether these

169

animals died from starvation, or injuries, or the goddamned boogie man. Okay?'

'Hey, sorry Detective,' WILKES said, 'but you need a vet for that.'

'No,' I said, 'I need you. You work for the county. A vet's a pain in the ass. I need you here to deal with the dead animals, any live frigging animals still around, *and* I need you to take a look at that horse.'

'We're not doctors.' WILKES shifted a cat sausage under his arm. Apparently he needed a free hand to carry on a conversation. 'We can't tell you what killed that horse any more than we—'

'Actually, we might be able to help,' MARTIN interrupted. He looked to be a few hours older and more sensible than WILKES.

WILKES glared at his partner, his jaw clenched. He had military-style buzz-cut hair, and biceps poised to rip through his uniform – reasons enough for me to dislike him.

'What?' MARTIN said. 'I know when an animal has starved to death.' To me, he said, 'We'll have a look, Detective.'

'That's all I ask. Thanks.'

'Whatever,' WILKES said.

'Oh, and there's a dog down by the pond,' I added. 'You might want to check him out as well. He seemed upset when I saw him.'

'Officer Clarkson's list shows him as deceased.' MARTIN glanced at a notebook.

Deceased? Really? Phil referred to a dead and rotting dog as 'deceased'?

'Must be my mistake,' I said. 'But if you get down there and you find a live dog, one horribly torn-up and seriously pissed-off chocolate lab, give me a shout, okay?'

'Fine,' MARTIN said. 'But we'll check on the horse first.'

'Good idea,' I said. 'And I need the cats that were shot. There are several on the porch downstairs, plus these three. I've got to have those ... um, just in case.'

'In case what?' WILKES asked. 'You think we're going to write you up for cruelty?'

'Just leave the cats, hotshot,' I said. 'On ice, preferably, if you have a styrofoam cooler you can leave me. If not, then make sure you let Officer Bryson know how to read this label system you've got on them.'

'Will do,' MARTIN said.

'Then you are free to hit as many barbecues as you like,' I said.

'We'll need to bring a truck in for the large animals,' WILKES said.

'*If* they died suspiciously.' MARTIN cut him off again. 'If not, we can drag them out and burn the corpses.'

'Really?' That surprised me.

'As long as you okay it,' MARTIN said.

'When? Tomorrow?'

'Unless something's screwy and they need to be seen by a vet,' MARTIN added. 'Blood work, that sort of thing.'

'All right. Then have a look at them, check out the dog down by the pond, and find me. I'll be around.'

WILKES' face reddened. 'You know, we don't work for you, Detective.'

To MARTIN, I said, 'Get him out of my face. Get him out of my face right this minute, or I am going to ram one of those motherfucking cats so far up his ass he'll be craving Purina Cat Chow all weekend.'

WILKES, looking for a fight, dropped his load of corpses. One bounced down several steps, unwrapping as it went. 'You got a real problem, asshole, you know that?'

Moving quickly, I stepped to my left and shoved WILKES as hard as I could with both hands. It was so brutal and unexpected there was nothing he could do except look horrified as he fell. He landed three steps down, tumbled another four or five, rolling through the shit I had stepped in that morning, and finally slid, spread-eagled, down the last few stairs to the living room floor. A handful of monogrammed food bowls clattered in his wake. He groaned a string of curses and rolled to his side, trying to get up.

I ran halfway down the stairs, then leapt the last five or six, too angry to realise I might break an ankle or fuck up Phil's evidence. I kneeled on WILKES' chest, leaned into his face and said, 'I have two dead people, probably three, at this house. There are dozens of dead animals here as well, and I cannot definitively rule out the possibility that they all died from an airborne biohazard distributed here by a terrorist who would love nothing more than to kill that entire stable of drunk hotties waiting for you at whatever keg party you're missing while you're here doing your job. I am a Virginia State Trooper and the homicide detective assigned to this crime scene, which means that I am God on this farm. I'm not here for fun, shitforbrains. I'm here on orders from my lieutenant and, in turn, our captain. So yes, right now you *do* work for me, and unless you want to be chasing down thugs stealing basketball sneakers from the fucking Foot Locker, you're going to get busy doing exactly what I say.'

Bryson came running in from the office. She looked at me and shook her head. 'Let him up, Sailor.'

'Sure,' I said. 'No problem. Young Officer Wilkes here slipped on his way down the stairs. But he's fine.'

MARTIN descended warily, looking numbly between Bryson and me. He had collected all six cat packages. 'Um ...'

'The horse, the dog at the pond, then me,' I said.

'Will do, Detective,' he croaked, kneeling to help WILKES as well as he could without spilling his grim cargo.

'Thank you,' I said and hustled back upstairs.

Bryson followed along. 'You're going to catch hell for that move.'

'Bullshit,' I said. 'I'll downplay it to Harper. And that other guy, Martin, he knows his partner's a dickhead.'

'You pushed him down the steps,' she said. 'Is there a way to downplay that?'

'I'm not a violent guy, Bryson, truly, I'm not. I may be a state cop, but I hate violence.'

'So you pushed him down the steps?'

'You're stuck on that, aren't you? Look, the way I see it, he wanted a fistfight. I didn't stand a chance against him, because I hate violence, and I'm not in very good shape.'

'So you pushed—'

'Didn't see it coming, though, did he?'

'Not much of a fair fighter, are you?'

'That was a fair fight,' I said. 'Fair, partly sunny, partly cloudy. Call it whatever you like. It's over; he's gone, and I'm not hurt so I can get on with my frigging job.'

She snorted disdain through her nose, a gesture that would never make the Boyfriend's Favourite Traits Tally. 'Are you okay?'

'I feel fine,' I lied.

'Well, if you don't mind me saying, you look like shit. You're all sweaty. Your face is torn up. You've got mud and shit all over your shoes. You look like you've been dipped in bad luck.'

'I *have* been, Bryson.' I gestured her back down the stairs. 'Right up until you told me about Carl signing Claire's Social Security cheques. Then my luck changed. Look, I just won a fight! I already lost one to a cat posse today. So from where I'm standing, things are looking better.'

'Then this should have you turning cartwheels.' She handed me a sheet of cotton-fibre letterheaded paper with *Hanover County Republican Party* embossed across the top. 'I just found it.'

'What is it?'

'It looks like a receipt, dated last month, for a ten-thousand-dollar donation to Bob Lake's campaign.'

'What?' I read, then reread the page. 'That's not possible. These people didn't have ten thousand dollars to spare for a political donation.'

'Call me crazy ...' Bryson looked almost happy to be here amidst the shit and dead bodies. She was proud of herself, deservedly so.

I read aloud: 'Thank you for your generous donation. Your contribution will help General Lake blah, blah, blah, and television ads addressing key issues for the Commonwealth, Hanover County, blah, blah, blah, appreciate your help generating enthusiasm for General Lake's campaign in the weeks leading up to the Republican National Convention.'

'Looks like the Bruckners were hard-and-fast Republicans.'

'Batshit-crazy is what they were,' I said. 'Look at this place: I've been in crack dens nicer than this toilet, and they're scraping together ten grand for a presidential nominee who doesn't give a shit about them?'

'Who knows? I just work here,' Bryson said.

'And you are doing a superhuman job, truly. While I've been out farting around, you're the only one uncovering anything interesting or remotely useful.'

She looked as if she had something to say, then thumped down the steps, kicking more plastic bowls out of her way. 'I want a steak,' she said finally. 'An ice-cold shower, a change of clothes, and a steak.'

'Done,' I said.

4:44 p.m.

I read each of Carl's citations, and all the faded newspaper clippings snipped carefully from the pages of the *Richmond Times-Herald*. The certificates and articles had been glued to matte paper inside three rosewood boxes. One contained Carl's Purple Heart, another, his Navy and Marine Corps medal, and the third, his Bronze Star. From what I could gather from the clippings, all three citations were earned on the same battlefield, maybe even the same day.

I made a few notes, including some terms, places, and engagements I'd never heard of before.

Pleiku. Montagnard. Gia Lai Province. 17th Air Commando Squadron. Major Steven Watts. LZ Nancy. MACV. Chinook CH-47. Creighton Abrams. McGeorge Bundy. Special Forces. Central Highlands. Robert MacNamera. I had heard of him. *September, 1968.*

'Hey, Bryson!' I shouted. 'Remind me when Carl was born?'

I heard her coming down the hallway, tired floorboards creaking as she walked. At the foot of the stairs, she opened a notebook, reviewed her scribbles and said, 'June, 1936. Why? What's up?'

'Maybe nothing,' I said. 'I'm heading over to the mobile lab to do an Internet search and check on Gretchen and Steve's progress. I'll be back in an hour or so and we'll take a break for some food.'

'Works for me,' she said. 'I could use a break. My good nature is wearing off.'

'Mine too.'

'Oh, and I forgot to tell you: the St James County sergeant wants to talk to you. He's out back with two officers and a game warden. The last I saw them, they were huddling in the barn, smoking cigarettes and waiting out the rain.'

'The guy from this morning? The shift sergeant?'

'Nah, he was the overnight. This is the day guy, Evans.'

'I'll catch up with him when I get back,' I said. 'He can hang around until then, or if he gets antsy, send him over to the Phillips 66 station.'

'Got it.' She disappeared through the kitchen.

My notes under one arm, I dug in my jacket for a smoke. My heart raced a bit in the wake of my assault on the muscle-headed Animal Control officer. I decided to take a break, just a minute to get my bearings and clear my head, before driving out to the mobile lab. Not sure how I'd explain the incident to Harper, I played out a few plausible explanations in my mind ... however, each of them ended with me shoving WILKES down the stairs.

Whatever. I'll deal with it when it comes across Harper's desk.

I leaned in to get a better look at Carl's Navy and Marine Corps medal. I'd never done anything even remotely—

The growl, resonant and threatening, came from down the corridor. I didn't need to look. Molly's bedroom door, a pink and purple pastel explosion, was closed. Bryson had shut it after photographing the cats Phil and I had shot earlier.

'He's in there,' I whispered to Carl's medals and citations. 'That sonofabitch followed me up here.'

Turning slowly, my Glock in hand, I approached Molly's room on tiptoe, the old wooden floor of the hall creaking as I moved. I was wondering whether I would have the balls to open her door and face whatever waited for me inside: bloodthirsty, tattered dogs. Ravenous, vicious cats. Screaming banshee demons. I shook my head, a minimalist gesture. 'No,' I murmured, 'not now. Not again.' The hallway light, a solitary bulb dangling from a frayed cable, shed uncertain light on the worn floorboards and the cracked plaster. I reached for the doorknob, my fingers numb. Faded photos of David Cassidy and Lee Majors watched me from where they'd been taped up thirty years earlier. The corridor smelled of wet fur.

Another growl, this one like the low rumble of distant thunder.

Don't open it, Sailor. Just walk away. It's too much to ask, too much for anyone. There's no shame.

'Sammy, come in.'

One day, I'd have to look in the mirror again. I wondered what I might say to myself when I did. Shrugging off the all-over lassitude that came either from embarrassing uncertainty or too much OxyContin, I holstered my gun, popped another pill dry, and padded quietly away.

The scrabbling sound of claws, scratching furiously at Molly's door, chased me down the stairs and onto the porch. I hustled, quickening my step towards the relative safety of the mobile lab. I'd been in the driver's seat all day, and I was looking forward to the anonymity of a crowd. Hopefully Bryson would choose a noisy restaurant.

The Virginia State Police Mobile Crime Scene Labs were forty-foot, high-tech, coked-up Winnebagos stocked with the absolute latest in forensic, photographic, chemical, communications, pathology and serology equipment. Designed for rapid processing of evidence on remote locations, the mobile labs had their own water supply and generators that could operate for days at a time without plugging in for a recharge. Labs were certified response units and command centres for crime scenes involving weapons of mass destruction as well as biohazard and bioterror attacks. With an onboard gas chromatograph and an infrared spectrometer microscope, these rolling chemistry sets were every drug dealer's worst nightmare. There was no amount of vacuuming you could do to hide trace evidence when equipment like that pulled into your driveway. I was especially interested in the lab's automated fingerprint identification system and its serology lab and DNA database access. I figured with a little luck and a quick hit on one of the latents Lourdes and Bryson had lifted from the fillet knife, we would have our suspect. Using the online DNA database Gretchen Kim and Steve Cornwell could dig up his records, have his DNA information available and filter through the evidence we'd brought out of the farmhouse; with any luck, we could have someone in cuffs by morning.

The pain in my ass was that each mobile unit had its own sergeant, a team of trained detectives certified to collect and process evidence on site, and two civilian technicians who, to be honest, did most of the work. I was neither trained nor certified to do anything more than polish the chrome on the lab; it was only because Phil Clarkson was a sergeant in CID and had received at least the basic training that he was able to request a mobile lab for the Bruckner case. What Phil had failed to report was that he would be leaving the scene for a few hours to watch his daughter play in a summer camp concert down on the James River, leaving me in charge of the state's two-million-dollar baby. Cheryl Baskin had said good things about Gretchen and Steve, but without Phil to lend credibility to my posturing I couldn't throw too much weight around inside the lab. I knew I'd have to be polite, ask nicely for whatever I needed, and be ready to hear the word *no*.

They'd parked the lab behind the abandoned station on Goochland Lane, a couple of miles from the farm. Two expandable antennae and a satellite dish had been hooked up on the roof and a retractable awning extended to provide a bit of shade out front. Seeing it up close, I was doubly glad we hadn't tried to get the lab up that muddy driveway. It would have been buried to the skirts by now, like some redneck's old pickup, and I'd be getting my résumé together – *chasing down thugs stealing basketball sneakers from Foot Locker.*

I parked beside the lab, careful not to run over the extension cord Phil had plugged in the back of the station. No sense firing up the generators if the old place was still wired up. The mobile unit looked like an alien spaceship among all the rusted junk, stacked tyres and forgotten machine parts tossed behind the garage.

I knocked and pulled the door open before anyone could answer. Overhead stereo speakers boomed symphonic music that sounded like a gang riot had broken out between the brass and strings.

One end looked surprisingly like the chemistry classroom at my high school back home: sinks, granite countertops, a pair of gas jets, and cabinets of a yellowish faux oak installed in a thousand cookie-cutter suburban kitchens. There were beakers and graduated cylinders, test tubes and a scattering of waterproof, plastic boxes with official-looking scientific symbols printed on them. The opposite end housed a communications and surveillance suite complete with radios, computers, satellite radar, a phone bank, and even a small conference table stacked with the evidence boxes from the Bruckner farmhouse. In the centre of the lab was a tiny room with a narrow door. DARKROOM IN USE glowed red when the door was locked from the inside. The unit had many closets, storage areas and cabinets; all sorts of equipment could drop down or fold away, like gizmos emerging from Inspector

Gadget's torso. It was a form-following-function masterpiece, and I understood immediately why detectives had to go through so much training to be able to play with it. There were enough latches and buttons, flashing toggles and levers to fill a week's worth of classroom exercises. I was out of my league; I silently promised myself I would not touch *anything*.

Under its own light, on a counter beneath an open cabinet, was the old handsaw Doc had pulled out of Claire's spine. It looked harmless enough, displayed on a roll of antiseptic white examination paper. Evidence labs had a way of mitigating the ugliness gathered up at crime scenes. The saw was just a saw in here. Beside it were Carl's Saint George medal and an engraved coin from a Marine battalion, the Eighty-Third. It had been in his pocket.

'Hello.' Steve Cornwell emerged from a door on the far end of the chem lab. He was tall, almost too tall for the lab, and exceedingly thin. I don't know how he got up for work each day knowing that his head would spend the next eight hours nearly hitting the ceiling. He wore a white lab coat that reached his knees – it would have dragged on the floor on me – and an open-collared shirt with three different-coloured pens in the pocket. With wavy brown hair and a bright smile, he looked tan and cool. 'You must be Detective Doyle.'

'That's me,' I said, shaking his hand. 'But please call me Sailor.'

He reached above my head and turned down the volume on the lab's stereo system. 'Sorry about that, but I lost the toss today. Gretchen picked the music.'

'It's Mahler.' Gretchen Kim rose from a comfortable office chair in the communications suite. 'His fifth symphony, my favourite.' Gretchen was the very antithesis of Steve Cornwell: petite, maybe five feet tall, if she stood straight as a ramrod. Long black hair tied in a ponytail was tucked beneath the collar of her lab coat. She wore khaki pants and running shoes with a VASP polo shirt, and like her colleague she looked professional and relaxed.

It's got to be the air-conditioning. I must look like an incinerated cadaver to these two.

As if reading my mind, Gretchen said, 'You look as though you've had quite a day, Sailor.' She shook my hand firmly. 'Can I get you some coffee or a Diet Coke? I'm afraid we're out of platelets and plasma.'

Tech joke. I get it: I look like death.

'Sure. Diet Coke, please,' I said.

She mined for one in a skinny fridge beside the darkroom as Steve ushered me to a cushioned chair at the conference table. 'So what can we do for you, Detective?'

I thanked Gretchen for the soda, and said, 'Actually, I'm here to borrow your Internet, but if you have an update for me, I'd be glad to hear it. I know Lourdes and Phil have already been by, so I don't want to interrupt again, but I'd love to know if you have any hits on our prints, especially that knife?'

'On the knife?' Steve retrieved a computer printout. 'So far only Carl Bruckner, Molly Bruckner, and an unknown. I cross-referenced the unknown with items Claire Bruckner most likely touched – the refrigerator, the photo in the master bedroom, her glasses case – so I think I can pretty much say the unknown was Claire. But there are still a few hundred prints to process, so the night is young. On the other hand, we do have both LiveScan and CardScan available, so we'll know right away if we get any hits.'

'Shit,' I said. 'Maybe he wore gloves.'

'Possibly,' Gretchen said, 'or like Claire, he was never fingerprinted, doesn't have any priors.'

I took a swallow of Diet Coke and masked a burp. 'Did you say you found Molly's prints?'

'Yup,' Steve said. 'She's got hits all over the place. She definitely lived there.' He and Gretchen chuckled at that – another tech joke.

'When would Molly Bruckner have been fingerprinted?' I asked. 'She's a seriously disabled person. Who would have fingerprinted her?'

'St James County Public Schools,' Steve read from his clipboard. 'She might have been involved in some kind of volunteer service, or maybe a job placement programme at one of the schools. Who knows? Maybe she slopped mashed potatoes or took out the trash.'

'She'd be fingerprinted for that?' I asked.

'Yes, sir,' Gretchen added. 'These days, you can't step foot in a public school without a background check, a photo ID and a tuberculosis vaccination.'

'And she handled the knife?'

'Sort of,' Steve said. 'It's not especially incriminating. I don't have a full palm print on the handle or anything. Rather, Molly had her right thumb and forefinger on the blade, near the tip. Decent prints, though, no doubt about the match.'

Disheartening news. I'd been hoping for a slam-dunk, open-and-shut investigation. Phil had, too: *That knife is the whole enchilada if we're looking for a killer.* I needed Steve or Gretchen to give me some hope. 'Any chance we'll find another match on that knife?'

Gretchen said, 'It's slim, but as long as we're running latents, something could come up.'

'But the killer would have to have touched the photo in the bedroom, the fridge, and Claire's glasses case, right?'

'That's correct, sir,' Steve said.

'Any chance Claire was fingerprinted and the unknown is a glitch in IAFIS?'

Steve shot Gretchen a look that said, *Should we humour this dope or not?*

Gretchen explained, 'Sailor, the IAFIS system is the FBI database. That's fifty-five million sets of prints. The odds are astonishing, but I suppose—'

'No,' I interrupted, 'you're right. He either wore gloves or he didn't use that knife. Fuck!' I pressed the cold soda can against my forehead. 'Sorry about that.'

'No problem, sir,' Gretchen said. 'This can be a frustrating business.'

'You need some ibuprofen, Detective?' Steve was already up and heading towards the chem lab.

'Please,' I said, 'as many as you can carry.'

'How about four? I can carry four.' He shook the pills into his hand.

'Thanks,' I said, and downed them with a swallow of soda. 'What else do you have going now? Any evidence of a biohazard? I didn't hear anyone screaming or calling for reinforcements, so I'm figuring not.'

Gretchen pointed around the lab like a flight attendant conducting a safety demonstration. 'Back there we have blood types. We've got Molly, Claire and Carl, and we're running the other samples to see if there are any mismatches. Steve's doing that, while I scan prints into the hard drive and run the decent ones through IAFIS up here. If we get skunked, I'll run the partials, but that takes longer. We've got fibre and tissue in the chem lab and we can run serology or pathology profiles for any samples that come back unknown. We've run field toxicology tests, quick stains for anthrax, smallpox, avian flu, your basic wipe-out-a-whole-farm-kind-of-toxins, and found nothing.'

'Anything else?'

'Apart from that we're really just getting started.' Steve sat across from me. His legs stretched to the opposite side of the aisle. 'But we have a pull-down bed up front, so we can take turns getting some rest and keep the lab running until Sergeant Clarkson gets back. All night if we have to.'

'We may have to,' I said, finishing the soda and digging for my notebook. 'You mind if I get on your Internet for a while?'

'Nope, help yourself.' Gretchen pointed to a laptop on a counter near the photo darkroom. 'The satellite is all hooked up. You just need to log into the CID network.'

'Thanks,' I said. 'I'm going to steal another Diet Coke, then I won't bother you at all, but please feel free to interrupt me if anything comes up.'

'That's fine, sir,' Gretchen said, 'but please don't worry about us. We're settling in here for a long weekend. It's no bother.'

I dragged the comfy chair over to the laptop and double-clicked on the VASP icon. From the corner of my eye, I saw Steve slip past Gretchen in the narrow hallway, heading up front to collect a file or a piece of equipment. As he sidled past, though, his hand brushed the swell of her tiny ass through the lab coat. He didn't say anything when it happened: no 'oops, sorry', no 'excuse me', nothing.

So that's it. That's why you two are the only people in America who don't resent being at work this weekend – and the state even provides the RV and the campsite, however disgusting the location.

I hid a smirk as I moved forward, pretending to hunt for a pen.

Gretchen looked at me questioningly.

'You got an extra pen?'

'Sure. Here.' She tossed me one and I saw the diamond on her finger, however well hidden by the examination gloves. Steve wore a white gold Claddagh, heart facing in.

And a convenient excuse, too. Ooh, sorry, honey, but I've got to go to work. Yes, I'll be gone all weekend. Huck says we see it all in this job. And he's right: two Mutt-and-Jeff lab geeks finding lust in a luxury camper with its own gas chromatograph. God bless America.

I'd never been someone who could get lost in the Internet for hours at a time. I have friends who log in and just wander from site to site, surfing or chatting all day. I tried it a few times, working late at the barracks or when we got lucky and hit a wireless router while farting around on a drug drop. It never grabbed me, though. I half-marvelled and half-frowned at people who hunted around long enough to find weird sites – except porn; as a former Vice cop, I'm an international champion at porn. But stupid pet sites, wacky cartoon versions of famous movies or political lampoon videos edited together from hours of news footage confounded me. What's the point? The potential in an information superhighway is astonishing, but what does Average Joe use it for? Wacking off, selling his couch, or watching grainy video of a dog jumping off a high dive to a waiting great white shark with a mole that looks like the baby Jesus. Welcome to the dark side of the information age, I guess.

I wanted to take off my suit jacket and enjoy the air-conditioning, but I was afraid I smelled so rancid that they'd toss me out. I caught a whiff of my shirt, my *new* shirt, and nearly swooned at the amalgam of dead, dying and decaying musk I had lodged in every wrinkle. I scratched at my bloody ankle and tried to ignore the itching, the cuts and gashes and the smell.

I typed in *Lennox-Gastaut Syndrome* and found a few credible-looking sites. I asked Gretchen, 'Can I print?'

'Yes, sir.' She pulled open a cabinet beneath the phone bank, exposing a networked printer. 'It comes out here.'

I ran off a few pages on the basics of the disorder, using the phrases myoclonic, tonic-clonic, tonic and atonic seizures, then tried some links. A children's hospital in Denver had an idiot-proof summary, so

I ran off most of the website, collected my pages and underlined a few things I wanted to ask Doc Lefkowitz specifically at the autopsies.

Next I Googled the words and phrases from Carl's boxes. I tried them all at once first, not really expecting much, but *Pleiku. Montagnard, Gia Lai Province, 17th Air Commando Squadron, Major Steven Watts, LZ Nancy, MACV, Chinook CH-47, General Creighton Abrams, McGeorge Bundy, Special Forces, Central Highlands, Robert MacNamera* hit paydirt straight away.

The search engine noted that once I'd worked through the top sites listed, I had another eight million to review if I really wanted the whole story.

'Eight million? You've got to be shitting me!' I found myself saying out loud. I had this weird propensity for talking to the screen. 'How is this something I've never heard of? Let's try again.'

This time, I just entered: *Pleiku, Montagnard, Gia Lai Province, Special Forces, Central Highlands, September 1968,* and added: *Captain Carl James Bruckner.*

It took some cross-referencing, but in around fifteen minutes Carl Bruckner's story had emerged, much of it from a website dedicated to the accurate archiving of the Eighty-Third Marine Battalion, part of the Eleventh Regiment of jarheads who mostly saw action during the siege of Khe Sahn, along the DMZ, and in the Mekong Delta. A link within a cryptic paragraph took me to an ancillary site, where I read the story of two of the Eighty-Third's platoons, diverted for one day to Gia Lai Province in the Central Highlands of South Vietnam.

I was immersed in the story, but my concentration broke when Bryson showed up.

Bryson knocked on the mobile lab's window, then opened the door. 'Sailor? You still here?' Inviting herself in, Bryson said hello to Gretchen and Steve then pulled a chair up beside mine. She looked road-weary, worn to the nub. 'Find something?'

I said, 'Yeah, but I dunno if it'll help us get to the bottom of anything. I've got some good information on Molly's disability but still no idea where she could be—'

'St James has got nothing. They've scoured the farm and contacted all the hospitals and day treatment facilities in the city. Their sergeant ran the phone records for me. None of the numbers matched any of the treatment centres in the region. There were a couple of calls to a family doctor; so I sent one of the deputies to roust her out for us. I didn't find anything in their personal papers that would lead me to believe any of the Bruckners had seen a doctor in the past year, but maybe she'll have some information. That was about an hour ago. Oh, and the Animal Control guys came back. The one named Martin said to tell you that you're out of your mind, because that chocolate lab's been dead for at least a week. The other guy, Wilkes—'

'The one I nudged?'

'Right, him. He said to tell you he appreciated all your insights into police investigation and he looks forward to working with you in the future.' She smirked.

Apparently, Bryson had never seen state troopers acting inappropriately before. I couldn't wait to get her out with Uncle Hucker.

I said, 'I'm sure that's exactly the feedback he had for me. What else do you have? Any other calls? Anything helpful?'

She kicked an evidence box covered with scribbled notes in indelible marker. 'Maybe. I brought along another stack of papers, mail and personal files, some notebooks, memos and things from the office. This guy Carl was some kind of office packrat. There's shit in here dating back to the early '70s.'

I frowned. 'Anything look promising?'

'A lot of war stuff.'

'Really?'

'Yeah. Memos and letters, some notes, diaries – scrap paper, mostly. A lot of it about some battle or fight, whatever, that he was in, some-place called—' She tried to sound out the spellings.

'Pleiku?' I offered, hoping for a connection.

'Yeah, that's it, Gia Lai Province.' She bent over the box and rifled through a couple of dozen clippings and official-looking documents.

'Good.' I rotated the computer screen for her. 'I'm just Googling Pleiku now. It happened in September 1968. Maybe with what you've got we can piece this together. I've gotta tell you, the more I read about Carl Bruckner, the more I think he might have been quite something in his day. Annapolis grad, Marine officer, multiple tours in nasty locales: this guy saw action all over the place.'

'You keep the AC on in here and I'll be happy to stick around all night. Some of the St James deputies helped me get police tape around the farmhouse and the barn and across the driveway by that little pond. The place is secured, so I've got as long as you like to go over the rest of this stuff. It's still in the high eighties in the house, even with my fans working overtime.' Bryson slapped at something on her forearm, then opened the collar of her uniform blouse, revelling in the air-conditioning. She wiped grime and sweat from her face and rubbed her palm on her sleeve. 'As for the phone, you've never seen a family make fewer calls than these people. There were months when they called out three, maybe four times – shit, Sailor, I make four or five calls a day that I don't even remember. I guess maybe it's not surprising, with these Southern-fried banjo-pickin' country folks out here.'

'I don't know about that,' I said. 'Carl may yet surprise us.'

'So what have you got?' She leaned back in the chair and eyed my empty Coke can. 'First, though, I need you to buy me a drink.'

I fished one out of the fridge. 'There's a site here cataloguing the deployments and battles of the Eighty-Third Marine Battalion. These poor bastards saw some of the worst shit over there, names even I recognise: Mekong Delta – that's where Phil was – Khe Sahn in the north, and this one, Pleiku, that didn't go well, apparently.'

'I've got it here, too.' Bryson unfolded a yellowed clipping from the *International Herald Tribune*. 'The dateline is September 20, 1968; the story's out of Budapest. It says Marines from the Second and Third Platoons, Alpha Company, Eighty-Third Battalion, en route from Khe Sahn to Bien Hoa in the Mekong Delta, were decimated during a routine supply mission from Pleiku Air Base to an undisclosed LZ ... what's an LZ?'

'A landing zone, often bulldozed right out of the jungle. Engineers would level an area, use it for a while, then let the forest reclaim it when they moved on. Agent Orange helped.' Steve Cornwell cracked a can of his own and pulled up another chair. 'You mind?' He raised his eyebrows at me.

'No, you're welcome to join us. You know anything about Vietnam?'

Gretchen Kim called from the serology lab, 'He wasn't even born until Jimmy Carter was already out to pasture. How the hell could he know anything about Vietnam?'

'No one invited her.' Steve grinned. 'Actually, my dad is retired army. He served two tours with the Air Cavalry, in the Central Highlands, Kontum Province, not far from Pleiku. I've heard him mention it a couple of times, you know, after a few beers.'

'Like eight or nine?' Bryson asked.

'In that ballpark, yeah.' Steve pulled the tab on his soda can with lean surgeon's fingers that seemed mismatched with his NBA physique.

'Great,' I said, 'that makes you our resident expert. Go on, Bryson.'

She wiped her forehead on her wrist, all decorum forgotten, and read, 'While sources remain undisclosed, Alpha Company Marines were allegedly transporting 150-millimetre howitzers via Chinook CH-47 choppers to a remote hilltop in the Central Highlands near Ban Me Thout, where Army Special Forces have been living in country, collaborating with and training local Montagnard forces ... whatever the hell those are. Sorry, I added that bit. All right, where was I? Oh yes, so en route, Marine platoons came under fire from NVA, I'm assuming that means North Vietnamese Army, moving east from the Ho Chi Minh Trail into the Central Highlands in an effort to reach the South China Sea and split South Vietnam in two. Lovely. Um ... what else? The sling-loaded howitzers were reportedly lost, along with two Chinook choppers, twenty-two members of Alpha Company, and—'

'Wait,' Steve cut her off. 'Wait just a second.'

'What's the matter?' I said.

'That's not right,' he said, 'Marines don't resupply Army Special Forces. Air Commando Squadrons, the Air Cavalry – where were they? This doesn't make any sense.'

Bryson handed him a stack of memos, notes and Xeroxed pages. 'Here,' she said, 'make yourself useful. I'm just reading what it says in the paper.'

'It might be bullshit,' Steve said, 'you know what I mean? Bullshit – propaganda, noise from the State Department to cover up a mission gone bad. You figure the wheels came off the wagon out there somewhere so Robert MacNamera and his crew drafted some hooey about Marines supplying howitzers to ghost soldiers – those Special Forces guys were frigging ghosts, living off the land in little groups, eating snakes and spiders and shit. Who knows what these Eighty-Third jarheads were really doing?'

'I bet a six-pack of Milwaukee happiness that Carl Bruckner knows,' I said. 'Keep reading, Bryson, and you, Steve, see what you can find in that stack.'

Bryson flipped to a second page. 'There's not much else, Sailor. Survivors were airlifted to Pleiku, including – holy shit, there it is: the company commander, Captain Carl Bruckner, who allegedly sustained serious injuries during the ambush.'

'I've got something, too,' Steve interrupted. 'It looks like a memo from Bruckner to MACV *and* the Secretary of the Navy, dated November 23, 1968. You guys know about MACV?' Steve glanced at me, read the ignorance I tried to hide, and said, 'Basically, it's in-country administration for the war, out of Saigon. Officers, under General Westmoreland until 1968, then General Abrams, called the shots. But I ask again, what was a Marine company doing flying howitzers to a bunch of Army Special Forces? I can't figure that. Anyway, this memo from Bruckner is all about some NCO named Kyle Hanson. It sounds like Hanson was a hardass, a lifer, one of those NCOs who eat their own roadkill and shit incendiary devices. My father had a couple who worked for him: career guys who didn't need sleep or food or shelter like normal human beings.' He read from Carl's memorandum: '"It was Sergeant Hanson, not Lieutenants Carver or Hodges, who was responsible for the safe return of the men from Second and Third Platoons. Hanson deployed along the tree-line, the Special Forces soldiers and Montagnards having cleared the hilltop in advance of our arrival. Despite heavy fire, Marines of Second Platoon held the western line, even while two Chinooks fell, one cutting a ragged path down the hillside, its rotors slicing through the emerald forest as it slid. Hanson freed me from—" Holy shit, listen to this: "Hanson freed me from beneath the sling-loaded howitzer, supported me on a full circuit of LZ-Nancy, and radioed the dustoff when I was unable to stand or reach our downed operator."'

'Mother of Christ,' Bryson whispered.

I typed LZ-*Nancy* into the search engine on the website I'd found on the Eighty-Third Marine Battalion. I half-watched the screen change as I half-listened to Steve Cornwell.

'"Given Sergeant Hanson's heroic behaviour under unanticipated superior firepower, and Sergeant Hanson's selfless leadership, even while Lieutenant Hodges lay wounded and Lieutenant Carver cowered selfishly, it is my recommendation that Sergeant Kyle Hanson, NCO, Second Platoon, Alpha Company, Eighty-Third Battalion, Eleventh Marine Regiment, be awarded the Navy and Marine Corps Medal, with all due honours, albeit posthumously." And it's signed, November, 1968, Captain Carl James Bruckner, Milano, Italy.'

'What was he doing in Milan?' Bryson asked.

'Probably recovering,' I said. 'You heard him. He said he'd been freed from beneath a sling-loaded 150-millimetre howitzer. I'm betting they're big-assed guns, fucking cannons, and they hauled them out into the jungle underneath those Chinook helicopters.' I showed them a photograph I'd found. 'Look at the size of that motherfucker. It's got twin rotors; each one's got to be forty feet across. That's a frigging flying apartment complex, not a helicopter. So they load a massive cannon on a sling beneath that thing. They arrive at LZ-Nancy, basically a hilltop in the jungle that some bug-eating Special Forces have bulldozed down to muck, and the NVA starts shooting.'

'Listen to this.' Bryson read from a handwritten notebook. 'The 17th ACS ... I don't know what that is.' She looked to Steve.

'Air Commando Squadron,' he said, 'the guys you'd actually expect to be supplying Special Forces hiding in the bush, not US Marines.'

'"The 17th ACS tore the hillside to shreds with M60 fire. The roar of the wind and rain were lost beneath the thunder of those guns. Anything alive down there should have been reduced to paste. Nothing could survive such a barrage. Nothing. From close range, an M60 could wipe out a continent. To this day I don't know how or where those soldiers were. It can only be that the Montagnards led our Special Forces to a hilltop already fortified with VC tunnels. Was it bad intel? Bum luck? A sell-out? It is my understanding now that Montagnard forces fought bravely, and the few I witnessed in action that morning appeared to be genuine allies of our colleagues in green. How a battalion of NVA reached that hilltop in the two minutes following an M60 barrage will remain a mystery to me for the rest of my life."'

Steve emptied his can. 'They must have had RPGs if one of the Chinooks went down—'

'Two.' Bryson dug back into the evidence box for another sheaf of papers. 'Two went down.'

'One of them while dropping a two-ton howitzer on Carl Bruckner,' I said.

'On his leg,' Bryson whispered.

'His leg.' I licked my lips, tasting the salty vestiges of Virginia summertime. 'Twenty-two men die, and—'

'Seventeen.' Bryson flipped a page in one of Carl's notebooks.

'Seventeen are wounded, including a platoon lieutenant.'

'The one who wasn't hiding, peeing down his leg, Carver.'

Steve crossed to the conference table and began organising pages into piles. He shoved two boxes of tagged evidenced out of the way to make space. 'Still, I don't get it. What are two Marine platoons doing in the Central Highlands while the rest of their battalion rolls south for Bien Hoa? How'd Bruckner get this assignment?' He looked over the stacks: Xeroxes, handwritten notes, typed memoranda, newspapers and official documents. 'What does it say on the web?' he asked me. 'Who was calling the shots? Who's the battalion commander?'

I scanned the website. 'Someone named Watts. Major Steven Watts led the rest of the Eighty-Third to Bien Hoa. When word reached him that Captain Bruckner's field trip had suffered such devastating losses, he returned to Pleiku, collected the remnants of Bruckner's command, and even gave a couple of field promotions right there on the tarmac. Someone named Hodges—'

'That's the lieutenant from First Platoon,' Bryson interrupted, tearing a page from a spiral pad and passing it to Steve.

'Okay,' I read on, 'so Hodges was flown to a hospital in Saigon, while Lieutenant David Carver was promoted to company commander, making captain in a field promotion. It looks like Watts pinned the citation on him before they regrouped and headed south for the delta.'

'Carver,' Steve stopped. 'The coward.'

'Right.' Bryson joined him at the table.

'So where was Carl Bruckner?' I asked. 'Did they ship him off to Saigon as well? How'd he end up in Italy?'

'Here it is.' Bryson held up a legal-looking memo with a Marine Corps emblem embossed in the upper corner. She read, '"Captain Carl James Bruckner, Marine Company Commander, Lloyd Hollis, Marine, Jerome Stansfield, Marine ..." The list goes on, but they were all apparently flown to the USS *Minnesota*, a floating hospital in the South China Sea, for evaluation, surgery and initial convalescence. Bruckner must have gone from there to a European base for therapy, prosthetics, who knows?'

Steve reached across to take the page from her. 'Either way, Carl didn't have anything to say about who took over after he was gone,' he said. 'He gets a howitzer dropped on him, possibly even from an exploding helicopter. His leg is reduced to Jell-O, and he has to be carried around the LZ like a child by his tough-as-nails NCO, who ends up dead, and when the smoke finally clears, the pansy-ass lieutenant gets the promotion, simply because he was the one who hid in the mud the whole time his platoon was getting its ass whipped.'

'That'd piss me off,' Bryson said. 'Enough to—'

'To what?' I asked. 'Complain about it from your hospital bed? I wonder why Watts didn't listen to Carl on that point. I bet that infuriated him.'

'Got him started writing all this mess.' She displayed two handfuls of scrawled notes.

'But where's the connection for us?' I asked.

Bryson didn't answer. Despite her sweaty, filthy hair falling over the headrest she was suddenly too feminine, too slight, too fragile to be a state trooper. She looked instead like a tired high-schooler playing dress-up in her father's uniform.

Steve Cornwell pushed pages around the conference table like puzzle pieces. After a long moment, he scribbled something on a sticky note and handed it to me. 'Sailor, do me a favour and type this into that search engine.'

The note read: *Major Steven Watts and Lieutenant Colonel Robert Lake.*

'Oh, shit,' I said. 'You think it's him?'

'He was at MACV under Creighton Abrams. I read about it in *Newsweek* last month. Abrams had been in South Vietnam for the better part of a year, just observing, consulting, whatever. He had plenty of time to round up a replacement staff of ass-kissers from the various branches headquartered in Saigon,' Steve said. 'Try it in that website you found. Just punch the names in and see if there was any link between them. There probably isn't.'

I hit the ENTER key and waited.

Gretchen Kim joined us from the lab, still suited up in rubber gloves and plastic goggles. 'What's going on?' she asked. 'What's the matter?'

'Hopefully, nothing,' I said, scanning the screen.

'Well,' Steve said.

'It could be him,' I said, 'he was a Marine general before he retired a few years back. He would probably have been a lieutenant colonel in the late 1960s, possibly that very ass-kisser who might have used Major Watts and the lowly Company Commander Bruckner for a political leg-up with the new sheriff in town.'

'Right,' Steve said, 'impress them with the size of your dick— oh, excuse me. But some things never change.'

'What are you talking about?' Gretchen was lost.

Bryson handed her one of Carl's notebooks, the battered spiral pad stuffed with bits of folded stationery. 'Lieutenant Colonel Robert Lake, later Marine General Robert Lake, and now Senator and Presidential Hopeful *Bob* Lake.'

'Bullshit,' Gretchen said, but she didn't get much behind it. She pulled her goggles down around her neck where they dangled like a cheap costume necklace. 'It's got to be someone else.'

I said, 'That would explain the clean suit and the ten-thousand-dollar receipt from the Hanover County Republicans. That wasn't a donation, Bryson. That was an entry fee.'

Gretchen said, 'Entry fee to *what?*'

Steve dug inside an old backpack stuffed beneath one of the fold-down benches. Finding the *Times-Herald*, he passed it to his lab partner. 'Tomorrow night, at the Jefferson Hotel,' he said. 'Every prominent Republican from the mid-Atlantic states will be there.'

Bryson said, 'It's beginning to look like old Carl was planning a reunion.'

'With the man who took his leg.' Steve draped an arm around Gretchen's shoulder, unaware or unconcerned that Bryson and I were sitting there.

'Holy Christ,' I said, 'things are coming apart around here, my friends. What the hell is this?'

Headed to Short Pump for dinner. Why not? We earned it today. I gotta get levelled soon, though. That Bruckner and Lake shit was an unexpected artillery shell, and I'm all over the place. Bad diet today, doesn't help. Coffee and chocolate bars for breakfast, Bruce Jenner's dream. Coffee all day, about 800 cigarettes, and what for lunch? Onion rings, a burger, iced tea. Four OxyContin. Was it five? Ibuprofen and Diet Coke so far tonight; I keep that up and I'll be a runway model. I need some starch, maybe a few beers to slow me down a bit, some bread, maybe potatoes.

Gotta call Harper, and soon. Maybe Huck, too – if he's down there with Lake's agents I should tell him one of their guests is dead, maybe from a biohazard, and he's all cut up, the part of him that wasn't buried in cat litter. Jesus, that's gonna go over well.

What a way to lose a foot: on orders from a bureaucrat licking another bureaucrat's boots, 500 miles from danger. Nice. I'd be pissed at Lake, too.

Short Pump – where the hell is Short Pump? Further out than I remember, maybe fifteen miles. That's the distance from Wibbleton to Wobbleton.

Where's my cell? Try Doc . . . no answer. What the hell? He's supposed to come out. Bryson's calling Lourdes. Huck, too.

Breathe easy. Just breathe easy. And drive, a couple of miles. Have a smoke.

Claire Bruckner dies, maybe weeks or months ago. She's interred by her family in the master bedroom so they can continue to deposit her social security cheques. Colourful. Felonious, but I don't give a shit.

Then Carl dies. He's been defrauding the government for months, but it's the same government that picked his name out of a hat for a milk run into the jungle where he lost his foot and most of two platoons of Marines. He's poor, dirt-poor, a dad with a retarded daughter who can't wipe her own ass *without help. A fifty-year-old daughter, a hundred pounds overweight, with a Minnie Mouse hairbrush and her pants bagging around her ankles while she sings BINGO.*

Yup. I'd be angry, too.

Okay, so old Carl defrauds the government to make ends meet so he can keep feeding his retard giant daughter. He's all right signing Claire's monthly deposit slips, because fuck 'em, this is the same government that took his foot, the same government that's seriously considering promoting the very same asshole who sent him out to lose his foot, probably, most likely because Lake was fishing for a leg-up with Creighton Abrams.

So far, so good.

Then the gods defecate on everything.

Carl dies. Does he die making plans with terrorists to kill Lake at the Jefferson Hotel? Does he die sniffing the very biological hazard he plans to deploy at the Jefferson? Let's say he does. Fuck him. Soldiers lose feet and bureaucrat cowards get elected president; it's the way of the universe. You don't like it; move to Antarctica.

So who cuts up Claire's body with the saw? Who fillets Carl? What happens to the slices? Are they cat food? Why does a terrorist cut up a body and feed it to cats? Was it Molly? Did she cut strips out of her father's body and feed them to her cats? Jesus shitting Christ.

Slow down, Sailor. Where's Doc? I have questions for Doc. What killed Carl? The knife isn't the whole enchilada, Phil. What killed Carl; that's the whole enchilada. And what killed Claire, for that matter? Heart attack? Stuffy nose? Stock market, Stanley Livingston?

If Carl and his animals died from a bioattack, are terrorists heading to the Jefferson Hotel to kill Bob Lake tomorrow? That is the motherfucking question; isn't it? Did they kill Carl because he didn't have the cash to buy the weaponry, the vial of anthrax? He ponied up ten grand to get in the door, that left him strapped. He was a Marine officer, he probably could have tracked down some nasty pharmacists with some nasty shit to sell. Did his dealer kill him because he was broke? Kill everyone? Horses, goats and cats too?

Is there going to be an attempt on Lake's life tomorrow? Or was Carl the only one? Is someone else hiding on the grassy knoll, someone I don't see yet? I can't be calling Harper. I need to slow the planet down, think things through, get them to make sense in my head before I embarrass myself with the lieutenant. I mean, why screw up a potential career-ender with a stuttery punch-line?

Or ... heh, heh ... is Molly Bruckner going to kill the presidential candidate? Could she do that, Molly, who can't wipe her own ass, could she kill Bob Lake? Could Carl do that, compassionate, father-of-the-year Carl?

Where's Doc? No answer again. Leave a message.

Slow down, Sailor. Maybe some radio.

Come on over to Ashland Chrysler. Prices there have n'er been nicer. Look away! Look away! Look away! To Ashland.

That's Ashland Chrysler. Just fifteen miles north of Richmond on Route 1 in Ashland.

Right. Yes, I know, you shitforbrains, southern-fried douche bags. The general's coming. The general's coming.

Wait ...

The general is coming.

The general is coming.

Molly wrote that. Or was it Carl?

Because Bryson had uncovered evidence of Carl Bruckner defrauding the government to the tune of Claire's $789 Social Security cheques, I let her choose whatever she wanted for dinner. Naturally, she picked an upscale place in Short Pump, not the chicken and beer joint I would have chosen about two doors down from the barracks.

Lourdes was on his way from Henrico, and Bryson had stopped to hit the showers at Division. After fourteen hours at the farm, she didn't smell any better than I did, and she needed to switch out cars before heading home.

I arrived at the restaurant first. The Flatiron Grill is a western-themed, steak-and-potato place with enough creative epicurean inventions and off-the-beaten-path salads to attract young professional couples from Richmond: emaciated New Age women dragging carnivorous Neanderthals out to dinner before hitting the boutique shops in the mall.

I grabbed us a booth near the back and ordered a beer from a college-age waiter in a tightly knotted tie. His Tom Selleck moustache dangled too far over his upper lip; I fought the urge to hold him down and trim it. He wore a long-sleeved shirt, despite the heat, and tried too hard to be polite about something as simple as a beer.

I looked over the menu for a few minutes, distractedly guzzling the beer, ordered a second and decided to take another mental lap around my unexpectedly eventful day.

Sometimes, when I think back over factors that have led to successes in my life, I hone in a few sure-fire common denominators. I've never been lucky. I'm not keeping notes, but I've got to be several hundred dollars in the red on the scratch tickets I pick up every now and then at 7-11. And I've never been the best at anything, ever. I found a few competitive events in athletics I could manage without terminally embarrassing my ancestors, but while I wasn't the kid picked last during gym class, I generally knew him well.

Rather, my successes came from the rare good teacher who connected with me, an occasional good coach, and my own ongoing focused effort. Hard work had always been the only option for me. I'm not a multi-tasker or an out-of-the-box thinker – whatever the hell that is – but I can throw myself into the deep end of any job, any investigation that means something to me. It's the only strategy I know: work it to death, put in the hours, push the rock up the hill, and the lights will eventually come on.

So the Bruckners had me in knots.

Felony fraud, terrorism, post-mortem mutilation, missing persons: all multi-dimensional, unanticipated factors complicating and confusing my virgin murder case.

The beers were slow to take hold so I ordered a third. This time, when Moustache Boy dropped it off, I saw the telltale whorl of a rouge and olive tattoo peeking out from under his cuff: another young person using skin as a permanent canvas. *Well, you asked for it, Chumbly. Better invest in a bunch of those long-sleeved shirts. Adulthood catches up with all of us.*

The Flatiron Grill has an open kitchen where sweaty chefs and sous-chefs in whites scurry around in a strangely algorithmic dance as they grill huge slabs of beef and mix up fancy Technicolor salads large enough to take home in a bucket. I sipped beer number three as if it had special significance as I watched the hustle and bustle of the naked kitchen. It was eerily like watching one of those Discovery Channel shows on animals that live, screw, eat and hunt in a pack, a pride, a flock, a busload, whatever. Everyone working on something, every slice, toss, slab and drink with its own part to play in the overall production. Here was a team tackling one problem after another, yet even observing as closely as I was I wouldn't have bet on who was in charge.

I watched for a while longer, wondering why my own team wasn't working as smoothly in our approach to Carl and Claire's deaths.

That was my fault. I tallied another factor that had been notoriously absent from my life's successes. 'No leadership skills,' I said and lifted my bottle to the kitchen staff.

'Who doesn't have leadership skills?' Huck sat across from me, took my beer, and drank it down. 'You? Shit, Sailor, I could've told you that. It's one of my favourite things about you.'

'Huck!' I immediately felt better; just having him around boosted my spirits. 'Thanks for coming.' I waved for Moustache Boy.

'What's doing, buddy? Wait. Lemme guess: you're neck-deep in corpses and you want to come back to the life-affirming task of chasing down thugs, drug dealers and porn kings?'

'Yes, and hell no.'

'What happened?'

'I'm over my head,' I said. 'I've got fifty-three problems, no solid leads, and no idea where to start.'

'Who's coming?' Huck loosed his hair, tugged it into a ponytail and retied it with a length of rawhide. He wore a baggy-sleeved paisley shirt under a black leather vest and faded jeans with holes in the knees. He had three days' stubble on his cheeks. I figured he carried a gun in an ankle holster. Most of Huck's uniforms came from a second-hand store in Shockoe Bottom. He looked like any loser you might find dealing dope in the street.

I said, 'Kay Bryson, Bob Lourdes, Phil Clarkson, if he can get a pass from his wife, and maybe Doc Lefkowitz. I've been trying to reach him for the past half-hour, but there's no answer. He was at the farm this morning, stayed for a while, and then sent his guys out to collect the bodies. I told him we'd take a break for dinner. He said he'd be by with whatever he knew so far.'

'He's working in the lab today?' Huck seemed surprised. 'What the hell for? They gonna be less dead on Monday?'

'I dunno,' I said. 'He seemed upset by the whole thing.'

'Upset? Doc? Nah.'

'Well, maybe not upset, but more ... unnerved. His wife's away for the weekend so he said he'd head for the lab to get a running start on the autopsies for me.'

'On July fourth? That's nice of him. What had him upset?'

'Unnerved.'

'Whatever—'

Moustache Boy appeared.

Huck said, 'A beer for me, and ... ah, hell, just keep 'em coming.'

'Right away, sir. You still waiting for others?'

'Yeah,' I said, 'we've got at least two more coming.'

'Anything while you wait?'

'Yeah,' Huck said, 'I'd like a plate of nachos with as much chilli, chicken, jalapenos and sour cream as the chef can fit in a snow shovel. I'd like Cameron Diaz to come in here and sit on my lap, and I'd like you to get Pink Floyd back together, just for one summer.'

Moustache Boy smiled; the hair on his lip almost reached his teeth. 'I'll get right to work on that, sir.'

'Thanks.' Huck peeled the label off my empty bottle. 'So what had him *unnerved*?'

'Dead farm animals,' I said. 'Doc says animals don't just die like that, of starvation. I guess; they'd break out, find grass and water. Hell, there's a pond a quarter-mile from the house.'

Huck stopped peeling. He looked like he had been given bad news. 'The animals starved?'

'I dunno. They looked like shit, all torn up by an army of starving cats, and most of them were too thin, ribs sticking out, and bandy-legged. They might have been neglected for months—'

'But eventually died from the same thing that killed your mom and pop victims,' Huck finished.

'Exactly. So Doc took all kinds of blood and snot samples and left in that German tank he drives. I haven't heard from him since.'

'Okay, I'd be worried, too.' Huck pulled out a smoke, looked around the restaurant and grimaced. 'Oh, not another of these frigging places, is it?' He didn't wait for me to answer but crammed the pack back into his pocket. 'What's going to keep my heart beating?'

'Beer and grilled cow?' I tried.

'You'd better hope,' he mumbled, then for good measure added, 'homicide-investigating pansies, picking yuppified, no-smoking, eco-logically friendly, candy-ass restaurants—'

'There may be worse news,' I said.

202

'Worse than that?' He accepted a beer from Moustache Boy and said, 'I'll have another when you get a chance.'

'But, sir, I just—'

'Son.'

'I'll be right back, sir.'

'Alrighty.' Huck gulped down half the bottle. 'What's the worse news?'

'My dead farmer, Carl Bruckner, might have been plotting an assassination attempt on Bob Lake tomorrow night. I know it sounds far-fetched, and I can't prove anything other than the fact that he was planning to attend. But if I can link him to the guest list at tomorrow's dinner—'

'Can you?'

'Yeah,' I went on, 'and if I can show that he died from an airborne biohazard—'

'Along with all the animals out there?'

'Right, then, I think we ought—'

'Did you call Harper or Fezzamo?' The serious veteran investigator, the one Huck generally sublimated beneath his good-time ex-hippy façade, was breaking through.

'Did someone give you twenty bucks to interrupt me tonight, Uncle Hucker?'

'Did you call them?'

'Not yet,' I admitted. 'I talked with Harper earlier today but that was before I stumbled onto any of this information. I told him that the Bruckners might have died from an airborne agent, but I hadn't connected Carl to Bob Lake yet.'

'What did Harper tell you?'

'He said he didn't want to get the CDC, FEMA or the NIH involved until Doc made the call.'

'Hmm, smart of him.' Huck scooped nachos onto a small plate, drowned the whole works with salsa and started eating with his fingers. With his mouth full, he said, 'That keeps the VASP out of trouble with Lake's campaign assholes. We didn't call in the cavalry; one of the medical examiners did. That's smart politics.'

'But that was before I knew—'

'Right—' he cut me off again, '—before you knew that Carl was going to the Jefferson Hotel tomorrow night, but who cares? What difference does that make? It might be a coincidence, and maybe the guy's a big supporter who happened to die of honest murder, just like any other shithead we scrape up. Harper doesn't want the State Police to look like we'd cry wolf to divert attention from Lake's shindig.'

'I understand that.' I grabbed some nachos. 'But as I was saying, I have a connection between Bruckner and Lake, and it's not good.'

'Shit.' Huck looked over his shoulder at the kitchen staff, still engaged in their modern dance. 'This food had better be damned good.'

'Why's that?'

'Because if what you're saying is true, we're both looking at a long night.'

'You can say that again.' Kay Bryson pulled up a chair beside me. She had changed into civilian clothes and even with the grilling meat and Huck's jalapenos she smelled clean, with a hint of whatever musky perfume she'd had on earlier. She wore her hair down over a crimson silk blouse that had one too many buttons unfastened at the neck. It was going to be hard not to look down her shirt. Like Huck, she was in worn jeans and boots – although hers were dressy; Huck's barely matched one another.

'Well, hello, Officer Bryson.' Huck raised his bottle to her. 'I understand you've had quite a day.'

'You're not kidding.' She helped herself to nachos. I couldn't remember if she'd taken a break for lunch; she had to be famished. 'It'll be months before I get the last of that stink out of my uniform, my car ... even my motherhumping hair!'

'You did a nice job.' I fumbled the compliment. 'Finding those deposit slips and that notebook, it would have been two weeks before I made those connections.'

'Yeah, thanks.' She shrugged it off. 'But none of it leads us any closer to a suspect, or to finding Molly.'

'What's in the notebook?' Huck asked.

I dug around in my briefcase for it. 'See for yourself. Then we can decide if it's enough to call Fezzamo. I don't mind calling Harper back. He's half-expecting me to check in anyway.'

Huck paged through Carl's writings while Bryson read the menu. Moustache Boy seemed happy to linger at the table now that there was a blouse to peek down. I watched the flat-screen TV above the bar. A news story about Bob Lake on the campaign trail came on. Lake, looking trim and tough in a way that screamed *retired military*, stood at a podium decorated with a National Rifle Association crest. He gripped the edge of the lectern, pointed at the camera, and said, 'I call upon my years as a United States Marine, my years as a Marine officer, and my years serving this country from the Pentagon and overseas, in South Vietnam, in South Korea, in Europe and Africa, and finally in the Persian Gulf. I call upon that experience when I pledge to keep all Americans safe at all times.'

Huck read from Carl's notebook, flipping randomly through the scrawled notations, margin sketches and scribbled ravings. 'It was Watts and Lake, the two of them working together. Watts made contact with Lake at MACV. I'm certain of it now. September 9, 1968. That was when it had to be. We were heading south, had stopped for fuel. Watts called HQ and they worked it out. The two of them knew that there were reserve ACS units available for the base in Pleiku – we all knew it. There were Air Force units all over South Vietnam. Why break up the battalion? What would motivate a man of Steven Watts' credibility and honour to break up his own unit, to send his own men into harm's way, and to risk the very core and culture of his command by sending the message that he was willing to arbitrarily and capriciously deploy men, HIS MEN, at the beck and call of the Lt Colonel? What Marine does that? What Marine makes that decision? POLITICIANS make those decisions, NOT MARINES!'

On the flat screen, Lake continued, 'I saw Marines through some of the bloodiest battles in Vietnam. I sat with them in field hospitals and wrote to their mothers when they died. Earning their trust and respect was the most challenging leadership task I've undertaken in my forty-nine years of public service. I will not falter when it comes to our national security. I will not falter when it comes to fighting terrorists. And I will not falter when it comes to defence and our military.'

Huck flipped a page. 'Watts made Lt Colonel, and Lake got his full bird. I lost a leg. Twenty-two Marines lost their lives. Another seventeen were wounded, sent home. My company was ravaged. Carver made captain in my absence, a damnable shame, a TRAVESTY! Watts did it, right there at the air base at Pleiku, said he wanted to keep morale up in the wake of our losses. Carver! If Sergeant Hanson had lived, he'd have greased them both, right on the tarmac, greased them and eaten their hearts. Sergeant Kyle Hanson: let the records show that he was a hero.'

The Lake story gave way to baseball highlights.

Huck closed the notebook. 'Jesus, Sailor, this guy was pissed.'

'No kidding, cousin.'

'So what if it's Lake himself?' Huck suggested.

'What do you mean?' Bryson asked. 'You think Bob Lake would even remember Carl Bruckner, forty years later? I don't mean to piss on the parade or anything, but those two went in slightly different directions after Vietnam.'

'Stranger shit happens all the time.' Huck finished the nachos and pushed the serving plate to the edge of the table. 'Lake gets wind of the fact that Bruckner's planning to fry his ass down at the Jefferson tomorrow night, so he sends a goon out to the house to take care of business beforehand. Lake would have thought of it as a pre-emptive strike.'

'Fancy,' Bryson teased him.

'Hey, I was in the Air Force before signing on to look for joints in high school lockers,' Huck said. 'I speak military bullshit.'

'Sure. And you were stationed at Seymour Johnson Airbase. Can you fuckin' believe that? Seymour Johnson! And you guys want us civilians to take you seriously!'

Bryson thought about it for a second, then nearly spewed beer foam all over the table, laughing too hard to say anything.

'Go ahead,' Huck said, 'go right ahead and make fun of the elderly among you. That's fine; I'll be all right.'

Bryson scribbled on a cocktail napkin, as if writing helped. 'But why would Lake kill Bruckner with an inhalant? And then why stuff him in a hope chest full of cat litter? That's not ever going to make sense to me.'

'Actually, that's the part that seems feasible,' I said. 'They get there, kill Bruckner, then find Claire upstairs—'

'—in the bed, or on the floor with the handsaw in her back?' Bryson looked confused. Her forehead wrinkled in endearing trait number eight or nine, or wherever I'd reached on the Boyfriend's Tally. Either I was horny as hell, or Kay Bryson was one of the most stunning non-traditional beauties I'd ever met.

'In the bed. They see that she's been interred in cat litter, so they stuff Carl into the chest, because it complicates things just enough that a room full of investigators will sit around and ... ah, fuck it,' I said. 'None of that holds water.'

Huck said, 'And you've got to remember that if they killed Carl with an inhalant, they were in and out. They might have come in after dark, opened a vial and left. The whole thing might have taken no more than five seconds.'

'Would that have killed all the animals, though? The ones in the fields and the barn too?' Bryson asked.

'Probably not,' I said, 'not any of the biological hazards we're familiar with, anyway. Most of those have deadly results at ground zero, but nothing I know of could kill a horse in a closed barn fifty yards away, especially given the rain we had last week. I just don't see that happening.'

'And they wouldn't bother dicking around with the body,' Huck said. 'Why stuff him in a box of cat litter when you know our techs are going to discover the cause of death in a matter of hours? It might throw us off for a day or two, but eventually we're going to see it as a bullshit manoeuvre. And, you've also got to remember that even the highest paid goons don't stick around after they've released a deadly biological killer into the air, certainly not to fart around with a corpse.'

'So when did Carl's body get into the hope chest?' I asked. 'We know he's only been dead for a day or two. Doc took scrapings for larvae, but from the blowflies on him, he's still pretty fresh.'

Huck frowned. His furrows were not nearly as attractive as Bryson's. Or maybe I *was* just horny. He said, 'Something's not right. We've got to back up a bit. What if Lake's got nothing to do with it? Let's say

Carl puts the word out that he wants to purchase a bioterror agent, something he can release into the air at the Jefferson Hotel. I haven't read enough of this manifesto to know if he was serious, but any one-footed shithead with a manifesto and a ten-thousand-dollar dinner ticket merits suspicion. He hates Lake; that much we know, and he blames Lake for losing his foot and his men out in the jungle. He's a Marine so he probably knows how to get his hands on some anthrax or a vial of smallpox – but why go to the trouble?'

'What do you mean?' Bryson waved to Moustache Boy and gestured around the table: *three more.*

I said, 'He means Carl was a tough old jarhead with a dead wife, a fruitcake daughter and a mortgage he couldn't make, not without Claire and two healthy feet. He must've felt the world slipping out from under him after Claire died, especially without her Social Security. Granted, he might have marshalled all his resources to buy a ten-thousand-dollar plate, but he wouldn't have used a biohazard. Carl Bruckner—'

'—would have gone down fighting.' Bryson got it. 'His .45 was oiled and loaded. It was probably the same one he carried from Pleiku Air Base that morning in '68. Of course, he would have wanted to use it—'

'—or his bare hands,' Huck said. 'I've been at the Jefferson all day, and I wouldn't want to figure a way to get a sidearm into that place. No chance. The Secret Service has the whole area cleaned out. I had a Coke and some French fries this afternoon and I went into the lobby to throw the bag away, but there's not even a trash can in that place. I just don't see Bruckner getting in there with his gun.'

'Could he have help? Someone inside?'

'I don't see how,' Huck said. 'You can't get a stick of gum past the Secret Service. It's not like the movies; these bozos will cripple you in a hurry. And Lake's personal security guy and one of his assistant assholes are already at the hotel kicking butts and shoving everyone around. The personal assistant, he's a real gem, some faggoty bureaucrat in an expensive suit – probably couldn't find his ass with both hands ... Carver, David Carver, that's his name, another retired jarhead from Nam.'

'Oh rats!' I grabbed my cell and started for the door.

'Where you going?' Huck stood, but he didn't follow me out.

'To call Harper,' I said. 'David Carver is one nail too many in my coffin.'

10:11 p.m.

The Flatiron Grill was bustling late into the evening. Bob Lourdes had shown up late and ordered a sixteen-ounce sirloin, rare. It bled all over his plate, tinting his mashed potatoes the same dull rouge as Moustache Boy's hidden tattoo. Lourdes wore cargo shorts and a golf shirt that might have fitted his little sister. His hair was perfectly coifed over his tan face, and his biceps flexed every time he lifted his drink.

Phil didn't show; he must have gone home to play Super Dad for his daughter. Good for him.

I had stopped counting beers – maybe in the neighbourhood of eight – and was on the verge of giving up on the Bruckner investigation until morning. I had sneaked an OxyContin, against my own best counsel, half an hour earlier and was spiralling into that glorious pharmaceutical stupor that made me feel like a fifteen-year-old.

Bryson looked good enough to slather with hot sauce and eat, but some thimbleful of good sense, probably left over from my days in preschool, kept my mouth shut and my hands in my lap. Besides, it wasn't long after Lourdes arrived that she surreptitiously slid her chair a bit to that side, and shifted her drink to her left hand. It was a subtle gesture, but a clear indication that Lourdes was on the menu and I was an overweight drunk who still smelled like cat litter and dead people.

I tried Lieutenant Harper twice, leaving messages I'm not sure he received. His phone cut me off once, then told me, mid-message, that the cellular customer was not available. I figured I'd try again later, but then I took my meds and drifted away.

Huck and I played out every possible scenario on the Bruckner case: from natural causes – *maybe he crawled into the hope chest and died* – to a full-on terrorist plot to assassinate Bob Lake and ensure President

Baird a second term in the White House. Nothing made sense, and after a while and a couple of dozen drinks, no one cared. We'd put in a long day; we would start caring again after breakfast. For now, our thoughts scrolled down to more drinks, more food, and the possibility of getting laid before dawn.

Huck stood up. 'I gotta piss. Come with me.'

'What are we, sorority sisters?' I complained but went with him anyway.

'How's Jenny?' he asked, holding the door open. 'Kids okay?' He wasn't slurring; Huck never slurred. He was an intergalactic champion when it came to alcohol abuse.

'Fine. They're fine. Ben's good. Anna's doing great, growing fast,' I said. 'Why?'

'Just wondering.' He stood at a urinal, cleared his sinuses with a snort and spat onto the blue puck.

'Actually,' I stood next to him, 'I think Jenny might be … ah, fuck it … might be, you know, out and about when I'm working.'

'Bullshit.' He dug a cigarette out of his vest, lit it with a match and blew smoke at the tile wall. 'Jenny'd never fuck around. She's not the type.'

'No?' I wanted to believe him, was willing to take anything he said as gospel.

'What makes you think so?' He zipped up, washed his hands.

'Honestly, I dunno. I found a bunch of notes and scribbles around the house, RML. I don't know what it means, but I figure it's initials, you know, like seventh grade. She's got them written all over the place, but nothing right out in the open. It's a few pages into the pad by the phone, on the back of an envelope in the trash can, on a little anklet she's been wearing. No T-shirts, billboards or anything, but RML, it's all over our house.'

'RML?'

'Yup.'

Huck rubbed his hands under the dryer then finished them on the ass of his jeans. 'She know anyone with those initials? Any friends or co-workers who might have come on to her while you were out chasing bad guys?'

'I can't think of anyone.' I leaned in to the mirror. I looked shiny with sweat and oil, as if I'd been basted for Thanksgiving. Splashing handfuls of water on my face, I rubbed my skin hard with a paper towel. 'I don't know everyone at her office, but still, she's just had a baby. She's carrying around twenty pounds of baby flab, and her boobs seep milk anytime I even look at them. Who'd want to have an affair with her? I mean ... *now* ... who'd want to have an affair with her *now*? Before she was pregnant, sure, but now just isn't the time to attract horny single men.'

'You'd be surprised,' Huck said, 'some dopey, romantic asshole thinking he's in love with her, with Anna and Ben, the whole bucket of suburban bliss.'

'Jesus, Huck, ease off a bit. I was hoping you'd make me feel better.' I *was* slurring, and I missed an easy jump-shot into the trash can with my paper towels. 'Fuck, man, I'm shit-faced. I need to back off.'

'You shouldn't have hit that OxyContin, young Skywalker. You're going to be asleep in ten minutes.'

'You saw that?'

'I'm a Dope cop, Sailor. I'd have had to be dead to miss it.'

'Yeah, well, it's just that one. I'm a little wired. It'll help me sleep.'

'You got any more on you?' he asked, testing me.

'Nah,' I lied. 'It was just that one.'

'You're not bullshitting your Uncle Hucker?' He crushed the cigarette and flipped the butt into the toilet.

'No, no bullshit. Just that one.'

'All right. Don't beat yourself up over Jenny. She loves you. I know it, even if you don't, dipshit. You get this murder in the can and then take a few days, no pills, no beer, just her and the kids. Get yourself back upright. It can happen.'

'You ever manage it, Huck?'

That stung him. I don't know why I said it, maybe because he had pushed me about the pill.

Huck shrugged. 'A couple of times before I let go of the wheel entirely. So you need to listen to me. I know.'

'That's what Doc told me this morning, the same damned thing.'

'He's no dummy either.' He leaned against the sink and fired up another cigarette.

'You're not supposed to be smoking in here, you know that?'

'Hey, I figure if they arrest me, I won't have to drive home.' He inhaled deeply, then tossed the rest into the toilet. 'There. Happy?'

'Not really, no,' I said.

Huck ignored me. 'Where is Doc, anyway?'

'I tried calling him a few times. I hope he's okay.'

'Ah, he's a tough old bastard. He's probably neck-deep in some newfangled chemistry project that's going to simultaneously solve your case, determine Carl's cause of death, exonerate Bob Lake, and—'

'And get Pink Floyd back together.' I slugged him in the shoulder. We were fine.

'For one heavenly summer,' he sighed. 'Then I can die.'

'Come on.' I stumbled into the door, propping it open. 'People are going to start talking if we don't get the hell out of here.'

At the table, Lourdes and Bryson sat even closer together. He said something mildly amusing and she threw her head back, flipping her hair off her shoulders and laughing, too hard. *Oh, yeah. They're done.*

Huck dragged a crust of bread through the last of Lourdes' blood-red gravy, chased it with a swallow of beer, and said, 'Bobby, my boy, are you on duty tomorrow?'

'Nope.' Lourdes leaned back in his chair, stretching for Bryson's benefit. His chest filled his shirt, but his stomach was flat as a sheet of newsprint. How was that possible? When I drank a half-dozen beers, my stomach looked like it had been inflated with a hand pump. Lourdes ate a sixteen-ounce steak, a generous scoop of potatoes, three pieces of bread and six or seven beers and his frigging pants were still baggy. Fucking cyborg. He flexed his arms behind his head, and said, 'I'm off until Monday, but I'll come back to the farm tomorrow morning if you don't mind, Sailor.'

Yeah, I do mind, you brown-noser.

'That's fine,' I said, 'although I might be at the hospital in town if I ever get Lefkowitz on the phone. I think he's doing the autopsies in the morning.'

Lourdes looked as though I had just invited him backstage to meet

Clarence Clemons. 'Really? Oh, Sailor, c'mon man, can I come with you? I'll take notes, photos, bag evidence, whatever. Can I stop by, or maybe ride in with you from Division?'

No. Shove off. Earn your ticket, dopey.

'Um ... sure; I'll call you in the morning,' I slurred. 'Are we done here, folks?' Our table had the lived-in look of a fraternity basement.

Bryson giggled. 'Yes. Let's get out of here, *Bobby*.'

'Hey, don't laugh. My mother used to call me Bobby.' Lourdes pulled Bryson's chair back. She took his arm, more for balance than to flirt. 'Unless I was in trouble.' Lourdes put a hand in the small of her back, not on her ass, not yet. 'When she was angry, I was Robert, sometimes even Robert Michael. I can remember her standing on the porch one day when I'd accidentally shot my brother with a BB gun. "Robert Michael Lourdes! You get your skinny ass inside this house right now!"' He helped Bryson navigate her way through the chairs, turned to Huck and me, and asked, 'You guys need a ride? You okay?'

'Yeah, we're good,' Huck said with a smirk.

'Fine,' I said, 'see you two in the morning.'

'Thanks for today, Sailor!' Bryson called over her shoulder. I appreciated hearing it. Maybe she was going home with the prom king, but even ruined on cheap beer, she realised she had learned something.

From me. That's funny.

'Get some sleep,' I said. 'Phil will be out there by eight. I'll call if I hear from Gretchen and Steve.' That was a lie. Nothing short of an edict from Congress would get me back on the phone tonight.

Huck gave me a drunken hug. 'Call me tomorrow when you hear from Doc,' he said. 'I'll be down by VCU all day, working the crowds.'

'I will.' I checked my cell phone. I had two missed calls, both from Jenny. 'Thanks, Huck.'

'Where you heading tonight? Not home, I hope.'

I swallowed a mouthful of tangy spit. 'You know.'

'You want a ride?'

'Nah. I'll make it.'

'Okay. I'm gone. Peace on Earth.' Huck slipped Moustache Boy a twenty on his way out. For an old Dope cop, he had a good heart.

I sat long enough to pay the bill, sign the receipt in an illegible scrawl that would have Harper cursing my mother, and finish my last beer. I stared at my cell phone for a few minutes, willing myself to dial Jenny. I knew if I did I'd find a hotel nearby and sleep like a corpse until morning. Some part of me wanted to, truly. But I didn't.

I dialled Sarah.

'Hey.' She was awake.

'Hey,' I said. 'What are you doing?'

'Oooh, someone's had a case too many,' she teased. I imagined her on her couch in one of my old T-shirts, her tan legs stretched out. 'Where are you?'

'Short Pump. You want some company?'

'You going to get killed on your way over here?'

'Nah, God watches out for children and drunks and professional hockey players from Ottawa.'

'Is that right?'

'Yeah, it's in the Bible. You can look it up.'

'Come on over.'

I flipped the phone shut and tried not to think of Ben and Anna, tucked in and sleeping – Ben especially, waiting for me to come home. He asked about me before falling asleep. I knew he had and wondered what lie Jenny told him. *Daddy's fighting crime in the big city. He's flying over Richmond right now. Oh yes, he is!*

'Okay,' I said to no one, 'gotta go. Gotta get up in the morning. Bryson and Phil, Doc and Lourdes. Everyone's coming back tomorrow. More to do. Lots to do. So sleep well, Bobby, you douche bag. Bobby who shot his brother with a BB gun. Robert Michael!' I staggered up, grabbed the edge of the table until my feet and my brain connected, then headed out front, mumbling, 'Bobby, Robert Lourdes, boinking Bryson and shooting his brother with a BB gun. Robert Michael, you get back in this police car right now. Robert … Michael.'

Robert Lourdes. No. Robert Michael Lourdes. RML.

What did he say this morning?

'*Actually, I've been up your way a lot recently, some training at Quantico, tech and database stuff, mostly.*'

And Jenny, when she found out he was at the scene?

'The goodlooking kid from Henrico. He's nice.'

'Holy shit.'

I hadn't cried since my father died, an old wound that had scabbed over years ago. Leaning against my car in the mall parking lot, afraid I might puke, I ripped it open, let the loose threads holding me together stretch and then snap. I cried out loud, bawling like a kid, unable to get hold of myself.

Two gang thugs, looking strung out and dangerous, materialised from behind a pickup truck. They came up fast, one flanking me.

'Hey, cracker, ya got a match?'

Still crying, I drew my .45, levelled it at one, then the other. 'Get the fuck away from me! Go on!' My face was streaked with a greasy amalgam of sweat, snot and tears. Drunk, stoned and waving a gun like a madman, I blathered something unintelligible, waiting for either of them to draw on me.

One of the thugs fled into the night. The other backed away slowly, his hands raised. 'Y'all made a mistake tonight, motherfucka. Ya should'a killed me. I'll be back for yo' ass.'

'Fuck you, you dumb sonofabitch; you don't know an unmarked police car when you see one? Go back to high school before you get yourself killed.' I coughed and wiped my face on my suit sleeve.

Outside the halogen circle thrown by the overhead light, the teen felon faded away, whispering, 'You know Marie forgives you. You know she does. You've got to find that girl, Sailor. Find Molly.'

Crying, coughing, I slid against the door of my cruiser until I felt the warm macadam. My pant legs rode up and my jacket bunched between my shoulders like a half-assed straightjacket: a drunken marionette, his strings all knotted, I lay there a while, my gun forgotten.

My cell phone buzzed some time later. It was Doc, throwing me a rope.

I rolled over, dug in my coat for my keys and ignored the phone. Doc could wait.

I pray when I'm drunk. As a Catholic, I grew up believing that it wasn't appropriate to talk to God. He didn't listen unless it was in church with a priest, one of His bullpen pitchers, in the pulpit.

But like most Catholics, I ignore that rule and talk to God whenever I want to. And most of the time, I want to after I've finished eight or nine beers. I don't suppose I'm that different; for the Irish Catholics in my family at least holy water and Jameson's whiskey are essentially interchangeable. My father honestly believed the only reason Jameson's didn't appear in the Bible is because Jewish scholars didn't know how to spell it.

That night, I prayed all the way up Monument Avenue. I enjoy going into the city that way, past all the brick row houses with their gleaming white columns and their neat postage-stamp gardens. The monuments rolled by, one each block:

First Arthur Ashe, who wasn't a Civil War hero but could have whipped them all with one arm duct-taped behind his back—

—*Dear God, please look after Anna and Ben tonight. I should be home with them. I know.*

Then Matthew Fontaine Maury, whoever the fuck he was—

—*Help Jenny find peace and happiness without me at home. Keep her from feeling lonely, and let her know how much I love her.*

To Stonewall Jackson, religious zealot—

—*Please Lord, keep Jenny, Anna and Ben safe, happy and healthy until I can be with them again.*

And Jefferson Davis, certifiable lunatic—

—*Let them sleep safe and happy, knowing how much I love them.*

To Robert E. Lee, the best West Point ever managed to graduate—

—*In Christ's name I pray. Amen.*

Then J.E.B. Stuart, whose joyride cost Lee the high ground at Gettysburg, and arguably, the war—

—*Thank you, Lord, for the life you've given me. Thank you. I know I should be content with what I have. I know I shouldn't . . . I ought to be better about forgiving myself for being human and fallible, but I struggle sometimes to . . . ah, I don't know*—

'I dunno.' Drunks shouldn't pray.

West Grace Street. Sarah Danvers.

Somehow I manoeuvred my cruiser into a parking space, cranked the air up and closed my eyes. Trying to relax, I drifted on buoyant memories.

'No, Sailor, no, it's Sociology.' Marie Doyle spun on her toes, wrapping herself, damsel-in-distress style, in the hallway phone cord. 'I'm not sure if I'll end up going to law school, or maybe teaching. I've always liked history. I did okay in high school, even in AP Euro with Harold Hardass Hanley. So I figure with Sociology behind me, I could go either way. I've got a really cool prof here, had her for a couple of classes. She's the one who's hooked me on it. I like the Anthro stuff, too. But that textbook sucked grasshopper snot, twenty pounds of bullshit about ancient cultures. Mom wants me to come back and teach at Freehold Catholic. Can you imagine that? Me and old Hardass Hanley sharing a classroom, or hanging out in the teachers' lounge swilling coffee?'

She unravelled her bonds, then spun again, coiling herself, shoulders to knees. 'I've got one more exam this afternoon, Brit Lit – I can't believe I stuck around this week to write about Ford Madox Ford. Who gives their kid a name like that? Then I'm hitting a Christmas party at Mitch's fraternity, but not late, because I want to get packed and out of here early tomorrow. You're coming early, right?'

Marie listened, bouncing now on the balls of her feet. 'Seven-thirty? How about eight-thirty? Early is one thing, but seventy-thirty might leave a scab.'

She listened again. 'Okay ... uh huh ... yes, I'll take you for doughnuts, Sailor ... yes, the place down on Fillmore, but then we have to hit the mall on the way home. I want to get something for Dad ... I dunno ... all right, but you have to split it with me, because I'm broke, but I want to get him something nice ... because it's the last Christmas of the millennium ... nope, it's not snowing yet, but it's supposed to tonight and tomorrow.'

Marie was barefoot in torn Levi's and a John Elway jersey, and her still-wet chestnut hair hung in strands over her shoulders. Her youthful skin was pale, winter-white, a stark backdrop for her hazel eyes. Slight, with sinewy muscles from years of running cross-country, she wore a brace on one foot, not the toe-spinning foot.

'It's okay,' Marie said. 'I've been off it for a couple of weeks. Coach has me pool running ... you've never heard of it? I'm not surprised. It's the most mind-numbingly boring physical movement known to western culture. I'm telling you, Sailor, you'd kill yourself. I put on this jacket, basically Bugs Bunny waterwings for grown-ups. I jump in the deep end of the pool and I run ... yes, shithead, I run ... for hours, days, weeks. It feels like an eternity. But it's completely impact-free, I'm assured ... of course there's other people around. It's the university fieldhouse; there are hundreds of people around ... I'm sure I look foolish, but I'm already in trouble for skipping indoor track. If I don't heal up by spring, I'm risking my scholarship.'

She waved to a pair of co-eds, bundled up in pea coats and heading for the stairwell. 'Okay, I gotta go. But I'll see you tomorrow ... call me if you're going to be late, Sailor, but don't be late. I want to get home in time to see some friends before dinner ... I will ... all right ... *all right*, already. Be careful driving ... okay, see you tomorrow, Sammy.'

Sunlight on snow lit the corridor with winter brilliance. Marie tried walking normally back to her room, but she was limping after a few steps. Apart from the twinge in her ankle, though, she felt good. Pool running all morning had her wiped out, spent like only endurance athletes can manage. She wanted a big breakfast – greasy dorm food was one of life's more agreeable rewards – before hitting the library for an eleventh-hour cram session on *The Good Soldier*.

Carla Phelps, Marie's roommate, was still in her pyjamas. Sitting up in bed, she frowned down at an open textbook. 'Verisimilitude,' she said as Marie limped to her own bed.

'Um ... probability, likelihood ... the appearance of truth.' Marie tugged her ankle brace tight, then slipped cotton socks onto her naked feet.

'That your brother?'

'Yup,' she said, 'he's picking me up in the morning. You sure you don't need a ride?' Marie found a hairbrush on her desk and started combing out tangles.

'I'm going with Debbie and that new guy she's dating from Sigma Chi: Bucky, Billy, Barfy, whatever.'

'The beefy, stupid-looking one with the blue sweater? From dinner the other night?'

'That's him: nice ass, nice pecs, but no one manning the lighthouse,' Carla said. 'Perspicacious.'

'Ah, perspicacious.' Marie brushed, tugging through shower knots. 'Having sharp or acute mental perception, an exceptional understanding. You know, Carla, for eight bucks I can buy you a dictionary.'

'Yeah, but this is more fun,' she said. 'I like finding ones you don't know.'

Marie pulled her hair into a ponytail. 'It's the ones *you* don't know that you should be worried about.'

'Ontogenesis.' Carla pointed an *I've-got-you-now* finger like a lawyer on cross-examination.

'That's not a real word,' Marie scoffed.

'Sure it is.' Carla held the book open. 'See? Right there: ontogenesis.'

'That's a bullshit made-up word. It probably only exists in that textbook.'

'I'm writing it down,' Carla said, matter-of-factly. 'I found a word that Marie Doyle, vocabulary savant of James K. Polk Hall, doesn't know.'

'Congratulations.' Marie stuffed two notebooks, a brick-like text, another pair of woollen socks and a pack of gum into her backpack. She put a portable CD player into her jacket pocket and draped a set of headphones over the back of her neck. Pulling leather gloves on, she said, 'I'm going to the Down Under for an espresso, then to Riverside Hall for breakfast—'

'They have the best eggs,' Carla said, highlighting a passage in yellow.

'They *do*.' Marie sat on the edge of her bed. 'You'd think they'd all be the same, but there's someone in that kitchen who works magic. Then I'm heading back to the Down Under for another espresso—'

221

'Junkie,' Carla interrupted again.

'Hey, everyone self-medicates.' Marie quoted one of her textbooks.

'I prefer beer,' Carla said. 'I figure I've got to die of something.'

'Then I'll be in the library until my exam at three.'

'You going to Pi Kapp later?'

'After dinner,' Marie said. 'I'm going to take my test then catch the bus into town. I've got to find licorice ropes.'

'What the hell for?' Carla looked up at that.

'For Sailor,' she said. 'He's coming all the way out here from Rutgers to pick me up – I've got to get him something.'

'I thought he liked the doughnuts from that little bakery down on Fillmore.'

'He does, but he loves licorice ropes.'

'So I'll see you back here before dinner then?' Carla asked.

'Sure.' Marie found her keys and zipped up her coat. 'What are you doing today?'

'You're looking at it, cousin.' Carla gestured as if the entire world lay at the foot of her dormitory bunk. 'I've got a Human Development final tomorrow morning, but if I read through lunch today, I can take a break to watch *Joe Versus the Volcano* on cable. Then Oprah's on.'

Marie pursed her lips. 'Sounds like a special day for you.'

'You're a fine one to talk, Miss Licorice Ropes.'

Marie started into the hallway, then poked her head back. 'Ontogenesis: of or relating to an organism's origin or evolutionary history.'

'Show off!'

'But it's still a bullshit word.' Marie waved and disappeared down the corridor.

'How was your test?' Carla brushed on pale blue eyeshadow.

'I dunno.' Marie held three sweaters in front of the mirror, alternating each beside a pair of cream pants she'd draped over a desk chair. 'I spent all day finishing *The Good Soldier* by Ford Madox Ford, and the two essays were on *A Passage to India* and *The Golden Notebook.*'

'Neither of which were written by this Ford Marcus fellow, I take it?'

'You really need to think about branching out a bit, Carla. Cognitive Psychology sounds awfully interesting, and I love the way you know the difference between learning disabled and ADHD, whatever that is, but you're missing some pretty decent courses.' Marie decided on a charcoal sweater over black herringbone pants, about the nicest cold-weather outfit she could pull together from her phonebox-sized closet. 'I've got to get ready in a hurry,' she said. 'I don't have much packed and I don't want to have to do it all when I wake up tomorrow.'

'Uh huh, sure. You tell yourself that, sweetie.' Carla fastened a thin chain around her neck, made a face in the mirror, and opted instead for a strand of fake pearls.

'What do you mean?' Marie played with her hair, hoping the right toss might convince it to come down as something spectacular.

'You'll be waking up at Pi Kappa Phi. It's the Walk of Shame for you tomorrow. Just make sure you get your slutty little ass back here or I might just be forced to entertain that goodlooking brother of yours for you.'

Marie blushed into the mirror. Carla was right; it was the emerging psychologist in her. Mitch Rivers was tall and lean, and somehow tanned, even in northeast Pennsylvania in December, and he was strikingly handsome. A Political Science major, Mitch was the son of two lawyers, the grandson of two lawyers, and sole heir to a modest but healthy law firm on Philly's south side. He was a junior at East Stroudsburg and a real workhorse; and he hoped to hit the LSAT out of the ballpark and earn himself an invitation to Temple Law. Marie would be happy to follow him there, even happier to join him for co-ed naked one-on-one wrestling after the party. It'd make a lovely parting gift for her holiday break.

'I can't help it,' Marie said. 'I try to behave myself, but he's just so—'

'Delicious and nutritious,' Carla said. 'I'd slather him with melted chocolate and die happy.'

'There's an idea,' Marie said. 'But not with my brother, okay?'

'Then hurry home, slutty, because if he arrives before you, I'm answering the door in a thong.' She painted red lipstick on her lips, then kissed at herself in the mirror. 'You think the bullwhip will scare him away?'

'Sailor?' Marie tugged at her bra, cursed and tugged the other way. 'Carla, the only thing that scares Sailor is a woman who seriously cares about him. The bullwhip, the chocolate, the thong thing, that's all right up his alley.'

The phone rang in the hallway.

'Oh, really?' Carla tried on three different shoes before deciding which she liked. 'Well then, take your time tomorrow, Marie, truly. I'll look after the Navy man when he gets here.'

Marie toyed with her belt. 'I shouldn't have eaten that pasta. These don't fit right now.'

'Oh, stop it, will you?' Carla chided. 'I'm thirty pounds heavier than you and I ate the slobbering meatballs. In ten years, you'll be able to parallel park on my ass.'

The phone rang again.

'You look great, Carla, especially in those shoes.'

'You think?'

'Hell, yes.' Marie stabbed a diamond stud through her ear. 'Debbie's going to have to suit up in goalie pads and a mask to protect Bucky, Barfy, Beefy, whoeverheis, from you tonight.'

Carla smiled at herself in the mirror. It was just what she needed, a little boost to help her hit the parties with a thimbleful of self-confidence.

It was tragic, Marie thought, what a few pounds could do to a young woman's self-esteem.

Carla said, 'But I'm not staying out late, and I can't get too hammered. I've got to get up for that Human Development test.'

'After humping my brother to within an inch of his life,' Marie reminded.

'Of course, after *that*.' Carla checked herself again then hustled for the phone, shouting to the corridor, 'Why doesn't someone else ever answer this damned thing?'

Marie leaned into the mirror, smoothing out her make-up and eavesdropping on Carla. It was easy to do; voices in the tiled hallway travelled like screams through a cavern.

'Hello, James K. Polk Hall. Come on over and Polk me!' Carla listened a moment, then said, 'Hi, Sailor, it's Carla ... no, she's here. Will I see ...? Oh ... um, yeah. Hang on.'

'Ah shit, Sailor,' Marie whispered to her reflection.

'Marie!' Carla called. 'It's my Navy man, but sadly, he wants to talk to you.'

'Coming.' She slammed her cosmetics case closed.

'Let me guess,' Marie said, 'you can't make it.'

She tugged absentmindedly at the sparkling stud in her left ear. 'How long will you be there?' she asked. 'Is that true, or is that the beer talking, Sailor? ... Really? What's her name? ... You don't sound like you; so there might be something to it ... How late will you get here? ... Yeah, I guess. I mean, what else can I do?'

Carla mimed *ride with us* in college co-ed sign language.

Marie said, 'Hang on, Sailor.'

'Come with us,' Carla said. 'We're passing close enough by New Brunswick. Tell him to sleep in, screw this trollop all he wants, and come out to meet us at the diner on Easton Avenue, right by 287.'

'You sure?'

'Yeah, sure, what the hell. It'll give me someone to talk to while Debbie's jerking off Barfy in the front seat.'

'Maybe we'll let them have the back.' Marie's face brightened.

'Even better,' Carla said. 'I've got my final at eight-thirty. It should take me about twenty-six minutes to write down everything I know about Human Development. I figure we can be out of here by nine-thirty, ten at the latest.'

Into the phone, Marie said, 'She'd better be worth it, Sailor ... yeah, I've heard you say that before ... no, with Carla and Debbie ... um, at the diner on Easton Avenue by ... okay, you know it ... eleven-thirty.'

Carla nodded.

'Eleven-thirty should be fine, but then lunch is on you, loser ... okay ... well, I *don't* love you—'

'Tell him to give her a good one for me,' Carla said, gesturing with her fist.

'Carla says you should wear a condom ... oh, bullshit ... not true

225

love, you drunk shithead ... see you tomorrow, *Sammy* ... I can call you Sammy if I want.' She hung up. 'That is one disappointing brother I have.'

'He's a college senior,' Carla explained, 'it's the last winter break of the whole freaking millennium starting tomorrow, and he's got his eye on some horny sophomore—'

'Junior.'

'Junior,' Carla went on, 'probably with big tits and a low-cut sweater.' She looked down at herself with disdain. 'I need to change.'

'Then we're getting drunk together.'

'Like it's 1999, sweetie! It *is* 1999!'

'That's true,' Marie limped behind Carla. 'Do you think we'll drink as much in 2000?'

'The year 2000?'

'Just 2000. Calling it *the year* 2000 all the time makes it sound too important.'

'Will they be serving keg beer in the year ... sorry, in 2000?'

Marie laughed. 'I'm sure they will.'

'Well, then I imagine things will be just fine.'

'Good.' Marie toyed with her hair then let it fall loose over her shoulders. 'What charming pick-up conversation are you using tonight?'

Carla frowned, considering the question as if paging through a Rolodex of possibilities. 'I think I'll go with eponymous foods from around the world.'

Marie snorted, then covered her face with both hands. Giggling, she said, 'I'm sure that Beef Wellington will have them lining up for you, Carla!'

Sarah answered the door in grey sweatpants and a ratty Hokies T-shirt. 'Holy shit, Sailor. What happened to your face?'

Fading, fading, fading.

'Hello to you, too.'

She dragged me inside by my lapel. 'And you smell like you've been in the river. What the hell have you been up to? Does this have something to do with Doc and his crazy phone calls?'

I fell into an easy chair that slid several inches across the floor with a noisy squeak. 'Let's see. First, I lost a fight to a posse of starving cats. I haven't been in the river, but the night is still young, so I'm not ruling it out. I'm almost positive this has something to do with the phone calls you're getting from Doc, however crazy, and I hope you'll fill me in on those once you've brought me fifteen ibuprofen and a half-gallon of Neosporin. And I've not been up to much other than investigating what might be a double homicide or a terror attack, a kidnapping, a missing persons case, or a cult killing, Egyptian-style.'

She looked at me as if I'd broken out of a psych hospital.

I burped up beer, nachos, salmon and jalapeno. 'But other than that, Mrs Lincoln, how was the play?'

Sarah tugged at my sleeve. 'Let's get you out of this suit. I don't suppose you have another at the barracks, so we need to try and clean this up a bit. It smells like something the road crew scraped up.'

'It's wool. In July. Tell me you don't love that about being a woman: no wool in July. I've been coated in a thin layer of filthy sweat for the past eighteen hours.'

'Like I said, we'll clean it.'

'You know a Chinese laundry with reduced rates for insomniacs?'

I settled in the chair and let her undress me. 'Because we can't just throw this in the sink. It's *fawn* for Christ's sake.'

'In-home dry-cleaning.' Sarah yanked my tie free and unbuttoned my shirt. 'It's time you woke up and smelled the new millennium. And it's brown, not *fawn*.'

'In-home ... really? They have that?'

'Right here in River City.' She was working on my pants. I tried for a hard-on, but that wasn't happening, not yet anyway.

'What's with Doc?' I leaned back far enough for her to get my pants down. There was nothing sexual in her movements; rather, she seemed genuinely irritated with me.

'I dunno,' she said. 'He called me in tomorrow morning, early. I'm trying to get this goddamned chapter written. I stayed here this weekend, gave up a trip home, so I could write it. I've got two hundred pages of notes and statistics and frigging literature review spread out over the floor of my dining room, and Doc calls me into the lab.' She slapped at a mosquito or something on her cheek. 'Ouch. Damn it.'

'It's got to be my bodies,' I slurred. 'They're all fucked-up. Doc tried to call me a little bit ago, but I didn't get the phone.'

'He leave you a message?'

'I dunno.' She pulled my socks off with a grimace. 'I don't care. I'm too shitfaced to care. I'll care again tomorrow.' I leaned forward far enough to brush her hair away from her face. It was wispy and delicate, the only remotely pleasant thing I'd seen all day.

'Don't.' She backed away. 'Your ankle is all bitten up. What is that, spiders? Gnats?'

'Whatever lives in a muddy pond.' I scratched at my leg while she pulled my shirt over my head. My arms and legs felt as though someone had filled them with tapioca pudding.

'Your toothbrush is in the bathroom. And you can sleep on the sofa. But I have to get some work done tonight, especially if Doc's going to burn my whole day tomorrow slicing up some corpse—'

'Corpses.'

'Even better,' she groaned. 'I'm never going to finish. My adviser wanted a draft of chapters four and five last Monday. She was going to take it with her this weekend. Do you know how huge that is? Taking my notes on vacation with her? And I'm farting around in the lab.'

Sarah looked good, better than Bryson by a country mile. I was glad Lourdes had moved in on my fantasy. They could have each other. 'I think Jenny's having an affair with a cop,' I said suddenly.

Shit. Where did that come from?

'News flash, Sailor.' Sarah frowned. '*You're* having an affair.' She collected my laundry in a rumpled heap and stomped down the hallway, mumbling, '... are you? ... whatever this is ... ? Fucking laundry service.' I heard her throw the dryer open with a clang. 'You take any pills tonight?' she called from the laundry room.

'Today.' I nodded down at my boxers. My roll of flab, stretching the waistband taut, was embarrassing. 'Today. Tonight. Enough that I'm seeing and hearing things, disturbing things.'

She ignored me. 'Bring me your underwear and that shirt. Then get in the shower. I've got a pair of sweats you can wear while I wash these.' She leaned far enough into the hall for me to see 'I'm-pissed-at-you-Sailor' creases in her forehead.

I complied without argument. 'All right. All right.'

Naked, bleeding, drunk, filthy, and tattooed with insect bites, I sat on the shower floor and let icy water massage my face.

I found a half-acre beach towel under Sarah's sink and dried off in the mirror. I sucked my gut in, hoping for an improvement, but I ended up looking like a fat guy trying to Vegas a hottie in her dorm room.

'What's she doing sleeping with you, fatso?' I asked my milky, bloated reflection. 'She's got to be blind.' I grappled with a pair of pink sweatpants, hiking them over my ass. She'd left them because she was angry. I hadn't been around in a couple of weeks, hadn't called or sneaked down here to visit her. No surprise she was upset.

That's fine, Sarah. I'll wear them: my married man's hairshirt. What a pretty fuchsia.

I guess I couldn't blame her. She'd come to Richmond to gather data for her dissertation. From what I'd seen of the process, it was like the homework assignment from the Black Lagoon. She'd written a few chapters, worked fifty hours a week in the lab for five months, and then paid some maths geek to run numbers through a computer programme so complicated I couldn't even decipher the directions. Covariate analysis. It sounded like two homos checking each other out in a doctor's office.

Now Sarah was near the end, Paperzilla almost done. She didn't have a research grant or a teaching job for fall semester, her lease was up in a month, and, perhaps worst of all, she was twenty-eight with a married boyfriend and no place to go. I'd been gone for a while, trying to make good impression on the Homicide Division *and* my wife. But did Sarah really think it was going to last for ever? That I was going to leave my family, move onto some liberal-ass university campus or into some strange town where she could scrape larvae off dead bodies?

But I didn't want it to end tonight, not yet.

I slunk back through the kitchen and collapsed on the sofa. Wrapped in the towel, I adjusted the pillows, stretched my fat pink legs as far as I could and closed my eyes.

The bed started spinning within seconds and I was tumbling ass-over-handlebars into oblivion.

'Fuck.'

Sarah sat in the dining room, clackety-clicking at her laptop with her back to me. 'What's the matter?'

'Spins,' I said.

'Read, puke, or drink some water.' She didn't turn around.

To myself, I said, 'Not very appetising, any of those, really.'

'Go puke.' She turned the lights down in the living room. 'Then you can pass out. I'll leave your clothes in the morning, or if you're up early, you can give me a lift to the hospital.'

'I don't want to throw up.' I rolled over. 'I'll just lay here for a while. You go type. It's all right.'

Sarah surprised me and came over to sit on the edge of the couch. Lifting my shoulders with both hands ...

Christ, that feels nice.

... she shifted far enough to cradle my head in her lap.

'Hi,' I said. 'Nice to see you.'

'What are you seeing and hearing?'

'What?'

'You said you were hearing and seeing disturbing things.' She ran a soft fingertip over my cuts and scratches. 'What things?'

'Images, words, frigging ghosts, all about Marie, at least I think they're about Marie. Maybe they're all wrapped up with this shitstorm investigation, or maybe … I dunno … maybe they're something more.'

'Who's Marie?' Her forehead wrinkled again, better this time, almost painfully endearing. I wanted to tell her I loved her.

But I didn't. *No one falls in love, Navy boy. You hear me?*

'Marie,' I said, feeling myself sink into the blessed softness of her thighs. Her old sweatpants smelled of laundry detergent and Chinese food.

'Who's that?'

'My sister.' I nuzzled my face under her breasts and thought *now is a fine time to die.*

'I didn't know you had a sister.' She played with my lower lip. 'God damn, Sailor, are these bites? Did a cat bite your face?'

'Marie. It was a long time ago – well, ten years, six months, and two weeks ago. Marie was at East Stroudsburg while I was at Rutgers. I was a senior; she was a sophomore. It was two weeks before the Millennium celebration.'

'Was?'

'Was,' I confirmed. 'I was supposed to pick her up for winter break. I talked to her a couple of times on the phone, just bullshit, you know. She had plans to go to a party with her friends. She was falling for some pre-law suburban scion whose frat was throwing a kegger to kick off winter break.'

Sarah tucked a throw pillow behind her back. 'So what happened?'

'She died,' I said simply. 'They all died. Marie, her roommate, Carla, and two friends, Bart Mikelson and Debbie Randall. It snowed that night, and they ran into shit traffic on Interstate 80 coming east into Jersey. Bart was driving, a Saturn, frigging aluminium and plastic piece of shit. You ever ride in one of those things? You can take it apart and put it back together again, like a big jigsaw puzzle.'

'They hit ice?'

231

'Snowplough,' I slurred, 'a Pennsylvania Department of Transport-ation snowplough, a big motherfucker that hit Barry's rolling soda can like an armoured prehistoric creature. The impact must have been unbelievable.'

'Jesus.'

'No, he wasn't there,' I said. 'They'd taken 611 south along the Pennsylvania line. You ever been up there? It's a nice drive through the Delaware Water Gap, with the sun coming up over the Appalachian ridge above the river. It's pretty. Anyway, the Delaware was a frigging steel-grey ribbon. There were chunks of ice floating in it. That's what I remember most clearly, those fucking icebergs. People always talk about water as blue. Kids colour it blue on maps, but water isn't blue. Sometimes it's grey, ugly, fucking frozen-assed grey. And you'd never think there'd be icebergs in New Jersey; you know? That's like an Arctic thing, but there they were, the Jersey state troops: pulling Bart Mikelson's Saturn out of the river onto a flatbed truck, with a whole scattering of icebergs floating by, like you'd see in a movie or on the Discovery Channel.'

'I'm sorry, Sailor.' She placed a hand gently on my chest, fingers splayed. There was nothing romantic in her touch.

'Hell, it's not your fault,' I said.

'I don't think it's yours, either.'

'Ah, but there you'd be wrong, my dear.'

'How do you figure? You weren't there.'

'Exactly.'

She changed the subject. 'Did Marie go to the party that night?'

'I hope so.' I was getting groggy, fogging up fast. 'I like to think she did. I picture her there, dancing and drinking cheap beer with her friends – the best nights of our lives. Maybe she hooked up with Mitch Whatshisname; he's a lawyer now in Philadelphia. I found him on the Internet a couple of years ago. She could have done worse.'

Sarah moved a coffee table with her toes and propped her feet up. She trailed a finger through my hair. 'What kept you from picking her up? And why are you still beating yourself up about ten years later?'

'A woman I met that afternoon.'

'You met a girl and never went to get your sister? Just left her stranded?'

'Yup. If you can believe it,' I said. 'The campus was half-empty, everyone scattering for the holidays, and I'm hanging around trying to finish a Criminal Justice paper that had been due two days earlier. I stopped by the library to dig up a book I needed, and ka-blam: there she was, feeding dimes into a microfiche machine.'

'Love at first sight?'

'Nah. But it was something nice, something warmer and more comfortable than anything I'd felt in my lifetime.'

'Sounds like love to me.' Sarah cupped the side of my face in one hand, pulling me close against her breasts. I didn't want to talk about love. Dredging up Marie had spoiled anything I desired ... or deserved. I flashed back on scores of meetings with the VASP psychologist, the way my heels clicked off the polished corridor at Division Headquarters sounding like Sarah's laptop keys as she hammered out Paperzilla.

'We talked in the library for an hour or so,' I went on. 'She finished running her microfiche copies and we went for coffee at a little place near the main campus. Coffee turned into dinner. Dinner held on for drinks, and so on. We spent the night in my apartment. My roommates had gone home already. And it was as if we had been there before, as if we had known each other, kissed, made love, slept together a hundred times before that night. You know what I mean?'

'No,' Sarah whispered.

I let it go. 'The next morning, she came with me. We slept in, read the paper, had sex all over the place again, and headed up Easton to the diner for a late brunch with Marie.'

'But she didn't show,' Sarah sighed.

'It snowed that night – I told you that already. You ever have sex with someone when it's snowing outside? It's always better. Don't ask me why.'

'With you, dumb-ass,' Sarah said. 'The first night we met.'

Fading.

'Right. Sorry.' I rolled onto my side, found her bare foot near my face and massaged it gently. 'Anyway, Route 80 coming into New Jersey was a mess. Some skier heading back from the Poconos slid his Honda into the concrete barrier and closed down two lanes of eastbound traffic. Bart took 611 south; any of us would have done the same thing. Crossing the bridge from Portland to Columbia, they slid, just a bit, but it was enough to get them T-boned by one of those titanic ploughs coming west into Pennsylvania. Amidst the wreckage they found a box of doughnuts from a bakery I loved, a little place right near the campus. Marie was bringing them to me; I'm sure of it. Best goddamned doughnuts in the world, they really are.' My sister's memory was slathered all over me, adhering to my skin like the layers of oily sweat I'd worn all day.

'Holy shit, Sailor,' Sarah whispered.

I cried. I didn't care. It was easy to cry when I thought about Marie. She had been so many things I wasn't and would never become – just plain enthusiastic about life was foremost on that list. What made things worse now was that I had Ben and Anna. I never imagined I would want them to meet anyone as much as my sister. That was one I hadn't seen coming ten years, six months, and two weeks ago.

My tears soaked Sarah's sweatpants. I kept a death grip on her foot and waited for the worst of it to pass. To Sarah's credit, she didn't say anything. She was smart. I liked that.

Eventually, she said, 'What happened to the girl?'

'I told you. They all died, hopefully on impact, but probably not. That bridge isn't very high. If it had been on the Interstate, the fall alone would have ...' I choked again, and buried my face in her lap.

'Not them ... the girl, the one from the library. What happened with her?'

I shifted onto my back and wiped my face with Sarah's beach towel. 'You know what's funny? I married her. It was Jenny, the love of my life. Can you fucking stand that? Can you?' Something between a laugh and a shriek escaped my throat. I balled up the towel and held it over my face, afraid I might do it again.

Sarah tucked a pillow under my head. 'Let me get you some water.'

'And one of my pills,' I said. 'They're on the coffee table, there in that matchbox.'

'Are you—?'

'Yes, fuck it, I don't care. I'll never sleep now. I need one, please, Sarah, another one, anyway.'

She glanced at her dining table, strewn with doctoral wreckage, looked back at me, then acquiesced. 'All right. I'll get you a blanket, too.'

'Thanks.' I popped the pill, sucked the sweet coating off, then ground it to powder on the coffee table. The smooth bottom of an old ceramic mug made for a workable pestle. Sarah looked as grimly disgusted as anyone I'd ever seen. 'Fuck it,' I mumbled, and snorted the chalky powder as far into my sinuses as I could, given a head full of snot and tears. Any bed-spinning need to puke was immediately washed away in a thudding wave of yellow, green and blue. My eyes watered, and I knew in a heartbeat how easy it would be to get indefinitely hooked on that little procedure.

'Never again, Sailor,' Sarah whispered, her arms folded over her perfect breasts. 'Never again in my presence.'

'Right,' I waved her off, 'whatever, sorry.' I chugged the water and sneezed a handful of oatmeal-coloured snot into my hand.

There was more. A bit more. Then I could sleep.

Sarah covered me with a quilt; it was all at once the blanket I wanted with me in my coffin. Screw the fancy suit or the trooper duds; just wrap me in this quilt and toss me into the River Jordan.

I wiped my nose. 'Marie's death hit my father worse than anyone. That surprised me at the time, because I always thought of my mother as the one who was closest to us, but Dad was ruined, torn to bits by it.'

'Do you think he blamed you?' Sarah sat on the edge of the couch, careful not to touch me.

I draped an arm over her thighs and tucked my hand in the small of her back. Thankfully, she didn't shrug me off. 'Think? I *know* he blamed me. He couldn't help it. I had fucked up: it was my job to go get her – one simple, stupid request, and I couldn't pull it off. My life as his son ended that day. Oh, he still loved me; that infuriated him. But we both knew without him saying a word, not even sharing a glance, we both knew that my time as his son was over. He didn't even come to my wedding.'

'He can't—'

'You don't understand, Sarah,' I cut her off. 'He didn't want to do it. It just happened. Do you know that after Marie died, my father lost the ability to feel with his fingertips? It was the strangest thing I've ever seen. All the soft, delicate things in this world to touch, the things to appreciate: a warm coffee mug, my mother's hair, the gritty feel of sand at the beach. They were gone. He was always burning his fingers on the stove or the barbecue; he had blisters all the time.'

'How is he now?' she asked. 'Did time help?'

'Time killed him,' I said, my nose still running. 'But enough of him died in that river with my sister that the rest was a formality. He just gave up. Whatever was holding him here was no match for what pulled him away.' I sniffed hard to keep from leaving tracks on Sarah's sweatpants. That would be too much, one too many shots to the head.

She tucked the pillow beneath my head, like I was some kid she had to babysit. 'Sleep now. I'll wake you before I go to the hospital.'

'Thanks, Sarah.' I wanted to say it again. *I love you.* Even if it wasn't true, she'd earned it tonight, looking after my sorry ass. Maybe that's why I kept my mouth shut.

PART II

Saturday, July 4th

Molly Bruckner

9:13 a.m.

I woke to my cell phone buzzing on the coffee table. Sarah's living room was brilliant with obnoxious light; it couldn't have been more than a mile from the rising sun. I winced, shut my eyes against the day and rolled onto my stomach.

Three deep breaths were the extent of my pain-free morning; then brutal, throbbing agony erupted everywhere at once: my head, shoulders, neck, lower back, legs and balls. And my motherfucking lip, where that fucking cat had bit me; that hurt.

Get up.

The beach towel had fallen to the floor; I reached for it, crammed a handful into my mouth and screamed, a muffled howl, until my lungs ached. My sinuses felt like they had been raked raw with a rusty fork.

Get up, shithead. You did this to yourself, snorting hillbilly heroin. Lovely.

I listened for Sarah moving around her bedroom or in the shower, but though brightly lit, her apartment was cool and quiet: Sarah was either gone already or still unconscious. West Grace Street, normally boisterous with morning traffic, was silent too.

Right. It's Saturday. July fourth. VCU's deserted for now. Later, Bob Lake will have them mobbing this place.

My phone buzzed again; someone was looking for me. I held the towel against my lip, hoping that might help, and sat up. A sneaky bout of vertigo blindsided me and my vision tunnelled. Sarah's apartment went fuzzy, then filled with tiny bursts of yellow and green fireworks.

Get up, Sailor.

I threw my shoulders forward, figuring I'd either find my feet or somersault onto the floor and wait for the paramedics. Nailing the dismount, I was up. Puke-sweat already dotted my forehead and coated my naked shoulders and back, despite the tomblike chill produced by Sarah's air-conditioner.

Not dead yet!

I needed to throw up, badly, with that achy, sick-all-over feeling that normally just comes with the flu, but as an experienced drunk, I fought it off. I could puke later.

My phone buzzed a third time and when I finally focused on the display I saw that it was Doc. I said to the empty room, 'Hang on one second, Lefkowitz. I've got to get my sea legs, then I'll call you back.'

I padded into Sarah's tiny kitchen to find a mug of cold coffee next to a bottle of ibuprofen and a sticky note with *Gone to the hospital* written in neat block letters. 'Ah, Sarah, you read my mind.' I swallowed four ibuprofen and chugged the coffee, holding the mug tightly with two hands, like a five-year-old. It was still lukewarm; she couldn't have been gone for more than half an hour. I sucked in a decent breath through my nose and exhaled out my mouth. 'All right, but just one for now,' I told myself. I filled the mug with tap water and went back to the living room for my matchbox. 'One ought to blow out a bit of this fog. Then I'll find something to eat.' The pill went down chalky, a harbinger of a shitty day. I cleared my sinuses into the back of my throat and spat lumpy green snot into the empty mug.

Okay. Get to work.

Sarah hadn't straightened up the mess on her dining table. I didn't want to move anything, or else risk incurring the corrosive wrath of a pissed-off doctoral candidate who knew where every scrap of scribbled data had been assigned. But I needed a place to write; so I closed down her laptop, unfolded my own notebook and punched the message button on my cell.

Five messages waited for me. The first was from Doc: *Sailor, it's Lefkowitz. It's about 10:45. I'm sorry to be calling so late, but I'm just getting back to the lab. I ran up to Quantico for a few things and need you to call me or come over here as soon as you can, any time tonight. Also, I need a number where I can reach the techs in your mobile unit. I think Sergeant Clarkson said he was calling for one. They have samples there that I do not, and I need them to run a few serology and pathology tests for me right away. Call me back, please.*

Doc had called again that morning: *Sailor. Call me. It's Doc. I'm at the lab. It's about six-thirty. You're probably sleeping, but I need you down here. I called the lab at Division, and they put me in touch with your mobile techs, Steve and Gretchen. I'll try to get Captain Fezzamo now.*

'Fezzamo? Shit! What the hell's going on?' I hit DELETE and listened for the next message. A sensation, not unlike free-falling through space, roused itself in the pit of my stomach.

Sailor, it's Harper. Where are you, son? I need you at that farmhouse right goddamned now. Call me on my cell. I'm heading into Owen's Marina and will be on scene in the next couple of hours. Fezzamo's not quite coming unglued yet, but I need to give him a hell of a lot more when I call back. I need to hear from you pronto. Call my cell.

'Christ, what happened? Is it Molly? I bet she turned up frigging dead last night.' Dreading what I might hear next, I hit DELETE again, and listened. It was Clarkson at the mobile lab. He whispered harshly over the crowded noise of Gretchen Kim's orchestra music: *Sailor, where the fuck are you? We screwed up. I'm at the mobile lab. Harper's on his way, and he's pissed. Doc's calling the fucking health department, and you know for frigging sure they're going to get the Feds down here. Call me back, as goddamned quick as you can.*

'Why's he whispering in his own lab? Who's there?' I pushed REPLAY MESSAGE and listened again, this time to the background noise. There was something else, behind the music. I closed my eyes and listened again.

It was Gretchen. I heard a thud, like a book or a notebook dropped on a table, then a few muffled words followed by one I could make out clearly: 'Aerosol.'

'Aerosol. What's aerosol?' I saved that message, then moved on to the fifth. It was from Sarah, calling on Doc's cell phone from the lab at MCV. Like Phil, she whispered. Apparently, Doc didn't know that I had slept at her apartment, not yet. I could hear him, though, saying something in the background. Was he shouting? Yelling to someone? At someone? Sarah's voice drowned him out: *Hey, Sailor. Wake up. You've got to get over here. Hurry up, sweetie. We need you.*

I folded my notebook and pushed back from the dining table. Still in pink sweatpants, naked from the waist up, hung over, I was struggling

241

to keep the contents of my stomach in my stomach. And they needed *me* at the scene, in the lab, and at the hospital.

'Harper and Fezzamo.' I stripped naked and half-jogged down the hall to Sarah's laundry closet. She had hung my clothes up; my suit looked pretty good, not quite professionally cleaned, but a couple of touchdowns better than it had looked and smelled when I left the Flatiron Grill. 'What the hell are we doing calling Harper and Fezzamo? Doc and Phil have lost their goddamned minds. You don't do that. You don't call them before calling me. What'd we miss? A basement full of aliens? A Tomahawk missile?'

I was halfway into my pants when my phone buzzed in the living room. I hobbled and jumped down the hall. The display showed LT HARPER.

'Not yet.' I hustled back for my shirt, tie and jacket. 'Not until I talk to Lefkowitz and Clarkson. Then I'll call you.'

I found a banana and a bran muffin in the kitchen; they'd keep me alive until lunch. With my tie stuffed in my suit pocket, I bit back the banana peel, grabbed my car keys and ran into West Grace Street and the stifling Richmond morning.

With lights and sirens I made it from West Grace to the hospital on Clay in less than five minutes. Saturday morning traffic in the city was always light, but this morning the downtown streets were as empty as West Grace and Monument, outside Sarah's place.

I punched Doc's number on my cell as I pulled up beside the main entrance.

Sarah answered before the end of the first ring. 'Sailor!' She sounded upset. 'Where are you?'

'Out front,' I said. 'What's going on?'

'Get in here,' she said. 'Doc can tell you. I'm running to the lab upstairs. I'll be back shortly.'

'Okay, are you—?'

'Did you get your suit?' Her voice cracked.

'No.' I tried to lighten the moment. 'I decided to stay in your little pink PJs. I thought it might add something to the investigation.'

'Sailor!'

'Yes, yes! Jesus, yes, Sarah, I got my suit. What's wrong?'

Now she did cry, just a gasp, then a pause to catch her breath. 'Fuck!'

I pushed through the double doors and crossed quickly to the elevators. 'I'll be down there in a minute. Wait for me.'

9:41 a.m.

I'd only been inside the basement morgue at the Medical College of Virginia a few times in my career. What stood out for me about the facility was the stark juxtaposition of state-of-the-art labs and equipment with penny-pinching accoutrements: cheap exam curtains, never-say-die Berber carpet, 1970s orange and green floor tiles, and battleship-grey filing cabinets, desks and office chairs lined up like artefacts from a lost generation. Branching off the main hallway were the doctors' private offices, autopsy rooms, an X-ray facility, and several disorganised labs, their polished granite tabletops crowded with microscopes, test tube racks, notebooks, laptop computers and a veritable battalion of chemistry oddments. Throughout the facility wall space that wasn't lined with faux-panelled cabinetry was stacked, floor to ceiling, with bookcases, each overflowing with notebooks, doorstop-sized textbooks and miles and miles of scholarly journals. A row of gurneys, bedding neatly folded, waited along the hall like cabs at a taxi stand.

The MCV morgue was a physics anomaly: always a cool seventy degrees and bathed twenty-four hours in garish fluorescent light, it was robust to the passage of time or the changing seasons. It might be two a.m. or high noon, blowing a gale or frozen solid outside. Only the wall clock at the end of the main hall, a bright yellow disc sporting a pharmaceutical company logo, noted the passing hours. Weary overhead speakers piped in lyrical orchestra music, not that raucous stuff, Mahler, whatever, I'd heard in the background at the mobile lab.

A pair of med techs in scrubs and surgical masks poured coffee from an ancient percolator tucked inside a token lounge with windows looking onto the corridor below the false sun clock. A lone futon, an old Sony television and a stack of outdated news magazines were the

244

room's only décor. The techs, one of whom wore a surgical hat with colourful frogs all over it, stopped when they saw me. Froghat pulled his mask down to sip from a Boston College mug. He watched me pass with a cold look.

'Hey guys,' I called, 'Lefkowitz in his office?'

'Um ... yeah,' Froghat said. 'Just down the hall.' The other tech stood frozen, the coffee pot in one hand, his surgical mask still tight about his mouth and nose.

'You gonna drink through that thing?' I joked.

'Um, no. Uh, I guess not.' He tugged the mask down and forced a smile.

What is this? I thought, then tried another joke. 'So ... how's business?'

'Holiday weekend, you know.' Froghat chuckled. 'We're running a group rate, Fourth of July sale.'

'Great.' I waited an awkward moment, then said, 'All right, well, I'm off to find the Doc.'

'You Doyle?' Froghat asked.

'Yeah.' I wanted to keep moving, to avoid another confusing conversation with strangers who somehow knew my sister or who sent me off to find Molly Bruckner. But I stopped. 'Sailor Doyle,' I said. 'What can I do for you?'

Froghat just nodded; the rainbow of frogs on his head leaped along. 'Down the hall to your left.'

'Thanks.'

Now I was famous. They'd been discussing me at the morgue; my mother would be so proud. Harper was angry. Doc was calling Fezzamo. Clarkson was whispering in his own lab, and two bleary-eyed techs mainlining caffeine knew who I was. So much for an easy by-the-book investigation to break my cherry.

I glanced at my cell.

Shitty signal down here. They'd have to wait.

No one else moved through the corridor. I figured the skeleton staff was sleeping in, even on the holiday weekend when the morgue might see a spike in corpse traffic. I passed the gurney-sized elevators and hoped Sarah might emerge, but the illuminated numbers above the door showed that she was still on the fifth floor.

My stomach rolled; I needed to find a bathroom. If Lefkowitz was working on Carl and Claire Bruckner, I would be a goner, hurling seventy-five dollars worth of Flatiron Grill food in less than five minutes. I hoped Doc had a deep trash can. The OxyContin was just taking hold. While I could sense that familiar, teenage invincibility revving up, I still felt like a kid who had pounded half a bottle of his father's bourbon before eating a bowl of grilled hamster.

I found Doc's office. The door was ajar; I knocked twice before peeking in.

He wasn't there.

A rear window looked onto an adjacent autopsy room. I let myself into the office and checked out back. Doc stood beside an autopsy table, hunched over a lumpy white sheet, dictating notes into a hanging microphone above the slanted steel table. Like the techs in the lounge, he wore scrubs and a surgical mask. I didn't hear water trickling through the table's drain, so I assumed the post-mortem was over. A raised counter ran the perimeter of the examination room. Along the far wall, I could see where Doc had lined up what looked like stainless steel brownie trays, each one beneath a hanging clipboard and filled with irregularly shaped brown and grey organs. Regretting every time I had slept my way through Professor Hynoski's Anatomy & Physiology lectures, I didn't bother trying to identify them. The small ones, looking like balls of wrinkled socks, those were probably Claire's. There was a digital balance and a tray of nasty-looking dart thermometers, like the one Doc had stabbed into Carl's liver, on the counter as well. *Weigh them, take their temperature, then leave them out on display. It's like an organ ward in here: just-born livers and kidneys all around!*

The examination lights were bright but focused on the body; the rest of the room lay in relative darkness. Only a green-hooded desk lamp cast soft light on a folding table, beside a deep sink. The table was piled high with notebooks, flanking a row of microscopes and a legion of Pyrex dishes with what appeared to be sundry tissue samples. A test tube rack filled with stoppered and labelled blood had been stored behind the glass front of a small refrigerator.

That was Sarah's station: blood, tissue, microscopes, three-inch notebooks, serology chemicals – a salad bar of things I'd never understand.

I watched Doc for a few minutes. It was impossible to see his eyes from here, but the stoop in his shoulders as he bent over the table, dictating to a stenographer who was probably in a beach lounger sipping mimosas about now, was alarming. He looked tired, old, as if he'd been at this all night and had burned the last stores of energy his body could summon. I didn't know why. With a home in Windsor Farms and a thriving practice in Chesterfield, Doc Lefkowitz didn't need to be the one stabbing thermometers into stiffs all over central Virginia. I vowed to buy him as many brandies as he could drink before calling in a Med-Evac.

Doc looked up, stopped his dictation and waved me inside. I slipped out the back door of his office into the cold, antiseptic cave of the autopsy room. My stomach fired a warning shot up my oesophagus: the cold helped, but that smell would get me in the end. I remembered that aroma from Rutgers: the smell of preserved frogs and cow's eyes.

'Morning, Doc,' I said. 'Sorry I missed your call last night. How's it going here?'

He rooted around in a cabinet and emerged with a fresh set of scrubs. 'Sailor, I need you to put these on.' His scrubs were special-order, sporting the orange and blue logo of the New York Mets.

I laughed. 'No thanks, Doc. I don't plan on getting my hands dirty. How about if I just watch, and maybe run for coffee every now and then?'

He stepped into the brilliant glow of the exam lights and tugged his surgical mask down around his neck. His face was pale and damp, despite the cold, his eyes bloodshot and weary. 'I'm afraid I must insist,' he said.

'Damn, Doc, you okay? You look like—'

I never finished my thought.

Doc pulled the small surgical hat off his head. It was ringed with a discoloured line of sweat, like high tide marks on a seawall. But it wasn't the sweat or the bloodshot eyes or the deep worry lines in Doc's face that shut me up.

Doc Lefkowitz had shaved his head bald.

I swallowed, just to buy myself some time. This was either going to be funny or deadly serious. I hoped for funny, but the chances were slim.

'Doc,' I started. 'I know you're getting older, but isn't this a bit—?'

A muffled gasp and shattering glass cut me off. I spun towards Doc's office to find Sarah Danvers standing over a broken Erlenmeyer flask, her arms full of Xerox pages, more notebooks, boxes of microscope slides and at least one legal pad full of multi-coloured writing. Like Doc she wore scrubs, gloves and a surgical mask.

Also like Doc, Sarah had shaved her head clean in what was clearly a hasty operation. A trickle of blood snaked down her left temple; while the top of her head was marked with a connect-the-dots map of nicks and cuts where she had finished the job with a trembling hand. Sarah looked different: embarrassed, strikingly less confident, horrified that I might see her this way. Her lip quivered as she dumped her load onto the folding table with a crash.

'Sailor,' Doc said.

I ignored him.

Sarah glanced at me over her shoulder then straightened up the mess. She flushed, looked away, then glanced back again, as if I'd caught her coming out of the shower or dancing in her underwear. Without hair, she was pale, sickly, too thin, and, again like Doc, tired to the point of collapse. Stress and fear deepened the lines in her face. She rolled her shoulders forward, victim-like, and hunched over her table as if waiting for someone – *me* – to beat her senseless.

Dumbstruck, I stood rooted to Doc's floor. 'Are you two all right?'

Sarah didn't answer. She pushed past me and hurried through Lefkowitz's office and into the corridor. I heard a plaintive cry as she disappeared.

'Doc?' I whispered. Now I was frightened.

'Come sit down.' He handed me the scrubs. 'I have a lot to tell you.'

The breath left my lungs. I felt all at once limp and exhausted. 'But ... we can't ... Doc ...?'

'Take your suit off. Strip down. You can throw your clothes in that biohazard container. I need some of your blood, and I'll check your lymph nodes. I'm going to give you a dose of gentamicin and then, for your own safety, we need to shave your head.'

'Come on, Doc, what is this bullshit? I'm not throwing my suit away – I'll get it cleaned, hell, *twice* if you like, but I paid—'

'Sailor!' he shouted, then quickly lowered his voice. 'Sailor, please try to understand: I'm not *asking* you, son. Get out of your clothes now, and come sit down. I'll explain as well as I can.'

He was shouldering something awesome, and it scared him. He said, 'You're not ready for what I have to tell you, but I have to tell you regardless. To face the day today, you're going to need to grow up about ten years in the next fifteen minutes. I don't doubt that you can do it, and believe me, I care. I honestly do.'

I turned towards his office and the corridor beyond. Listening for Sarah, I felt utter defeat take me. 'Doc,' I said, 'Jenny and I ... I mean ... Jenny's the love—' I let it go; it sounded too much like bullshit.

'You don't answer to me, Sailor,' he said. 'The day I'm perfect, I'll judge you. All right?'

'I'm sorry.'

'I know.' He tapped a cheap aluminium stool with the toe of a six-hundred-dollar loafer. 'Get undressed.'

I slipped out of my jacket, emptied my pockets onto the counter and kicked off my shoes. Standing there in my boxers in Doc's autopsy room I was acutely aware of my body: my pale flesh, my cuts and bruises, my insect bites, my sagging belly and skinny arms. I was glad Sarah had run out; it would be just as embarrassing for her to see me this way, sober and scared and falling apart. It was like being trapped in some ironic short story in which *I* was next in line for Lefkowitz's slanted table.

I pulled the scrub bottoms on, but waited on the starched, uncomfortable-feeling shirt. I didn't want it full of hair clippings.

'Have a seat.' Doc plugged an industrial-sized set of sheep shears into an orange extension cord; they buzzed to life.

'Not until you tell me what's going on,' I said, trying to sound like I retained any control of the Bruckner investigation.

'I'll tell you as we go.' The phone rang in his office. He ignored it to stare me down.

'Fine. Fuck it; it's too hot for hair, anyway. Maybe I'll look better with it shaved.' I grudgingly sat astride the stool. Doc circled behind me. 'All right, what's happened?'

The shears hummed and buzzed over my scalp. A massive clump of hair, a handful that said *there's no going back now*, fell into my lap. I turned it over in my hands then dropped it to the floor.

Doc worked quietly for a moment, then said, 'It was 1348 when the first ships arrived in England, importing from the Mediterranean what the English came to know as *the great mortality* or *the fierce mortality*. Within two years, millions had died; some estimates put it as high as half the population. At first the Scottish thought it was God punishing the English, and they actually gathered an army together with the intention of invading their weakened neighbours, stupid Highland bastards. All they succeeded in doing was capturing the illness themselves. When they retreated from the border, the Scots carried death with them to the furthest forests and valleys of their homeland, decimating their own.

'There was no place to hide. Conditions were miserable, especially in London where the Thames was a sewer, a source of drinking water, a laundry and a public bath. City streets ran with shit, literally, and bacterial infections thrived in the moisture and filth. That spring had been damp, unseasonably rainy, even for England, and the city was like a Petri dish all summer.

'Children were lost by the tens of thousands, dying sometimes within a day or two of infection with *the great mortality*. Parents often left their children alone; they were too terrified even to sit with them through their final hours. The elderly were abandoned as well, or forced into the street at the first sign of infection. Prisons, sheltered hamlets, monasteries and farms weren't spared. Actually, many of those self-contained communities were ravaged even worse than the big cities, sometimes losing all their inhabitants in a matter of days. Some believed it was the beginning of the Apocalypse; a largely illiterate populace always looks to God when things go wrong. Marathon penitence sessions were organised to appease the Christians' angry

Lord, but all that accomplished was to exacerbate the problem. Large groups of people coming together only intensified the rate of infection. Others, naturally, blamed the Jews, and angry mobs attacked and dismembered hundreds of my ilk before the smoke had cleared on the mid-fourteenth century. But that was nothing new for us, after all.'

'You're talking about the plague, right? The Black Death and all that?' I ran my hand over my naked head, feeling the occasional bit of bristle, all Doc had left me.

'Top marks, Sailor,' Doc said. '*Yersinia pestis*, a zoonotic bacteria carried in the blood of rats and transferred from rat to human by—'

'Fleas.' I thought back to the Bruckner farm and the number of times I had slapped at my neck, my wrists, my face. 'Jesus motherhumping Christ – Doc, are you suggesting that the fleas at the Bruckner farm are carrying the plague, that those cats were infected with this whateveritis *pestis*—'

'*Yersinia*,' he said. 'I don't know. It could be something simpler.'

'Terrorists.' I remembered Gretchen Kim in the background of Phil Clarkson's phone message. 'An aerosol form of plague, something Carl Bruckner might have purchased from a terror organisation, something he intended to use tonight, at the Jefferson Hotel, at the Bob Lake fund-raiser. Am I right?'

'It's possible,' Doc said, 'but unlikely, given the circumstances.'

I didn't know what to think. Mechanically, I brushed the hair from my shoulders and pulled the surgical tunic over my head. 'That's why you were calling Fezzamo. That's why you worked on the Bruckners all day yesterday. Isn't it? And that's why you went ... wait, where did you go?'

'Quantico,' he said. 'I needed to pick up a few things from their lab, emergency items, pathology and serology equipment we don't have, even here: gram-negative coccobacillus and bi-polar stain assessments, Wright, Wayson and Giemsa stains for Sarah, along with specific ELISA kits for the plague bacillus we're chasing.'

Doc might as well have been speaking Sanskrit. 'What's an ELISA kit?'

'An enzyme-linked immunosorbent assay kit.'

'Naturally.'

'We have a few of them here; we are a research institution, after all, but if this infection spreads, we'll need more, possibly a lot more. And to answer your next question, no. I didn't know any of this when I was at the farm yesterday. So don't get pissed at me for withholding my fears. If I had thought you were in danger, I would have pulled your entire team off that crime scene in a heartbeat.'

'When did you know?' I asked, turning a slow circle, looking for something productive to do with myself.

'Very late last night,' he said. 'I tried calling, but you were—'

'Shitfaced,' I whispered.

'Unavailable,' Doc corrected, ushering me gently back to the stool. 'Sit down. We're not done yet.' He unwrapped a syringe and a pair of stoppered test tubes he'd found in a drawer and prepared to take a sample of my blood.

'Doc.' I watched him work, as if from across the street. My vision tunnelled and I thought I might lose my balance and fall off the stool. 'Do I have the plague?'

'Probably,' he said, 'but the medication I'm about to give you should take care of it. Phil Clarkson, Gretchen Kim, your young friends Officers Bryson and Lourdes, they have all either been taken to local hospitals or are at the mobile lab receiving treatment.'

'Inoculation from whom?' I asked.

'Not inoculation, treatment.' Doc raised a gloved finger at me. 'There is no inoculation for plague at this time. Knowledge from an epidemiological perspective is alarmingly inadequate. Our only hope is to treat everyone as if they're infected. However, the CDC can get thousands of doses of gentamicin here inside twelve hours; at least that's what they claim. I'm not sure anyone's ever dialled them up with a genuine order before, and certainly not on July fourth. Those two variables could complicate matters considerably, especially if we begin to see exponentially increasing infections and dramatically decreasing doubling times.'

I didn't know what any of that meant. 'Doc, who's treating my troops?'

'For now, a team of first responders and doctors from Richmond and, I believe, Henrico County. Shortly, I expect to hear from the CDC that they're taking control of the entire crime scene. That might have been them on the phone when you came in. They'll want to isolate and provide medication to anyone you and your team came in contact with last night. If there is a silver lining to this whole affair, it is the fact that we have the index case right here.'

'Index?'

'Carl Bruckner,' Doc said, 'as far as I can gather, the first person infected. His wife, Claire, died months ago of a cerebral haemorrhage. I'll have a more accurate estimation of the exact month of her death when I get the lab reports back in a few weeks. I couldn't wait that long on the sputum and blood samples from Carl, but luckily, I happen to have Sarah, my own biochemist, this semester, and she has a cognate in histopathology. Right now, our first responders will be establishing a quarantine area, probably out near your mobile lab. I understand Phil Clarkson went to a concert last night down on the James. That's troubling. Hopefully, Sarah's tests will determine that he isn't infected.'

'He wore a mask most of the day,' I said, going numb all over. 'Does that matter?'

'As my granddaughter would say, "fingers crossed", Sailor, fingers crossed.'

Sarah appeared beside her row of microscopes. Her face shone in the examination lights. She'd washed it, scrubbing away the tear streaks, but her eyes remained puffy and red. I looked at her and tried to think of something comforting to say. All I came up with, however, was, *Thank God I didn't go home last night . . . to my wife and kids. Thank you, God.*

Doc stuck my arm. I watched him fill both test tubes with my blood.

While he worked, he said, 'By the end of the seventeenth century, when the last of the plague was finally cleansed from Europe, tens of millions of people had died, more than Stalin purged in the Soviet Union, more than Hitler killed in the death camps, that reprehensible little cocksucker. In the fourteenth century in England, up to two hundred people a day were marked for burial in common graves. One of Vienna's most picturesque streets, Der Graben, which runs to the front door of the city's proud Stephansdom cathedral, was named after a massive grave for plague dead, right there in the centre of town. Sometimes the bodies were stacked four- and five-deep, all awaiting burial. Legend also has it that plague bodies were fired from catapults into walled cities, closed bastions hoping to escape the pestilence. I suppose you could say that *Yersinia pestis* was the world's first bioterror agent. Death was quick, quick enough to inspire the Italian poet, Boccaccio, to write: "Victims often ate lunch with their friends and dinner with their ancestors in paradise". By the turn of the twentieth century in India, nearly a million people a year were dying of plague. Worldwide estimates reach as high as two hundred million total.'

'Is this spreading through Richmond?' I asked. 'Is there some kind of pandemic about to begin?'

Doc pursed his lips. 'That's a tough question, Sailor. We have to time the interval between contact with our index case, young Carl here, and the onset of symptoms in those of you who were infected.'

'Yes or no?' I pressed. 'Am I going to be responsible for the deaths of ... any ... innocent people in Richmond this week?'

'Of bubonic plague?' Doc shrugged. 'Hopefully not.'

'But ...'

'But pneumonic plague or septicaemic plague could tear through this region in a matter of days, and unfortunately, domestic house cats, while not enzootic mammals like prairie dogs or rats, can transfer the pneumonic version of the plague to human victims.'

He handed my test tubes to Sarah who busied herself with a brown chemical bottle with a black rubber stopper. It looked like something from an old film about a mad scientist with a hunchbacked assistant. Doc said, 'We'll be downright screwed if we discover a pneumonic strain out there. We have no way to contain it, especially if it's of the drug-resistant persuasion.'

'Holy fuck! Holy fuck, Doc! What are you saying? What are those things? What's the difference?'

'Come here.' He adjusted his surgical mask, gave me one and nodded towards a box of rubber examination gloves. I grabbed a pair and wrestled them on, tearing one in the process. I cursed, tore it off and pulled on another more carefully, though my hands were shaking.

Lefkowitz drew back the sheet to reveal Carl Bruckner's body, lying prone on the stainless steel surface, his opaque grey eyes staring at nothing, his purple wrists and fingers looking as if they'd been dyed with grape juice, except for the tips which were still black with finger-print ink. The top of his skull had been removed and sat, forgotten, in the irrigation trench along the edge of the table. Carl's mouth hung open and I could see three silver teeth, glinting brightly in the overhead light. He was smaller than I remembered, almost diminutive on the slanted table. I imagined Claire would have looked like a child when displayed here, her mummified remains already shrunken to a leathery husk.

Carl's ribs and sternum were cut away and his insides removed. Now he was waiting patiently for samples to be drawn from his organs, his stomach contents to be examined, his blood vessels split, his brain weighed, and his intestines drained. Later, one of Doc's assistants, perhaps Froghat himself, would return all of Carl's organs to his abdomen, sew up the Y-shaped incision in his chest and return the top of his skull to its rightful place.

What wouldn't be returned today was Carl's missing foot, his link to Bob Lake, David Carver and the Central Highlands of Vietnam. The whitish knuckles of callused, hastily sewn skin gleamed. Were a missing foot and a decimated platoon enough to drive a former Marine to terrorism? And not just a Marine, but a Marine *officer*, a full-on patriot ...? Did Carl have enough influence with paramilitary groups, anti-American organisations, even Middle Eastern extremists, to pur-chase an airborne version of the plague that had ravaged Europe in the fourteenth century? Could he have sprayed it arbitrarily throughout the Jefferson Hotel in the hope of killing Bob Lake, exacting some kind of half-assed forty-year-old vengeance? I shuddered as I admitted to myself that the pieces of this puzzle were falling neatly into place, whether I approved or not. Carl Bruckner was looking more and more like he really was a broken-down dirt-poor one-legged assassin with a wild plan to kill a presidential candidate – the likely next President of the United States of America.

Lefkowitz leaned over the body, feeling for something. He looked like a baker kneading dough.

'What are you looking for?' I asked.

'Ah, here it is,' he said. 'Come feel this.' He guided my hand beneath Carl's arm and I obediently pressed into the soft flesh with my fingertips until I felt a bump, like a gobstopper or a large gumball, then another. A few inches higher, almost inside Carl's armpit, I found a third, the largest, about half the size of a golf ball.

Doc said, 'If you roll him up on his side, you can see that one.'

I slid a hand under Carl's shoulder and lifted. I nearly pissed my scrubs when I felt a hand close over mine. It was Sarah, helping me rotate the body.

She took hold of Carl's elbow and lifted his arm to an impossible position. Clearly Doc had dislocated the old man's shoulder getting a look at whatever it was I had felt.

'There,' she said, 'see it?' The blood that had trickled from her temple was gone; only a tiny scab remained where she had nicked herself. She wore a look of grim determination; the seductive woman I had met at the CID Christmas party was gone.

'Christ, what *is* that?' I pushed on the golf ball and it squished backwards into Carl's armpit, then bounced forward again. 'It looks like a bad bruise. What's that colour? Is that dried blood?'

'That is what we call a buboe. What you feel under Mr Bruckner's arm are swollen lymph glands. The discoloration of that large one gives us an idea of how far along Carl Bruckner was when he died.'

'Not very far?' I guessed. I had been expecting the Black Death to look significantly more ominous than just a bruise – albeit a bad bruise – and a swollen lymph gland.

'Not very far, no,' Doc said.

'So what killed him?' I asked.

'Seventy-five years of beef, cheese, mayonnaise, eggs, bacon, and the finest North Carolina tobacco.' Doc smiled for the first time since I arrived. 'He had a massive heart attack two days ago, and by my estimates – as fatigued as I am this morning – approximately fifteen to twenty hours *after* contracting *Yersinia pestis* infection. The plague bacteria had time to take hold, but not time enough to kill him. Carl Bruckner is a journal article, hell, a whole chapter all by himself, a classic reminder to always, always, *always* be thorough.'

'Hold on a minute,' I said, 'so what am I seeing here? Carl had bubonic plague, and I'm guessing that means it's the kind of plague that has buboes. How is pneumonic plague or September—?'

'Septicaemic,' Sarah supplied.

'—right, septicaemic plague – so how is it supposed to take out Richmond if Carl's here and everyone who was out at the farm yesterday has been treated? Who's actually *got* pneumonic plague?'

Doc helped Sarah roll Carl onto his back. 'I take it you never found the daughter, Molly?'

My heart lurched. *Find Molly.* How many of my hallucinations had given me that order in the past twenty-four hours? 'Um ... no,' I said, 'not yet.'

'No body?'

'No.' Neither of them were blaming me exactly, but our failure to find Molly Bruckner, a disabled fifty-year-old with a severe seizure disorder and the mind of a child, was entirely my fault.

'Then we have to assume – and by *we*, I mean as well as us, Captain Fezzamo, the Virginia State Police, CDC, the World Health Organisation and FEMA, all of us, in fact – *we* have to assume that she is carrying a highly virulent strain of pneumonic plague.'

I scratched my head, itchy from the unaccustomed shave. 'How did she catch it?'

'From her father, most likely, though cats can spread plague too.' Sarah pulled off her gloves and ran her hands over her own bald pate. She spoke softly, looking down at Carl's open cranium rather than at me, the man who'd brought the infection into her spotless apartment. 'Pneumonic plague is spread by breathing bacteria into the lungs after coming in contact with a bubonic victim. The buboes are painful, and they usually result in death themselves, but the pneumonic version, in the lungs, or the septicaemic version, in the bloodstream, are even worse. They are unstoppable.'

Doc added, 'Molly Bruckner is at least three or four days past the point of infection. If she's still alive, she'll be succumbing slowly to bubonic plague, while spreading incurable pneumonic and septicaemic strains all over St James County. Anyone she talks to, breathes on, brushes past, all of them are at risk of inhaling the bacteria. Nothing can save them.'

'Or those they encounter afterwards?' I asked.

'Exactly,' Doc said. 'Granted, there's an incubation period – we'll need to calculate that – but I'd just as soon not have to.'

Sarah said, 'The last major plague epidemic occurred in 1910 in Manchuria. More than five thousand people were infected, and most died within twenty-four hours of symptoms' onset. A few, a deadly dangerous handful, lived for up to twelve days, spreading the disease until they passed away.'

'Jesus,' I whispered, 'and you think Molly's doing that now?'

'Yes,' Sarah said, '*if* she's still alive. You've got to figure that she's lying dead out there somewhere. She might have been scared by those cats and wandered off, maybe died in the woods near the house. She could be anywhere, Sailor.'

I shook my head. 'St James was all over that place with a blood-hound. If she was dead, that dog would have found her in two minutes in this heat – hell, he'd've smelled her from Nags Head!'

'That's a good point,' Sarah said. 'You're probably right.'

I turned back to the other conundrums I had yet to solve. 'So who tried to saw Claire in half? Why were those strips cut out of Carl's back? Was there someone connected with the family who wanted to turn both Bruckners into collectors' items? Mummies to hang on the Christmas tree, maybe? I can't believe it was Molly – could she really feed her father to her cats?' I gripped the raised edges of the examination table, propping myself up. I badly wanted Doc to cover Carl's body with the sheet again.

'Those are questions for you to answer, Sailor,' Lefkowitz said. 'I don't know where the plague bacteria came from; I'll do some reading on it this morning and have an update for you later today. If Carl was working with a terrorist organisation or some paramilitary group, then who knows what might have happened. It's my job to determine and describe the causes and conditions under which Claire and Carl's deaths took place. I've done that. The homicide investigation, if there is one, is all yours. Well, it was – by now it might have been swallowed up by any number of competing federal agencies.'

'Competing?'

'Competing, collaborating, whatever. It's going to be a shitstorm, as you younger people might so eloquently say.' Doc smirked.

'There's something missing,' I said, 'some key element that will make this all come together. I just can't figure it out yet, except that Carl wanted to kill Bob Lake and as many people close to Bob Lake as possible in as gruesome and vengeful a manner as possible.'

'Maybe Molly can tell you,' Sarah said. 'Maybe Molly *will* tell you.'

'We have to determine where she might have gone,' Doc said, 'because by now she'll be experiencing violent, flu-like symptoms. She'll have a high fever and nasty delusional periods. She'll feel like she's been run over by a car, with real bad all-over body pains, and – most troublesome from our point of view – she'll be having coughing fits, spraying infectious sputum everywhere. If she reaches Richmond, Sailor, we'll have a major tragedy on our hands. Thousands … hundreds of thousands could become infected in a matter of days.'

'Do you think she's heading for the Jefferson Hotel?' Sarah voiced what we all had been thinking.

From Wibbleton to Wobbleton is fifteen miles. From Wobbleton to Wibbleton is fifteen miles. From the Bruckner farm to the Jefferson Hotel is fifteen miles. The stickman genrele is coming. Stickman Genrele Robert Lake is coming to the Jefferson Hotel, only fifteen miles from the Bruckner farm. Retired Marine Genrele Lake.

My legs went rubbery and I felt vomit churning in my stomach. I ran for the sink near Sarah's table as she cried out, 'No, not there!'

I leaned over to find a half-open plastic specimen bag, a big one filled with what was either a massive South American snake decomposing rapidly, or Carl Bruckner's intestines. I couldn't avoid breathing in three-day-old Bruckner guts with last night's revelry. My eyes rolled back in my head, and I collapsed, puking, to Doc's floor.

Back on the road, I rolled for the Bruckner farm, trying hard not to think about bald Sarah Danvers and that night in December when, shitfaced, she invited me to her apartment. If I'd been sober I might not have leapt so willingly, might not have been so desperate at the idea of sex with her, might not have ended up in an affair, and might not have carried plague into her house last night. *But it wasn't your own house, shithead, was it? She's the reason you didn't go home last night and infect your own family, your* children. *So be careful what you wish for.*

I don't know how fast I was going – as fast as my car could on those rough, twisty back roads. My head was still swimming, and my tongue tasted like yesterday's socks. Two hits and one gentamicin shot into the day and I didn't feel any better. My chest hurt too – that was new. I didn't know if it was the goddamned plague, which begins with flu symptoms ... talk about finding the road to Hell on the Equator. Or maybe I was just feeling the after effects of the worst day of my life – *okay, second worst* – and my body was simply tallying its scorecard for the past twenty-six hours.

I don't know. It felt like flu, and what else feels like flu?

Plague. Lovely.

I glanced down: 108 miles per hour. 'You're going to get killed, Sailor,' I said out loud. 'Slow the fuck down. It's only fifteen miles, the distance from Wibbleton to Wobbleton, from the Bruckner farm to the Jefferson Hotel. The general is coming! No, no, no. Not the general, the *genrele*.' I did my version of Frenching up the word, figuring that was how to say it: 'Yup, the *genrele*. Robert Lake, David Carver. Gia Lai Province. LZ Nancy. And Carl Bruckner's foot. The *genrele* is coming, and Carl's got a surprise for him. Don't you, Carl? Welcome, *Genrele* Lake, I'd like to introduce you to my daughter, Molly, my fifty-year-old, batshit-crazy, retarded daughter. What's that around her mouth and nose? Oh nothing, just coagulating plague-infested sputum. It's lovely on crackers.'

Still a few miles from the farm, I Steve McQueened around a tight corner, stomping the brakes and dropping the cruiser into low. I turned through the skid, then rode the gas again. The engine wailed in protest, threatening me audibly with imminent collapse.

Before creeping back over ninety, I punched Doc's cell number on my speed dial. Not surprisingly, it went straight to his voicemail.

'Doc, it's Sailor. I'm almost back to the farm and I'm thinking some of this through. I need you to call me at the mobile lab in about five minutes.' I peeked at my watch. 'I can't figure how Carl imagined this whole thing going down. Was he planning to send Molly to Richmond? To bring her there? Daddy's little girl. Just catapult her body over the dais like some mediaeval land owner?' I swerved to avoid a fallen branch, dropped the phone in my lap, then fumbled around for it. I didn't know if I had lost him, but continued anyway, 'How would she get there, Doc? There's no way she can drive ... Did she know the way? The bus schedules? Could someone else be helping her? I need to talk to Clarkson. Call me back when you can.'

I hung up, uncertain how much of that Lefkowitz had got. 'Call Phil.' I rubbed a hand over my head and came away with a palm flecked with shorn hairs. 'No, screw it, you'll be there in a couple of minutes. Just watch the road.' I cranked up the air-conditioning until it roared as loud as the engine. 'There's going to be hysteria. We won't be able to keep a lid on this. Word'll get out. People are going to riot.' I fished into the pocket of my scrubs for a smoke. 'And I've got the plague. Not crabs, lung cancer, not even the fucking trots, but pandemic-strain plague. And guess what? *I* introduced it to Richmond!'

I flipped open my phone, tried to remember Phil's number, then slapped it shut again. 'Fuck it.' Dense Virginia forest flashed past my window in a mottled green and brown blur. I inhaled deeply on the cigarette, held the smoke a moment to calm down, then exhaled a guilty whisper. 'Thank you, God. No matter what, no matter. Thank you for keeping me out last night, away from Jenny and the kids. Look after them for me today. Please God.'

11:06 a.m.

Cresting a blind rise beneath a low-hanging archway of elm branches, my cruiser about lifted off the pavement. My stomach flopped like it used to on the kiddie roller-coasters at Seaside Heights a hundred years ago.

A St James County police car had been parked diagonally across both lanes of whatever back country road I was on. Lights flashing, the uniformed deputy ran up the street towards me, waving his arms over his head.

'Holy shit!' I stomped the brakes and fought to keep the ass end from fishtailing into the raspberry bushes. I opened my door, already yelling, 'Stupid motherfucker! Don't they teach you anything at the frigging academy any more? You don't close a road behind a blind hill! Jesus Christ!'

He wasn't hearing me. Still jogging towards my car, he shouted, 'This road's closed! You're going to have to turn around.'

'Stop!' I yelled. 'Stop right there!'

He didn't. Clearly, he had seen too many slasher films to take orders from a bald lunatic in hospital scrubs on a country road.

I drew my Glock, levelled it at him and shouted again, 'Stop right there, dumb-ass!'

The deputy, no more than twenty-five, threw his hands up. 'Whoa! Whoa, mister! What the hell?'

'Just stop! Don't come near me. Stop where you are.'

'What? Wait. I don't ...?'

'I'm Detective Doyle, from CID Homicide.' I found my badge on the dashboard and waved it at him.

Seeing I was a cop, he got pissed in a hurry. 'What the hell are you doing drawing on me, asshole?' His hand fell to his own hip.

'Saving your fucking life is what I'm doing.' I dropped my gun on the front seat. 'I'm infected. Don't come up here. You got a wife? Kids?'

'What?' He looked confused now, but at least he wasn't coming any closer.

'I'm infected,' I said again. 'The farmhouse up there is my crime scene. I was at the Bruckner place all day yesterday. Didn't they tell you anything? The guys at the mobile lab, by the old Phillips 66 place on Goochland, did they not brief you this morning?'

'No, no, they didn't. They just called to say I should come down here and—' He looked back and forth across the lane, then said, 'Shit, no.'

'It's all right,' I said. 'You got a wife?'

Like any cop, he didn't welcome references to his family while on duty, not from anyone, anywhere. His face reddening, he said, 'Yeah. Why?'

'Then don't be a hero today. If they call you up anywhere near that farmhouse, you play deaf on the radio. You understand? Or just clear the hell out of here and pretend like you got a call from a dying relative, anything. Don't go up there.'

What I was telling him went against everything he had been trained to do, not to mention several of his direct orders. I could tell, even from twenty paces, that half of him wanted to tell me to go screw myself, while the other half was confused, scared witless. He finally asked the right question. 'What're you infected with?'

'Plague. Old-time fuck-you-up plague.'

His mouth lolled open for a second, his eyes wide. 'Hey, maybe I should call … are you … ? I think I ought—'

'What's your name?'

'Jeffries, Ken Jeffries.' He took off his hat and wiped a sleeve over his brush-cut hair. It came away wet. The farms and forests northwest of Richmond were gearing up for another scorcher.

'Deputy Jeffries, I'm Detective Doyle, Sailor Doyle, Virginia State Police. There is a potential plague pandemic spreading right now from the Bruckner farm. Obviously, your brass and my brass don't want anyone to know, and that's probably a wise decision. You're doing a nice job out here, and I suggest you keep on doing it – once you've moved your car out of this gulley. Don't let anyone pass going north. And if that's all you do today, you're one of the fortunate ones. If your sergeant calls you anywhere near the old Phillips 66 station, or worse, up to that farm, I want you to ignore him. Okay? Fuck it, it isn't worth dying for. This is someone else's mess. Stay clear of that place for a couple of hours and the CDC will probably come in and take the whole thing over anyway.'

'I don't know if I can do that, Detective.' Embarrassed at how frightened he had looked, Deputy Jeffries tried to regain a measure of his bullshit, tough-guy exterior.

'It's your choice, Jeffries,' I said, 'but today is not a day for heroes.' I got back in my cruiser, passed him on the shoulder and continued towards the farmhouse.

I encountered two more roadblocks before reaching Goochland Lane and the Phillips 66 station. I tinned my way through both of them without a problem. Jeffries had called ahead.

The Phillips 66 had been turned into a command post: with a second mobile lab, half a dozen state and county cruisers, multiple unmarked units, three ambulances and a rescue squad truck, the parking lot was full for the first time in decades. Flashing red, blue and white lights coloured the cracked plaster and concrete, turning its mildewed walls a roiling rainbow of colour. About a quarter-mile south on Pitcairn several news vans had been blocked by St James deputies. Their camera crews jockeyed for the best place to set up, working the long-distance camera shot.

Phil Clarkson stepped from our mobile lab. His grey suit and yellow tie were accessorised with a surgical mask and examination gloves. His pale face was damp and splotchy with razor burn, and his tension palpable from across the parking lot. Phil hadn't had much hair to begin with, so shaving his head didn't change his appearance much. He stopped about fifteen feet away. 'You get a shot?'

Eat shit, Phil.

'Good morning, Phil,' I said. 'Yeah, Doc stuck me a few times down at the morgue. He gave me pills too, something to help the gentamicin.

He says it'll kill this thing off in about ten days.'

'Good.' Phil tossed me a mask. 'Put this on, anyway. There's no access up at the farm, unless you're in a hazmat suit. You got one?' His voice cracked. He was frightened, and trying hard to keep his composure. This was obviously more than he had ever tackled with the Roanoke City PD.

'You all right?' I felt like an idiot in scrubs and wing-tips.

'We fucked up bad, Sailor,' Phil said. 'We should've called, should've let someone know. I mean—'

'Hold it there, Phil.' I pulled the mask over my face. 'We didn't ask for this. We can't be held accountable for finding those buboes on Carl's body. That's Doc's fuck-up. We did our job.'

'We didn't call for help!' Phil shouted.

'We didn't *need* help.' I stayed calm. This was still my crime scene, technically. I couldn't afford another meltdown this morning. 'We gathered evidence, worked with Doc's office, shared our concerns with Animal Control and even called in the mobile lab to expedite the assessments. I left a message for Harper last night to note my concerns and to justify keeping the lab open overnight. This bullshit this morning is Doc's nightmare. I don't know how quickly plague pandemics are usually detected around the world, but the fact that Doc located the index case within twelve hours of visiting the crime scene has got to count for something. Our job – yours and mine – was to investigate a homicide, which is exactly what I think we should do.'

'You don't know,' Phil whispered.

'Know what?'

'We've been benched. We're under quarantine, you, me, Lourdes, Bryson, the Animal Control officers, everyone they can find who was in that house yesterday. We're not going anywhere.'

'Where's Harper?' I asked, ignoring the fact that I might be ordered to sit on my hands all weekend.

'On his way,' Phil said. 'Fezzamo's up at the farm now with a researcher from the Bioterror and Infectious Disease Lab at Quantico, some scared-looking suit named Hurtubise, and a rep from FEMA, Dr Novosel something. He's pretty pissed, wants your ass in a hoagie roll with chips.'

'FEMA, Jesus. What are they doing here?'

'Nothing yet.' Phil shrugged. 'It's too early. Everyone's mobilising at once. No one knows what's going to happen this afternoon?'

'The CDC here?'

'That's the state ME's call, but I'm sure they'll be on the horn together this morning.'

'What kind of news coverage are we getting?'

'Gretchen and Steve have it on the TV.' Phil turned towards the lab. 'Mostly local stuff so far. Fezzamo wants to have a statement prepared before the national and cable channels get hold of it.'

I followed him in. 'Any helicopters?'

'Not yet,' he said. 'I don't think they know what to look for. They could fly over the Bruckner farm all day and not see anything but techs in hazmat suits. They'll probably think a meth lab exploded.'

'Or run some bullshit story about anthrax or local militia wanting to overthrow the government.' I climbed the steps into the combination RV and crime scene lab. Gretchen Kim and Steve Cornwell were writing names on small pieces of sticky paper and attaching them to a wall-sized map of the greater Richmond area. Steve spoke on the phone, I guessed with Doc or maybe Sarah.

Into the phone, he said, 'Until we find someone who exhibits symptoms, we won't have a baseline for our first interval ... yes, I understand, but they would all have been infected at approximately the same time yesterday morning ... they are all here now except Detective Doyle—' He saw me come in, paused to look me over, then said, 'Never mind. He just got here ... uh huh ... I understand ... that's correct; her name is Grace Wentworth. She's the principal at Jefferson Middle School in Richmond ... we can find the dispatcher and the road officers Detective Doyle encountered at Division Headquarters ... thanks, Sarah ... no problem; we'll call back shortly.' Steve hung up. 'We have to find Grace Wentworth and any teachers or clerical staff on duty yesterday afternoon.' He wrote Wentworth's name on a sticky note and hung it on the map near the intersection of I-295 and Route 1, Division Headquarters. Several stickies marked the same spot: Shantal Carmody, Dave Stephens, Tony Cotillo and Cheryl Baskin.

Gretchen Kim adjusted her surgical mask, and said, 'Good morning, Detective.'

'Hi Gretchen,' I said. 'So what's going on?'

Her eyes lit up; she tried to smile at me, despite the mask. 'Sergeant Clarkson has been helping us retrace everyone's steps yesterday. The CDC, FEMA and the World Health Organisation will expect us to have timed the interval between Carl's infection – which we figure was three to five days ago, but we note down as six a.m. yesterday, when we can confirm contact with uninfected subjects – and the onset of symptoms in the first victims who encountered him after that. For example, if Officer Lourdes, who made initial contact with the index case, began showing symptoms at six a.m. today, and Sergeant Greeley, who had contact with Officer Lourdes at nine p.m. last night, begins showing symptoms at nine p.m. tonight, we'll know we have about a twenty-four-hour incubation period for this particular strain of *Yersinia pestis*. Twenty-four to forty-eight hours are normal for colony formation, but we can't be certain. Plague epidemiology isn't something we get to study every day.'

I saw where they were headed with this. 'And those times let us know how long we have to get everyone treated, because after twenty-four hours—'

'Right,' Gretchen said, looking over a legal pad full of names and times. 'Things get more difficult.'

'And you expect that these intervals will begin to get shorter?' I asked.

'Not necessarily,' Gretchen said. 'Everyone infected with this strain of bacteria will probably begin demonstrating symptoms at about the same rate, accounting, of course, for differences in overall health, whether the victim is already on any antibiotics, and a few other variables.'

'The problem is not the time of onset as much as the exponential nature of the victims' contacts,' Steve added. 'If you aren't contagious for thirty-six hours, then we don't have much to worry about. You're here; you're treated, and we can eliminate everyone you encountered since yesterday morning. However, if you were contagious after ten hours or fifteen hours, then we have to assume anyone you were with last night or this morning is infected as well.'

267

'My family,' Phil said quietly.

That's it. That's why he's given up.

Gretchen continued, 'So for now, we're trying to make contact with anyone you might have infected yesterday, because Carl can't tell us how long after he encountered the bacteria that he began exhibiting symptoms.'

'Lefkowitz says he died of a heart attack about fifteen to twenty hours after infection.' I took a seat and looked over the dozens of bits of sticky paper Gretchen and Steve had already affixed to the map. It was a real-life example of exponential growth, a stats professor's dream.

'That's true,' Steve said. His head nearly scraped the ceiling every time he stood upright. 'But Doc can't know how long Carl was infected before he began exhibiting symptoms, even with underdeveloped buboes. If this strain of bacillus works as quickly as Lefkowitz fears, the greater Richmond area and maybe even central Virginia are in deep, deep trouble. Fifteen hours takes us all the way back to the first St James officers on the scene, to Grace Wentworth, everyone on duty at Division Headquarters yesterday, the staff at that diner you visited – it's a lengthy list. And God help us if even one infected person, just *one*, drove up to DC or flew out of Richmond Airport. It's more than I can imagine.'

Gretchen said, 'Why did you … ?' but thought better and let the rest of her question muffle inside her mask.

'Why did I what?' I asked. 'You got something on your mind, Gretchen?'

'No, Detective, sorry,' she said.

'Good,' I said, trying again not to get angry. My actions, directives, decisions, everything I did yesterday would be called into question eventually. An embarrassing degree of scrutiny was just beginning.

Phil said, 'They're wondering why you went to Division and then to lunch yesterday, why you left the crime scene to meet with Dr Wentworth.'

'Oh, are they?' I said.

'Yes,' Steve whispered, avoiding my gaze.

'Well, lemme see,' I started. 'I went to Division yesterday morning to

268

collect what I thought was a helpful fax from the National Personnel Records Center in St Louis. I met Dr Wentworth, because I felt she would have useful information on the Bruckners, especially Molly, and finally, I went into the city because at the time, I didn't know I had the fucking plague, and because I goddamned felt like it! Any other fucking questions? Huh? Anyone else want to sit in the driver's seat on this?'

'No,' Gretchen muttered, 'but we do need to find Dr Wentworth right away.'

I took a breath, struggled to inhale deeply through the mask, then pulled it off my face. 'Sorry guys,' I said. 'It doesn't do us any good for me to lose my temper, but you two focus on the epidemiology, and I'll focus on the homicide investigation.'

'You have a number for Dr Wentworth?'

'It's in my phone,' I said. 'I'll go get it. I need a smoke anyway.'

'Wait' – Steve grabbed my arm – 'here it comes.' He released the MUTE button on the television remote. An attractive Channel 9 reporter, dressed in a conservative suit, her hair pulled into a bun, stood flanked by a thick patch of elm, oak and hickory trees. She held a microphone and a small pad and stared into the camera in mock consternation. She had no idea what was happening, but she tried to sound convincing regardless. As the camera panned, I could just make out the flashing lights, the mobile lab and the rusted Phillips 66 sign overlooking the parking lot outside.

'Why doesn't she sweat?' Phil said. 'I'm soaked through to my shorts and she's not even flushed.'

'She's a television reporter,' Gretchen said. 'That makes her an android.'

'Oh well, that explains it.' Phil dug in the lab's fridge for a water bottle, gripping the handle tightly to hide his trembling fingers.

Frowning for effect, the pretty reporter said, 'Police and rescue officials have refused to comment on what appears to be a recent double homicide here in rural St James County. I am reporting from the corner of Pitcairn Road and Goochland Lane, just west of the Hanover County line, where an elderly couple, Claire and Carl Bruckner, were found dead inside their nineteenth-century farmhouse.

Deputy Medical Examiner Dr Irving Lefkowitz and techs from the Medical College of Virginia were on the scene yesterday to assess and transport the bodies to Richmond for autopsies later this week. While police spokesperson Lieutenant Edward Harper remains silent on the causes of death, he assures us that the homicides were not the result of armed intruders or a drug transaction gone awry, leaving us only to speculate that the victims knew or were possibly related to their attacker. As you can see from this vantage point, there are numerous state and county police cruisers, at least three rescue squad teams, and two of the Virginia State Police Mobile Lab units. Several officers appear to be wearing hazmat suits. No county offices have reported a hazardous materials spill in this area today, so significant unanswered questions remain as we continue to follow this emerging story. We will have more details when they arise. From rural St James County on this Fourth of July morning, this is Jessica Beech.' The reporter brushed a lock of hair away from her forehead and said, 'Back to you, Mike.'

Steve said, 'See? They don't have anything solid, nothing confirmed.'

'And Harper is keeping quiet, at least so far,' Phil added. 'That's got to have come directly from Fezzamo. There'll be hell to pay otherwise.'

'Whatever,' I said, genuinely not caring if Captain Fezzamo's reputation with the news media took a hit today. 'I'll get Wentworth's number. I want to call my wife and get my smokes anyway.'

The news programme went to commercial as I stepped outside into the merciless heat. Before Steve muted the sound again, I heard the irritating strains of 'Dixie', reminding everyone in Richmond that Ashland Chrysler was having a Fourth of July sale all weekend.

I jogged a couple of steps to escape from that infuriating bastardised version of the South's palsied national anthem. 'Too hot to buy a car, anyway,' I mumbled. 'Two hillbilly retards in an orange racecar … stupid motherhumping—'

I stopped twenty feet short of my cruiser. 'Holy shit. Holy shit!' My skin chilled into goose pimples and I weathered another warning clench of dizzying nausea from my stomach. It'd be dry heaves this time.

The Phillips 66 parking lot was abuzz with activity. State and county officers talked on radios and cell phones, poured over maps and satellite photos or moved about in hazmat suits, some hauling biohazard boxes containing cats, goats, sheep, perhaps even a few chickens that had died from complications due to respiratory infections or attacks by starving cats.

I watched them work without really registering what they were doing. Unlike the chefs at the Flatiron Grill, the Phillips 66 lot was full of confused Keystone cops, no one quite sure what to do. It was too early in the investigation; they'd been called in three hours before they were really needed. No one knew anything except that members of my team had contracted a bubonic version of *Yersinia pestis* at Carl and Claire Bruckner's farm, that their daughter Molly was missing, and that Ashland Chrysler could match or beat any sticker price in the metro area through Monday night.

'Phil!' I shouted towards the lab. A handful of cops and technicians turned to listen.

'Yeah?' Phil stuck his head through the door. His humiliation was as red in his cheeks as Carl's livor mortis.

'I'm running up to the farmhouse,' I said.

'You can't.' He stepped outside. 'Fezzamo's orders.'

'I'll worry about Fezzamo.'

'You got a hazmat suit?'

'Yeah, in my trunk.' I climbed into my car, cranked up the air-conditioning and stomped the gas pedal. 'Two hillbilly retards in an orange racecar.'

Rolling slowly past the red cinderblock hovel with the buried pickups alongside the driveway, I called Jenny. She answered on the third ring.

'Hey, baby! You didn't call last night.' She sounded like a worried wife trying hard not to sound like a worried wife. 'You okay?'

'I'm fine, Jenny. Listen, I have about two minutes, and then I'll have to call you later. But please do me a favour and stay in today.'

'Stay in? What do you mean?'

'You watching the news?'

'No, Sailor.' Now she laughed. 'You know that if the TV is on around here, it's an animated bear singing about how to avoid strangers with candy. What's going on?'

'Nothing I can tell you about right now,' I said. 'Just please promise me that you'll stay in today – and no guests, nobody. All right?'

'You're making me nervous.'

'Nervous enough to stay inside?'

'What's going on?'

'Hopefully, nothing. But don't believe what you hear on the news. I'm hoping everything's fine, and I'll get back to you as soon as I can.' I tried to flatten the tremor in my voice, but she caught me. The gap between us might have grown in the past few years, but when the smoke cleared, no one would ever know me as well as Jenny.

'You don't sound right, Sailor. You get any sleep last night?'

'Not much,' I lied. 'We had the mobile lab going late, and I had to run to the morgue this morning. The two dead bodies I told you about yesterday are causing a bit of a stir. There's an old connection between them and Bob Lake, but more than that, I don't really know too much.'

That seemed like enough information to placate her, at least for now. She lowered her voice to a conspiratorial whisper. 'Is this some kind of political scandal?'

'Yes.' I decided to run with that, anything to throw her off the awful truth. 'I suppose it is, and with Lake coming to Richmond tonight, we're trying to keep the whole mess quiet.'

'Why do I have to stay in?'

'Because I'm asking you nicely,' I said. Any tension in my voice now would be abundantly familiar to her.

'Okay, okay,' she said. 'But I want Edward Norton to play you in the movie when this all breaks.'

'I'm sure he'll be happy to help us out,' I said. 'How are your children?'

'My daughter is being an angel, but your son is missing his father and whining about not seeing you at the ool yesterday.'

I turned onto the dirt drive leading up to the Bruckner farmhouse. Someone had tied yellow police tape across the lane. I drove through it. 'Can I talk to him?'

'Sure,' Jenny said, 'hang on.'

I stopped beside the pond where I had hallucinated my encounter with the dead stray. Waiting for Ben, I peered into the brush, hoping to find the dog's inanimate corpse, rotting in the heat.

Ben picked up the phone. 'Hi, Daddy!'

'Hey monkey-face! How are you doing?'

'I'm waiting for you, Daddy. When are you coming home?' No one could sound quite as disappointed as a four-year-old boy.

'Pretty soon, buddy, but definitely tonight; I promise.'

'You missed the ool. I swam with Mommy, but she couldn't come too far out, because she had Annie in the floaty chair.'

'Did Annie like the water?' I wiped my eyes. There had never been time for the things I should have been doing, but somehow I'd always found ample time for jerk-off bullshit. Did Carl feel like this about Molly once? Did he love her like this? Did my father love me this much? Or Marie? That he did. That much I knew. But I could one-up my father in the long run; I could do this better.

273

Ben got distracted, said something to Jenny, then giggled so hard, I laughed along with him. 'Ben,' I said. 'Ben! Are you there?'

'Sorry, Daddy.'

'That's okay, monkey.'

'Will you wake me up when you get home later?'

'I will.'

'Me and you.'

I pressed my lips hard together and swallowed before answering, 'You and me.'

'Bye, Daddy. I love you.'

'I love you, too, buddy. Tell Mommy I'll call her in a little while.'

'Okay, bye.' He hung up.

I sat looking into the tiny LCD screen on my phone, where the word DISCONNECTED blinked at me. 'Yeah, I know,' I said.

I was about to flip it closed when the writing changed. Between flashes, the word DISCONNECTED morphed through fuzzy pixels to: FIND MOLLY, SAILOR.

'Okay,' I said to the empty car. 'I'll find her. I know where she is.' I rolled down the window. 'You hear me, Molly? I'm coming! Don't be scared; I'm on my way!'

I got out of the cruiser and fell to my knees in a dusty rut. 'Hang on, shithead. It's not much longer now.' I grabbed two handfuls of damp ferns and held on. 'This must have scared the shit out of those poor bastards back in the fourteenth century, though. Hallucinations: those would have been the Devil. Nice.'

Jenny, the love of my life, the reason I never picked up my sister, Jenny my wife is fucking Bob Lourdes. RML. Robert Michael Lourdes. I'll feed him some coagulating sputum. Dickhead. But I've gotta get through the day first. I've got to get this bottled up.

'That's it. That's it. Keep your head in the game, Sailor.' I let go the ferns and used the open door to heft myself up. The scrubs I had borrowed from Doc's autopsy room didn't have an adjustable waistband so my .45 kept pulling them halfway down my ass. I lit a cigarette, inhaled a lungful of contentment, fixed my badge to a neck lanyard and popped the trunk.

I hadn't lied to Phil: VASP regulations since the September 11 attacks required me to have a hazmat suit in my car. It was zipped into a nylon bag emblazoned with the VASP crest, the FEMA logo, and a patch from the Department of Homeland Security, a veritable crowd of state and federal executives encouraging me to don that ridiculous space suit and march brazenly into the war on terrorism.

Sod them. I was already infected with plague. That was enough patriotism for one morning. If I was to track down, apprehend or even kill Molly Bruckner today, I'd just as soon do it in my borrowed New York Mets pyjamas.

I dug around beneath an old raincoat and a spare Kevlar vest to find my nylon tactical belt. I made sure it had two extra ammo clips, a pair of handcuffs and a canister of pepper spray, along with my old road holster. It needed a quick adjustment to accommodate the extra pounds I had picked up since Ben was born. Strapped on, it looked pretty comical with my sweaty surgical scrubs and my muddy wingtips, but it made me feel better.

I finished my smoke and lit another instead. The OxyContin pumped me full of bright yellow happiness, and the cigarettes were North Carolina candy. I would have sold what was left of my soul for a Scotch, but that would have to come later. My thoughts were a beat or two behind my vision, but like any lunchtime drunk with a good buzz, I felt confident I knew what I was doing. I stuck my cell phone into the breast pocket and hooked my handheld radio onto a belt clip.

My Remington 12-gauge stood in a quick-release stand between the two front seats of my cruiser. I stared at it through the open door for almost a minute before deciding that I wouldn't need it. I had forty-two rounds for my handgun; if I wasn't able to bring down Molly Bruckner before she reached a populated area, then I wasn't much of a cop.

DISCONNECTED.

The phone's admonishment flashed in my mind's eye. I wallowed in a moment's self-pity over Jenny's affair with Bob Lourdes, her RML. I cursed myself for not asking her outright, but I didn't know what I would have said if she confirmed it for me: *That's fine, honey, because I've been humping Sarah Danvers, a younger, sexier, smarter and hornier woman than you'll ever be, and I've been at it for six months.* I tried to put it out of my head, that whole bucket of bullshit, but it dug in: Molly's disappearance, Marie's death, Doc's disappointment, Phil's embarrassment, Sarah's look of shock and horror, the way her baldness made her hollow-cheeked and emaciated, too thin. All of it found a solid purchase in my mind and threw my timing off, confused me and enhanced that senseless-all-over feeling I was getting as the OxyContin mingled with the gentamicin Doc had stabbed into my shoulder. And beneath it all, bubbling at a low boil, was Carl Bruckner, the enigmatic ex-Marine with his anti-Lake manifesto and his missing foot. Was he a caring father and a forgiving war hero, suffering the cruel circumstances of his time in the Central Highlands? Or was Carl a vicious criminal, bent on revenge and willing to sacrifice his daughter for a thimbleful of payback? And how much was he like my own father? Dad had lost his daughter and given up on life. I never blamed him, because in the end, his decision to come apart made twisted sense to me.

The pieces spiralled around one another, trying to fit.

Carl had died before losing his daughter.

Marie had died before Dad.

Molly had developed Lennox-Gastaut Syndrome as a toddler.

Dad had lost the ability to feel with his fingertips.

Carl and Claire had raised Molly in what Dr Wentworth called a loving, caring home.

Fragments of conversations, memories, questions and ideas thudded and banged around inside my head. Less than half of it would be useful in solving the Bruckner case, but I wouldn't be entirely in focus again until I either gave up on the connection my mind seemed determined to draw between Molly and Marie or until I discovered what intangible threads were holding them together. My hallucinations, all the interchanges and encounters I'd had over the past thirty hours, seemed determined for me to find the link, whatever it was, that had random encounters spinning into psychotic episodes all with a missing sister/dead sister common denominator.

DISCONNECTED.

Yes, I suppose I was, but should I have been surprised at that? The OxyContin label almost never reads: *take 11 and attempt to solve homicides*.

I rubbed a hand over my newly smooth head and watched a state police car, an unmarked sedan, bump and jounce over the pond road. I guessed it was Captain Fezzamo, Old Fezziwig, returning to the mobile lab to alert the governor and the Board of County Supervisors that we were a day late in stopping a potential plague epidemic because one of his rookie investigators had fucked things up like an international champion.

He pulled over when he saw me.

'Mother of God, Doyle, you look like hell.' Fezzamo hauled himself out of his car with both hands. He was an unimposing figure, six inches shorter than me, with bushy eyebrows, a trim moustache and greying hair combed straight back off his forehead. He was weighed down by an enormous stomach and I always imagined him sitting with his secretary, scheduling official responsibilities around meals.

I thought, *Damn, he does look like Vito Corleone, Uncle Hucker. You're right!*

Fezzamo wore an expensive suit beneath a zip-up hazmat outfit that he had opened far enough to push back the head gear. His shirt and jacket were soaked through and his face was moist, but he donned a surgical mask before approaching me. To alleviate his anxiety, I tossed the cigarette into the mud and pulled my own mask back into place. We looked like two rejects from a seventies sci-fi movie.

'Did Dr Lefkowitz make you shave your head?' Fezzamo leaned awkwardly against the front fender of his car. At about sixty years old, he didn't look like much, but he had earned every bit of that scrambled egg on his hat brim. He had been investigating murders before I was born. Talking to him one-on-one was like getting physics tutoring from Albert Einstein.

'Yes, sir.' I tried to keep my thoughts together, using every strategy I'd ever run past a hesitant bartender at two-thirty a.m. 'Just this morning. Apparently I was bitten by enough of those fleas to merit the medication, the haircut and the new duds. I'm still not sure how I'm going to explain to my wife that I've left a Brooks Brothers suit in the biohazard trash at MCV hospital.'

'You get out of this alive and she'll forgive you, Doyle. Don't worry about that,' he said. 'But, son, I wish that you had called us yesterday. I know you were out on your own for the first time, and I'm not too happy with Phil Clarkson, either. He should have known better than to sneak out of here without tying up all the loose threads. But we've got a gargantuan shitstorm coming, and there's nothing we can do to stop it, except to find that daughter and to burn this whole goddamned place to the ground.'

'Captain, please don't blame Phil,' I started. 'He was just—'

'Now listen, Doyle.' Fezzamo raised both palms at me, as if I was one of his grandchildren. 'I'm the goddamned captain, and I'll be pissed off at whomever I choose. Today, I choose you and Phil. You've got two dead bodies; that's fine, but these animals with all that shit coming out of their noses, that's either terrorism, or it's a demon from Hell.'

'We called Animal Con—'

'I know you did, Doyle' – the captain waved me off – 'and it's nothing personal, and Lieutenant Harper probably should have thought twice before sending you out by yourself, but what's done is done. I need you to get back to the quarantine at the lab, to stay on whatever medication Lefkowitz gave you, and to get healthy as quickly as you can. I don't know much about you, but Harper seems pleased with your work so far. You got out here and got over your head in a hurry; so the take-away message for you is to call for help when you need it. You understand?'

I tried again to defend myself and my team. 'Captain, our plague victim, Carl Bruckner – who Doc's calling the index case – died of a heart attack less than twenty-four hours after contracting plague. It was a one-in-a-million shot, and Doc didn't catch it at the scene. The fact that he worked all night, drove to Quantico and diagnosed the *Yersinia pestis* infection as quickly as he did is a testament to him certainly, but it's also a testament to my team's work at this scene yesterday. Now, I think that you ...' I let my voice fade. I didn't know what I thought Fezzamo should do, and he clearly didn't care what I thought anyway.

'Doyle, do you know who I just got off the phone with?'

'No, sir.'

'David Carver. Do you know who David Carver is?'

I reached inside the car for my notebook, then decided I didn't need it to retell Carver's tale. 'Actually, yes sir, I do. David Carver was a platoon officer in a Marine company under Bob Lake's command in 1968. Lake was apparently a Marine liaison who started at MACV when General Abrams first travelled to Vietnam to await orders to relieve General Westmoreland of his duties. Carl Bruckner's company, and Carver's platoon, took heavy losses in the Central Highlands near the South Vietnamese city of Pleiku. I'm guessing that as Bob Lake was promoted, he was able to draw his personal staff from officers in the country at the time. I am not certain whether he developed a relationship with Lieutenant Carver in 1968 or if it was later, but that's where they first came into contact with one another.'

Captain Fezzamo was obviously impressed with my information.

'That's very good, Doyle. I can see you've managed to get some homework done in the past twenty-four hours. Excellent. Now, I don't know all that about Vietnam, but I will tell you that David Carver is probably going to be the next White House Chief of Staff and a powerful figure in the Republican Party. Of course, half of me doesn't really give a shit, but the other half is not interested in having anyone like Carver blaming the Virginia State Police for screwing up their little party at the Jefferson later tonight. We're a key state in this election, Doyle, and this year we could go either way. Our failure to contain a plague epidemic will ruin us, even if everyone is treated and not a soul dies.'

'It's my understanding that David Carver didn't serve with much bravery in battle,' I added, as if that meant anything to Fezzamo forty years later.

'Hell, Doyle, neither did I! But you're missing the point. I am not about to have ... actually, no, now's not the time.' He pushed off the fender with one hand, as if to leave. 'I want you to get back to the lab. You're under quarantine. While there, I need you to tell Gretchen Kim and Steve Cornwell absolutely everything about your actions after you left here last night: where you went, whom you met, how many waitresses brought you drinks, how many nurses you diddled, how many parking lot attendants you told to fuck themselves, everything you can remember. And then, Doyle, you're off duty. You'll stay in quarantine until the CDC or FEMA lets you go home, and then I want you home until you finish every one of those pills Lefkowitz gave you.' He found a pen in his shirt pocket, then said, 'He did give you some pills to take, didn't he?'

'Yes, sir,' I said. 'Do you need something to write on, Captain?'

'No, I don't.' He stepped closer, taking me by surprise. Looking into my face, he held up his pen, and said, 'I want you to watch the tip.' He moved it slowly back and forth near my left eye, then repeated the process on the other side. 'Okay, good.'

My whole face felt numb, and it was hard to track on the pen tip. I suddenly became acutely aware of how much I was sweating in the humidity, which only intensified the water works on my forehead and face. I tried not to get upset. Telling the captain to back off would have been a career-ender this morning. I was already in enough deep shit. Fezzamo was being kind while working out a plan to cover the VASP's collective ass. Harper would be another story. He'd have steam blowing out his ears by the time he finished with me.

'You stoned, Doyle?'

'Jesus Christ, no!' I feigned offence. 'Why?'

'Your pupils are bouncing like basketballs,' he said. 'If we were on the road, I'd have you in cuffs already.'

'I've not taken anything, sir.' More sweat ran between my shoulder blades. Then a flash of brilliance came to me. 'Well, that is except for whatever Doc gave me in that shot.'

'He shot you up, too?' Fezzamo asked.

'Yes,' I said, 'I guess it's part of the treatment – maybe I'd gone too many hours to risk starting with the pills alone. I can't remember what he called it, but he said it might make me feel a bit strange.'

This stroke of genius on my part appeared to appease the old man. 'That probably explains it,' he said. 'Go on back to the lab. There's a pull-down cot in the front and plenty of air-conditioning. Take a nap, a long one. You look like you've been attacked by a werewolf, and your skin's the colour of city snow. I'm surprised Lefkowitz let you come back out here at all.'

'He wasn't too keen on the idea, sir, but I think I know where Molly Bruckner might be going, sir. I need to get another look in her bedroom, if I may.'

Despite the grandfatherly concern, Captain Fezzamo was finished hearing anything I had to say. My career as a homicide cop had taken a hit. He walked like the Michelin Man back to his car, wrestled himself and his hazmat suit into the driver's seat, and said, 'I don't want you in that house, Doyle. The FEMA tech is out there now with one of the researchers from the Bioterror and Infectious Disease Lab at Quantico. They're deciding just how angry to be with us. If you think you know where that girl is, or even *if* she's infected, you follow me back to the Phillips 66 station and tell it to Gretchen and Steve. But given what Bryson pulled from Bruckners' office yesterday: those writings, and that ten-thousand-dollar-receipt, every trooper, county deputy, EMT, Boy Scout and off-duty janitor from here to the Jefferson Hotel is going to be out looking for her. It's only fifteen miles; we can cover every inch of it. You don't need to worry any more, Doyle. You take it easy, get well, and stay the hell out of contact with anyone else. You understand me?'

'Yes, sir.' There wasn't much left to say. I'd been relieved. I got back in my cruiser, pulled a K-turn on the narrow drive and waited for the dust cloud behind the captain's sedan to settle before following him out.

Something moved in the bulrushes beside the pond.

'Ignore it,' I said out loud. 'It's just another stress-induced, fatigue-induced, pharmacological hallucination – a harmless by-product of an inconvenient pill problem. There is not a dog over there, Sailor. Just look away.'

My phone buzzed once.

'Don't do it.'

Against my better judgement, I flipped it open. Text scrolled up the LCD screen:

YOUR SISTER FORGIVES YOU.
YOUR SISTER FORGIVES YOU.
YOUR SISTER FORGIVES YOU.
YOUR SISTER FORGIVES YOU.
YOUR SISTER FORGIVES YOU.
YOUR SISTER FORGIVES YOU.
YOUR SISTER FORGIVES YOU.
YOUR SISTER FORGIVES YOU.
YOUR SISTER FORGIVES YOU.
YOUR SISTER FORGIVES YOU.
YOUR SISTER FORGIVES YOU.
YOUR SISTER FORGIVES YOU.

I slapped the phone closed and stuffed it back in my pocket. 'Who cares?' I shouted, shoving the cruiser into park. 'Who cares if Marie forgives me?' I punched the combination airbag and horn on my steering wheel until my knuckles ached. 'What does this have to do with anything? *What?*'

In a show of focused frustration I popped two quick OxyContin, swallowing them dry. 'Fine. I already failed Fezzamo's field sobriety test. I might as well go down in flames!'

The shadow slipped from behind the bulrushes and darted along the periphery of the little pond, vanishing into the brush where I had left the mutilated stray the day before.

'Okay, okay. I'm coming,' I said. 'I'm coming.'

12:11 p.m.

I heard the dog growl before I reached the pond's edge.

'I hear you, Scooby, you putrefying pain in my ass, and I'm going to shoot you; so get ready for the trip to dog heaven, shithead.' I drew my .45, chambered a round and pushed, shoulder first, through the stand of rushes. 'All right, come out and take your medicine. Where are you, you malignant, fucking tumour in my rectum?'

He growled again, from further along the north side of the pond. I heard a rustle, a loping footstep as if the dog had run off, and then, distinctly, a child's laugh, an unmistakable giggle, lost after a moment behind a swelling chorus of locusts.

'Molly!' I cried and ducked through the raspberry thorns and poison oak throttling the path to the rotting hickory stump that had marked the end of my progress the day before. 'Molly, are you in there?'

Locusts drowned out everything but my laboured breathing and the sound of my wingtips sloshing and sucking through the mud. Clouds of no-see-ums attacked my face and head and I held a hand up high in the hope that the old wives' tale about them converging on the highest point might be true. After braving an initial wall of thorns, a couple of dozen bloody scratches and a pair of muck-sodden shoes, I entered a small clearing dotted with colourful wildflowers. A muddy embankment tapered sharply down to the water, where a forgotten Barbie doll struggled to free herself from thigh-deep murk. A large flat rock, lying half in and half out of the water, made a perfect picnic or reading spot. I imagined Molly down here often, enjoying the sun with half a dozen cats in tow.

There was no sign of the stray dog, nor any lingering scent of him either.

Did Bryson say they had disposed of the corpse? Or was it still out here?

'Rover, Fido, Shithead, Lassie, whoever you are!' I yelled across the clearing. 'Come on, boy. I've got a nice bone for you. Come out and see Daddy, you canine nightmare!'

Nothing.

A thatch of sunflowers towered over the east side of the clearing, shivering in the light breeze with an unnatural scratching sound. Looking closer, I discovered a piece of drawing paper that had blown between the heavy stalks. It rustled a scratchy whisper with each gust. I tugged at one corner, and it ripped off in my hand.

'Shit.'

I tried again, this time pushing the happy yellow sentries to one side to release a piece of faded pink construction paper. It was another of Molly's drawings, with the same bearded stickman, his sabre drawn for battle, astride the same white horse. The words *the genrele is coming!!!!* had been scrawled across the bottom in the same careful but crooked writing as the pictures Phil and I had found in Molly's bedroom. The locusts quieted and the no-see-ums swarmed up near the tops of the sunflowers, granting me a moment's peace. I stared down at the drawing, my fingertip tracing the outline of Bob Lake's beard, his purple cutlass-like sword and his ten-gallon – *fifty*-gallon – cowboy hat.

'Christ, how could we be so stupid?' I asked of no one, then dialled Phil Clarkson.

He answered on the first ring. The signal sucked, so I wandered back and forth across the clearing, hoping to find a place where I could hear him. I finally stepped onto the rock, jutting like a promontory over the surface of the pond. The locusts roused themselves again and I pressed a finger in my free ear, hoping to close out the rest of the world.

'Where the hell are you?'

'Phil, I know where Molly's going. I was pretty sure of it before, but now I'm convinced.'

'You've got to come in here. Fezzamo's pissed. He doesn't show it, but he's disappointed and he wants you back here right away. Jesus, Sailor, you're carrying plague. You can't be out running around. What are you thinking?'

'Phil, I need you to listen. Get on the phone. Get a few guys. We don't need the whole goddamned National Guard or the Green Bay

Packers. We just need a few guys, maybe that warden and his blood-hound from yesterday.'

'He's infected – they're all infected, Sailor, and it's going to hit the news any second now. One of the St James deputies said something to someone, and the media is calling every five seconds. The CDC is here now to handle all the communication, the quarantine, and the plan for treating anyone exposed in the past twenty-four hours. Anyone in contact before that could very well be fucked. Anyone who doesn't know they've been in contact could very well be fucked, especially if they ignore the EMS announcements and continue to go about their business. Gretchen Kim says the worst is going to come once people think things are under control, while a few ignorant, even unwitting, carriers continue to spread this shit to people who believe they're in the clear. Fezzamo is heading south for a press conference in the next half-hour. There's going to be mayhem, Sailor. It's a fucking mess, and you're calling for a bloodhound?'

'Yes.'

He sighed. 'Where?'

'East of the farm. Molly's heading east, not south.'

'How do you know?'

From my father.

'Because Carl loved her, Phil. Just like any father … like any father loves a daughter, like you and me, for Christ's sake.' My voice trembled; I cleared my throat to hide it. 'He didn't use her as an agent of terror. It probably broke his heart to know she was infected – *if* he even knew before he died.'

'How do you know this?'

'Think about that house, his life, those pictures on the wall, all of it. Here was a guy with a dying farm, a disabled daughter, and a mummified wife duct-taped into a makeshift tomb upstairs. Think about the inscription on the door. They weren't crackpots. They were poor. Carl didn't bury his wife because he was broke, plain and simple. Sure, it's a back-assed way to get rid of a body, but he had to have Claire's income. He'd save the money on the funeral, sign the deposit slips for Claire's Social Security cheques, and use the cash to care for Molly. This guy wasn't a criminal; he was desperate. Who knows how long he thought he'd live? It can't be very long. So he fucks the same government that took his foot, and he does it to care for the daughter he loved more than anything.'

'The retard.'

'Don't call her that.' I felt stupid chiding him. 'She isn't retarded. She's disabled. Molly's a basket case, a full-on space shot, but that doesn't mean her father didn't love her. And it sure as hell doesn't mean that her father was about to use her as a living biological weapon. She's an innocent child trapped in a fifty-year-old body, and she's not going to the Jefferson Hotel, I'm sure of it.'

'Where's she going?'

'East.'

'What's east of the farm? Nothing at all.' Phil was humouring me. I figured he'd chat with me about my theory for another minute or two before telling me to get my ass back to the lab.

'Right, there's nothing. For about fifteen miles, there's not a damned thing but swampy valleys and forested hills. From Wibbleton to Wobbleton is fifteen miles. From Wobbleton to Wibbleton is fifteen miles.'

'Holy Christ, Sailor, you've blown a gasket. You need to come in here. We'll call Doc.'

'She's not going to the Jefferson Hotel, Phil. Tell them that.'

'It won't matter,' he said. 'They're already mobilising every cop, soldier, Secret Service agent and EMT in the Richmond area to work crowd control in the city, to staff the quarantine areas over in Henrico, or to find Molly Bruckner. The search is going to be massive. There's nothing I can say to change that. Every inch of countryside between here and the Jefferson is going to be examined under a microscope.'

'They're not going to find her.' I jumped from the rock to the clearing and started east through the thickly wooded forest that covered most of the open space between the Bruckner farm and the I-95 corridor fifteen miles away.

'Okay, so where the fuck d'you think she's going?'

'Out towards the Interstate,' I said. 'She'll be on foot, and she has up to a two-day head start. I think she was here by the pond yesterday; don't ask me how I know. So hopefully she hasn't covered much ground yet. I'm going to follow the easiest path through the woods here, at least to the next cross-street where I'll call you again. If I find some sign that she's passed through, I'll call you back and you can bring up a satellite image of the whole area.'

Phil hesitated, then said, 'Sailor, this is madness. Come in. I'll talk with Harper for you. None of this was your fault. You don't have anything to prove.'

'Trust me, Phil, I'm right about this.'

'Do you have a fever?'

The question threw me. 'Um ... I dunno ... I don't think so.'

'Are you shivering? Have you got diarrhoea? Does your body ache all over?'

I don't really know, Phil, because I've taken enough OxyContin to kill your dog – and your neighbour's dog too.

'I'm fine,' I said, 'admittedly a little tired and shaken up, but it isn't every day you learn that you're carrying the plague – a pandemic strain of a bacteria that's killed more people than all the wars in human history.'

'Come in, Sailor. You need help.'

'I need a bloodhound between here and the Interstate, Phil.'

'Why there?'

'Well, not the Interstate, per se. Molly's heading for Ashland, Ashland Chrysler to be exact. It's on Route 1 just south of town.'

'Do you have any idea how insane that sou—?'

'Wait,' I interrupted.

A friendly breeze blew off the pond, tickling the razor stubble on the back of my head. Between locust choruses, I heard it again, distant this time, but definitely coming from the east: a low growl and an innocent giggle.

'I'll call you later, Phil.' I snapped my phone shut. No sooner had I broken the connection than the phone buzzed again, just once. I didn't bother looking this time. I knew what it said.

12:33 p.m.

Running. I hated running. Back in high school I had played football, because everyone from my town played football. Our fathers and grandfathers and uncles and cousins had all warred up and down the same gridiron at Freehold Catholic High School, and I was no different. I didn't mind the passing, catching, tackling, even the locker room antics: the pranks and the homophobic, communal-shower bravado. Most of those bits were fine. What ruined football for me was the running.

Central New Jersey in the summertime was muggy and thick. All those people in their cars, clogging up the Turnpike, the Parkway, even the local roads to and from the tunnels and bridges spanning the Hudson to Manhattan. Millions of commuters passed by my parents' house every day and all that carbon in the air made New Jersey summer a season in Hell. The sun never really shone in Jersey in July; rather, a bright yellow refraction burned down on us until the first cool breezes of September pushed the smoggy clouds of cheap unleaded exhaust out to sea.

Football practise started around the first of August, six or seven weeks after the last baseball game of the spring season. Since I rarely ran further than the distance between my bedroom and the upstairs toilet, I quickly lost whatever lungs I had built up during baseball season. By August, I was as out of shape as any diabetic propping up the counter at the local McDonald's. After two weeks of double sessions, most of my teammates were back in fighting form, ready to take on central Jersey's other harpy footballers for the entertainment of our parents, grandparents, friends, and especially our cheerleaders.

Not me.

By mid-August, I was wiped out, devoid of all desire to compete.

The only reason I never quit was because my father watched me play with such pride. Games were on Saturday mornings – none of the Catholic schools had money for stadium lights. We would drive up to Irvington, Patterson and Newark to check out the Friday night games at the bigger city high schools, where watching football under the lights was like making a pilgrimage to a holy city. Sixteen- and seventeen-year-old players, same age as us, looked professional, sprinting faster, tackling harder, passing the ball further than any Saturday morning team we'd ever seen. And when they scored, they kicked the point after, just like the Jets or the Eagles or the New York Football Giants, no two-point conversions because all the kickers were off playing travel-league soccer. It was magical, and we drove home afterwards, an open pizza box on the back seat, envisioning what feats we ourselves would accomplish the following morning. No one ever said it out loud, but those nights driving south on Route 18 were the times when we really felt like heroes.

Never on Saturdays. Because if Friday nights were for epic gridiron battles and romantic escapes with Homecoming queens, Saturday mornings were for soggy cereal, cartoons, and fumbled football played by clumsy oafs in thrift-store uniforms.

But I played, and I ran, because my father was up there watching me, elbowing his friends in the ribs whenever I did anything even remotely athletic. He'd have a Coke and a hot dog, and he'd keep an arm wrapped around my mother and a proud look on his face, win or lose. For me, that was worth the August double sessions. After the game, he'd talk strategy, picking apart every key play as if John Madden himself might stop by, looking for insight. And I played along. Actually, I never wanted those conversations to end, but there are only so many ways to say *next week you should try harder not to suck*.

My mom would make pot roast, Uncle Paul would bring Aunt Stacy and my cousins over to watch the college games, and Marie would hang on my every word as if I were a Super Bowl MVP regaling a Sports Center host with my thoughts on the game.

It was blue-collar, middle-class, suburban, hard-working, conservative, call-it-what-you-will America, and it was just about the best time in my life.

Even with all the frigging running.

After graduation I went to Rutgers and quickly discovered beer – also one of the best times in my life, but for entirely different reasons. My roommates and I would drink for fun, drink for sport, drink in celebration, drink in commiseration, drink on Fridays to blow out the academic week, drink on Sunday afternoons to say farewell to the weekend and on Sunday nights to brace ourselves for Monday. Beer flowed through our dorm like an amber river, and except for the occasional drunken frisbee competition, there was no running.

Now, running east through the Virginia countryside, I regretted every damn one of those beers, every slice of pizza, every box of Krispy Kremes, and every morning I ever woke up, hungover, to watch joggers run by my house.

With temperatures in the nineties and vicious pre-storm humidity swaddling St James County, I ran over the rocky, uneven ground lugging a fourteen-pound gunbelt, fifteen pounds of flab, a loaded Glock 21 at my hip and a pair of mud-encrusted wingtips on my feet. I wheezed like an emphysemiac, coming dangerously close to passing out, but somehow I kept moving, one foot in front of the other ...

I had started running when I heard Molly giggle from the underbrush. I wasn't fooling myself into believing that it actually was Molly, any more than I believed that the dead dog had been growling, but I wanted to find out what was behind the bushes, beneath the trees, what it was that connected everything to my sister's forgiveness or Molly's disappearance. Had any of the people I'd met actually said those things? Probably not – but I had heard them, just as I had heard Molly giggling, just as I'd seen my cell phone displaying increasingly cryptic messages.

I pounded, flatfooted, through the woods, wanting this ordeal to end. It was easy at first, because I didn't think I'd have to go very far. The answers had to be here, even if Molly was already well on her way into Ashland. After a mile or so I stopped, to suck in a few desperate breaths. It was pretty obvious I couldn't sprint the fifteen miles to Route 1, but I had to keep moving.

With my hands braced on my knees I bent over and hacked up a lungful of plague-infected phlegm. I spat it at a pin oak, breathed in painfully and started down a muddy rise to a babbling creek. Sweat stung the cuts on my face and the nicks on my bald head, so I fell to my knees and dunked my head and shoulders into the muddy water. It wasn't that deep; I banged my forehead against a submerged rock, but I didn't care. The cool water was a blissful reprieve, and I dunked my head twice more before I pulled myself together. It was hard not to drink my fill, but I figured however picturesque, the creek was likely mostly farm run-off, and one deadly infection was enough, even for a holiday weekend.

'You gotta walk, Sailor,' I said. 'You try running all the way to Ashland and your feet will be blistered to Hell and back, you'll get too dehydrated; shit, your heart may simply—'

I stopped. Cold water trickled down my spine and soaked into the waistband of my boxers. I sat on my haunches, looking like an escapee from a psych hospital, and blinked my eyes into focus. There, on the opposite bank, was an unmistakable footprint in the mud. I wiped my eyes on the back of my wrist and stood slowly. Only one kind of shoe left such a footprint. I had worn them myself for years, tugging them on after every one of those Saturday morning football games.

Converse All Stars. *The yellow ones sported fresh stains: cat blood.*

'Molly's closet,' I said to no one, and started running again.

She had been there recently. The rain yesterday afternoon – *what time was that, after lunch, right? After I dropped Dr Wentworth at her car, next to that prehistoric fucking snowplough behind Division Headquarters* . . . It had been an apocalyptic storm. The creek would have been running high, much higher up the bank, certainly above that footprint.

So Molly had come this way in the past twenty-four hours, more recently, most probably. It would have taken time for the creek to resume its normal course, for the saturated mud to dry up a bit. She was a big woman, a hundred pounds overweight, easily, and if she had stepped over there right after the rainstorm, her footprint would be deep, not shallow and defined. So when was she here? Last night or this morning?

I really hate running, but I kept at it now because of some cop gene that says *I'm close, damnit, and I'm going to see this end*. I huffed and puffed my way up a short draw to a massive soybean field, at least half a mile across, and flipped open my cell phone to dial Phil.

The LCD screen mocked me again, this time flashing up NO SERVICE. I flipped it closed and stuck it back in my pocket, ignoring it when it buzzed a few seconds later. I knew what it would say. This was the right direction. I could call Phil later.

At the edge of the field I stopped and shaded my eyes, straining to see to the east. I hunched down and scanned the tops of the soybean plants, hoping to catch a glimpse of Molly's body, but somehow I knew she hadn't fallen, not yet.

I waved at a cloud of no-see-ums and slapped a mosquito off my cheek. I had come two hundred yards from the creek and already I was overheating. 'Maybe you should have drunk a little of it, Sailor,' I said as I jogged on into the hazy sunlight.

1:17 p.m.

Forty-five minutes later I came to a gravel road running north–south through the fields and lush wooded hills west of Ashland. I figured I had come about three, almost four, miles since the creek, though I had seen no sign of Molly, nor any evidence that she had come this way. I lit a cigarette and tried to ignore the sense of doubt creeping up on me from the shadows. If I was right and Molly was heading towards Ashland, I'd need help finding her once I reached the outskirts of town. More roads offered more opportunity for her to get lost and less likelihood that I'd be able to track her down on my own. While there was little chance of me catching her out here in the boondocks, I was hoping some stroke of Hail Mary luck would lead me to her before she hit the suburbs and started an unstoppable plague epidemic. I needed help.

Half a mile back I had noticed a housing development sitting on a landscaped hillside. The uptight gated community with its cookie-cutter mansions sitting on identical rectangular lots was the only landmark other than the gravel road that I could use to give Phil an idea of my position. I'm no Boy Scout by a couple of furlongs, but I thought I'd managed to keep a fairly direct path to the northeast, and assuming I could keep it up, my twelve-minute-per-mile pace would have me in Ashland before four p.m.

I looked down at the burning cigarette in my hand that I didn't even remember lighting and thought, *this might have been a mistake*. I needed a pee, and tried not to be shocked at the acrid smell and dangerous shade of brownish-yellow; I already knew I needed water.

I flipped open my phone and saw that I now had a weak signal.

'Sailor?' Phil sounded exasperated.

'Yeah, Phil, listen, I've got a shitty signal and a dying battery, so I don't have time for any bullshit. I need a dog or a couple of dogs, and as many guys as you can spare. Have them fan out, north to south, and start moving west through the farms outside Ashland. I'm on a gravel road about four, maybe four and a half miles east-northeast of the Bruckner farm and about a mile north of what looks like a new development, suburban sprawl stuff, Richie Rich places, maybe with a golf course. I'm going to continue towards Ashland and hope to find some sign of Molly, maybe crossing one of these big soybean fields.'

'Sailor, you don't get it,' Phil said. 'I don't have any authority. I'm in quarantine. I'm off this case. The story is all over the news. Richmond is in a frigging panic. The Secret Service is looking for you; they want to question you, and the CDC is screaming for your head. They figure they can't get this thing bottled up with you out running around. You gotta come in. Just turn around and come back.'

'Phil!' I shouted. 'I found one of her drawings out here, the stick-man on the horse, like the ones in her room. The general is coming, the general is coming! Remember? Well, it isn't General Lake – Molly doesn't know Bob Lake from Luciano Pavarotti. She's heading to Ashland Chrysler to see Robert E. Lee and his horse, the big white bastard that's been on television every ten minutes for the past three weeks. I know she's out here, Phil, and if you're waiting for her to show up in Richmond, you're watching the wrong roads.'

There was silence for a moment, then Phil said, 'I'll try to get a helicopter. We'll send someone to pick you up. You might be delirious. It could be—'

I hung up and dialled Huck. Before connecting, my phone flashed LOW BATTERY at me.

'Yeah, I know, I know,' I said. 'I didn't plug it in last night; so fire me.'

'Hey, kemosabe!' Huck answered. 'There are a lot of people looking for you.'

'Spare me the details, Uncle Hucker. I need a favour.'

'Where are you?'

I repeated what I had told Phil.

He said, 'I'll see who's on duty up at Division, but just about everyone's been rousted already. The local cable company activated the emergency broadcast system, encouraging everyone to stay put. The CDC is trying to track down everyone who's had contact with any of the investigators at the farm yesterday. They're setting up quarantine and treatment centres in Henrico and Hanover, and I think another one's down in Maymount Park. It's already a cluster fuck, and they've only been at it for a few hours. There was a huge pile-up on Grove Avenue in front of Retreat Hospital, people rushing the emergency room for inoculations, and I just heard over the radio that a doctor's been shot outside his family practice over in Chesterfield. Everyone with a computer is researching this thing, trying to order whatever medications they need to ward off the plague. Google's a hell of a lot faster than the CDC or FEMA. When I spoke to Harper, he told me the governor's probably going to close I-95 in both directions through the city, rerouting all traffic around 295. Because we were out at Short Pump last night, most inbound traffic on 64 has trickled to nothing, but we may send cruisers out to close the westbound lanes beyond the mall. Two Middle Eastern men have been shot by the canal, and all the Islamic leaders they can find inside the Beltway have been on the news denying responsibility for this thing. Helicopters are flying all over the place, broadcasting images of people going batshit crazy. There was a fight outside a CVS over on Cary Street that erupted into a minor riot. City PD responded, and everyone ran. They're convinced we're all infected, anyone in a police uniform. Can you believe that? It's on every channel – local, national, the cable channels. But no one actually knows anything yet, so it's just noise, getting everyone fired up. The FEMA director's coming on in a few minutes with some executive director from the CDC. I heard that they might announce some kind of regional spray campaign, you know, to kill all the fleas up there along Goochland and Pitcairn. Fezzamo was on the local channels, and they're replaying that every ten seconds, but no one trusts him, because they're hearing that it was state troopers introduced the infection to the Richmond area.'

'Jesus,' I whispered. 'And the deadliest one is still out there.'

'You said it, boss.' Huck went on, 'The search for your girl Molly is shaping up to be one of the biggest manhunts in Virginia history.'

'Then why is no one listening to me?' I shouted. 'I know where she's going, but I need help containing her before she gets to Ashland. There's still ten miles of woods and farms between here and the Interstate. It's a shitload of space to cover, but if we can catch her up here, we might keep anyone else from becoming infected.'

'I'll see what I can do, Sailor.' He didn't sound convinced. 'This deal at the Jefferson tonight has politicised this whole scenario unnecessarily. Us state police are looking like we knew something and didn't act on it. Bob Lake's handlers are crying foul; so to make up for it, everyone has been deployed along the roads and highways coming in from the northwest. They figure Carl Bruckner had a hard-on for Lake and Molly's on her way to exact some kind of forty-year-old vengeance. Until they corral her, I don't know what resources I can send your way, but I'll try to wrangle a few of the Ashland town cops to pull on their wellies and give you a hand.'

'Just tell them she's here,' I said, 'somewhere between Ashland Chrysler and wherever the hell I am, out along the St James–Hanover line.'

'Will do, kemosabe.'

'Where are you, by the way?'

'Quarantined at MCV hospital with your buddies Bryson and Lourdes. They gave me a shot the size of John Holmes' wiener, and I've got a bottle of pills I'm supposed to finish over the next ten days.'

'You'll be all right,' I said. 'Lefkowitz told me that'd do the trick. Did they cut your hair?'

'Over my dead and broken body will they touch my flowing locks! They agreed because I hadn't been in immediate contact with any fleas, I didn't have to get a haircut, but they did shave Lourdes and Bryson. She wasn't best pleased.'

'This is my fault,' I said, 'all of it, Huck. I really fucked up.'

'Bullshit. You can't have seen this coming. No one could. I've been on the job twenty years and I would have done the same damned things. I'll call when I know something,' Huck said. 'Sorry I can't be out there to help.'

'You think I'm crazy?' I asked.

'Why? Because you don't believe that a father would use his daughter as a living agent of vengeance? No, Sailor, I don't think you're crazy.'

'Well, that's one, I suppose.'

'When Melissa, our oldest, was eighteen months old, she came down with pneumonia. Sandy and I were still married at the time, still happy; you know the story. Anyway, the doctors kept Melissa in the hospital for six days. She had an IV in the back of her hand – she was too small for one in her arm – an oxygen tube in her nose and a pulse-ox clip on her fingertip that registered her oxygen level every thirty seconds. For six days my wife and I watched those little red numbers blink and change, sometimes going up, sometimes sliding down, every thirty seconds for six days. We took turns sleeping, in case Melissa woke and needed anything. But we never missed a beep, never missed a number. Sandy and I don't talk much now, but I know I can speak for her too when I say that even on the day we die, neither of us will ever be that scared again. I didn't know Carl Bruckner, but if what you told me last night, that he buried his wife in cat litter to save eight hundred bucks a month to support his kid, if that's right, then I can't imagine that he'd send his daughter on some kind of idiot suicide run, not if Carl had even just a shot glass full of whatever it was that kept Sandy and me staring at those damned little red numbers for six days.'

'Like the red eyes of Satan,' I said.

'What's that?'

'Nothing, Huck. Thanks.'

I hung up and switched off the phone to preserve the battery. An impossible chill passed on the air, and the skin on my forearms tightened into goose pimples. 'Uh oh. This is a problem,' I said as I rubbed my arms to warm them up. I felt a layer of sweat, but still I was cold. 'I've got a frigging fever,' I said. 'Not good, Sailor. This is not at all good.'

My muscles didn't ache, and apart from the pain in my lungs, I felt fine, no other flu symptoms – I figured I had to credit the OxyContin for that, though, probably could've fallen off a building right then and not felt it. Flu symptoms wouldn't make a dent in my armour for another hour or two.

Though Doc's shot might help me in the long run, flu symptoms – *plague* symptoms, maybe time to call it what it was – they'd drain my strength in a raging hurry, especially jogging cross-country like this. I jumped over a narrow drainage ditch running along the gravel road and landed hard on the forest floor beyond. It was at least another ten miles to the outskirts of Ashland; I had to hope Uncle Hucker could get the local PD mobilised to give me some help out here. I had been to the Ashland Police Station. It wasn't big, but add in a game warden and a dog or two and they might be able to sniff out Molly before she reached town. From Wibbleton to Wobbleton is fifteen miles ...

I covered another five miles in a state of dehydrated delirium. My twelve-minute-per-mile pace had risen to twenty-something, but there was nothing I could do about that. Not even with a gun to my head could I have moved any faster. The one main thoroughfare I remembered crossing was Route 33 – at least, I think that's what it was. This far out of the city, though, even that had narrowed to a quiet two-lane road.

Doc's scrubs were sodden, my shaved head was sunburned and painful and the multiple blisters on my feet were broken and bleeding; my socks were soaked through with sweat and blood, and serrated pain lanced up my lower leg with every step. I had dozens of mosquito bites on my arms and neck, and I silently wished septicaemic plague on every one of the bastards that swooped in for a taste of my infected blood.

But worst was the pain in my knees and lower back: the pain of dehydration. I had burned so much lactic acid that my muscles were on the verge of shutting down. I didn't have enough electrolytes in my system to keep myself upright much longer, and unless it started raining Gatorade and bananas, I had only a couple of miles left in me, then I'd be crawling. I had had nothing to drink after the water I'd cleaned out my mouth with after puking on Doc's floor all those hours – days, it felt like – ago. I cursed myself for not grabbing even a bottle of water from the mobile lab.

My OxyContin wall had crumbled enough that I could now sense the early tendrils of plague reaching out to envelop me. Aching muscles and a rail-spike headache were difficult to ignore, but for the pain in my feet which was so excruciating that I almost managed to block out these lesser problems.

I sang every inane song I could remember from Ben's favourite CD. Jenny kept it in the minivan and it played constantly, in the background, even when I ran weekend errands by myself. The songs were catchy, repetitive, and easy for toddlers to sing, and it was that repetition that kept me going now as I staggered, hunched over, through the woods.

I sang, 'Mrs James has a cow in the barn, cow in the barn, cow in the barn. Mrs James has a cow in the barn, early Sunday morning. Mrs James has a bloody foot, a case of plague, a sunburned head. Mrs James has swollen knees, early Sunday morning.'

I pushed through a stand of rubbery saplings only to discover that God had dropped a pile of rocks here, each one as big as my house. I picked my way around and over them, glad to be climbing because it wasn't running ... not that what I was doing could be classified as running any more. I caught the faint aroma of grilling meat: goat, or something cloven-hoofed from the Old Testament. *Bible-Q – delicious!* As hungry as I was, the smell made my bowels clench up and threaten to cramp.

As I dragged myself over a rough crest I found myself looking at a ramshackle farmhouse across a narrow pond. It was a mess, even worse than the Bruckner place, but to me it was Mecca. 'Thank you, God,' I said, 'I'm gonna make it. *Thank you.*'

The pond stretched too far south to skirt; fresh water, clean socks, dry shoes and industrial quantities of aspirin were too close to take the long way around. I descended from the rocky moraine near the north edge of the pond and would have thrown myself in if it hadn't been covered quite so thickly in aromatic green algae. It would be crammed with leeches, too, so no thanks.

I made my way around the muddy shoreline, climbing on all fours up a steep embankment towards what looked to be the skeletal back side of a row of corn bins, long since rotted away to kindling.

Up the hill, Sailor, crawl up the hill and just throw yourself over the back wall of the corn bin. That's it: from there, you can shout for help. Now, just crawl.

The embankment was the result of a hundred years of erosion which was slowly washing away the entire farm. I wasn't surprised that the bins had been abandoned. They lay so close to the edge that a full load of corn might have toppled the whole row down the muddy slope into the pond. Beyond the bins, an ancient flatbed truck was parked beside the hatch door to a storm cellar. No grass grew around the house; rather, the yard was sun-baked, kiln-dry clay, hardened over two hundred years of neglect. A lone goat had been tethered to a metal rod beside a massive maple tree that had probably once cast shade down on an embattled Robert E. Lee.

The genrele is coming!

Other than me, nothing moved. I pulled myself up wearily, stumbled a few steps to my right, overcorrected left, and tried to shout.

'Hey!' I croaked. 'Help me! Someone!'

I staggered to the lowest of the corn bins. The rear slats had either fallen off or been harvested for minor repairs around the dilapidated house. It stood about waist-high. I grabbed hold of the uppermost slat and tried to throw one leg over, but the rotten wood gave way beneath me and I tumbled into the bin with a groan.

'Sonofabitch,' I cursed into the scattered layer of cow corn left on the ground. 'Just my shit luck to pick the one with rotten—'

The first snake bit me hard on the wrist, coiled and struck again. Another bit my ankle. I kicked viciously at it with my heel. It was a monster, a speckled diamond-headed fucker as thick around as my wrist.

I sat up and screamed, 'Jesus Christ! What is this? Jesus, help me!'

They were everywhere. I felt another bite deep into my thigh – this one was a cottonmouth moccasin, a giant. There were rattlesnakes, water moccasins, copperheads, dozens of them, all slithering, trying to escape, or to defend themselves against me.

I drew my gun and started firing everywhere, emptying the clip. I definitely hit two, watching their bodies tearing open and flopping against the slat sides of the corn bin. I might have killed others, but I couldn't be sure.

Terrified, I wrestled another clip from my belt, but I got bitten again before I could reload and I was shaking so much I fumbled the new ammo clip. I watched it fall near a diamondback rattler that struck at it then slithered away. A rainbow-coloured snake, something I thought I had seen on the Discovery Channel, slid over my foot. I kicked it towards the rattlesnake, hoping it hadn't been the last one to bite me.

There was nowhere to go and too many to shoot. A copperhead struck at the sole of my shoe; I stomped hard on its head, feeling it crunch beneath my heel, then took a step forward and threw myself over the front wall of the bin. Like the rear slats, they collapsed to splinters beneath me and I fell, screaming hoarsely for help.

The bright afternoon sun faded to black and I felt heavy-bodied, poisonous snakes slithering around and over my body as I lost consciousness, my mind howling a silent scream.

I threw the football to Dad. He had a great arm for perfect spirals. I could never get it right; mine always wobbled like an injured duck in flight.

In the back yard of my parents' place in Jersey, summer was about to give way to fall. While still warm during the day, the evenings were cool enough to sit outside, to mow the grass without sweating or toss the football around in anticipation of the coming season.

A bee, maybe a wasp, stung me in the ass. It hurt, but I ignored it. The rare game of catch was too richly packed with everything I wanted from life as a ten-year-old. Shrugging off a bee sting was easy.

Dad dropped back and lofted one high enough to clear the rooftop. I scurried around like a confused crab, trying to guesstimate where it might return to Earth. When I made the catch, the impact knocked me down on the wasp again. He stung me a second time, harder, as if I'd made him mad somehow. It had to be a wasp to be that pissed off.

I reared back and heaved the ball as far as I could. Dad was on the opposite side of the yard, a good twenty feet further than I'd ever thrown before. But in the wake of my acrobatic catch, I wanted to make a decent pass, to spiral one like Phil Simms hitting Mark Bavaro across the middle.

I didn't make it. The ball bounced twice before Dad scooped it up. But his smile as he tossed it back made everything right in the world.

The wind creaked like an unoiled spring.

'Not bad,' Dad said. 'That's further than you've ever thrown it.' He had a way, back then, of finding a positive angle on anything. The house could have burned to cinders and he would have told Marie and me that we were lucky we weren't inside at the time or that we were fortunate to have Uncle Paul and Aunt Stacy to help us out.

I tried to catch the ball on the run, like Bavaro, but another wasp sting, this one deep into my left butt cheek, threw me off stride. I chased the ball into the stand of scrubby cedar bushes lining the Davidsons' yard next door.

Marie banged through the screen door, its hinges creaking like the wind, though I'd never heard the wind creak before. 'Daddy, Sammy, Mom says you have to come in.'

'One more, Dad!' I threw as hard as I could, but the football barely covered half the distance across the lawn. 'I'm never going to get this.'

'Sure you will,' Dad said. 'You throw as far as any ten-year-old kid I've ever known. You've just got to keep practising. You'll get it.' He looked taller than usual, leaner, his neatly trimmed hair, what my mother called Paul Newman hair, blown about a little during our game. He wore long pants every day of his life, except for the beach, the only time I'd ever seen him in shorts. That was strange. Given my choice, I would wear shorts everywhere: to school, to my wedding, to job interviews, and heck yes, even to my funeral. But Dad was a Dickies guy. He had about five pairs, but neither Marie nor I could tell one from the other. After work, he'd strip down to his Dickies and a white undershirt. He'd drink a beer, read the paper – I never in my life saw him read a book – and chat with my mother or help Marie with her homework.

He wore a white T-shirt now. I watched the muscles along his bare arm flex as he bent down to pick up the wayward football from the closely cropped grass. He wasn't Mark Bavaro, but he looked strong enough to take on the world. I wanted nothing more at that moment than to be with him for as long as I could, to find a way to keep the late afternoon sun high in the sky.

He flipped me the ball and said, 'You and me.'

I didn't know what it meant; so I said the first thing that came to my mind: 'Me and you.'

The wind creaked again, like a door in a haunted house. The wasp stung me in the upper arm. I swatted at it absentmindedly, unable to look away from my father as he started up the lawn towards Marie. 'Wait for me,' I called.

Dad turned, his smile fading. 'No,' he said, 'you've got to find Molly. You know why. Go now, Sammy.'

'She's like a baby. Right? Just a little girl?'

'You know.'

I rolled onto my side and threw up on the floor.

My stomach empty, I puked anyway, my whole body contracting with each dry heave.

I was lying on a collapsible cot, and the springs creaked noisily with my every move. It was one of those foldable models that lifted you just a few inches off the floor. I tried to sit up, but a sudden burning in my lungs knocked me back.

The room smelled of musty grandmothers and mothballed blankets. The wide plank floors were pitted from decades of work boot traffic and too little varnish. An empty bookcase stood against the wall near the entrance to what looked like a dark hallway, and a row of wooden pegs protruded from the whitewashed plaster beside the front door. Despite the summer heat, each peg held a different flannel overshirt, the heavy kind farmers and deer hunters wore through autumn. Several newspapers were tossed about the room, scattered on the floor as if by a breeze. Sundry crosses decorated the walls, *Christian Absurdism*, and from my cot I could see three or four framed pictures of Jesus. They were the kind of images I would expect in a Baptist vestry, with a serious-looking Saviour backlit by a sunburst of yellow or white and giving the peace sign, or whatever it was when he held up his fingers like that. In one, Christ's burning heart was emblazoned on his chest with a bit of flame below a little cross. I'd seen the image back at Rutgers; one of my dorm mates had drawn a burning joint in Christ's hand and written *Wanna drag?* in a cartoon bubble over his head. It hung in our dorm for two years before some God Squadder pulled it down during a party.

An old milk crate stood beside the cot. An array of medicine bottles and intravenous needles were arranged on a clean white cloth. Someone had injected me; I guess that accounted for the wasps.

A tattered plaid sofa was pushed beneath twin windows looking onto the yard. The goat, still tied beside Robert E. Lee's maple tree, paced the length of his chain. From my cot I could see that the sun was less bright, but still high enough in the sky for me to make it to Ashland before dark. I watched the goat disinterestedly for a moment before realising that the upper edge of the sofa was shifting slowly from left to right.

'What the hell?' I wheezed. 'Holy shit, it's a snake! Hey, anybody? There's a big snake in here!' I couldn't tell what kind it was; the light wasn't good in the low-ceilinged room, but I could still see it was the biggest snake I had ever encountered outside the zoo. I sucked in a painful breath and tried again. 'Anyone! Can you hear me?'

A squat woman with a flat face waddled in from the hallway. She might have been sixty or maybe three hundred; it was hard to tell from the shape she was in. Her short hair was greased flat against her head and down the back of her neck. She had no teeth that I could see, and her lower lip was tucked beneath her upper, making her look as if she was trying to swallow her own chin. She was easily as big around as she was tall, and with thin ankles and small feet, she looked like an enormous medicine ball, one that had sprouted legs and wandered away from the gym. In one hand she carried a leather-bound Bible, and like Claire Bruckner, she wore a gaudy wooden cross on a heavy gold chain. It bounced on her flour-sack breasts as she walked. Without hesitation she picked up the snake – it was at least six feet long – and draped it over her shoulders.

'Thank you,' I rasped.

She looked down at me with expressionless eyes and said, 'Hap by vis?' A line of spittle dribbled down her chin and dripped onto her cross.

'I'm sorry, I didn't ... What?'

She held the Bible out to me. 'Hap by vis?'

'Um ... I appreciate you bringing me inside, ma'am.' I rolled over, trying to get up. 'I'm a Virginia State Police officer, and I'm trying to track down a fugitive who might have come this way.'

'Da gur, hmm,' she said, nodding. The snake lifted its head to look at her. I thought for certain it was going to eat her, head first, and

307

then slither away into some dark corner to digest for the next thirty-six years.

'I'm sorry, I don't understand.' I pressed down hard on my chest. My wrist was swollen and red. Twin puncture marks showed where I had been bitten. The wounds still stung, as did the bites on my thigh and lower back. But nothing hurt as much as my chest. I coughed up a mouthful of phlegm, remembered my infection and tried to warn her. 'Ma'am, please don't come near me. I'm carrying a disease, and it's nothing you want to catch, trust me.' I coughed again, and as flecks of yellow light burst before my eyes I fell back onto the cot.

'Da gur hap gur by vis, hmm,' she tried again.

I waved her off. 'Just a minute— I just need a minute and I'll get out of here.'

'Y'all aint goin' nowheres, son. Thanks be to God.' A dowel-thin man, also about sixty years old, dragged a wooden chair over beside my cot. 'Breathin' hard: that's how y'all knows y'all bin bit by a coral snake. That's coral snake, breathin's hard. Coral snake. Praise Jesus.' He spoke fast, religious comments added almost as codas, but at least I could understand what he was saying. He was shirtless, his oversized work pants – *I bet they're Dickies* – held up by worn leather suspenders. His bandy arms, neck and sunken chest were covered in hundreds of pockmarks, each scar a healed version of the wounds on my wrist: snake bites. Like the woman with the speech impediment, he wore his hair short and pressed fast against his balding head with some kind of grease or petroleum jelly. His skin was as pale as turned milk and he smelled of body odour, tobacco and the reptile tent at the Stafford County Fair.

'What's happening to me? Why can't I breathe?' I mumbled.

'Coral snake's a bad'un. T'others, they ain't nuthin' to worry 'bout. Give y'all shots awhiles back. Praise Jesus. Lot of serum. Worried 'bout y'all going into shock, but y'all, yer a tough'un. Thanks be to God. Praise Jesus. Cottonmouth got y'all twice. That don' hap'n much. They don' bite much, them cottonmouths. Coppahead too, praise Jesus. A'course, coral snake's a bad bite. Takes time. Thanks be to God.' His voice was a real smoker's rasp.

'Did you give me the antivenin?'

308

'Hmm,' he said, 'Leroy's brung y'all in. Leroy. Praise Jesus.' One of his eyes was refusing to behave, turning towards the window before focusing on me again. I tried not to look at it.

'Thank you,' I said. 'May I have some water?'

He nodded to the woman, who disappeared down the hall. She returned with a pitcher and a glass that had started life back in the 1970s as a Flintstones jelly jar. She poured out water and handed me the glass. The snake was gone.

'Can you help me sit up?' I asked.

'Hmm. Thanks be to God. Praise Jesus.' The old man slipped an arm under my shoulders and eased me to a sitting position.

I felt a little better after drinking half a dozen glasses of water and dumping another on my head, cooling my sunburn. The woman, who'd been sitting on the couch with her hands in her lap, watching me in silence, chuckled at this.

'Y'all look fo' that girl,' the man said. It wasn't a question.

'Yes,' I said, 'I have to find her before she gets to Ashland. I saw that truck outside. Can you drive me? Or maybe let me use your phone? I won't report the snakes if you like. I mean, I don't know anything about snakes, but I think you probably saved my life. And I could use two or three pairs of sports socks and a handful of aspirin. My feet are pretty torn up. I'll pay you. I don't have much with me, but I'll come back, or I'll send a police car out with some money ...' I regretted saying that. These two didn't look like they welcomed police officers too often.

'Y'all gotta stay. Praise Jesus. Y'all ain't ready. Could still stop y'all's heart. Lots of serum. Dangerous. Thanks be to God.'

'You don't understand, Mister ... ?'

'Burgess. Burgess Aiken.'

'Mister Aiken, I can't stay here. I have to get—' I felt around the cot, on the floor, looked at the bookshelf, the window sills. 'Where's my gun?' A sense of icy dread coiled itself around my heart.

The old woman opened her Bible and began to read aloud. 'Fa thu say Law, ty boo incur, a ty woo greev. Ta non tow plee ty ...'

Burgess Aiken beamed. 'Oh, yay, Momma. Them's a good'un. Praise Jesus. For thus saith the Lord, thy bruise is incurable and thy wound is grievous. There is none to plead thy cause, that thou mayest be bound up: thou hast no healing medicines. That's all Jeremiah, chapter thirty.' He quoted the verse from memory in impeccable King James English.

I tried to stand. Everything hurt. 'Where's my gun?' I braced myself, waiting for him to push me back onto the cot. I wasn't anywhere near ready for a fight, but I reckoned I had about eighty pounds on the old man. If it came down to a wrestling match I could try to use weight to my advantage – though I dreaded touching him and his necrotic tattoos. 'Where's my gun?' I asked again as my vision blurred. The faded floral pattern of the stained wallpaper looked like snakes coiling incestuously.

Burgess ignored me and gestured for the woman, Momma, whoever she was, to choose another scripture. She flipped a few pages, raised her fold-away chin proudly and read, 'Fa t'indinat t'Law up'n nates, hist foo up'n all y'amee …'

I leaned against the wall as he hurried into the hallway, where I could hear him thumping and banging around. I wondered if he'd be returning with my gun, probably to shoot me, but he bellowed through the wall, ''Nother good'un, Momma: Isaiah thirty-four! For the indignation of the Lord is upon all nations, and his fury upon all their armies: he hath utterly destroyed them, he hath delivered them to the slaughter. Their slain also shall be cast out, and their stink shall come up out of their carcases, and the mountains shall be melted with their blood! Praise Jesus! Thanks be to God!'

Then he screamed. He didn't bring my gun or my phone, but instead he returned with two vicious-looking snakes, one, a cotton-mouth, wrapped about his forearm, the other, an eastern diamondback rattlesnake, the same one that had tried to bite my ammo clip, in his hand. The diamondback was at least five feet long and looked about as irritated as a serpent can get. Burgess held it about five inches below its head, close enough to control the snake, but not close enough to keep it from biting him if it chose to.

He waved the snakes in my face, babbled something I didn't understand to the frightening fat woman on the couch, then said, 'Y'all have seed the news. Y'all seed the size of the armies. Y'all know that

He is comin' back. He, the Redeemer, the Righteous One, it is His time! Thanks be to God!' Burgess threw his head back and howled at the cobwebbed ceiling.

Momma read us another verse. 'Bab'n grey fal, it becud habshon a devs ...'

Burgess, in the throes of religious ecstasy, recognised this verse too and after only a few words, brandishing the snake at me like a venomous sword, he cried, 'Y'all seed the wars! Y'all seed the armies! Momma reads the Word! Thanks be to God! Praise Jesus! The Word of God in Revelation eighteen! Babylon the great is fallen, is fallen, and is become the habitation of devils, and the hold of every foul spirit, and a cage of every unclean and hateful bird! For all nations have drunk of the wine of the wrath of her fornication, and the kings of the earth have committed fornication with her, and the merchants of the earth are waxed rich through the abundance of her delicacies! Don't misunderstand the Lord, Officer Doyle—'

The sonofabitch went through my pockets. He read my ID.

'The Lord will show y'all the way to Heaven!' He wrapped the cottonmouth about his neck and began dancing and hopping around the room.

Medicine Ball Momma looked immensely pleased with this. I didn't know if the snake had bitten him; Burgess didn't show any sign of knowing even that the cottonmouth was there. He held the rattler aloft with both hands, waving it at me, caressing his face with it, bringing it dangerously close to Momma, whoever's momma she was. I pushed myself away from the wall and tried to get past him, but he poked the snake in my face and shouted, 'One more! Y'all gotta hear one more, and y'all'll understand. Thanks be to God.' His eyes rolled back in his head and he babbled, spat and grunted another inarticulate message to the Holy Spirit.

I tried once again to sidle past him, but my reflexes were slow, my brain addled to the consistency of mashed potatoes. The rattlesnake's tail vibrated, a maddening blur, and the sound was deafening in the small room.

Burgess cried, 'Read 'nother, Momma!'

Taking her cue, Momma turned the page. 'Behud, wid grey play ...'

Burgess wheeled on me, abandoning his lunatic dance, and stared me down. He whispered, 'That's a better'un, Momma. Praise Jesus. Second Chronicles, chapter twenty-one. Thanks be to God. Behold, with a great plague will the Lord smite thy *people*, and thy *children*, and thy *wives*, and all thy *goods*!' He emphasised each victim with a threatening wave of the rattlesnake. The cottonmouth had slithered onto the couch and was now coiled beside Momma, watching the room warily. 'Do y'all understand me, Officer Doyle? Y'all are gonna go nowheres after that girl tonight. She is the plague upon the land. She is the wrath of God. She will lay waste to the armies. And y'all will be right here, right here with Momma, me and Leroy.'

'Mr Aiken—' I backed away as far as I could in the small room. My hands found the edge of the empty bookcase and I pressed myself against it, happy for its solidity. 'This isn't the Book of Revelation, Mr Aiken, this is a disease. I have it, and you – you and your ... your Momma – you might have it too. I have a treatable version, Mr Aiken: there are drugs that will cure it, but Molly Bruckner, the woman you met, she does *not* have a treatable version. She is carrying a deadly form of plague, and hundreds of thousands of people are at risk if I don't find her. Do you understand what I am saying to you?' For the first time in hours I felt clear-headed, mission-focused. Now all I had to do was make Burgess Aiken and his Momma understand me.

He looked askance at me. 'Hmmm. Praise Jesus. Thanks be to God.' Scooping up the cottonmouth with one hand – *as easily as my father scooped up that old football* – Burgess disappeared again down the hallway.

I turned to Momma. 'Please,' I said, feeling the pain of a dozen different injuries, blisters and infections. I had no clue what the anti-venin might be doing to my body, especially as it was mixed with the aftermath of who knew how many OxyContin – *ten*, I had taken ten already – and a massive shot of gentamicin.

Could still stop y'all's heart.

I raised my hands to Momma. 'Please, ma'am,' I said again.

'Hap by vis?' She held her Bible up again.

My mind had been a few beats behind all day. It was slow to start now, but I concentrated on what she was trying to say. Burgess hummed, sang and shouted down the hall, searching for something. I worried what it might be.

'Hap by vis?' Momma used both hands to roll herself to her tiny feet.

'Do I what? Do I ... shit ... what? Do I have a Bible verse? Is that it?'

'Ha, ha!' She clapped her hands and flashed a toothless grin I would see in my nightmares for the rest of my life.

'A Bible verse? Are you kidding me? Mrs Aiken, Momma, I was never very good at getting myself up for church on Sundays.' I pushed hard on my temples. It was difficult to breathe, like having Uncle Paul sitting on my chest; his favourite game when I was a kid: tickle the dead. 'Bible verse. Do I know any Bible verses? I don't ... We Catholics don't really read the Bible, ma'am, we only know Bible verses if we pay attention at Mass, and – well, look at me. Do I look like I paid ...? Wait a minute.' I froze, remembering something. The sustained white noise of the pissed-off rattlesnake was still audible, but it was muted now, coming from down the hall. I closed my eyes and tried to picture the licence plate on Dr Wentworth's car. 'I've got one!' I shouted. 'I do! I have a favourite Bible verse! God damn us all to Hell!'

Momma's eyes lit up. Apparently mine was a soul worth saving. She looked at me expectantly.

'It's Proverbs, chapter twenty-two, verse six.'

Momma didn't need to open the Bible. Instead, she loosed her gruesome smile and said, 'Tra a chy way he'o ...'

I took over. 'Train up a child in the way he should go: and when he is old, he will not depart from it.'

She reached out with a stumpy, gnarled hand and brushed my cheek.

I said, 'Mrs Aiken, Carl and Claire Bruckner didn't train Molly up to become a plague carrier. They didn't train her up to kill thousands of innocent people. Do you understand why I have to find her? She's like a little girl. I have to bring her back to her parents. I have to bring her back to her fa—' My voice got lost somewhere in my throat. I stared out the window at the Aikens' lone goat, looking like live

313

bait for a reticulated python. 'Her father,' I whispered, 'I have to bring Molly home to her father.'

Momma sucked her bottom lip into her mouth. It vanished entirely. 'Da gur hap gur by vis, hmm.'

'No, Molly wouldn't know any Bible verses. She needs us – *me* – to find her.'

Momma Aiken turned on her axis and shuffled towards the door. The rattling sound along the hallway grew louder, and I watched the entryway with a wary eye. She moved one of the flannel shirts to reveal another wooden peg, a few inches below the others. My gunbelt, cuffs, final ammo clip and cell phone hung there together.

'Thank you, Mrs Aiken.' I strapped the belt on just as Burgess appeared carrying rope, duct tape, and the coral snake that had nearly paralysed my diaphragm. I drew my Glock, jammed a clip inside and pointed it at the middle of the connect-the-dots map of scar tissue across his chest.

'No, Momma, no!' Burgess shouted. 'He is of the armies of Satan, the armies who battle all that is righteous, and he gotta stay by us, Momma. That girl gotta reach the marketplace, reach the merchants and dealers of death as the very wrath of our Lord.' To me, he snarled, 'Y'all are going nowhere, son,' and threw the coral snake at me.

I squeezed the trigger, and blew the top of Burgess' left shoulder off. He screamed something that sounded like *Joy!* and tumbled in a screaming heap halfway down the hallway.

The coral snake was flying at me, a rainbow-coloured blur headed straight for my face. It would bite me again; I knew it. My lungs would seize up and I would die a terrifying death, probably convulsing outside in the dirt as the Aiken family goat watched. But Momma Aiken was quicker; she threw her pudgy hand out and snatched the serpent from the air. It bit her at least once before she was able to drop it and I stomped on its head and kicked it under the sofa for good measure.

'Shit,' I said, and helped Momma to the cot. She sat heavily, but with composure, holding her arm down, keeping the bite marks well below the level of her heart.

'Okay, be ite,' she said. Burgess screamed for Jesus to save him and for God to strike me dead, and I felt like shooting him again, just to shut him up.

Straining for breath, I said, 'How do you know it'll be all right? I don't know which of these ampoules is the right one, and these needles are all infected with my blood. We can't stick you with one of these, Momma. You'll have plague then for sure. Do you understand?'

Calmly, she picked up a needle, drew a measure of clear serum from a small ampoule of what I assumed was antivenin. She checked and double-checked the level, then rolled on her side and tugged down on her pants and underpants. 'Okay, be ite,' she said again, and inclined her head.

'I don't know what to do.' My breath caught in my chest and I felt like an idiot. Snakes slithered from under the furniture and down the hallway. Burgess kicked his feet wildly, refusing to get up, but still shouting scripture at the ceiling, as if God was in one of the upstairs bedrooms.

'Be ite.' Momma gestured towards her ass again. It was as big as a drive-in screen; Christ knows I couldn't miss.

'There you go,' I said, closing my eyes and praying for the best. I withdrew the needle and tossed it onto the milk crate. 'Are you going to be okay?'

'Okay,' she smiled again. 'Be ite.'

'Be ite,' I said and rose to leave. 'I've got to take your truck, but I'll bring it back later tonight. I'm going to call an ambulance for you as soon as I get rolling. Please stay still and keep that arm down until the paramedics get here. Burgess was hit in the arm. He'll be fine.'

'Be ite,' Momma said again. 'Bi vis, plea.'

'Your Bible?'

'Plea.'

I handed it to her. 'Thank you.' There was water left in the pitcher. I chugged what was left, then offered to refill it for her, but this time she waved me off.

My feet were on fire as I staggered through the door and down the wooden steps to the muddy driveway. And there, standing beside the flatbed truck, was a bearded giant armed with an axe. He didn't attack me, but it was clear I would have to go through him to get to the truck. In a flash I knew what Burgess had screamed when I shot him – not *Joy*, but *Leroy*: three hundred pounds of muscle and unkempt, bushy hair, all farm dirt, dungarees and determination. I'd have to shoot him six times before he'd even realise he'd been hit.

I tried diplomacy. 'Leroy, your … *parents* … they need you inside, right away.'

He didn't move. 'Y'all haint takin' ma truck.'

'I'll bring it back tonight, Leroy, I promise – Hell, I'll get the State Police to buy you a new one, Christ knows I will!'

'Don't y'all blaspheme here!' He raised the axe.

I drew my .45 again. 'Okay, okay! I'm sorry, it slipped out! I'm from New Jersey; it happens.'

He didn't think that was funny. 'Y'all haint takin' ma truck. Shoot me if y'all wants, but I haint movin'.'

I lost my patience. 'Listen, you fucking glandular disorder in dungarees: *I am taking that truck into Ashland*, and I am leaving in the next thirty seconds. I will bring it back. I'll fill the tank. I'll even have the State Police buy you a new one; you can pick the fucking colour, but if I have to shoot you to save thousands of people from the fucking pneumonic plague, then I will do it, Leroy. Don't test me.'

'Be ite, Roy.' Momma Aiken appeared on the stoop behind me. 'Be ite.'

'Thanks, Mrs Aiken.' I shot her a grateful look, then said to Leroy, 'They need you inside. I'll send help as soon as I can.'

He sighed, then flipped the axe towards a woodpile behind the house. 'Awright, but hold up.' Leroy opened the driver's side door, rooted around beneath the front seat and emerged with a six-foot-long emerald boomslang, my parting gift from the Aiken family.

'Any other surprises in there?' I asked.

'Secon' gear sticks a bit is all.'

'Thanks,' I said as I tugged open the dented, rusty door and stepped up on the running board. I looked back at Momma Aiken. 'Thank you,' I said again.

'Find Molly, Sailor. You know where she is. Go on now,' Momma said with near-perfect articulation.

316

Leroy, who didn't appear to have heard her, stomped up the porch steps to examine the bite marks on his mother's wrist.

'I will.'

'Find Molly, Sailor.'

My vision fogged again; I wiped my eyes. 'It means nothing, doesn't it? My faith, my drunken prayers, all my talking out loud to God?'

Momma Aiken cast me an unconvincing wave. 'Be ite.'

I got the flatbed rumbling down the gravel drive before I looked back. Leroy and Momma had gone inside the farmhouse. I held my shaking hands in front of my face and scraped up a deep breath from somewhere. I couldn't hear Burgess screaming over the rumble of the big diesel engine.

It was eight-forty p.m. according to the dashboard clock. I had lost more than five hours, but I had gained a truck.

If Ashland PD hadn't found her, Molly would be in town by now. I didn't know what time Ashland Chrysler closed, or when their stick-man Robert E. Lee would ride off to Appomattox on his big white horse, but I was betting it would be at least nine p.m., after the Fourth of July fireworks.

8:42 p.m.

The old flatbed chugged and wheezed its way southeast, down a rutted dirt lane between two corn fields. Twilight gave way to gathering darkness and I judged the distance to Ashland by the glow of electric lights behind a sloping ridge to my left: probably another four or five miles. When I reached the end of the lane I'd have to pick my way northeast until I found a paved road.

Squinting against the darkness, I used the last determined rays of bruise-purple sunlight to search the fields, looking for an errant shadow or a dead body.

Could still stop y'all's heart.

I felt the coral snake's iron band tighten around my chest and made myself count breaths as my tongue thickened, and my neck swelled. I'd never been in anaphylactic shock before; I didn't know what it would feel like, sneaking up on me. I was pretty sure Burgess had injected me with at least three antivenins and I would have bet he hadn't checked any labels to see if they could be used all at once, let alone in tandem with a double-dose of gentamicin, or on plague victims. Any one of those variables might mean the end of me.

I was truly frightened, for the first time since Lieutenant Harper had called me the previous morning to send me on this fool's errand. My face bruised and torn, my arm oozing blood, my feet in agony from countless blisters rubbed to raw flesh, my head, legs, shoulders and back ached with a vicious throb deep down in my bones.

I checked my armpits and groin, feeling for swollen lymph glands, what Doc had called buboes. I didn't find any, but the swelling in my neck had me panicked. It was either the result of the plague infection, or it was a combination of too much snake venom, too much antivenin and the pharmaceutical cocktail currently running riot in my blood. Whichever way, I was probably screwed.

'Could still stop my'all's heart,' I said, wiping my forehead on a bit of greasy rag lying on the seat beside me. 'But if there's another frigging snake in here, Leroy Aiken, I swear I'm coming back there to kill the lot of you. And if I'm dead, I swear I'll haunt you all to Kingdom come.'

I leaned over to check the floor on the passenger side, looking as far as I could under the seat. The truck bumped through the shallow ditch beside the lane, tore through a stand of saplings and crushed a lone mailbox.

'Goddamnit!' I tried to shout. I gripped the wheel with both hands. 'Watch the road, Sailor, you dumb-ass. That's all you need: add a traffic accident to your list of fuck-ups.'

The first of the Ashland town fireworks lit the night sky. They were close enough to see clearly, but still far enough off that I couldn't immediately hear the distant crack and boom of the explosives. My father had taught me that old algorithm for storms: watch for the lightning flash and then count Thomas Jeffersons until I heard the thunder rumble; every Thomas Jefferson meant that the lightning was another mile away. In college I learned that light travelled nearly 190,000 miles per second, while sound lumbered along at 770 miles per hour, the tortoise and the hare of Physics 121. I figured the firework flash was pointless; only the timing of the explosion would give me an idea of how far away I was.

I watched for a flash, then counted, 'One Thomas Jefferson, two Thomas—'

The thudding boom reached me as a wimpy bang.

'Okay, so what's that? Basically two seconds? If sound travels at 770 miles an hour, that means it travels about 125 miles in ten minutes. That's around 12 miles every minute, so that's— one-sixtieth of 12 miles every second.'

The arithmetic calmed me a bit, distracting me from the burgeoning reality that not only was I lost among the farms and fields north of Richmond, but I was about to die somewhere in a stolen truck loaded with poisonous snakes.

'Counting two seconds makes me two-sixtieths of 12 miles. I guess that's one-thirtieth ... ? Great, that helps: I'm one-thirtieth of 12 miles from Ashland, Virginia. Wait, that can't be right. That's less than half a mile. I must have been absent the day they taught division. Sorry, Dr Wentw—'

I flipped open my cell phone, saw that my battery indicator was empty but not yet flashing, and scrolled until I found her number. My hands numb – *like Dad's fingertips* – I fumbled the CALL button twice before getting it right.

'Detective Doyle?' She answered right away. 'Are you all right?'

'No, ma'am.'

'I've been quarantined,' she said, 'but I suppose you know that.' There was nothing accusatory in her tone; rather, she sounded sympathetic.

'I'm sorry.'

'It's not your fault, Detective, not at all.'

'It is.'

'Where are you?'

I blinked my vision clear. 'I don't really know, somewhere near Ashland. I'm following Molly.'

'Are you?' She said something to someone in the room with her, then said, 'The police and the Secret Service seem to think she's coming here. They're spread out all over Glen Allen and the North Side, trying to find her.'

'They're wrong, Dr Wentworth,' I said, 'but I don't have time to argue now. I'm calling with a question about Lennox-Gastaut victims. I've been having some ... hallucinations, delusions, I don't know what to call them – psychotic episodes, maybe – for the past two days, and I don't know why.'

'I see.'

I heard thirty-eight years of public school teacher, counsellor and administrator in those two words. 'Yes,' I said, 'and I'm calling because I'm wondering if you ever met a Lennox-Gastaut victim who was able to ... *do* things, make ideas or pictures appear in people's heads. Get people to say things they hadn't planned, in a voice that wasn't theirs. Is that crazy? Am I ... ? I can imagine what you're thinking, but I just had to ask, because—'

'Detective Doyle, I have worked with students with mild to severe cognitive disabilities for more than three decades. I have seen them do surprising, heart-wrenching and even tragic things, but I have never known any of them to be clairvoyant, or to be able to control other people's thoughts or actions. I'm sorry.'

I pushed the truck into neutral and coasted to a stop at the intersection of the Aiken farm drive and a one-lane county road. The fireworks flashed, spun, flickered and boomed over Ashland in the distance. I sat back in the worn fabric seat, feeling the old springs give as I shifted my weight.

'Detective? Detective Doyle, are you there?'

'I'm sorry,' I said. 'I'm sorry I didn't really listen to you yesterday. You were telling me much more than I heard.'

'I don't understand,' she said. 'Why don't you come down here, and we'll discuss it? The city is a right old mess, and many of the roads are closed, but if you can get to Maymount Park, I'm sure I can find someone here to help you feel better. You don't sound good at all, Detective.'

'I was wrong, Dr Wentworth, wrong about Carl and Claire, but especially about Molly, wasn't I?'

'That's impossible for me to know, Detec—'

'I was,' I said. 'Lots of people are.' My vision blurred. I might have been passing out or crying. I didn't know which.

'If you come down here, we can talk about it for as long as you like, Detective. I don't think you should be out interacting with people. You might spread—'

'It's okay,' I interrupted her again, 'I won't be out long. Thank you, Dr Wentworth.' I hung up, wrenched the truck into first gear and lumbered northeast onto the road, straddling the centre line to make sure I kept out of the ditch.

I see Molly on the stairs, cat bowls for FERGIE, BERT and MING on the worn treads. Carl's in the hall above, still out of view, but I hear him walking, one work boot and one aged prosthetic: clump, clack, clump, clack.

He calls, 'Come on up, sweetie. It's time to say good night to Mommy.'

'I'm scared, Daddy. Wibbleton. Daddy. I'm scared. Wibbleton to Wobbleton.'

Carl appears on the landing. He is backlit by a naked bulb overhead and flanked by pictures – newspaper stories and citations from his tour in Vietnam. He hands Molly a palm frond. 'You remember how to tie it into a cross? Mommy taught you. You tie it for her, sweetie.'

Molly cries. It's a terrible sound. 'Daddy scared. Wibbleton. I'm scared.'

Carl wipes his hands on his pants, beige Dickies, dusty with cat litter.

There were houses now, not many, but a few country places tucked here and there into the woods beside a stream that paralleled whatever road I found myself on. The fireworks boomed off to my right, and through the trees I managed barely one Thomas Jefferson between the flashes and bangs. It seemed strange to me that the town would go ahead with its fireworks display when all the major roads were most likely closed in all directions except for military, FEMA and CDC traffic – but those were bigger thoughts than I could manage given the circumstances so I focused instead on keeping Leroy's flatbed rolling towards town.

The land rose before me, climbing a wooded rise; the stream dropped off to my right, cutting through a gulley as it wound south towards the Chickahominy River. As I crested the short hill I saw the outskirts of Ashland come into view. The picturesque little town had an Amtrak station next to the college common. Scores of trains passed through each day, some stopping briefly, others roaring through at 115 miles per hour. How more children and drunk fraternity brothers weren't clobbered each year was a mystery to me.

I found a spot on the road where I could see above the treetops and pulled over. Molly Bruckner could be anywhere. The dark, western edge of Ashland spread out below me, the old part of town a bit further east and slightly south, towards the Interstate. Route 1 was a corridor of commercial light, an illuminated four-lane trail running south from Ashland until it blurred into the ponderous glow of the metro Richmond area fifteen miles away. I set the parking brake and rested again, content to take a minute to catch my breath and pull my thoughts together.

'You're never going to find her, Sailor,' I said as I peered along Route 1, hoping to make out something that looked like a car dealership, even from this far away. 'Give it up. Just close your eyes and let go. It'll all be fine. *Be ite.* Just let it go.'

Carl's on the tattered sofa. I don't know how long he's been there. A week, maybe two, certainly since the first pains in his chest, which he understands were just a harbinger of what's coming. He's made the decision to give up on Robert Lake and David Carver. They never would have paid anyway.

Carl's wet with sweat, and shivering. Yet there are no medicine bottles, tissues, bedpans, nothing. A fire-eating jarhead to the very end.

'Molly, sweetie, come in here, baby.'

She shuffles from the kitchen. 'Daddy, I'm hungry. The cats are mad, Daddy. Moose and Poopsie. Wibbleton. Wibbleton to Wobbleton. Daddy, so . . . I'm hungry, Daddy.'

'Sweetie, I need you to listen.' He reaches for her. Molly kneels on the rug. 'Can you listen to Daddy?'

'Cats are so mad, Daddy. Wibbleton. Moose and Poopsie. Chickadee. Mad, Daddy.'

'You just leave those cats outside, sweetie. Okay? They'll take care of themselves. You leave them outside.'

'Wibbleton. Wibbleton to Wobbleton.'

He caresses her cheek. 'Sweetie, Daddy's sick. Daddy's sick. I need you to listen, baby. Daddy needs you to go to Mr Henry's, across the field. Okay, sweetie? Go to Mr Henry's. He'll help you.'

'Mr Henry's hungry. Wibbleton. Daddy, I'm hungry.'

'Can you go to Mr Henry's, sweetie? Can you do that for Daddy?'

'Cats are mad, Daddy. Moose and Poopsie.'

Carl pulls her to him, hugs her to his chest. 'Daddy loves you, sweetie, so much. But tomorrow morning, you go to Mr Henry's for Daddy.'

Molly sobs, her face buried in Carl's flannel shirt. 'Daddy so . . .'

'Daddy's not mad, sweetie. Not mad, not ever mad.'

I drifted for a while as my legs and arms went numb. I might have slept. Leroy's truck was the most comfortable place I'd ever been, and despite the lingering smell of mould and singed oil, I let the bench seat wrap me softly in its caress. And I gave in.

My phone buzzed; I don't know how much later. It vibrated irritatingly long before I managed to reorient myself, to find it in the darkness and to flip it open with my dead fingers, *like Dad's, Sailor. They're just like Dad's.*

'Doyle,' I said, needing something to drink. I fished around for a cigarette but could find nothing. I figured Burgess must have stolen whatever was left in the pack.

'Sailor?'

It was Jenny.

'Hey, baby.' I tried to sound sensible, sober, not drugged or plague-infected.

'Where are you? I'm scared. Is this all ... ? Is this what you meant? All this? Jesus, it's terrible, Sailor. People are rioting. There was a run on the hospital at VCU. The city police shot two men who were infected and trying to escape a quarantine; that's just the ones we know about. The highway's closed. The airport's shut down. The CDC director is on television talking about exponential infection rates. Did you do this? Is this your case? Please tell me you're okay.' She sounded as tense as she did tired.

'I'm all right, Jenny.'

'Where are you?'

'Ashland.'

'Can you come home? Or are you ... ?' She didn't want to say it, but we both understood: if I had the plague I wasn't going anywhere near our home. I could die here on the side of the road after saying good-bye to my wife and children. Hell, there were fireworks cannonading the night sky above town. What better time to go?

'It'll be a while before I can come home,' I said. 'I'm trying to fix some things I messed up yester— Well, some things I messed up. I'll fix those, and then I'll be done.'

She was crying now.

'Can I ask you something?' I said.

'What is it?'

'Why Bob Lourdes? How did it happen? Was I away too much? Too distracted? Why him?'

'I don't understand.'

'RML, RML, RML. It's everywhere. Robert Michael Lourdes. You said yourself he was goodlooking, and he asked about you yesterday morning. Why him, Jenny? He's so—'

'What are you saying, Sailor? Do you think I'm having an affair with Bob Lourdes?'

This roused me a bit. I tried to grab the steering wheel to pull myself up, but my fingers didn't want to comply. 'Yes, I do, Jenny. I see it all over the place: RML. Who is that, if it isn't Lourdes? Who gave you the ankle bracelet? I didn't.'

'I know you didn't.' Her voice broke. 'Do we have to talk about this now? Please, can't it wait until tomorrow or whenever I can see you face to face?'

'No!' I tried again to shout. It didn't work. I wasn't angry; I was sorry. But I wanted the truth. 'No ... Please tell me now.'

She took a deep breath and said something to Ben. I strained to hear him, wanting to catch whatever he said in case I never saw him again. It sounded like *wormy*.

'Jenny, my battery's going, baby.'

'RML doesn't stand for Robert Lourdes or anyone for that matter. It's something else.'

'What?'

'Sailor.'

'Please.'

Another sigh. 'It stands for *Reclaim My Life*. It's ... it's a message, something I tell myself all the time. I scribble it on pads. I have it on that anklet. I write in on envelopes while I talk on the phone.' The word *phone* was lost behind a sob.

'*Reclaim my life*,' I echoed. 'Reclaim it from what?' I didn't understand.

'From whom.'

'Fine, from whom?'

'From you, Sailor! From *you*! I have to reclaim my life from you.'

The fireworks over Ashland flashed and flickered a thousand different colours, but the pop, boom and crackle had fallen silent. 'Reclaim it from me?'

'Yes.' She didn't try to say any more. I wouldn't have understood. After a while, she took a steadying breath and said, 'Please come home.'

'I'll be there as soon as I can,' I lied. 'But Jenny, would you do me a favour? Please? A couple of favours, actually—'

'What?' She sniffed hard. It was loud despite the weak signal.

'Please don't give up. I've had a rough couple of days, and I think that I ... just ... please don't give up, not now.'

'Come home, Sailor.'

'And please tell Ben I said: *You and Me*. Will you do that for me?' I asked. 'And I promise I'll get there as soon as Doc Lefkowitz clears me. I promise.'

'I'll do it,' she said. 'You know, this all goes back to Molly.'

It was a slap in the face. I sat up. 'What did you say?'

'Your sister, Marie. You never got past your sister, Sailor, and I can't do this any more: the pills, that woman, the booze. Any of it. I have to get my life back. I have to—'

'Jenny,' I cut her off, 'please, not yet. I need—'

My cell phone died. The word BATTERY flashed at me several times, then blinked out.

'Fucking phone!' I threw it out the window, stomped on the clutch and jammed the truck back into gear. Rolling northeast, I clicked on the high beams, looking for a right turn – any right turn. I needed to get over the stream, across the gulley and into town if I was going to cut the corner to Route 1 and Ashland Chrysler. I sucked air in hard through my nose and blew it out of my mouth, hoping to create some kind of vacuum in my lungs. The adrenalin of the past few minutes would wear off soon enough and I needed to get into town before I started drifting again.

The fireworks display ended with a crashing finale, clouds of cordite drifting west into the farmland, filling the corn and soybean fields with the smell of war. The gulley on my right grew deeper as the truck climbed another hill. The sides of the stream bed were lined with brush that eventually gave way to hardwoods and prickly cedars. The forest grew thick around me, knotting together overhead in a brambly ceiling. Something colourful flickered to my right, across the stream. It might have been more fireworks, a kid playing with Roman candles, or it could have been emergency lights, an Ashland police cruiser. I slowed, watching out of the passenger window, hoping to see it again.

Ashland still glowed in the distance, but across the stream from me, darkness reigned. The hillside tapered down to a sunken road, so if I had seen emergency lights, the car, ambulance, whatever, must have turned north, around the wooded hill across the stream, but beneath me, too far down for me to see anything now.

Across the stream . . .

'Holy shit!' I shouted, downshifting from fourth to third and ramming the accelerator to the floor. At top speed Leroy Aiken's flatbed might only have been doing fifty miles per hour, but it beat the hell out of jogging in soggy wingtip shoes. I reached the crest of the hill and saw what I knew would be there. A green highway sign read: *Ashland 1 mile.* Clinging to one of its metal posts, waist-deep in poison oak, was the white-haired banshee woman I'd seen in Molly's room. Her pale face shone the colour of raw bone as she pointed east with a gnarled finger. Her ebony topcoat billowed like a loose sail, despite the still summer night. She screamed a winter wind and the breath left my lungs, seemingly for good.

I stomped on the brake and the clutch simultaneously to make the turn and the old diesel screamed, oily smoke pouring from a dozen spot-welds as I cranked the big steering wheel around. For a moment, I thought I would miss the turn entirely, run off the road into the gulley . . .

'C'mon, baby, come around,' I urged, holding my breath as the back end skidded in a disconcerting fishtail. I corrected the front wheels, turning back as quickly as I could to break the skid and the truck slid to a stop in a cloud of dust and burned rubber. I found myself facing south, having spun almost entirely around. A glance back at the sign revealed that the shrieking woman was gone; only a ratty black trash bag clinging to the signpost fluttered in the wake of the flatbed's frenzied turn.

I coughed and saw stars, and cursed the pain in my chest. My numb fingers managed to get the truck back into gear and I started slowly towards the old truss-and-beam bridge spanning the stream, now at the bottom of a narrow but steep ravine. In the diesel's headlights, I saw what looked like the skeleton of a proper bridge, stripped by years and weather to its rusty bones. A worn, shield-like medallion hanging from the first cross-beam read *1817*. The macadam roadway ended at the edge of the bridge, which shifted abruptly from pavement to railroad ties, black with creosote and smelling of summertime behind a train station.

I didn't trust the bridge to support the weight of Leroy's big flatbed so I stopped at the edge, shouldered the door open and stepped outside with wobbly legs.

Across the bridge, two Ashland City police cruisers and an unmarked sedan, all with lights ablaze, took the turn at speed. Their sirens tore a ragged hole in the darkness.

I started running, as fast as weakened legs and injured feet could carry me, as ungainly as a ninety-year-old man and probably half as fast, but still I ran, because I had seen it all in my mind a thousand times over the past ten years.

Ten years, six months, two weeks, and one day.

The cruisers skidded to a noisy stop when they saw her. They must have caught sight of her before I did because they were out of their cars and screaming before I spotted her myself, trying to duck behind a rusty truss.

'Wait!' I said in a hoarse croak. 'Wait! Don't shoot her – she doesn't understand! She's not dangerous!'

The bridge was seventy-five yards across and Molly Bruckner was still a good fifty yards away. She needed to stay put for ten seconds. It wouldn't take me longer than ten seconds to run fifty yards and if I could just make it that far, they'd hear me – the Ashland cops, the very guys I'd begged Huck to mobilise. I had to get them to see me, *the State Police detective*, not the stumbling, out-of-uniform, stooped-over lunatic running at them, gun in hand, from an old farm truck.

'State Police!' I yelled, but my voice was gone. I waved my badge over my head, hoping it might catch a glint of flashing light.

One of them shouted, but I didn't hear what he said. Another replied, something that sounded like *wormy*, before dropping to one knee.

'Don't shoot!' I cried. 'Don't shoot!'

Molly heard this, saw me, and shuffled awkwardly in my direction. 'Ooh, Daddy say ... Daddy say. Wibbleton. Wibbleton. Cut the Christmas tree. Daddy say ... ooh, Daddy mad. Daddy say ...Christmas tree. Wibbleton. Wibbleton to Wobbleton. Daddy so mad. Daddy so mad. Wibbleton to Wobbleton, fifteen, fifteen miles.'

'It's okay, Molly,' I shouted. 'Come to me. Come on.'

As she got closer, I could see that she was a walking nightmare. The enormous pink shorts with yellow flowers revealed Molly's stubby, hairy legs, which were riddled with mosquito and horsefly bites, and drying scabs where I could only guess that she had been attacked by her own cats. Her flabby arms were the same, and I tasted acrid bile when I saw a couple of leeches attached firmly to the back of her dimpled upper arm. She wore Bugs Bunny gloves, for what reason I couldn't begin to fathom, but now I understood why we hadn't found her fingerprints on the handle of Carl's fillet knife. She dragged the green cardigan she had been wearing in the old photograph I'd found inside Claire's tomb; it was torn and filthy, stained with mud and drying algae and who knew what.

Molly's face bled; her elbows and knees were scraped open from too many downhill stumbles through too much thorny underbrush. She had furiously unkempt hair and a round, pie-plate face, flat and pale. She weighed probably two hundred and thirty pounds and had sweated through her Minnie Mouse T-shirt so much that it looked to have been died piss-yellow under the arms and beneath the collar. She smelled of vomit. When she wasn't prattling on about her Daddy being so mad, she made sustained vowel sounds in a half-whine, half-scream that made me want to either shoot her or shoot myself. She doubled over when she reached me and coughed so violently I thought she might pass out.

One of the Ashland police officers shouted at us again and I screamed back, but no sound came out. My vision tunnelled as I stood there on that narrow span, and I tried to wave the officers away, to get them to shut off the lights and the sirens.

One of them fired.

'No,' I cried, 'don't!'

I heard a voice scream, 'Wait!'

Another shouted, 'Get down. He's got a gun!'

There was another shot, a blistering pain in my hip, and a high-pitched whine past my face.

I squeezed off a round myself, aiming at nothing, then dived for Molly. She outweighed me by at least fifty pounds, but I wrapped my arms around her and shoved her towards the side of the bridge, trying to get both of us behind one of the slanted trusses. We stumbled, fell hard on the splintered railroad ties, and rolled for the shadows near the rail.

Through the confused din, there were more shots, more screams, and another lance of fiery pain, this one through my shoulder. I reached for Molly and she grabbed my forearms, swallowed her manic vowel song, and said, 'Daddy! Daddy so ... Wibbleton. Wibbleton to Wobbleton. Daddy so ... cut the Christmas tree.'

The rusty creak of tired metal rent the night, drowning out all other sound—

—and we fell—

I hit the water hard enough to knock the wind from my lungs, which was a stroke of good fortune, because my right leg shattered against an underwater rock. I would have been screaming for hours had I not eventually passed out.

Stark, astonishing cold – as cold as winter in Stroudsburg, Pennsylvania – stabbed at my skin as I tumbled over the pebbly bottom, delirious with pain, yet almost relishing the blissful confusion.

Strong arms grabbed me, dragged me to the bank, though my head stayed submerged for a long time. That was fine with me. I thought of the word *wormy*, and what it might mean.

Then I was out, watching cruiser lights flashing overhead, colouring the bridge beams and trusses in rolling waves of blue and red. I stared up for a long time, watching the rhythmic lights flash on and off, as disconnected as a pithed frog.

My leg moved and I screamed.

My left foot trailed in the water; my right was gone.

I swallowed what tasted like blood but what might have been river water.

Then Molly Bruckner was beside me, one of her pudgy hands splayed flat across my chest. She leaned over and said, 'Marie forgives you, Sammy. Your sister forgives you. It's okay. So do I.'

My vision faded; the sounds of the forest, the police shouting as they scrambled down the sides of the ravine, even the stream tumbling past, all of them quieted to a barely audible whisper. 'What did you say? Dad, is that you? Dad?'

Molly leaned over me again. Blood spiderwebbed her forehead and neck and her nose lay crookedly across her flat face. She whined, coughed down at me, and barked a helpless, miserable cry. She was hurt, frightened and lonely.

I felt sorry that I had no comfort to offer.

'Wibbleton. Wibbleton to Wobbleton. Daddy so ... Daddy,' she said.

Finally I tumbled away.

Molly struggles with Claire's body. It's board-stiff, but light. She tries to get her mother through the doorway, but she can't figure it out.

Housecats, transformed by hunger and plague, scratch and claw at her legs. She kicks at them, admonishing her few favourites. 'No Moose! No! Wibbleton. Wibbleton to Wobbleton. Get down Bert! Poopsie, no!'

Claire won't cooperate.

'Daddy so mad. Daddy cuts the Christmas tree. Daddy so mad. Cut the Christmas tree before it goes in the water. Daddy so ... Wibbleton. Wibbleton to Wobbleton. Wobbleton. Moose, no! Down! Bert, get down!'

She wants her mother and father to be together. Carl's too heavy. She's

331

strong, a powerful woman, but not strong enough to get Carl up the steps. She'll bring Claire to him.

'Cut the Christmas tree. Daddy so mad. Moose is mad. Cats hungry, Daddy.' She drops Claire and starts to cry, wailing, a sustained shriek that momentarily distracts even Moose and Bert, the hungriest cats.

'Cut the Christmas tree, Daddy. Santa says. Cut the Christmas tree. Wibbleton. Wibbleton to Wobbleton.'

Molly steps over her mother's body, kicking cats away. Her father's saw is in the barn. It's the one he uses to slice an inch or two off the Christmas tree trunk before mounting it in the tree stand.

Molly helps him, every year. They always do it together.

EPILOGUE

Tuesday, July 7th

*Medical College of Virginia,
Richmond*

11:06 a.m.

It was cold, not frozen-river cold, but extra-blanket cold. I woke to the sound of an aluminium desk chair being dragged across a tile floor, a vivid, shocking screech that would wake the dead.

Doc Lefkowitz saw my eyes flutter open. He shot me a guilty grin and whispered, 'Sorry.'

'S'okay,' I wheezed. 'Water?'

'Sure, sure.' Doc filled a plastic jug from a sink beside my bed. He opened a paper-wrapped straw, tossed the wrapper towards a bin and held the jug beneath my chin.

I drank a little, took a breather, drank a little more, and whispered, 'That's better.'

'You done?'

'Not yet.'

With Doc leaning close, I could smell his expensive Spanish cigarillos – *burning whale snot*. He wore New York Mets scrubs and had a surgical mask tugged down around his neck. He looked as though he had been awake for months.

'A little more,' he said, 'but not too much, not yet.'

'What day is it?'

'Tuesday.'

'Holy shit. Really?'

'You were out of it for a while.' Doc sat in the desk chair. 'Your leg needed surgery, and you'd been shot twice. It was touch and go for a while when you first came in. All that snake venom and antivenin in your system made for some interesting results. Reading your blood work was like checking the inventory at a pharmacy: OxyCodone, gentamicin, antivenin, ibuprofen, ethyl alcohol. It's quite a laundry list. You must have had a hell of a day.'

'Not one I'll forget anytime soon.' I tried to shrug but discovered that my shoulders were wrapped tightly in gauze and surgical tape. I lifted my head far enough to see that my right leg was also encased in hospital white. There was an IV in the veins on my left hand, and three layers of tape across the back of my wrist. It hurt when I moved it. 'Where are we?'

'MCV. You came in via Med-Evac from Ashland, Saturday night around ten.'

'How's Molly?'

'She died, about five-thirty yesterday morning.'

My throat tried to close. I gagged back a mouthful of tangy puke. Failure, utter and absolute, wrapped itself around me like a damp shroud. I would have been happy to have the floor of MCV hospital open and drop my broken, useless ass on the express elevator to Hell. I cried.

Doc didn't mind. He said simply, 'Sorry about that, Sailor.'

'How many others?' I wiped my face on my sleeve.

'Seventeen so far, and we have another forty-one in critical condition. While there is no inoculation for *Yersinia pestis*, an aggressive gentamicin regimen can cure the bubonic version of plague.' He kicked off his loafers and leaned back far enough to put his stocking feet on my bed. 'Sadly, there is no cure for pneumonic plague. Those infected by fleas at the farmhouse should be fine. We believe we've found them all, and the CDC has administered the necessary medications. The victims infected after the fact, either via contact with Molly Bruckner or with one of the infected investigators, are less fortunate.'

'Phil's family? His daughters?' *Don't say it. I'm not ready for another one. Don't . . . !*

'They're fine. Tested, treated and released.'

'Thank Christ for that.'

'I'm sure he appreciates it.' Doc winked.

'And the panic?'

He shuddered. 'It was downright nasty for a while, but there were scrolling alerts on all the 24-hour news channels and FEMA and the CDC took over the local Comcast channels. Once we started getting out clear, constant information it calmed down and by Sunday afternoon things were pretty much under control. They got the medication to us here at VCU, down in Maymount, and up in Henrico County, and any potential victims who had travelled outside the city got help from local law enforcement agencies. President Baird, determined not to miss a glorious opportunity to reassure this great nation – and the rest of the world – even interrupted Saturday night programming!' He laughed. 'You'll be pleased to know Bob Lake, not to be outdone, called a press conference of his own, and basically took credit for side-stepping a national pandemic. Go figure. In the end, we were able to open the roads and the airports by late Monday night. While it ranks among the shittiest weekends of my life, I am painfully aware that it could have been significantly worse. Your friends Bryson, Lourdes and especially Phil Clarkson were instrumental in identifying potential victims and in calculating the infection rates.'

'We lose anyone we know?' I asked, and regretted it right away. Doc and my team had done their best to save the Eastern Seaboard from my mistakes. Today wasn't a good day for me to be selfish.

Doc sighed through his nose.

'Doc?'

'I don't think Grace Wentworth is going to make it, Sailor. I'm sorry. She didn't have the strongest constitution to begin with, and she had fairly close contact with you Friday afternoon.'

Now, I didn't try to stem my tears. 'I was contagious by lunchtime Friday?'

'No, no.' Doc scratched at the stubble – several days' growth – on his chin. 'You were carrying fleas on you, on your suit, in your car, in your hair. She didn't have a chance of avoiding them.'

'Oh, Jesus,' I cried.

'I'm sorry.'

'Where is she?'

'Upstairs.' He nodded at the ceiling. 'This whole wing is quarantined.'

'I want to see her.'

'Give yourself a day,' Doc said. 'If you're up to it tomorrow, I'll wheel you down to the elevator.'

I didn't argue. There was no point fighting with Doc, especially flat on my back. 'Okay,' I said, 'so how did fleas give her pneumonic plague?'

'They didn't,' Doc said, 'but you've got to remember, bubonic plague is a vicious motherfucker, pardon my Latin, and not everyone responds to the drugs.'

'Fuck this fucking job,' I said. 'I'm going back to Dope.'

Doc grinned. 'Well, you were good at it. I'm sure they'd be happy to have you back.'

'Prick,' I said.

'Feeling better already, huh?'

'How's Sarah?'

'She'll be all right. She's not interested in seeing much of you any time soon, though.' He chuckled and looked again like an exhausted old man. 'She's a workhorse. She's been in the lab running tissue stains and serology tests since Saturday morning. I made her get some sleep Sunday night, but after a couple of hours on the couch in the hallway, she was back at it. There's a team of graduate students in from Tech. I know one of the professors from the Fralin Life Science Lab in Blacksburg. They leapt at the opportunity for this kind of field work. Sarah's done a nice job standing up to the CDC and FEMA, too. She's defending her work, protecting her samples, and keeping as much of the research and data here in the hospital as possible. I was worried for a while that the whole thing might get swallowed up by the Bioterror and Infectious Disease Lab at Quantico, but she went toe to toe with an irritated CDC director ... and won. Bringing the Tech researchers in was smart; it made the whole thing public.'

'Should make for an interesting chapter in her dissertation,' I said.

'Definitely something to talk about during her job interviews.'

I let my head fall deep into the pillow. The room was cold, but I welcomed it. Except for the stream, I couldn't remember the last time I had felt cold – *December 17, last year outside the* CID *Christmas party, that might have been it.* 'How many needed treatment?' I asked.

'A little more than seven thousand were tested and treated.'

'Bullshit!'

'Nope,' Doc said, 'no word of a lie. It's astonishing how many people were exposed just to you and members of your team. If we hadn't found those buboes on Carl's body, we'd have been looking at two hundred thousand by Monday, maybe even more. They'd have been leaves in the wind.'

'How's Huck?'

'He'll be all right. He's mighty pissed at you for shooting him, but to be honest, it wasn't much more than a scratch. I think he's going for the sympathy play with one of the nurses downstairs.'

I laughed, and my chest hurt. I silently promised never to go anywhere that had coral snakes, ever. 'How exactly is he suggesting that I shot him?'

'Ah, but you did.' Doc raised a finger at me in his familiar gesture. 'He was on the bridge with the Ashland Police and the Secret Service on Saturday night. He wasn't able to organise anyone to help you, so he broke out of the containment area he'd been assigned to, stole a car and drove to the police station in Ashland. All the way up there, he was on the phone with David Carver. Do you know who David Carver is, Sailor?'

I nodded weakly.

'And you know Huck was slated to work the Bob Lake fund-raiser Saturday night at the Jefferson Hotel, right? So he knew Bob Lake's handlers – hell, the whole damn Republican Party – would blame this entire mess on you, the CID and the Virginia State Police, if only for botching the containment. So he started Carver thinking that the Secret Service could grab a share of the glory when they collared Molly Bruckner, a deadly terrorist determined to assassinate Carver's boss.'

'And that actually worked?'

'Who knows?' Doc said. 'But I think we'd better prepare ourselves for a lifetime of listening to Huck refining his version of the truth.'

I managed a grin. 'I shot him?'

'In the shin.' Doc waved it off. 'To hear him describe it, you'd think he'd taken one in the chest defending democracy from a battalion of rabid Chinese infiltrators.'

'Ah, damn it, Doc, don't make me laugh,' I coughed. 'My lungs are going to fall out.'

'I'm just glad I'm older than you,' Doc said. 'It means I'll have fewer years to listen to him.'

'So I bet he saved my life.'

'He did that,' Doc conceded. 'But when you think about it, anyone infected with plague could have broken out of state quarantine, stolen a government car, made his way up a closed highway, convinced the future White House Chief of Staff to redirect Secret Service agents, conscripted two Ashland police deputies and their cars, carried you up a ravine with a gunshot wound in his leg and transported you to a hilltop where a Med-Evac chopper could rush you into surgery.'

'Right.' I tried to shrug again. 'Anyone could have pulled that off.'

'Yeah, buy him a beer, and he'll call it even.'

'Is he here?'

'Downstairs.'

I shivered, and Doc pulled a blanket from the end of the bed and draped it over me. I thanked him, then asked the ten-million-dollar question: 'So where'd the plague bacteria come from? Was it really an aerosol?'

'Nope. Naturally occurring sylvatic plague. It's rare, especially in this neck of the woods, but possible because of the weather we've been having and the enormous rodent population on that farm.'

'How can you know?'

'Because of the timing of the infections,' he said. 'It's what epidemiologists call "average serial intervals". You see, for Dr Wentworth to have become infected, she either had to catch the plague from you, to breathe in the aerosol itself, or to get bitten by fleas from the farm. We know she didn't breathe in any aerosol at the farm, so she had to have caught the disease from you somehow. That afternoon, you left the farm for lunch, went to Division Headquarters and—'

'And cleaned myself up in the sink,' I finished for him.

'Exactly,' Doc said. 'So if you were contagious, Tony Cotillo, Dave Stephens, Shantal Carmody and Cheryl Baskin would have contracted the pneumonic version of the plague. But none of them are sick.'

'So the fleas weren't on my body,' I said.

'At first, I think they were,' Doc said, 'because Jessica Thistle, a clerk at the store where you purchased a new shirt, she *did* become infected – but with the bubonic version, not the pneumonic.'

'So I carried fleas into the men's store but not into Division Headquarters?' I felt as bemused as I sounded.

'Oh, you carried them in all right, but they didn't infect anyone, which is a goddamned miracle, seeing as how every flea bite can transfer up to twenty-five thousand bacilli, every time. And infected fleas are ravenous: they're actually dying of starvation, because the bacteria block a tiny sphincter that closes off a flea's stomach, so they feed constantly; they're never full because the blood never gets to the stomach. And they spread bad news with every little nibble. You probably had them on your clothing or in your hair, but cleaning up in the locker room probably shed enough of them that your brief contact wasn't sufficient to pass on the infection to Tony, Dave, Shantal or Cheryl. It was a quiet day at Division so the janitors took the opportunity to deep-clean a little: the industrial bleach they used could kill an elephant, never mind starving fleas freezing their sick little asses off on the cold tiles, waiting for a nice furry body to come and rescue them ...'

'Grace Wentworth rode in my car,' I said, 'so there must have been fleas in my car.'

'Either that, or you were already contagious.'

'I thought you said I wasn't.'

'I don't think you were, but to be certain, we have to examine another case.'

'Sarah Danvers.'

'Exactly.' Doc held the plastic jug beneath my chin and gestured with the straw and I drank a few swallows to oblige him. 'You went to Sarah's apartment more than ten hours after your lunch with Dr Wentworth.'

'Jesus Christ—! *She washed my clothes ...*'

'And we have a winner!'

'So Sarah caught the plague from my flea-infested clothing – the bubonic version? Why didn't she catch the pneumonic version from me?'

'How close contact was it?' Doc looked askance at me.

'Not that close, I guess,' I said, remembering the feel of Sarah's thigh against the side of my face. 'I mean, I didn't kiss her or sneeze on her or anything.'

'She was lucky,' Doc said. 'Not kissing her – or sleeping with her – probably saved her life.'

I tried to arch my back. 'Can I sit up for a while?'

'Sure.' Doc used a remote control to adjust my backrest, then grabbed my forearm and helped me to sit up. 'So where were we? Ah yes, the fact that Jessica Thistle, Grace Wentworth and Sarah Danvers all caught the bubonic version of the plague after contact with you, but Tony Cotillo, Dave Stephens and the rest of Division Headquarters didn't, is what leads me to believe that it was the fleas you carried on your person or in your car that infected them.'

'Okay … But I still don't get how the plague could be naturally occurring,' I said. 'Couldn't an aerosol have infected everything? The insects, the animals, the cats, the people? Wouldn't that make more sense? They passed it on to me and then it jumped from me to the others?'

'Cats can give plague to humans, even pneumonic plague, but they don't give it to fleas,' Doc explained. 'These cats probably gave it to the sheep, the goats and any other small farm animals, especially if the cats attacked them for food. But the rodents – the rats, squirrels, chipmunks and field mice – they all contracted the disease from infected fleas. That place was infested with fleas, and every enzootic species of rodent—'

'What's that?'

'Enzootic,' he said. 'It means endemic, but for animals.'

'So the plague was endemic – enzootic, whatever – in the Bruckner cats?'

'Nope. Cats are epizootic; they eventually die of plague, just like we do. But mice, rats, even some squirrels: they are enzootic, and all the acronyms – the CDC, FEMA and WHO at least – are out there right now figuring out who the guilty rodents were. Combine the right kind of rodent and the right species of flea and an enzootic reservoir of plague bacteria can be supported for generations. Given our damp spring, this hot summer and the filthy conditions on that farm, I'm not that surprised that it happened.'

342

My brain obviously wasn't up to speed yet. 'So the plague's not extinct, whatever the word is?'

'Eradicated? No, there are thousands of cases of plague every year around the world,' Doc said. 'It's not advertised, because it's got such a bad rep: just the name, *plague*, strikes fear into the hearts of millions – as we've just seen. There's a handful of cases which occur in the American Southwest like clockwork – the victims out there contract the disease from fleas that live on prairie dogs. The bacteria probably came from fleas on rats in steamships docking in San Francisco more than a hundred years ago. You get a couple of bilge rats sneaking down a mooring line for a night on the town, and *ka-blam*.'

'But how did the right flea get to St James County?' I asked.

Doc shrugged. 'Who the hell knows? There're more than a hundred million cows, seventy million dogs and ninety million cats in the United States alone – and what? Half a billion chickens? Cows aren't great hosts for fleas, but they do get around. You'd be amazed at the ground domestic and livestock animals cover in trucks, planes and trains. And it's mind-numbingly high odds that the right flea would find the right field mouse right here in our back yard, but with twenty thousand bacilli in every flea bite, it only had to happen once.'

I shook my head. 'Plague. Gods of our fathers. The Black Death.'

'Yep, the very plague you introduced to the Richmond area when you purchased your shirt and went to lunch on Friday.'

'Hey!' I feigned offence. 'You came back to the city too.'

'That I did.' Doc threw up his hands. 'I'm guilty.'

'You saved us all, Doc,' I said, reaching for his hand. I felt teary all over again.

'Bullshit,' he said. 'But I'll let you buy me a beer and we'll call it square.'

'That's two beers this thing's costing me,' I whined.

A nurse knocked and poked her head inside the room. She wore a surgical mask, and an armband marked her as a CDC staff member. She had short cropped hair, as close to a Marine's high-and-tight as I could imagine on a woman, and mid-length sleeves revealed muscular forearms. When she spoke, however, I was pleasantly surprised at her lyric alto. 'I see you're awake, Detective Doyle. Would you mind a visitor?'

I glanced at Doc. 'Would I?'

'Who is it?' Doc said. 'Not his family. Not yet.'

Her face split into what I imagined was an uncharacteristic grin. 'It's Sergeant Harold Greeley, Dr Lefkowitz. He says he's coming in no matter what, but I can probably get an orderly to roll him back downstairs.'

Doc waved them in. 'That's fine. Detective Doyle and I both have our cyanide pills handy should he get out of hand.'

'Yes, sir.'

Nurse Lyric Alto held the door open for a grim-faced orderly who pushed Huck's wheelchair into my room. Huck had one leg elevated on the chair's adjustable support. Like mine, it had been wrapped tightly in gauze and surgical tape. Other than that he looked like a thinner, paler version of himself, and in good spirits at that. Huck took one look around my room and said, 'So this is what you get for shooting a former partner? Nice digs, kemosabe. I'm in an unfurnished garage down on Thirteenth. I had to tip the bellman a twenty just to get up to this level – whatever it is – superhero level.'

'How're you feeling, cousin?' I asked, certain I'd never been so glad to see anyone in my life.

'Well, let's see . . .' He frowned, pondering his list of ailments. 'Apart from being infected with the plague, *by you*, I should point out, my only complaint is that when I went to save your sorry ass, I was shot in the leg, *by you!*'

I rubbed a hand over my bald scalp and wondered how the hell Huck had managed to keep his salt and pepper ponytail. 'Hey, at least I wasn't aiming for you,' I said. 'Those guys you brought along – they were trying to kill me!'

'In their defence' – Huck held up his hands in a show of bullshit supplication – 'you didn't look much like a cop with your drunken gait, your bald head, your unintelligible babble and your racing flatbed stinking of diesel. And, to their credit, those Secret Service guys were really just hoping to be able to make the drive back to DC with a trophy head tied to the hood of Bob Lake's limo.'

Doc interrupted to ask, 'How's the leg?'

Huck tugged at a bit of tape that was coming unstuck from his bandages. 'My time in the half-marathon is going to suck this season,' he said. 'I suppose it's a good thing that the only running I had planned was back and forth to the bar. Otherwise, six weeks of rehab and I'll be back out there collaring gangs, thugs and dealers, everything a growing boy wants for Christmas.'

'Glad to hear it,' Doc said.

Huck changed the subject. 'Sailor, I've got to know.'

'What?' I asked.

'How the fuck did you manage to get yourself so thoroughly bitten by poisonous snakes? Did you stop off in the Amazon, or does God just hate you?'

I snorted through my nose. 'Uncle Hucker, I simply made the mistake of trying to jog across St James County in the summertime. That's all.'

'Religious zealots?' He winked at Doc.

'Yeah.' I frowned. 'How did you know?'

'We checked the registration on that clunker diesel you hijacked. It led to a Burgess and Catherine Aiken of St James County Road 7—'

'Road 7?'

'No joke, kemosabe. Road 7 in St James County, what folks in the big city would call: Holy Shit Rural.'

'That it was.'

'By the time St James deputies arrived, Catherine Aiken had succumbed to respiratory failure. The son, Leroy, had taken off, and old Burgess had thrown himself on the mercy of his snake collection down in the basement, some kind of half-assed lunatic suicide attempt, test of God's love, or some shit. I dunno. They had a hot-air incubation system down there to rival the Reptile House at the National Zoo, tropical snakes coming out of the cereal boxes. Last I heard, the forensic guys were digging a .45 calibre slug out of the plaster. You wouldn't know anything about that, would you, Bruce Willis?'

'That'd be mine,' I said. 'But if fear for my life is any excuse, I had a whole lifetime's fear during the brief but memorable time I spent in the Aikens' charming company.'

Doc said, 'Venomous snakes and illegal animal smuggling should be enough to take to the judge. I'm staggered at what you maniac Christians will do to praise Jesus. You never catch a rabbi wrestling a boa constrictor out of the Ark during a Shabbat service. *That* would be bad form!'

Huck leaned forward. 'My back is screwed up,' he said. 'Don't get old, Sailor.'

'I'll try.'

'So Phil Clarkson stopped by last night,' he said. 'He briefed me on the farm investigation. Jesus, what a tangled mess, huh?'

I said, 'You know it, cousin. The way I figure it, Claire died months ago – Doc's confirmed that much for us – and Carl started signing her Social Security cheques, depositing the money and committing fraud, which might just be the only honest-to-God felony that took place out there, if you can believe that. I have to check with the Commonwealth Attorney's Office to see what the law says about the internment of dead bodies in Virginia, but there might not be any actual law against burying your wife in cat litter and duct-taping the door closed.'

'How'd she get into the hallway?' Huck asked either of us.

I answered, 'Molly. She was a big girl, strong enough to heave me out of that stream. I guess when Carl died, she wanted them to be together. It was easier to bring Mom downstairs than to carry Dad upstairs—'

'Especially since Claire had lost about eighty pounds by then,' Doc added. 'She'd be completely dehydrated, no fluid left in her body.'

I said, 'Molly's problem was that Claire wouldn't fit through the door. She was as stiff as one of those damned railroad ties. So Molly went into the barn and found one of Carl's old handsaws. Who knows why she quit, but if I had to lay a wager on it, I'd say she was being attacked by cats at the time. Her bedroom, and the reading room where we eventually found Carl, they were the only places that appeared to have been closed off.'

'Did she cut those strips from her own father's back?' Huck asked, looking as though his resignation from the State Police might hinge on my answer.

'She must have,' I said. 'There were no prints on the handle, but the slice marks were consistent with that blade. Right, Doc?'

'That's right,' he said. 'When they brought Molly in Saturday night, she was wearing knitted gloves.'

'Bugs Bunny gloves,' I added.

'Maybe something she wore when travelling, or for emotional comfort – who knows?' Doc said.

'Holy Mother of God,' Huck sighed. 'She fed her father to her cats to keep them from eating her. I'll never sleep soundly again.'

'She had a severe cognitive disability after suffering a vicious seizure disorder for nearly fifty years. Who knows what was in her head?'

'A retard,' Huck said.

'Please don't call her that,' I whispered, guilt thickening in my bloodstream.

Huck shrugged an apology.

'Why not let anyone know that Claire had died?' Doc asked.

'Carl needed the money,' I said. 'He couldn't make ends meet on his Veterans' Affairs benefits and the farm alone. Molly needed the farm for quality of life. He knew he couldn't sell the place off and confine someone like his daughter to a condo in the city. So he defrauded the government. Fuck them, right? They took his foot and half his company in Southeast Asia. What does he care?'

'Do you think he was really going to try and kill Bob Lake?'

'That remains a mystery, Uncle Hucker,' I said. 'For some reason, he mortgaged himself to the hilt to buy that ticket. I think maybe he was planning to put Lake on the spot, to corner him, or David Carver, his old lieutenant, and demand enough money to see Molly safely cared for after his death.'

'Didn't he have his old .45 polished up and ready?' Doc asked. 'One of those 1911s, like Gary Cooper always carried in the movies.'

'He can't have been that stupid,' Huck said. 'He had to know he'd never have got it through the door.'

Doc nodded. 'Sailor's right: it was probably a blackmail scheme. He had all that documentation, not so much Bob Lake ordering his company into the bush, but more David Carver's failure once the shit hit the fan. Lake wouldn't want the world knowing his new Chief of Staff was a coward in battle. Hell, the two of them have built his campaign based on Lake's leadership and Carver's heroic service in the field.'

'Well, that's going to bite them in the ass,' I said. 'Someone out there will know. Someone will remember Carver's cowardice.'

'Probably right,' Doc said. He held out the water jug for me.

I managed another mouthful before asking, 'What's happening with Harper and Fezzamo?'

'The politics of bullshit, as far as I can tell,' Huck said. 'We've basically screwed the Republican Party out of a significant fund-raiser, not to mention a vital stump speech in a pivotal swing state. Bob Lake's staff is screaming for Fezzamo's head, and the governor might just give it to him. The spin on the story now is that we tried to cover up the plague infections because we didn't want a national mess while the TV cameras were pointed at Richmond for Lake's speech. The other side is trying to dig up what they can on Carl Bruckner as the angry, ex-Marine who lost his foot and sought vengeance forty years later. Neither side is daring to suggest that actual terrorists might have been involved, because neither side wants to look like they've no fucking idea what to do when terrorists test aerosol biohazards within fifteen miles of the state's capital city.'

'Lovely,' I said. 'Remind me to avoid the news while I'm here.' I toyed with my IV, freeing the loose coils from beneath my leg.

'Either way,' Huck said, 'are you up for dinner later?'

'Yeah, sure – but I'll need you to come over. I'm not quite mobile yet.'

'I'll be back,' he promised, spun the wheelchair like a pro, pulled open the door, and whistled for Nurse Lyric Alto. 'I've got a Percocet and a long nap waiting for me downstairs.'

'Thanks for coming up, Huck,' I said, again.

'Good to see you, too, kemosabe.' He grinned, and I could see the Mississippi riverboat gambler behind the tired eyes and the gaunt face. 'I'll be back for rice pilaf and Jell-O at five-thirty. Yum!'

'Done,' I said. 'See you then.'

The door swung shut behind him, but Huck caught it at the last second. Leaning back over his wheelchair, he said to me, 'Sailor, you do realise that we're quarantined here for the next two weeks, right?'

'Yeah, so?'

'So ... no cigarettes, not one.'

'Oh shit!'

'My sentiments exactly,' he said. 'So I suggest we enjoy the state-sponsored pharmaceuticals as much as we can while our bodies go through the happy torment of nicotine withdrawal.'

'Spoken like a true Dope cop, Huck,' said Doc Lefkowitz. He waved and Huck gave us a panicked look as the door swung closed. We heard him from the hallway, barking orders to Nurse Lyric Alto. 'Prepare to repel borders, Lieutenant. Haul away!'

Doc laughed a bit too long, then looked away from me and pulled his shoes back onto his feet.

Into the awkward silence I said, 'You don't want me to ask.'

'No, I don't,' he said, still looking at his shoes.

'I have to know.'

'I can't help you, Sailor.'

'It just doesn't add up, Doc,' I said. 'She breathed into my face. She talked to me. I hugged her, and when she hauled me out of that stream she coughed directly into my face. There is no possible way that I could have avoided that infection. How is it that I don't have pneumonic plague? Was the shot you gave me enough?'

He shrugged slightly, noncommittal. 'I don't know, Sailor, honestly.'

'She spoke to me,' I said. 'In perfect English, Molly Bruckner told me that my sister forgave me. She mentioned Marie by name, just like half a dozen other friends and strangers over those two days. What was that, Doc? What happened to me, and how is it that I'm still alive?'

'It's a miracle,' he said.

'You're a sixty-one-year-old Jewish doctor. You don't really believe in miracles, do you?'

'No.'

'She called me Sammy. Do you know that the only people who called me Sammy in the past fifteen years were my sister and my father, and they're both dead? I need to know what happened. Did my father speak to me? Did my sister?'

'Of course not.' Doc waved a hand in my direction as though he were dismissing a compliment. Though he wasn't convinced, he made a half-hearted attempt to explain. 'You were fairly well cooked on OxyContin. You were tired, stressed, hungry, dehydrated and overworked. You saw parallels between Molly's disappearance and your own sister's death. Maybe being so close to Carl, finding out all that you did about how he lost his foot and how he blamed Bob Lake ... maybe that information got mixed up with the drugs in your system to convince you that you were hearing things, seeing things.'

I remembered the stray beside the Bruckners' pond. I'd nearly shot it. *That* was seeing things.

Doc went on, 'Clearly you've never forgiven yourself for your sister's death, and your mind saw this as an opportunity to earn you a measure of redemption.'

'Find Molly.'

'Exactly.' Doc nodded. 'You bring Molly back to her father, and you're bringing Marie back to your own father. I'm no psychiatrist, but what the hell, it makes sense to me.'

'Can you lower me down, please, Doc?' I asked. My lungs hurt. He used the remote to ease the backrest flat once again and I tried to get comfortable. 'It seemed so real, so many times,' I said. 'I can't imagine it was just some kind of drug-induced psychosis, or brought on by stress.'

'Believe it,' Doc said. 'Then stay here this week, next week. Get your blood cleaned out. It'll be good for you. God's giving you a clean slate, Sailor, thanks to the Centers for Disease Control and the Federal Emergency Management Agency. You'll be clean when you leave here, and maybe even a non-smoker. I'd bet dollars to doughnuts that if your father did send you out across fifteen miles of humid Virginia farmland in your scrubs that he didn't do it for himself. He did it for you, and for Ben and Anna, and Jenny.'

I hadn't thought of that. 'I bet you're right, Doc—' I choked on the words, and lifted my arm so I could wipe my eyes on my sleeve. 'I bet you're right.'

'Sleep now,' Doc said. 'I'll call Jenny and let her know that you're doing all right.'

'Tell her I love her,' I said, 'and I'll call her later.'

'Will do.' He started for the door.

'And tell Ben I said—'

'You and me,' Doc cut me off.

'How did you … ?'

Doctor Irving Lefkowitz shot me a mock salute, turned on his heel, and said, 'Your sister forgives you, Sailor. It's important that you understand.'

My stomach rolled over. 'How do you know?'

He smiled. 'Would you forgive her if the tables were turned? Let it go, Sailor. Your life's waiting.'

He left without another word.

I closed my eyes and listened to the resonant hum of the industrial air-conditioner. 'I swear I'll never complain about being cold again. Never.' My voice sounded broken in the antiseptic room.

I didn't know what they'd been pumping through my IV – Demerol mostly likely – but I felt no craving whatsoever for OxyContin. 'You will, though,' I reminded myself. 'It'll be back for you. That's going to be a long goddamned field to plough, Samuel Doyle, a long goddamned field.' I silently promised to worry about it later, after some rest, and to tell Jenny everything: the pills, the nights with Sarah, the lies I'd concocted, anything she needed to help her reclaim her life.

'Our life?' I asked the empty room. 'How about our life, Jenny? Can I talk you into reclaiming our life instead?'

No one answered.

I might have slept for a while; I can't remember. Sleeping on my back has always been difficult for me, too much like resting in a coffin. Even napping on the sofa, I need to be on my side.

I tried, after a while, to roll over. Maybe I could roll my leg a quarter-turn in the traction straps holding it aloft; a quarter-turn would to it. I'd elevate my bad wing, roll up on my good side – if I had a good side – and sleep like the dead, or at least the very nearly dead. My IV hand stung a bit, and the dull, thudding throbbing in my leg, shoulder, hip and lower back was background music to the vicious pain of my blistered feet and my torn lip. It might have been the cocktail in my blood or the recent surgical meds, or maybe a combination of the two warring for control of my liver, but I couldn't get past the feeling that it was my ripped lip that was making me so miserable. There was no question in my mind that two million *Yersinia pestis* bacilli—

—old–fashioned fuck-you-up plague, you mean—

—had entered through those deep puncture wounds. Glad I had shot that cat, I was content to remember the tattered body somersaulting into the hallway, blown nearly in two.

Finally on my side, I knew I wouldn't last long; the angle of my elevated leg was too high. My hip felt as if it would come apart with an audible pop, adding hyperextension to my list of maladies.

'Shit and shit and shit on this. Now I'm frigging stuck over here.' I rolled my shoulders back with a grunt and reached for the hand-sized trapeze bar chained to a ceiling support above the bed. I pressed my gunshot shoulder into the mattress and freed my IV hand. 'All right, kiddies, don't try this at home.'

I cursed and heaved myself up, held myself for a second or two as I worked on rotating my leg back where it had been, and fell, panting, into the pillow. 'Oh, Christ,' I breathed through the agony, 'and now I have to piss, just my whoring luck.'

I stretched for the remote Doc had left handily just out of reach, down near my left knee. It had a CALL button. I'd get a nurse, get comfortable, take my piss – *Do I have a catheter in? I must* – and then sleep until my dinner date with Huck. Stretching, I could just brush the very edge of the plastic device with my fingertips. 'C'mon, you bastard ...' I clenched my stomach muscles, trying to ignore the blazing flare in my hip, and lunged.

'Gotcha!' I gasped and fell back onto the pillow. I closed my eyes, trying to shut out the pain, and fumbled for the CALL button. Then I pressed the UP button. The bed hummed as I felt myself rise slowly to a position that would have been mightily comfy in a Sunday-afternoon recliner but here felt like the lesser of two evils. I pushed the CALL button again and let my chin drop lazily onto my good shoulder. At least now I could see out the window, though the view was air-conditioning chillers on the roof across the street – it was still better than the whitewashed walls of my MCV cave.

'Okay.' I pressed CALL a final time, then dropped the remote. 'Okay, just a minute or two and someone will be here, Nurse Lyric Alto probably. You're all right. You just tried to do too much, a dismount with a difficulty level of seven point eight—'

The putrefying chocolate-brown Labrador retriever, the same dead dog that haunted the small pond at the Bruckner farm, appeared briefly from behind a green electrical box on the roof next door. He dragged one broken leg and limped on another that had been bent to an impossible angle. He managed to stand stolidly as he made eye-contact with me through the window. Even from this distance, I could see he was a ruin. Half his face had been torn away, and his massive, once-powerful chest was ripped open, a bloody tear that dripped black fluid into a puddle between his paws. He barked at me through dripping jowls, twice, then disappeared behind the fuse box.

'No,' I wheezed, 'no, no, motherfucking no!' I grasped the mini trapeze and pulled myself up but I couldn't get high enough. Panting, I found the remote again and pressed UP until I was bent over nearly double, then wrapped my swollen fingers around the handle and yanked myself as high as I could.

Something popped in my lower back; I tried to scream as my muscles locked and my grip slipped off the bar. 'Ah, damnit!' I croaked, and ground my teeth together. They were the only part of me that didn't hurt. I sat up, as high as I could, trying to get a look across the roof next door.

His paws were there, two furry nubs protruding an inch or two beyond the edge of the electrical box. *He's lying down. He's there.* I held on another second as the dog's snout, striped with a pattern of bone-deep slashes, came to rest between his forepaws.

'He's waiting for me.' I fumbled for the remote, found the DOWN button and pressed it just as Nurse Lyric Alto opened the door.

'Detective Doyle, are you all—?' She pulled up short. 'Good lord, look at you! What are you doing? You're going to hurt yourself, Detective – please, here, please let me help you. Did you roll onto the

353

remote? You're much too far up. You'll open your shoulder, your hip. We've got—'

'He's waiting ... over there.' I tried to point out the window but I was too exhausted to show her. 'He's waiting for me. I need Doc. Get Doc, please.'

The nurse supported my head and shoulders as she lowered the bed flat. 'You need to rest, Detective,' she said. 'I'll call Doctor Lefkowitz down for you after you've had a nap.'

'He's waiting for me. Please: tell Jenny. Tell Doc.' My breath rasped, and my lower back felt as though Burgess and Leroy Aiken had driven nails into it with a sledgehammer.

Clucking her tongue, Nurse Lyric Alto made an adjustment to my IV drip, and within seconds I felt myself let go. 'Waiting out there ...' I tried before drifting off. 'Tell Doc ...'

From far off I heard Nurse Lyric Alto, her voice a faint melody. 'Rest, Sammy. You'll be fine. You did fine.'

Acknowledgements

Growing up the son of a homicide investigator, I learned early in life that the Carl and Claire Bruckners of New Jersey would be daily topics of conversation around our family's dining table. No killing was too grisly, no dismemberment too grim to be described and discussed in sordid detail over bowls of my mother's lasagna. I'm sure we ate other entrees, but in my memory it's always lasagna, thick with bits of meat and sloppy with tomato sauce. My friends loved coming over for dinner. I thank my father, NJSP Captain Robert Scott, Ret, for bringing work home all those years. No episode of *CSI* could ever capture the essence of one Sunday afternoon, listening as he described the Major Crime Unit's latest investigation. Who knew that Jersey mobsters really do strip you naked, cram ceramic knickknacks down your throat, shoot you full of small-calibre bullets, and then boil you in your own bathtub as your house burns to the ground? *Shazam!*

I was fifty pages into this manuscript before I realised that I don't really know anything about post-mortem criminal investigation, bacterial infections or childhood seizure disorders. I managed a B in college Biology, only because my bean plants grew a few inches taller than the rest in the lab – a clear testament to light beer's usefulness as a fertiliser. I owe a debt of gratitude to Dr Peter Hurtubise, Dr Peter Novosel, and to Neil Beech for pointing me in the right direction on too many scientific and medical questions to list here. Thanks to Officer John Lavely from Prince William County, Virginia, and the Troop A detectives working South Jersey in the late 1970s, when a farmyard full of disagreeable cats made local news.

I thank the faculty and staff at Brentsville for being so patient with me, especially Stan Jones, who kept me honest on Vietnam. Anything I've fouled up here is entirely my fault, not Stan's, and I apologise to members of the US Marine Corps for misrepresenting troop movements through the Central Highlands and the Mekong Delta in late 1968. Thanks to Krista and Mike for reading draft after draft and to Chris Knoll, who knows all the spooky and groovy parts of the Bible from memory. Thanks, Uncle G, for keeping me plugged in to the new millennium, and special thanks to Mickey Mulgrew for getting behind this project from the very beginning.

I owe a debt of gratitude, as ever, to Jo Fletcher and the staff at Gollancz, and to Ian Drury, Agent 003.14, for championing *15 Miles* around the world while I stay home, making certain everyone knows how to find the Y-intercept.

Thanks again to Aunt Chrissy for her work distributing books throughout the Western Hemisphere, and thanks to Kage, Sam and Hadley, who make all of this worth doing.

Rob Scott
September 2009
Virginia, USA